PRAISE FOR

SIR CALLIE
—— AND THE ——
CHAMPIONS OF HELSTON

★ "An inclusive tale that affirms everyone's right to define themselves. **A must-have for every library.** This is an important book that will capture every reader's heart and imagination."
> —*School Library Journal*, starred review

★ "In this **uplifting debut,** Symes-Smith skillfully crafts an emotionally rich adventure starring an intersectionally inclusive cast of courageous characters."
> —*Publishers Weekly*, starred review

★ "A can't-miss, one-of-a-kind (for now!) page-turner, bursting with heart. . . . Among the best of the year—and a debut, no less."
> —*Booklist*, starred review

"**Fierce, heartfelt, and determined.**"
> —*Kirkus Reviews*

"**Young readers will find a worthy hero in Callie,** who displays boundless courage in defending both their convictions and their friends."
> —*BookPage*

"**Everything you could possibly want from a middle grade fantasy.** . . . Fierce, sharp-witted, and unapologetically queer."
> —The Nerd Daily

"**Symes-Smith has forged a razor-sharp story of bravery, emotional resilience, deep honor, and adventure!**"
> —Ash Van Otterloo, author of *Cattywampus* and *A Touch of Ruckus*

"This **warm hug of a book** is . . . **thoughtful, inclusive, and an absolute joy.**"
> —Jamie Pacton, author of *The Life and (Medieval) Times of Kit Sweetly*

"A groundbreaking, magical story about fighting for who you are. . . . **Callie is a character every middle-grade reader deserves to have on their shelves.**"
> —Nicole Melleby, author of *Hurricane Season*, *In the Role of Brie Hutchens . . .* , and *How to Become a Planet*

"Symes-Smith has created **a groundbreaking story with engaging, unforgettable characters,** whose personal journeys will mean the world to so many young readers."
> —A. J. Sass, author of *Ana on the Edge* and *Ellen Outside the Lines*

"**Sir Callie is the hero I needed while growing up.**"
> —H. E. Edgmon, author of *The Witch King*

ALSO BY ESME SYMES-SMITH

Sir Callie and the Champions of Helston

SIR CALLIE

AND THE
DRAGON'S ROOST

✦ ESME SYMES-SMITH ✦

LR LABYRINTH ROAD | NEW YORK

Text copyright © 2023 by Esme Symes-Smith
Jacket art copyright © 2023 by Kate Sheridan
Map art copyright © 2022 by Kate Sheridan

All rights reserved. Published in the United States by Labyrinth Road, an imprint of Random House Children's Books, a division of Penguin Random House LLC, New York.

Labyrinth Road and the colophon are trademarks of Penguin Random House LLC.

Visit us on the Web! rhcbooks.com

Educators and librarians, for a variety of teaching tools, visit us at RHTeachersLibrarians.com

Library of Congress Cataloging-in-Publication Data
Name: Symes-Smith, Esme, author.
Title: Sir Callie and the dragon's roost / Esme Symes-Smith.
Description: First edition. | New York: Labyrinth Road, 2023. | Series: Sir Callie; book 2 | Audience: Ages 8–12. | Summary: Realizing that resistance to the inclusive culture they envisioned still remains, twelve-year-old nonbinary hopeful knight Callie and their friends continue to fight for the heart of their kingdom.
Identifiers: LCCN 2023012464 (print) | LCCN 2023012465 (ebook) | ISBN 978-0-593-48581-1 (trade) | ISBN 978-0-593-48583-5 (ebook)
Subjects: CYAC: Gender identity—Fiction. | Knights and knighthood—Fiction. | Dragons—Fiction. | Fantasy. | LCGFT: Fantasy fiction. | Novels.
Classification: LCC PZ7.1.S995 Sj 2023 (print) | LCC PZ7.1.S995 (ebook) | DDC [Fic]—dc23

The text of this book is set in 12-point Macklin.
Interior design by Ken Crossland

Printed in the United States of America
1st Printing
First Edition

For Megan, who gave me wings,
and Liesa, who taught me to fly

AUTHOR'S NOTE

Dearest Readers,

Welcome back to Wyndebrel! Before you join Callie on their adventures, there are a few things to address.

First, you are going to meet a few new friends who use **neopronouns.** The same way Callie uses **they/them/their** and Willow and Elowen use **he/him/his** and **she/her/her** respectively, these characters use the pronouns **xe/xem/xir** (pronounced with a beginning "z" sound). Like Callie, these characters do not identify with the gender binary, and I can't wait for you to meet them!

Now, more seriously:

At the end of Book 1, we left our champions on the cusp of a hopeful future. But although the battle was won, the war is from over.

Healing is a long and difficult journey, with twists and turns that often feel like we are going backward. But slow progress is still progress, and healing from the kind of trauma that Callie and their friends have suffered is never simple. Each character, like each person, takes their journey at a different pace, and it is my intention that all readers be able to find themselves in one of our heroes.

That said, I urge every reader to consider their triggers and boundaries. *Sir Callie and the Dragon's Roost* is a triumphant adventure, but the battles are not only fantastical. Within these pages are depictions of violence, transphobia, and child abuse, as well as frank discussions concerning the well-intentioned but ultimately harmful efforts of adults.

This book is about deconstructing the stories we take for granted and discovering truth for ourselves. It is about enemies and allies and the bridge between them. It is about breaking down everything we think we know in order to rebuild ourselves into who we truly are.

If you are in need of extra help, here are some accessible resources:

Trans Lifeline: translifeline.org
Childhelp: childhelp.org
The Trevor Project, confidential helpline for
    LGBTQIA+ youth: thetrevorproject.org

In a world where those seen as "different" are persecuted, the bravest thing any of us can do is stay stubbornly ourselves.

You are enough and loved, exactly as you are.

—Esme Symes-Smith

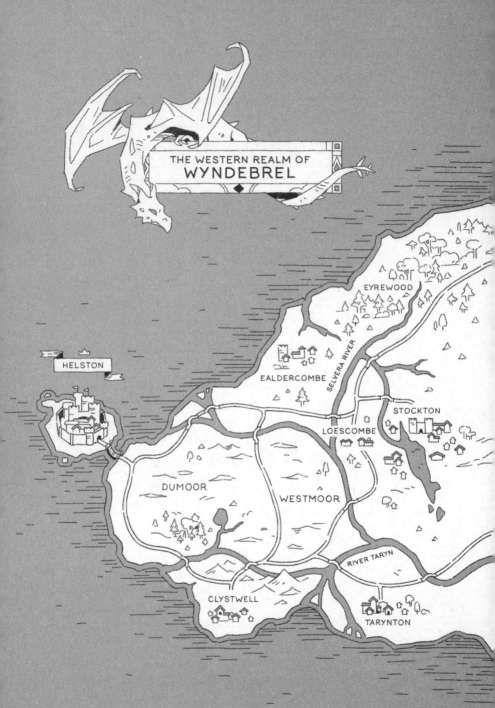

THE WESTERN REALM OF
WYNDEBREL

HELSTON

EYREWOOD

SELVERA RIVER

EALDERCOMBE

STOCKTON

LOESCOMBE

DUMOOR

WESTMOOR

RIVER TARYN

CLYSTWELL

TARYNTON

The Ballad of Sir Dorian and the Wyndebrel Beast

And lo! There he spied it,
A shadow lurking in the dark.
And Sir Dorian readied himself
To take up his righteous charge

Though he knew he might not make it
For dragons, they lie.
Their tactics are devious,
And so many die.

But Sir Dorian was smarter,
And his mission was true.
He felt no fear,
And he knew what to do.

The Wyndebrel Beast
Never stood a chance
Against the great Sir Dorian
And his champion's lance.

The first blow fell
Upon the dragon's writhing tail,
And the beast reared to attack
But was destined to fail.

Because right is right
and wrong is wrong,
And there is no monster
Who can stand up as strong

To the power of goodness
In a faithful knight's heart.
And defeating the dragon
Is only the start.

CALLIE

There are dragons in my dreams. There have been dragons in my dreams ever since we nearly got eaten in Dumoor Forest just a few short summer months ago. And every single dream is the same.

Kensa, bathed in flames, waiting for me. Calling me. Whistling for me like I'm one of the witch's wolves. My body reacts, moving toward the sound of its own accord, falling for the sweet tune that sounds like home.

Come away, little knight. You don't belong here. Come home.

I follow the song through the shadows. Birds join the chorus, their calls harmonizing with the dragon's song; their black-and-white bodies bumping against mine as they guide me through the darkness. Flock as thick as fog.

But I always wake up before the dream ends, leaving me

with nothing but confusion and an emptiness I don't under-stand.

This is where I want to be. Helston—with all my wishes coming true.

I have never wanted anything else.

I should be happy.

I *am* happy.

Aren't I?

TEO

"Stay close," Lara murmurs, and Teo trots to obey, sticking close to her side.

This is xir first mission for Dumoor, and Teo's stomach has been flipping between nerves and excitement all day. Xe's ready! Alis would never have let xem go if xe wasn't . . . but it would've helped if Kensa had been able to feign even a little enthusiasm. Instead, the older dragon stared at xem, long and hard, with an expression Teo almost read as grief before it dimmed to a low anger that xe didn't understand.

This was exciting! This was an opportunity to prove that xe had been worth taking in and taking up space. It didn't matter how insistent folks were that Teo wasn't indebted to anyone; xe knew how thin resources were stretched in The Roost and how much they risked taking in a dragon. Xe *has* to prove that xe's worth the trouble.

Teo wants to fight, to defend xir new home against the threat of Helston.

And besides, it is a great honor to be chosen by Alis herself. If she believes xe's ready, who is anyone to question her judgment?

It's going to be okay.

Teo's pointed ears twitch with every scrap of sound—a birdcall, an insect scratching at the dark bark of the trees, a horse's footfall—

"Wait." Xe grabs Lara's sleeve, forcing her to a stop; holding xir breath to listen for more.

Lara makes a motion to the others, and they all stop, waiting for Teo to tell them it's either safe to go on or not.

Teo closes xir eyes and listens, focusing on the sounds of the forest.

"There's ten of them," xe whispers, counting the hoofbeats in the distance. "Ten horses, all with riders. I can hear armor. And weapons."

Gillian curses under their breath. "Helston's getting bolder."

"That's one word for it," Lara returns grimly. Her knife is ready in her hand, freshly sharpened to a brutal point. Teo has seen what she can do with a blade, but even so . . . *Ten* Helston soldiers.

As the others silently ready themselves for the skirmish, Teo does the same. In the dappled shadows of Dumoor Forest, xe holds xemself steady and focuses on xir breath, the warmth rising in xir chest and spreading out from xir heart to spark into something sharp and powerful in xir throat.

Teo's wings might not have come in yet, but today xe feels like a real dragon.

Kensa would be proud.

Teo swallows.

Kensa should be here. Kensa *wanted* to be here, and when Alis gave xem a mission that sent xem far away across Wyndebrel, Teo was a little afraid that Kensa's fury would turn the whole of Dumoor to ash.

But Alis stood firm, her decision final: She needed Kensa elsewhere. And who was Kensa to refuse her?

Still, Teo wishes more than anything that the enormous shadow of Kensa's dragon-form would fall across the forest, even just for a moment. Just to know Kensa is watching over them all.

Especially as the sounds of the Helston riders get closer.

Gillian holds up their hand, the sign for *Wait and get ready.* They're just around the corner now, so close, Teo can hear the men breathing.

Xe shivers.

Teo's never been to Helston, never encountered the force spewing out across the bridge that everyone warns of. Teo knows xe's lucky. Stories of Helston linger like ghosts in Dumoor.

Gillian counts down silently with their fingers as the crunch of hooves gets closer and closer, mingling with the voices of the Helston soldiers, who don't care if they're heard or not.

When Gillian throws up a fist, Teo's fire collides with a rush of adrenaline.

Xe can do this.

Xe is ready.

Xe is a dragon.

For The Roost!

On Teo's right, someone shifts into a shaggy gray wolf with glinting yellow eyes. On xir left, Lara lunges with her knife in one hand and a flame in the other. Gillian slams their magic down, ripping the ground apart beneath the horses' feet before the soldiers even see them.

Horses scream. Men yell.

And the world erupts into chaos.

It's so much more than Teo expected. Too many sounds, too many voices, too many flashes of magic catching on swords. Too much. Too much to think through.

Teo scrambles desperately to bring xir magic to xir fingers, but every lesson Kensa ever taught xem is gone. Forgotten. Fled from the trees like a frightened bird.

If Teo could fly, xe would flee too, but xir feet are rooted to the forest floor.

Frozen.

The sword's blade glints in the sunlight as the soldier raises it, and Teo flings up xir arms with a yell—the last sound xe ever expects to make.

But the blow doesn't fall.

A choking sound, and Teo cracks xir eyes open to see Lara's knife in the soldier's throat and blood spilling from between the man's fingers.

Teo is no stranger to blood, but this is different. Xe's never seen someone die before.

Xe can't look away, watching the long moments between living and dying, like a candle snuffed out.

A shove to the chest and Lara screams, *"Run, Teo!"* She hurls the ball of light right into the eyes of the Helston soldier descending on them with a raised spear. "Go back to The Roost! Tell them we need help! Tell them—"

But she never gets to finish her sentence.

Lara's eyes go wide, her last gaze fixed on Teo, and then she falls with an arrow in her neck.

Xe can't move.

It wasn't supposed to be like this.

No one comes to help her. No one comes to help Teo. Everyone is fighting for their own lives, and everyone is losing.

It wasn't supposed to be like this.

It was only supposed to be a handful of soldiers. That's what the magpies said. Just a few unwelcome guests that needed to be seen off.

Something sharp zips past Teo's head, grazing xir ear with white-hot pain. Xe whips around, hands up, staring from arrow to archer.

The man, dressed in a crimson tunic bearing the gold sigil

of a rearing doe, stares Teo down in the near distance, face set grim. He doesn't see a ferocious dragon to be feared, nor a human child to be pitied.

When he looks at Teo, all he sees is a troublesome animal that needs to be culled.

The archer raises the bow and aims again.

The arrow won't miss this time.

"*Wait!*"

"What?" the archer demands in a growl, scowling at another man in an identical uniform.

Teo doesn't dare hope. Xe doesn't even dare breathe. Maybe if xe's still enough, xe can just disappear . . .

"Leave one alive, Captain said. Bring one back to the palace."

"Why? This kid's not worth anything to anyone."

"That's not what Adan said. Orders are orders."

The archer fixes Teo with a last scowl, then lets his bow drop with a disdainful huff. "I dunno whose command Adan's been following lately, but as you say. Orders are orders. Bind him up well. These Dumoor dragons are tricky."

The way he says "dragon" sends a tremor curling all the way through Teo's body. A dragon is a rare and beautiful thing, but on this man's tongue it is a condemnation.

Teo doesn't fight the hands that grab xem and drag xem through the bodies strewn across the forest floor. Dumoor bodies. Helston bodies. Young bodies. A boy, not much older than xem, stares unblinkingly at Teo.

Xe can't look away. Not until xe's hauled onto the waiting horse and xir face is shoved into the mane while ropes lash xem tight.

If xe survives all the way to Helston, it'll be a miracle.

No, not a miracle, Teo thinks as they start to move. A curse.

Helston is where hope goes to die.

CHAPTER
ONE

I awaken to the dragon's song seeping through the walls of my bedroom as new light filters through the gaps in the curtains like the rudest wake-up call.

I groan, rolling over and burying my face in my pillow, avoiding the day for just a few blessed moments longer. My whole body aches from yesterday's training. Don't get me wrong—it's the good kind of ache that confirms I'm doing what I'm supposed to do, but that doesn't mean my body doesn't yell at me for every bruise and every overworked muscle.

Getting up is the hardest part of the day. My bed in Helston is the height of luxury—soft and deep, and big enough to really sprawl out on. The moment I hit the soft sheets after a punishing day, I never want to get up again. Not for any knightly accolade in the world. I could lie here forever and ever and ever . . .

But that's not what I fought for.

That is the only thing that gets me moving.

I fought for my right to be here, to train with the best—to *be* the best—and there is no pillow soft enough to tempt me to throw all that away.

I drag my body out of its nest, forcing each bit of me to succumb to the lure of breakfast.

Breakfast.

The smell of Neal's cooking already drifts through the wall, sweet and buttery and crackling in the pan. Everything Neal touches turns to gold and my mouth *aches* in anticipation. While the rest of the palace takes their meals in the Great Hall, our little family holds on to our peace for as long as possible. We're all excruciatingly busy, so meals are the only times we really get to spend together.

It's totally *not* because whispers follow Neal wherever he goes, or because Papa gets weird looks when he and Neal are together, or that Helston's elite hate me because I got Peran kicked out, or that Elowen and Edwyn can't handle being near their mother even though she's technically following the rules and leaving them alone.

It's not because we stick out like a callused, chewed-down thumb in a handful of perfectly manicured fingernails.

But in here—when it's just us—none of that matters.

Our apartment is a haven, untouched by the storms raging around us. There are no politics, no wars, no complication. It's just us. Just family.

The people who love you exactly as you are.

Me and my dads and the twins. And Prince Willow whenever he can get away from his duties. If Her Majesty allowed it, he would move in permanently, but unfortunately, being the future king comes with obligations and responsibilities and all kinds of fun stuff, which means he's up on the dais with Queen Ewella, learning how to be a ruler instead of eating pancakes and playing with magic at our dinner table, listening to Papa cracking bad jokes and watching Neal roll his eyes fondly.

I wish the whole world was like this. I wish we were the norm instead of the exception.

I pull on my page's uniform—not the super-fancy velvet-and-gold one, but the hardier linen tunic that holds up against buckets of sweat. It's still fancier than anything else I own, still bright Helston crimson, and I always—always—fix my pin proudly on my chest. The Queen's Sigil, the doe rearing up on her hind legs, is the proof that I did it. I earned my place and I belong here now. The best shield against glaring eyes and curling lips that resent my existence.

I pull a brush through my orange hair until it's fuzzy, then bundle it up into a tail out of the way.

It doesn't matter what anyone else thinks. I am here. And I'm not going anywhere.

Finally, I buckle my belt securely, smooth out the last creases in my tunic, and grin at my reflection.

Sir Callie of Helston. The prince's champion.
I look *good*.

Neal's the best whistler in the whole world. I reckon he was a bird in a past life, and the sweet tune weaves through the apartment and binds my heart. Music and magic work in tandem, and the sparkle on Neal's fingertips perfectly toasts the bread until it's crispy on the outside and soft in the middle.

Even though the sun has barely risen, Edwyn is up too. A lifetime of early mornings and late nights is a hard habit to break, even if you need to catch up on your sleep. Getting Edwyn to rest more than five hours a night was a fight Neal insisted on winning, and they eventually compromised with seven, even if I know for a fact that Edwyn still wakes up unspeakably early. As long as he's not trying to train or work or worry, it's okay.

In the early days, Edwyn used to hide in the bedroom he shares with Elowen until a reasonable time to be awake—fearful of disobeying Neal. Now he understands a little better that it's not about obedience and he's not going to get into trouble because his body refuses to sleep for long. In fact, these early hours have become precious—a rare moment when Neal can bond with Edwyn without anyone else interrupting or causing trouble.

Because change is hard and progress is slow, and we're all struggling a little bit.

Elowen gets antsy when Edwyn is stuck in his head, and her anxiety makes him worse, and then Papa gets upset that all his efforts to make the twins comfortable and welcome aren't enough and believes it's all his fault, and that makes everyone uncomfortable, and it spirals into one big mess.

Or it did.

The spirals are smaller now, a few months forward; the messes, easier to manage. We're all learning to live with each other in our new normal.

A new normal that consists of food theft.

"Hey!" Edwyn whips around and glares at me as I stuff the piece of toast he'd just finished buttering into my mouth.

I grin, showing off my mouthful.

Edwyn rolls his eyes in disgust.

"Revolting child," says Neal fondly, swiping for me, and I giggle as he wrestles me to his side. "Didn't your father ever teach you manners?"

"Papa never learned his own manners. I was set up for failure."

"My darling lost cause." Neal kisses the top of my head and elbows me away from the rest of the toast before I can steal more.

Elowen glances up from the book open on the table—an encyclopedic tome titled *The Complete History of the*

Rise and Fall of the Age of Dragons, which feels like a mighty bold claim given that history is a constantly moving entity so even if it's complete one day, it won't be the next unless they're continuously updating it and who's got time for that?

"One day," says Elowen, "you are going to get arrested for all the food you steal."

"Nah." I slide into the chair next to her, pulling my legs up under me. "I'm too quick. Anyway, it's worth it. Stolen food tastes better. That's science."

Elowen rolls her eyes and goes back to her book, but there's a smile tugging at the left corner of her lips. She's not really mad.

"Is it good?" I lean almost fully over her book, looking at the densely packed paragraphs of minuscule writing. I grimace. "How can you even make *sense* of that before coffee?"

"Are you telling me you'll be able to make sense of this *after* coffee?"

"I don't even *like* coffee."

"Maybe that's your problem."

I stick my tongue out and Elowen's stern countenance breaks with a laugh. We grin at each other. It'll never stop being absolutely awesome having her living with us. Edwyn's pretty okay too, but El is *amazing,* and she gets more amazing every single day.

No one has ever worn freedom as well as Elowen does— taking the new opportunity for, well, opportunity and running with it like a flag billowing behind her. No longer restricted to the Queen's Quarters and the Chancellor's Chambers, she stretches herself across the whole of Helston, hungry for every new chance open to her. She studies magic—the pretty kind *and* the scary kind—with Neal, and joins the pages in their training, fighting as fiercely as any of us. She absorbs history and botany and beast-lore, healing and brewing and *everything*. Information is water and she's done being thirsty.

"Knowledge is the greatest weapon against prejudice," she told me once when I asked why she worked so obsessively. "I am never going to be caught unarmed again."

She is certainly making up for lost time and arming herself to the teeth. Give it a year, and she'll be a whole army inside one person. Goodness help anyone who dares stand in her way.

"This is *not* all for you," says Edwyn bluntly before setting the teetering platter of toast down in front of me. Well, technically it's in the middle of the table, equidistant from everyone, but—

I'm already reaching for my next piece. "Yeah, yeah. Sure, sure."

By a quick calculation, there are eighteen slices left and five of us, which means three pieces each except Papa will maybe have one, which means two left over, and neither Edwyn nor El ever takes more than exactly their share, which means one extra for me and Neal *if* Neal's hungry, which means at least four for me. Which is fine, I guess. I'll survive until lunchtime. *Just.*

Neal brings coffee for himself and the twins, and tea for me because coffee is the grossest thing anyone's ever invented, and four enormous mugs because who needs portion control.

He slides into the seat opposite and squints at me. "What're you doing up so early? Did you sleep badly?"

I shrug, focusing on what's going into my mouth so I don't have to worry about what's coming out of it. I haven't told my dads about the dragon dreams yet. I don't need the fuss. They're just dreams, but Neal and Papa take dragons *very* seriously. But Neal continues staring and waiting until I've swallowed every crumb and don't have any excuse to avoid the question. "Someone woke me up with their whistling. Not mentioning any names, *Neal*."

I don't tell him why it woke me up, or that Neal's tune is the same as the dragon's, or that it lingers in my head for hours after I awaken, or that my arms are still chilled with goose bumps.

Luckily, my response is enough.

"It's a big day today," Neal reminds me softly. "It's okay to be nervous."

I grimace and sink into my tea. "Not that big. And I'm not nervous."

Which is a lie.

I'm nervous every day, every time I take my place among the other pages on the training grounds. Even when it's a regular day with boring lessons I can do in my sleep, because I *know* everyone's watching and willing me to fail. Today's not so different, even if the stakes are higher. Even if it's Captain Adan's eyes that will be on me.

I grind my teeth.

More than worrying about being nervous, I'm worried I'll let my anger get the better of me and I'll mess up. Every time I look at Adan, I see Lord Peran, and it's like the captain is determined to continue Peran's work in his absence.

Unfortunately no one else sees it.

Captains are supposed to be strict, demanding no less than the best from those taking on the responsibility of defending Helston.

But Adan is different.

He's mean.

And he *hates* me.

Which is totally fine. Loads of people hate me, and if I worried about all of them, I'd be worrying for the rest of my life. No big deal. Or it wouldn't be if his opinion didn't matter quite so much.

See, it's Adan who decides who's gonna be moving forward and who has to stay behind, who graduates to squiredom and who's stuck as a page for the next year. And sure, I've only been a page for a few months and I love it more than anything, but I'm way ahead of nearly everyone, and at least on par with top students like Edwyn, and if they get to graduate and *I* get stuck behind, I don't think I'll ever recover from the humiliation.

"Everything happens in its own time, Callie," Neal reminds me, like he hasn't said the same thing every day for the last I-don't-know-how-long. "Just do your best, and your best will be enough."

Except every single one of us around this table knows that is a blatant lie.

The field is nowhere near level, and for people like me, like El, even like Edwyn, we're playing by a whole different set of rules, which seem to change every time we come close to getting our heads around them. I can only do my best, but we're not exactly being set up for success here.

An arm snakes around me to snatch the toast right out of my hands. "Quite right too!" says Papa cheerfully. "What're you all conspiring about without me?"

In his haste to stand to attention, Edwyn scrambles up so fast that his chair wobbles and nearly falls.

I catch Papa's grimace.

It doesn't matter how much Papa begs him to relax, or how hard Papa works to prove to Edwyn that he's safe, there isn't an instinct in Edwyn's body that will let him be anything less than obedient and respectful to the point of excruciating. He's looser around Neal, though even that took time, but Papa's the perfect storm of commander and surrogate father, and Edwyn hasn't exactly had the best experience with either.

And Papa *hates* it.

He takes every flinch, every wary glance, like a personal failure.

The early days were *awful*, and every step forward was paired with two steps back. I didn't think we were gonna make it through, but healing takes time. Healing is *messy*. It's only been a few weeks, and if it was years, that would be okay too. Guilting Elowen and Edwyn for not healing fast enough isn't the way to go about this, even if it's not intentional.

"It's not about you, Nick," Neal counseled. "They need to know they're loved and welcome *regardless* of how you feel."

Papa held his head in his hands and nodded. "I know. I'll do better."

And he has, even if it's plain as day how difficult it is.

"Take a seat, kid," he tells Edwyn cheerfully. "Before Callie eats *your* toast too."

I scowl. "*Hey!* You're the one who stole from me!"

"No one needs to steal from anyone." Neal rises, distracting Papa with a kiss and his own share of toast. "You're up early. Are you ill?"

"If I was ill, I would have an excuse to stay at home." Papa leans against the wall, as exhausted as if he's already gone through a whole long day. "Ewella wants us all around the table ready to go first thing. As if *more* time is going to do anything but make these lords extra crabby and uncooperative. I don't know why she doesn't just dismiss the whole damn lot of them and start fresh. We're never going to make progress if she still insists on deferring to Peran's men."

"Maybe if you actually accepted the position of chancellor formally instead of doing all the work for none of the benefits—"

"If I take chancellor, I give up my role as knight," says Papa firmly. "I'm not committing to a lifetime sitting on my ass at a damn table. No, this is just a favor for Ewella until she finds her feet. That's it. Then I'm going back out into the field. We need commanders far more than we need chancellors." He elbows me with a grin. "What d'you think, kiddo? You and me out on the battlefield. Sir Nick and the prince's champion?"

I punch the air with a cheer. "Unstoppable! Those dragons don't stand a chance!"

I chomp my way through the rest of the toast, deep in a beautiful dream of horses and swords and hard-won victories against Dumoor's fiercest. Me and Papa fighting back to back in gleaming armor beneath Helston's sigil as wolves and witches come bearing down on us under the swooping shadow of a dragon.

None of them stand a chance against the champions of Helston.

CHAPTER TWO

P eter's good, but he's not as good as I am.

I readjust my stance as he comes at me with grim focus and swings with a yell like we're on the battlefield, fighting for our lives, instead of on the training grounds dueling for Captain Jory's approval.

His sword barely clips mine as he goes hurtling past and face-plants in the dust with a *thunk* and a groan. Satin's blade might be marred by the jagged scar left over from my fight with Lord Peran. But far from being weakened, she is stronger than ever. We both are.

I smirk as the watching pages snicker. Even Peter's friends—the little clique of older boys who are under the mistaken impression that they rule the roost around here; all born and bred in Helston and, wow, can you tell they've never set foot on the other side of the bridge. They look down on anyone who has been here for less than their whole lives.

Goes without saying, they're not my biggest fans.

Peter picks himself up as quickly as he fell, shoving his dusty hair out of his eyes, and wheels on me, ready for another round. I squeeze Satin's soft leather hilt and brace for the attack, but Jory stops us with a clap of his hands.

"All right, you two, take a break and a breath and give someone else a turn."

Peter glowers and sheathes his sword, returning to his crew with his chin held high like I didn't just publicly humiliate him.

The good thing is it doesn't take much work to humiliate this lot. Just my presence is a personal insult to most of them.

"You're not making friends like this, you know," Edwyn murmurs, offering me a handkerchief to wipe away the sweat stinging my eyes. There is a warning in his dark blue eyes, but there's a spark of amusement too. I'm not entirely sure what kind of history those two have, but whatever it is, it means Edwyn enjoys seeing Peter eating dirt as much as I do.

"Don't care." I sheathe Satin, loving the sing as she slips easily into her scabbard. "Not trying to make friends."

I have enough of those. Don't need any more.

El's over on the other side of the court with Neal, dueling with magic the same way the pages are dueling with swords. It's just the two of them, despite the new rules stating that anyone with magic is now free to use it without fear of scorn or retribution.

I suppress a scoff.

Easier said than done.

The rules might have changed, but that doesn't automatically mean people's attitudes have. Helston doesn't like different, and that's never been plainer than the look on my peers' faces as they watch Elowen and Neal spar, their magic bright and burning through the air. Where the sight fills me with awe, the others watch Elowen and Neal with contempt, confusion. Fear. No doubt wondering how on earth they could be expected to combat such power with steel weapons.

Progress is slow, and the learning part takes even longer than the rules part. I know this, but I'm itchy for change. *Real* change.

The new era at Helston dawned with hope and excitement, leading the way into a future where both magical and physical forces can work side by side, as equals. Queen Ewella even charged Neal with the responsibility of creating a magical curriculum for anyone who wanted to learn, and granted permission to use the training grounds—going against all the increasingly loud voices of those who still saw Neal as an infiltrator, a witch's spy. The enemy.

Neal pretends not to hear the not-so-subtle muttering, or see the suspicious glances, but I can't ignore them. It took getting into several nasty brawls with bigoted kids of bigoted grown-ups before Neal told me to stop.

"Let it go," he said, carefully healing my third split lip of the week with soft magic. "They don't matter."

"Why don't you care?"

"What difference would it make to care? Nothing I—or you—can do will change people's minds. They have to learn for themselves."

"But what if they don't?"

Neal gave a small smile. "Their loss, kiddo. Give them time. They'll come around once they understand we're all on the same side."

I guess I get that. But I wish they would hurry up and understand it faster!

So far not a single person has volunteered for Neal's lessons except me and Elowen. Willow is busy round the clock learning the ins and outs of being a king or whatever, and Edwyn would still rather die than come out as magical.

At least that is easier to understand. When you've been taught that who you are is a punishable offense, it's hard to let go, even in a safe place.

But even though I understand that, I'm not patient, and faith doesn't come easily. We fought the battle and won, didn't we? We earned our progress and things should be better *now*!

I take the pause that Neal's been trying to teach me and breathe through my frustration, counting all the battles we've won and the things that *are* better.

Peran is gone. Elowen and Edwyn are safe. Girls are allowed to fight and boys are allowed to be magical, even if no one's taking the opportunity right now. Helston is healing, and healing takes time, and that's *okay*. Everyone is moving forward, and the proof is right in front of me. Just the fact that I'm here, training with the best to be the knight I know I am, is huge.

We have time.

I wipe my brow, then offer the handkerchief back to Edwyn. Or try to. He balks like it's been soaked in a pox.

"No thank you," he says primly. "You can keep it."

I shrug. "If you're sure."

"I am." Edwyn's voice is brusque, but there's a hint of a smile in there too, and I grin back.

Peter watches us from the sidelines with narrowed eyes flitting from me to Edwyn and back again like he's trying to work out some equation.

I touch Satin's hilt meaningfully—the universal sign for *You wanna go again?*—but Edwyn gives a subtle shake of his head and repeats the mantra I've been trying to practice ever since I joined the pages in their training: "His issue, not your problem."

I pull a face. "Rude of you to throw *that* back in my face, but whatever."

Edwyn smirks. "You shouldn't hand out advice you're not prepared to take, Sir Callie."

I'm all ready to initiate a scuffle when Jory claps his hands and Edwyn snaps to attention so fast I'm shocked his spine doesn't break.

"You're up, kid."

"Yes, sir."

I plonk myself down on the ground and get comfy as Edwyn takes up his position opposite his opponent. Even though Edwyn is almost a whole head shorter than the other boy, I already know how this fight's gonna go. For better or for worse, and mostly the latter, years of Peran's brutal routine have made Edwyn unbeatable. He can take every hit without stalling, can go longer without sweating, and watches for every minuscule crack in his opponent, ready to pound the weak spot until they break.

Losing is not an option.

Edwyn grounds himself, readying his body for the first attack. This is his personal method—letting his opponent strike first to get a good idea of what the opponent has to offer, and then turning it right back on them with twice the skill.

The first blow sends Edwyn skidding in the dust. Taking three measured steps backward, Edwyn sweeps his sword in a wide arc. The two blades meet with a clash, but less than a heartbeat later, Edwyn dips and strikes. His opponent stumbles with the effort of dodging the blow, and from there Edwyn is relentless. The attack comes in a volley of brutal blows that beats the boy farther and farther back, nearly sending him right into the collection of onlookers.

Then a shadow falls.

My jaw clenches in time with my fists.

Captain Adan.

Peran's *dog*.

Though "dog" is way nicer than he deserves.

As far as I'm concerned, Adan should've been sent across the bridge with his master. Between him and Lady Anita, it's like Peran's still here. The ghost of Helston. Except no one else can see him. Just us.

And the ghost manifests in the shadows on Edwyn's face.

He falters, needle-sharp focus broken, and his opponent snatches the chance to deliver a ringing two-handed blow right across Edwyn's chest, sending him crashing to the ground in a cloud of dirt and dust.

With a triumphant sword point at his heart, Edwyn coughs and raises his hands with a gasped, "I yield."

I sprint to offer Edwyn a hand up as his opponent returns to the collection of pages, flushed with the surprise of his win. Edwyn's face is a grimace of pain, but he ignores my hand, painstakingly maneuvering himself onto his knees before trying to stand.

"I'm fine," he mutters before I can suggest otherwise.

"You did good, kid." Jory comes up and squeezes Edwyn's rigid shoulder. "No one can win them all. You had him, right up until that moment."

Unfortunately, Jory doesn't come alone.

"You mean the moment he lost?" Adan scoffs. "If this is the best of Helston's future, we might as well surrender to the witch now."

Jory matches Adan's glare point for point, despite nearly half a foot in height difference. "One defeat does not make a failure, Adan. They are kids, they are *learning—*"

"Make them learn *faster*. And turn out the hopeless. It would be a kindness to put them out of their misery." Adan turns a contemptuous sneer on Edwyn. "For all our sakes."

As I watch Edwyn shrink, my temper finally snaps. "No one is hopeless. Least of all Edwyn. And you'd know that if you gave him a chance and didn't try to scare him into losing every time."

"Knights shouldn't get scared."

"That isn't true!"

"Callie—"

"No!" I sidestep Jory's placating hand. Neal and El are watching us too, but I don't care if I'm causing a scene. "It doesn't matter how good Edwyn is, Adan's already made up his mind! And knights *do* get scared, and pretending they don't just makes you a bad leader!"

Adan looks just about ready to pop a vein. Or take a swing at me. Or both. Probably both.

He bares his teeth. "You're not a knight yet, little girl. And you forget who decides when you're ready to graduate. I expect my squires to be quiet and obedient. Edwyn might be worthless, but at least he has those qualities. What do you have to offer?"

Rage bubbles hot in my blood. "I'm not a girl," I say through gritted teeth. "And if you think I'm gonna be the kind of squire who shuts up and follows bad orders—"

"Then you will stay here and watch as everyone you know moves forward without you," says Adan bluntly. "Honestly,

Jory, I pity you. Not even the most skilled master can create gold from dirt. Her Majesty set you up for failure."

Elowen storms up to stand beside me, anger blazing as hot as the magic in her fingers. I can't believe anyone ever dared suggest that magic was a worthless power. "The only person who's dirt is *you*."

I snort but Edwyn winces as he says, "Elowen, don't—"

Adan draws himself up, outrage glinting in his eyes. But his anger isn't directed at Elowen. Instead, a slick smile curls on his mouth as he looks down at Edwyn. "A knight who needs his sister to defend him . . . Is this really what Helston has been reduced to?"

Neal stops at Elowen's side, his own face a picture of anger. "Speak to Edwyn like that again, and you will meet me on the dueling ground."

The laughter dies on Adan's face. There is nothing left in his expression but the deepest disgust. "It would be my pleasure, *dragon*. You know I've been waiting for the excuse to run you through. This is a *Helston* matter. Stay out of it."

Dragon. The insult zips through my blood like lightning. I've been hearing it more and more lately, whispers following us through the palace, the implications plain: *Liar. Traitor. Enemy.*

Neal breathes through the insults and ignores them. I try to do the same. I'm not as good at it as he is.

"My children *are* my business," he says firmly. "I will not apologize for defending them."

Adan's bark of laughter is a harsh bray. "*Your* kids? I

suggest you don't get too attached. Folks around here aren't too happy with you being allowed near our children. And looking at this group, it's plain to see why. Your days of freedom are running low. And you two—" He looks down on the twins. El glares back, but Edwyn's chin is deep in his collar. "You both know this cannot last. You will be returned to your places soon enough. I advise you not to get too comfortable."

I am so close to exploding, my vision's gone fuzzy, but before I can even open my mouth to yell at him, the sound of bells rings through Helston.

I stop. Everyone stops. Even Adan freezes.

It's not like the chiming celebration that runs during the tournament, or the bright sound that begins every day. This is low and pounding, and I feel it in my chest more than I hear it in my ears. It sounds like the sea—booming and wild.

And then the spell breaks and everyone moves as one.

"What's happening?" I demand, yelling to be heard over the chaos.

It doesn't do any good.

"Take your kids home," Jory orders Neal, moving to herd the pages into some semblance of order. "Stay inside and wait for Nick."

"That's not an answer!" I shout. "What do the bells mean?"

Elowen's hand is on my arm. "They mean the company has returned," she says grimly. "It means defeat."

All the hairs on my body rise. Fear runs through the pages

31

like a vein, and the anxious muttering turns to panic. One of the boys starts crying.

"The dragons are coming! They're gonna attack! The castle's gonna fall!"

The older pages do their best to help, to calm the younger ones.

Everyone except Peter, who backs away, shaking his head when Jory reaches for him.

"I can't," he says, voice brittle and shaking. "My cousin . . . He was with them. I have to . . . I have to make sure he's not—"

"Peter!"

But he's already gone, pushing against the tide of people.

"Is that what this is?" I ask. "The company returning? But that's a good thing, isn't it?"

"Those bells aren't good," Elowen whispers. "The last time they rang was when Prince Jowan was brought home. These bells mean death."

Death.

My head rings.

"Come on, Callie, quickly." Neal's hand on my back urges me away but I don't move.

I'm a knight. I can't run from danger. I can't hide from death.

I have to meet it head-on.

"I'm going down to the bridge!" I shout behind me, already on my way. "I'll meet you back at home."

CHAPTER
THREE

There's already a sizable crowd by the watchtower looking out across the bridge to the moors, though the only sounds are the constant tolling of bells and the vicious roaring of the wind, snapping at hair and clothes and cloaks.

Just like everyone else, I ignore it, pushing my way through the wall of grown-ups to try to catch a glimpse of what they're looking at.

"Callie." A hand grabs my shoulder and drags me back. Papa glares at me, fiercer than he ever is with me. "What on *earth* are you doing down here? Go *home*."

He's using his dead-serious voice, but I swallow hard, jut out my chin, and tell him, "No. I want to know what's happening."

Papa pinches the bridge of his nose. "I will tell you all I can later. It isn't safe for you here—" Then he looks up and curses emphatically as Neal and the twins push through to join us. "For goodness' sake, go home. We don't know what's coming—"

"We're not being attacked," says Elowen. "That's not what those bells mean."

"I know that, Elowen, that isn't what I'm afraid of."

I fold my arms. "Then what?"

Papa's green eyes flick across the anxious crowd, and I don't need to hear his explanation to understand. A frightened Helston is a dangerous Helston.

"We'll be careful," I promise. "But we've a right to know."

Papa gives me a long hard look, then sighs, defeated. "Fine. But stick together and be *quiet*. And if there's any sign of trouble, get home." He nudges my nose with his scarred knuckles. "Got it?"

I nod my promise, hoping I don't need to keep it.

We nestle together, our mismatched family, as nervous speculation flies through the gathered court; then the crowd behind us parts and Queen Ewella sweeps briskly through, cutting a path as easily as a hot knife through butter. Her chin is held high, her expression cool and calm. Her dark hair is braided in a crown about her head, and her long crimson-velvet gown brushes the ground like a breeze.

Two steps behind, Willow hurries along in his mother's wake.

He catches my eye as he passes, and I give a small wave and an even smaller smile, but Willow doesn't return either. On the outside he looks like the perfect crown prince—crimson-and-gold tunic gleaming in the sunlight, long black hair sleek about his shoulders—but his face looks like he has absorbed every ounce of fear in the kingdom. He looks like he's about to throw up. Haunted.

I move automatically to be by his side, but Papa's hand on my shoulder holds me still. Now is not the time to break protocol.

Silence falls when they reach the bridge, save for the snapping of flags and the moan of the wind. Even the bells stop tolling, leaving an empty space where the sound was.

We all wait together to count the returning men.

How many rode out yesterday? I try to remember and hate myself when I can't. It didn't seem important at the time. I didn't know any of the riders personally and I knew nothing of their mission. I was so caught up with my own life that I just didn't bother to pay attention.

Now I wish I had.

I wish I had been there as they'd saddled up, to bid them luck and give them my hope they would come home quickly and safely. I wish I had looked at all their faces and committed each to memory.

Next time I will. I swear it.

Queen Ewella shares a murmured conversation with Adan, then with a quick glance summons Papa away from us.

Willow lingers awkwardly behind the grown-ups, alone and ignored, and I want to shout to him to come over here where he belongs, with us. If he's only there for decoration, he might as well be with people who're going to take care of him. Anyone can see that he's in dire need of a hug right now.

Then the fragile stillness cracks.

It starts with murmuring, shifting, pointing across the chasm. Then hooves hit the bridge, and the salt-worn wood squeals.

Without Papa to hold me back, I break free and wriggle to the front of the crowd, where I can get a clear view of the bridge.

Six horses.

Two soldiers.

Two.

Only two. Out of ten.

There is no triumph in the returning troop. They pick their way across the bridge carefully. Defeated. The man in front looks singed, his tawny brown skin marred with burns. The younger one, pale and ginger and covered in blood, stumbles behind. His eyes are haunted and unseeing; he depends on his horse to guide him.

For half a moment I wonder why they aren't riding, especially when they're so visibly battered they can barely make the last steps into Helston.

And then I realize why.

Every single horse has a rider, strapped down and concealed beneath cloaks. Not moving. Not breathing. Not living.

My stomach turns.

At a nod from Queen Ewella, soldiers and squires rush

to meet the returning party, taking the horses and helping the younger survivor before he falls. His Helston uniform is barely recognizable beneath blood and dirt and soot. They cake his tunic, his skin, his hair. The whites of his eyes are stark in contrast.

He pauses a moment by the queen, who touches his shoulder and murmurs something inaudible, before allowing himself to be helped away to heal.

The older scout, a man called Colin, is in just as bad a shape, but he shakes off the offer of assistance and makes an unsteady bow to the queen.

"It was as we feared, Your Majesty," he says, voice a burned rasp. "They were waiting for us. They knew we were coming. We didn't stand a chance."

A woman shoves through the crowd, eyes wild, fair skin blotched with tears. "Danny! Where is Danny?" Her violet dress drags on the ground as she searches desperately from horse to horse.

Danny, at least, is a name I can put a face to. A spotty-faced squire, newly appointed, grins in my memory, teasing every girl who crosses his path.

There is no one like that here now.

Queen Ewella attempts to usher the woman away herself with gentle hands. "Lady Dahlia, go home. As soon as we know, I promise I will—"

Lady Dahlia rips away the nearest cloak, and the cry that follows freezes my blood and feels like my own.

The picture of Danny in my memory contorts and twists until all that remains is the broken body draped across the horse. He doesn't look like himself, just a poor imitation made by an unskilled craftsperson. Waxy and unlifelike and too small. Squires look like grown-ups to me, unreachable in age and bigger than I'll ever be. But that's not true, is it? Danny is—was—sixteen. Just a handful of years older. Just a kid. Just like us—

"Come away," says the queen more firmly, pulling Lady Dahlia back and replacing the fallen cloak, shielding the boy from view. Then she searches the crowd and beckons. "Peter."

I hadn't even noticed him standing right beside me.

The command forces him from the horror he is trapped inside just enough to drag his gaze from the covered body. "Majesty?"

"Take your aunt home and make sure she is looked after. I will visit later."

He bows shakily and puts his arms around Lady Dahlia, murmuring comfort.

She ignores him.

"What happened? Who did this to him?" she demands, voice ragged through her tears, and rounds on Colin. "How could you let this happen? He was a *child!*"

"Lady Dahlia, your son was a fine squire, more than ready—"

"Then *how* did he fall?"

Colin falters, and I catch a swift glance to Adan before he

speaks softly. "There was no hope. They knew we were coming. It was a trap. A *slaughter.*"

Queen Ewella's face is hard. "A witch's attack."

Colin nods. "They stalked us from the first moment we set foot out of Helston. We could feel her eyes upon us, like we were being followed by specters." He shakes his head. "We should've paid more heed to our instincts. We should've turned back."

Adan grips his shoulder hard. "You did Helston proud. All of you. You showed courage in the face of wanton cruelty and cowardice. You followed your orders to the bitter end, and the fallen will be honored as the heroes they are. We will see them avenged, their murderers brought to justice." He turns to Queen Ewella and makes a low bow. "With your permission, Your Majesty, I would like personally to oversee the mission to bring Dumoor to its knees."

I catch Willow's eye, and he confirms the uneasiness in my chest. Anything Adan oversees can't be a good thing.

"We will talk strategy later, Captain Adan," the queen replies. "At present, we must concentrate on mourning our fallen and honoring their sacrifice. Bring them inside and take care of them. We will begin funeral preparations at once."

"Wait," says Colin as servants start flocking to the horses. "We didn't come back empty-handed."

He moves to the very last horse, a tired piebald mare, and jerks the cloak off its load.

My stomach flips.

Bound tight to the horse's neck is a kid. They are motionless, could easily be mistaken for another corpse if it wasn't for the ragged sound of terrified breathing.

"Careful, Majesty," says Colin as Queen Ewella steps forward. "I know he looks small, but he's dangerous. They all are. Even the youngest ones. Witch's weapons, all of them. We're not even sure if this one's human or another one of her shifting creatures."

Adan cuts the bonds and the kid falls. *Hard*. But they barely hit the ground before a soldier hauls them to their feet, arms locked behind their back. A dirty cloth is stuffed in their mouth. Gagged.

They cringe when Adan approaches but the soldiers hold them still and Adan grabs their chin, forcing their head up.

My feet move before I can stop them, closer, forward, straining to see—

Gold-yellow eyes in a tan face darkened with blood and bruises snap to me and I freeze.

I've never seen eyes that color before, like there's something burning under the surface.

Adan drops the kid. "What would you have us do with him, Your Majesty?"

Queen Ewella pauses, assessing the kid with an expression I cannot read, then turns abruptly away with a curt, "Bind him. Take him down to the chambers before he hurts anyone else. Any trial can wait until after the funeral."

"As you wish."

On Adan's orders, soldiers move to tie the boy's hands, and something snaps inside me.

It's too familiar and too recent because isn't this exactly what they did to us?

But Neal gets there first.

"Wait! Stop! I know Dumoor, and they *don't* use kids. Something isn't right. Please, at least have all the information before you condemn this child."

Adan tilts his head. "Something isn't right?" he echoes. "You suggest there is a right and a wrong way to commit murder? Would you like to inspect them yourself for *evidence* of what your mistress has done?"

"I will work with you to tell you everything I know about Alis and Dumoor," says Neal, fighting and failing to keep his voice steady. "I will give you everything I have, but please do not convict this child for the crimes of adults." He turns to Papa. "Nick, tell them!"

But Papa's not looking at Neal. He eyes the encroaching crowd uneasily; the angry buzz growing like a disturbed swarm, and all that anger focused on Neal.

Words like "magic" and "danger" and "always knew" pop in the air.

And then, worst of all, repeated whispers of *Peran was right*.

Papa moves quickly, taking Neal by the arm. "Get the kids home," he orders, so softly I barely hear him. "And stay inside. This isn't helping."

Neal's voice turns desperate. "Nick—"

"Go," Papa insists. "Now."

But Neal holds his ground, and it's a shock to realize that he's shaking. "Don't let them hurt him. Promise me, Nick. Protect him."

"You would protect the enemy over your own?" says Adan loudly for the benefit of the crowd. "Your Majesty, isn't this proof enough that he is still in the witch's pocket? And no doubt the corruption has spread to Sir Nick—"

Papa wheels on him with a snarl and his sword in his hand. "Shut your mouth, Adan, before I shut it for you."

"Enough!" The queen's voice is a boom of thunder, and her face is a storm. She glares between Papa and Adan. "Helston is in mourning, all else can and will wait. Neal, take the children home. I will hear nothing more from any of you. *Dismissed.*"

CHAPTER
FOUR

Neal bundles us all into the apartment—me and Willow, El and Edwyn—securing the door with his own glowing seal. No one can get in without permission. He doesn't speak. He doesn't look at us. Just moves in a daze toward the kitchen.

Elowen elbows Edwyn in the ribs and mouths, *Tea*.

The boys overtake Neal and busy themselves with the very important task of tea-making so El and I can take care of Neal.

"Come sit down."

"I'm fine, Callie."

"You're not," I tell him bluntly. "You're very not fine."

"Do you know that boy?" Elowen asks, gently ushering Neal into the living room and onto the sofa. She sits on one side and I take the other, perching on the arm to look down at Neal.

"No," says Neal. "But that doesn't matter. You shouldn't have to know someone personally to care about them. I don't understand," he growls, pacing. "I realize it's been a long while since I left, but I *know* Dumoor. I know their limits and they don't use kids. Not like that. If that boy is one of hers, then something has changed. Something is wrong."

"Can we really expect the enemy to play fair?" I ask, then wince at the look Neal gives me.

"There are two sides to every battle, Callie, remember that. No one fights believing they are in the wrong."

"They killed our soldiers, Neal!"

"And Helston killed theirs."

"Yeah, but—"

"Listen to me. You are going to be a knight. It is your *duty* to understand that nothing is so simple as right and wrong, good and evil. The enemy are people, just like you and your friends. You think Dumoor isn't feeling the loss too? You think there isn't someone out there terrified that their kid didn't come home? That could've been you, Callie. You could've been captured and locked up just as easily as that boy. The enemy in their eyes."

I shiver. I can imagine it, clear as anything. Me with my hands tied behind my back and surrounded by folks who want me dead. Papa and Neal not knowing if I'm alive.

"I get it," I whisper. "I'm sorry."

"No need for sorry." Neal hugs me tight. "Just promise me

you'll keep your eyes wide open. Follow your own head be-fore you follow anyone else. That goes for all of you."

I hold tighter to Neal, waves of nausea crashing through me. My stomach doesn't like the thought of Helston and Du-moor being the same, not when I'm flying straight toward pledging my loyalty and my life to one of them.

"They're not really gonna hurt him, though, right? They're sticking him down there just to make sure he doesn't cause any harm?"

Neal combs his fingers gently through my hair. "Even if they don't touch him—and I wish I could believe they won't—locking a magical being underground for an extended period of time will do more damage in the long term than anything they can do to his body. Magic needs light and fresh air. With-out it, magic dies. Those cells were designed for a reason."

"To contain the magical." Edwyn sets down two steaming mugs of tea, his expression wiped blank. He stands to the side, arms wrapped tight around his middle. "To *torture* the magical."

"That can't be true," says Elowen with a waver in her voice as Neal nods. She clenches her skirt in trembling fists. "If there was a way to kill magic, Father would've—"

"He did," says Willow, gingerly carrying the rest of the tea. "Or he tried to, at least."

Dread thunks like a stone in my gut. "On *you*?"

Willow's nod is small. "On both of us."

Elowen stares at her brother. "You never told me—"

"Of course I didn't," Edwyn says tersely. "I didn't want to worry you."

"*Worry me?*"

"It didn't matter. It was never for long. I was fine. I was always fine."

I catch Willow's eye. "Fine" is a very subjective concept, especially as far as Edwyn is concerned.

"Regardless," says Edwyn through the horrified silence. "My point is that the chambers have a specific purpose. Father used them, and now Her Majesty does too. I wouldn't be surprised if they are utilized more regularly after today."

"No!" Willow looks desperately between us. "That's not . . . She can't know. Not truly. If she did, she would never—"

"Wouldn't she?" Elowen snaps back so sharply Willow flinches. "It seems to me that she's as afraid of magic as the rest of them."

"Papa will make things right," I say as Willow sags, clutching his tea to his chest. "He'll explain everything and she'll understand. Everyone's on edge and at their worst right now. Once everything calms down, it'll be better."

The others bob their heads miserably, believing me just about as much as I do.

Helston is not an easy place to have faith.

Willow and I suffer the endless wait for Papa's return in the twins' room. It's not what *I* would call homey, with nothing personal but the shared wardrobe of clothes and a few books stacked beside Elowen's bed. There is nothing on Edwyn's side but Edwyn himself, lying on his back and staring dully up at the ceiling.

Elowen and Willow sit on her bed as she braids his hair and I pace like a horse forgotten in its stall for too long.

Once again, the world is turning without us and we're just expected to go with it.

"How long are you going to let it grow?" Elowen asks, curling Willow's plait and holding it in place at the back of his head. "You could wear it as a crown once it gets below your shoulders."

Willow sighs. "I'd like that, but Mother's been bothering me to have it cut."

"Why?" I demand, more sharply than the conversation really warrants. I don't care. I don't have much goodwill to spare right now. "You've been so excited to let it grow long."

Even that's an understatement. Since Peran left and his rigid command on Willow's presentation was lifted, Willow's been near-obsessed with finding a look that is entirely, uniquely his own. I'm fairly certain that's the biggest reason he spends so much time in our apartment—so he can rifle through Elowen's wardrobe and have her teach him all the intricacies of gowns and embellishments.

He wears them well, the skirts flowing as naturally as

47

water on his body. If Edwyn wore El's clothes—if *I* wore El's clothes—they would be an awkward costume, but Willow looks like he should've been wearing dresses his whole life.

So far his clothing experiments don't leave this room, but Willow's hair is something else entirely. It's smooth and sleek like his mother's, and just as beautiful when cared for properly. The longer it gets, the more elaborate styles Willow begs Elowen to teach him.

Willow hunches up with a sigh, reaching back to lovingly touch his braid. "She says it draws too much attention."

I burst out laughing. "You're the crown *prince*! Your whole being draws attention!"

But Willow doesn't return the laugh. "The wrong kind of attention. Apparently I've been the subject of several disputes within the council chamber. Some of the lords are unhappy. They're saying it isn't appropriate for the future king to look like a—"

"The lords can shut their mouths," I tell him firmly, and that at least raises a small smile on Willow's lips. "If they can acknowledge that you're gonna be king, they can acknowledge you can look however you like!"

"You'd think, wouldn't you?" says Willow. "But even my hair is political. It's ridiculous. And it's only going to get worse."

Edwyn pushes himself up on his elbows. "What do you mean *worse*?"

"Not worse as in bad," says Willow quickly. "Nothing's wrong, nothing's . . . bad. Only . . . she wants to have me crowned younger than is tradition. Imminently. It won't make a difference. She'll still be regent until I'm of age, but I'll be"—the lump in his throat is visible as he struggles to swallow—"king. She says it will protect me."

"Isn't that what you want?" I ask. "You're gonna be king eventually anyway."

"But not yet! I—I don't even know who I am yet, let alone King Willow." He grimaces around the title as though it tastes bitter on his tongue. "Anyway, it doesn't matter, it's happening and that's fine. There are bigger issues in the kingdom than me wanting to wait a little longer. I can't complain, not when my people are being slaughtered." His eyes go suddenly wide and his chest heaves with the first throes of panic. "*My* people . . . I'm responsible . . . They're going to . . . They're going to look to me . . . And I . . . I—I can't. And that boy . . . And Neal's right, no one sets out to be the villain, do they? They're just like us, and the . . . th-the council wants to— How can I send out my people to die? To kill? Because that's what's expected, isn't it? That's my job." He puts his head in his hands, pulling away from El. "No wonder Father left. I wish . . . I wish I could leave too. I wish I could run away, somewhere no one would find me. I wish I could just disappear. Like Father."

I sit beside him and wrap my arms around his shoulders. "I don't think you really mean that."

"No. I don't. But I wish I did."

"Yeah, I get that."

"It's going to be okay. Papa's gonna work things out and your mum will come around. It's just . . . messy right now."

Willow nods against my shoulder, but Elowen scoffs behind me.

I fix her with a glare. "What?"

"And how long are we supposed to wait? Helston's been in shambles for years, and that's always the excuse grown-ups use. Just wait. Just be *patient*. Sit still and shut up and wait for *them* to make things better."

"That is their job, El," says Edwyn.

"Then they should be more competent!"

I scooch backward, close enough that our knees bump. "It's better now, though, isn't it? Compared to before, I mean. With your dad?"

El's eyes flick and catch Edwyn's on the other side of the room. "Yes," she says stiffly. *"Better."*

⊢━━━━

Papa always comes home late these days, but tonight he's even later, even more worn down, even more defeated.

He won't even look at us as he sheds his cloak into Neal's hands. As hungry as I was for information, by the shadows on his face I'm not sure anymore if I want to know.

Neal finds the courage to ask first. "What happened?"

Papa's eyes flick to me, to Willow, to the twins, all watching anxiously and waiting to be told that everything's okay. And he shakes his head again with a mumbled, "Later."

My gut twists. Papa doesn't keep secrets. He doesn't keep things from me just 'cause I'm a kid. That's not how we do things.

I stand up tall. "No, not later. We've been waiting and it concerns all of us! *Please!*"

Papa hesitates, more than half looking like he's going to disappear into his bedroom and shut the door. But even though everything else is wrong today, he's still him and we're still us.

He sits between me and Elowen, with Willow and Edwyn on the floor, Neal standing at his side, and takes a deep breath.

"Things aren't good," he begins like that's news. "This has got people spooked. *Really* spooked. Ewella is afraid that this is going to undo all the progress she's managed to achieve with magic, with tolerance, with change. This isn't just about the Dumoor kid, it's about all of us. She has to put on a show and make people feel safe. A frightened mass is *dangerous*. She has to play the long game."

Neal asks the question that's on all our minds. "What does that mean for us?"

"I don't know how long it will last," Papa tells him honestly. "And yes, things are going to be a bit different for a while." He looks around at us, taking in our family with an apology set deep on his face. "We're all going to lie low until this blows over. Every single one of us." He looks very pointedly at me. "I'm dead serious, Callie. It's gonna get worse before it gets better, and I won't see you hurt. You hear me?"

I nod slowly. I hear him. It makes sense. That doesn't mean it sits right, though.

"Magic lessons have been put on pause," Papa continues. "I'm sorry, truly, but I do think it's for the best right now. And honestly, I want all three of you to stay inside until I'm sure it's safe again. Willow, I wish I could include you, but I think your mum's gonna want to keep you pretty close. Know you are welcome here anytime you like. Day or night."

He takes stock of each of us in turn. "I know this is going to be a hard time, but as long as we stick together, we can weather whatever they throw at us. Right?"

We bundle up tight. I hold on to El's waist with one arm and Willow's with the other, burying my face in Papa's tunic. Even Edwyn lets himself be part of the hug.

"Right," I whisper.

CHAPTER FIVE

For days, our door stays shut, and only Papa leaves; heading out too early and coming back too late, and staying too tired and disappointed always. He doesn't tell us what goes on during the endless council meetings. The most we hear are vague murmurs through the walls after he and Neal go to bed.

Elowen presses her ear to the wall and translates for me and Edwyn.

"Neal wants us to leave," she whispers. "He is angry that Sir Nick is keeping us trapped here. He says it isn't safe. Sir Nick insists everything's going to be okay and we just have to wait it out."

"Papa's right," I say, winding one of Elowen's ribbons around my fingers like a web and pulling until my fingertips lose their color. "We can't run away just because things get tough."

No way am I leaving. I fought too hard for too long just to be here. If there's a fight, I want to be part of it. It's my duty. My job. I am a Helston page, destined to be a Helston knight. This is where I belong. Just like Willow.

Helston just needs to heal.

I hope Papa can make Neal understand that.

⚔

Stasis ends with the toll of funeral bells before first light.

Neal helps Papa with the finicky clasp on his black cloak. It's deathly early in the morning; the sea mist is thick over Helston, obscuring any hope of a sunny day. Elowen and Edwyn are dressed almost identically in black with silver detailing; Edwyn's tunic is free of creases like it's never been worn, and Elowen's dress falls long about her ankles.

My own tunic is like my formal page's uniform but black and somber, and I feel like a shadow when I put it on. Only my orange hair keeps me from disappearing entirely.

I'm nervous at the thought of rejoining Helston in a way I never was before, even when I spent whole weeks locked in my room. It's different this time—more dangerous and less personal.

"I don't think my presence would be appropriate, Nick," Neal says, picking the lingering lint from Papa's cloak. "It would be best if I stay behind."

"It would be worse if you were thought to be hiding," Papa

argues, catching Neal's hand in both his own and raising it to his lips. "And you have *nothing* to hide. You should be there, with us, as a family. Show them all that we are not afraid."

Neal's expression softens. "But I *am* afraid. And you should be too. You know as well as I what these people are capable of when driven by fear—"

The next kiss is on Neal's lips. "I would like to see anyone try anything," says Papa.

But, like Neal, I can't help but feel Papa is missing the point.

We join the procession from the palace to the highest cliff in Helston, with a clear view of the moors to one side and the sea to the others; keeping close together in a tight-knit unit.

I've never been to a funeral before and I have no idea what I'm supposed to be doing or thinking, so I just go along with the flow, making sure I don't lose my family. There aren't as many tears as I was expecting, just stony, somber expressions and fierce glares that turn on us. On Neal.

I keep his hand tight in mine and squeeze; his pulse thumps hard against my fingertips. But even I can't stop myself thinking about the mark on his side. The mark of the witch. The enemy who slaughtered our people.

I feel like I did when I first realized that Helston wasn't my friend, except this time I don't know how I'm supposed to claim my place and prove that I belong. I don't think there's anything I *can* do.

The air outside is thick with fog speckled with ice, like

we've been plunged into winter despite it barely being autumn. Everyone clutches their cloaks tighter around themselves, staring up at the sky like they don't recognize it, like the weather is a Dumoor attack.

"It doesn't feel right," Elowen breathes, the words forming ghosts. "It feels . . . magical."

"Hush, El," Edwyn warns.

I agree with Edwyn. If her magic starts sparking, I don't think anything could contain the mob. If Helston starts thinking there's more magic in the air, who knows what chaos will ensue. We're in survival mode. Get to the other side of the day. Get to tomorrow. Keep going until things are better.

Keep going.

It's a long journey all the way up to the hill. Queen Ewella waits beside Prince Jowan's statue, her face fierce and stoic as her black hair streams behind her in the punishing wind. Willow is on Jowan's other side. His tunic is almost identical to Edwyn's, though there's a touch more silver and his cloak looks much thicker. The crown nestled in his hair sparkles like frost.

His hair, so proudly grown, has been clipped short above his ears.

My breath catches in my throat and I nudge El. "Look what they've done to Willow."

She looks and her lip goes between her teeth. "I told you," she whispers. "I told you we were going backward."

We huddle together in the wind as a member of each family who lost someone stands and speaks of their loved ones. The speeches run together, tragic ballads of unique bravery and lost hopes. There are no tears apart from Lady Dahlia, who sobs into her cloak as her husband speaks of the son they lost. The way they talk, you'd think he was a seasoned knight with decades of mighty deeds under his belt. Not a sixteen-year-old squire on his first ride out of Helston.

Just like Prince Jowan.

Just like us in not so long.

My breath struggles in my chest.

I have never feared battle or injury. Knights fight. That's what they're for. That's what I want. And it's not like I've ever been under any illusion that this path wasn't dangerous. People fall all the time.

But—

I swallow.

It's not supposed to be us.

We're supposed to survive. Win. Live.

I don't care that to the other side we're the enemy. I know we're the heroes. The victors. We're fighting for right and good, and we're supposed to win! That's what all the ballads say.

But the ballads aren't the whole truth, are they? They're just one shiny side of a messy story, bloodstained, tear-stained, muddy.

It isn't always the bad guys who lose.

Like Prince Jowan.

If the ballads are to be believed, he should've lived and he should be here now.

Ballads are just stories and this is real and dangerous, and every battle comes with a possibility of not coming back. Of losing. Of dying.

I never worried about Papa. I was miserable when he rode out but that was because of *me*, because it meant months alone with Mama. I always knew Papa would come home. And he always did.

I had no idea how lucky I was.

How lucky I am.

My whole body shudders and Papa squeezes me closer, and I'm grateful for the physical proof that he's still here with me. Still alive.

The thought of anything less hurts too bad even to nudge with my mind.

Willow shifts at his mother's side, and I can see his hands twisting behind his back, not quite hidden. He looks like a real prince up there, every hair, every inch of his tunic perfect. The gold crown bright against his raven-black hair. And he looks absolutely miserable. The weight of the kingdom already rests too heavy on his shoulders, even with Papa and the queen to help him.

Once the words run dry, we all stand at the edge of the cliff. On the sand below are five pyres, one for each of the recovered fallen, their bodies wrapped in thin shrouds that make them look like ghosts.

Helston's best and bravest.

Queen Ewella faces them, her long hair whipping in the wind, raising both arms high. "Helston will be forever indebted to you for your sacrifice." Which makes it sound like it all happened on purpose, intentionally, like they knew what they were heading into.

Fire blazes from her palms and the whole court flinches as it engulfs the pyre. There is no struggle for the flame to catch in the wood, even with the sea spattered wind doing its best to blow it out.

Nature has nothing on magic.

And we stand back and watch the fallen burn.

The heat is intense and the smell is worse. The court cringes from the smoke, lords and ladies covering their faces with their cloaks. I hold my breath for as long as I can before giving in and using my own cloak.

Queen Ewella never turns her face away, nor does she cover her face. Her dark eyes follow the smoke spiraling up and up to mar the clouds; then she raises a hand high and lightning flies from her fingers, cracking and fierce, to stab through the clouds as straight and true as an arrow.

When she speaks, her voice is thunder. "Let this serve as your only warning. To all who dare ride against Helston, to all who underestimate our strength, to all who seek to tear us apart, we will not sit still and silent as you threaten us. We will meet you and win. You will take no more of our children, and you will pay for what you have stolen in the blood of your own." She turns back to her people, expression grim, and tells us softly, "From this moment forward, Helston is at war."

The five of us are the only ones who do not cheer.

CHAPTER
SIX

Any pretense that we're kids at school ends in that moment.

No more games. No more playing.

This is life and death, and if you're not better than your best, you'll die and take all your friends down with you.

There are no guarantees. No promise that we'll win, but I'm ready to do my best.

We all are.

Even the littlest pages have a newfound solemnity. We're soldiers, and none of us are willing to be the weakest link. Adan takes over from Jory and every day is a new fight, a new hell, just to stay on our feet.

Edwyn and I return home late in the evening, battered and exhausted, and it takes Neal and El all the way to bedtime to heal us enough to sleep. Every day, Neal gets angrier and quieter, and his arguments with Papa after we go to bed grow more insistent.

"This isn't *safe*, Nick. Not for Callie, not for me, and certainly not for the twins. They deserve better. They deserve—"

"It will be better, love," I hear Papa tell him through the walls. "Everything will settle down soon enough. Have faith."

"Faith in whom? Ewella?"

"Me."

A long pause, then, softly, "You know I do."

"Then be patient. Fear brings out the worst in people, you know that."

"I do, but why should we be the ones to suffer for it?"

Papa pauses, his silence strained. Then, "I have a duty. I cannot run away again."

"And the children?"

"Try telling Callie not to fight." I can hear the smile in Papa's voice. "This is what they've been working toward—"

"But not yet," Neal insists. "They're twelve. They're not a squire yet. Stop treating them like they're older than they are! Let them be kids!"

"A knight's life is not easy. This is what they want."

I move away from the wall, my heart thuddering. Papa's right. Of course he is. He knows me better than anyone does, even Neal. This is what I've always dreamed of—a life of danger and duty. That's what knights do. That's what I signed up for. Sure, it's not exactly happening the way I thought it would, but nothing ever does. And that's okay. It's hard and I'm hurting, but it's supposed to be hard, and no one can learn to fight without getting hurt.

Neal just doesn't understand.

Nor does Elowen.

Every day she gets pricklier. It doesn't help that she stays inside the apartment with Neal day in and day out, the suspicion surrounding all things magical at an all-time high. She has endless hours to brood over everything that's wrong with Helston and blow it all out of proportion.

"Is this really the kingdom you want to serve?" she demands of me and Edwyn as she tends to our bruised skin and bleeding knuckles. "They're going to kill you before you even make it out onto the field."

"It's special circumstances, El." I hiss as her magic touches the stinging scrape on my elbow where my opponent knocked me to the ground. "If we weren't at war, it'd be different. We have to be ready to fight at a moment's notice, and that means stuffing years of learning into—"

Her eyes flick up, brows arched. "A few weeks?"

I shrug. "I guess. It's fine."

"It's not."

"It is!"

It has to be.

It's not like we have any choice.

And it's not like we have time to think about it. Even

Peter doesn't waste time picking on us, as needle-sharp focused as the rest of us as we go through our drills over and over; strength and resilience over form and footwork.

Fight for Helston.

Protect Helston.

Our duty to Helston.

To the Crown.

To each other.

No longer individual rocks but a single, impenetrable stone wall.

And with the single entity we've become, the race to graduate first is forgotten.

We all go together.

Every single one of us, whether we're ready or not.

I am ready, obviously. Edwyn and Peter and the older pages are ready. But I can't help looking at the little ones, the boys who only arrived in Helston just a short while ago, who are barely used to being away from their parents and holding practice weapons, let alone fighting for real.

I watch them struggle and fall. I watch their tears and their determination. I watch Adan and his men break them down into something usable if not durable.

It's in those moments that I wonder, distantly, if maybe Neal might not be completely wrong.

But it's too late now.

This is the choice we all made.

It was never supposed to be easy, even if it wasn't supposed to be quite this hard.

"We will prepare to ride out in one month," Adan tells us, striding up and down the lines of kids holding themselves ramrod rigid as per order. "You are expected to be ready. You will not be excused if you are not."

Jory stands at the side, head turned away like he can't bear to look at us.

"The ceremony will take place in three days' time, during which not only will you be anointed squires of Helston but you will pledge loyalty to our newly anointed king along with every knight and squire in the kingdom."

My whole body tightens. *King?*

I steal a glance at Edwyn beside me. To anyone else, he would appear utterly impassive, but he and I have spent more time together in the last few months than most people do in years, and the twitch of his eyebrows gives him away; shock matching my own.

So, it's really happening. Helston will have a twelve-year-old king served by twelve-year-old knights.

And that's the solid strategy the council came up with after months of nothing?

Sounds on brand for them.

But I'm determined to see the best in it. I know I'm ready, and Willow is the only person in the whole world I am happy to kneel for. To give my life for.

It could be much worse.

Even if the ceremony isn't special and only for me, that doesn't mean it isn't just as important or something to be proud of. Every time disappointment nudges at me, I kick it away with a hiss. Just because Neal won't be there like I always imagined he would be, doesn't mean it isn't something worth celebrating.

Just because the ceremony is only taking place because Helston is desperate for bodies who can hold swords, doesn't mean I don't matter.

It's fine.

This is what I always wanted.

Everything is . . . it's fine.

The Throne Room is a spectacle of royal pageantry, banners bearing the queen's crest billowing from every eave.

It would be pretty awesome if only I could breathe.

I stand crammed in with the other pages. More than a hundred of us. The little ones, the big ones, and everyone in between. There's no organized roster; the only priority is getting everyone into the single room, its air thick with sweat and perfumes.

The Throne Room has never felt so small.

Edwyn and I stick close together. No easy feat when the bustle seems determined to split us apart. But it's hard for him, being back in this room, especially with so many people here. It's hard for me too; impossible to keep my head from going backward to the last time we were here, on our knees before the court.

I try to suck in a breath and focus on the present, mimicking Edwyn's posture and his blank expression. But where his eyes are fixed frontward, mine can't stop moving. My gaze roams across as many faces as I can scan, taking in the nerves, the fear, the excitement in my peers, and the anger in the expressions of the grown-ups.

The tension in Helston has thickened to the point of unbearable since Queen Ewella declared war on Dumoor, like we're all warhorses pawing the ground and champing at the bit, desperate for the order to charge down the enemy.

I can't stop my fingers from fidgeting.

This is supposed to be everything I've worked for, everything I've dreamed of.

We are not on trial. We are being *honored*.

But it sure doesn't feel like it.

Papa is all the way up at the front, standing at attention beside the two thrones. He's dressed up fancier than I've ever seen him, and looks way more serious than I'm used to. On the left breast of his tunic is the chancellor's pin. The tower flanked by the two hounds.

The pin worn by Peran not so long ago.

He did it. He gave in.

He doesn't look like himself.

Neither does Willow.

He's shrouded in ermine and gold; the crown on his head slips down around his ears, the ridiculous size of it making his eyes appear huge and his body tiny. It doesn't matter what kind of ceremony Queen Ewella puts together; it doesn't matter if she makes every single person in the whole world kneel before him.

He looks like a little kid playing dress-up in clothes borrowed from his parents' closet, about to go stomping off in boots ten times too big.

And then I realize what Willow reminds me of.

Me.

Tied into dresses by my mother and made to perform a role I would never master.

Doing his best to be what everyone wants him to be.

But his best isn't enough.

It will never be enough.

This is wrong.

This is wrong.

Suddenly I can't breathe. My tunic clings in all the wrong places, and the collar is buttoned too high and too tight, and I can feel sweat being squeezed out of me.

"Stop fidgeting," Edwyn murmurs.

I try.

It's not like I can stop the proceedings. The thought is almost laughable. It's happening. It's done. And I'm just one insignificant page in an army of hundreds. A single weapon in an extensive armory.

I am nothing on my own.

There is nothing I can do.

Her Majesty stands and the room falls silent.

Queen Ewella smiles, her rich brown eyes sweeping across each of us. "Welcome," she says. "And thank you. I know these last few weeks have been difficult for all of us, and I have been impressed by the level at which you have all applied yourselves to your studies. Dedication and determination are everything we look for in young knights, and all of you are more than ready. Helston is lucky to have you. And I am lucky that my son will step into his rule with such a strong force at his back. Look at you all now—I will rest more easily knowing that Helston is in your hands."

I steal glances at the faces of my peers, wondering if anyone else is not quite 100 percent on that kind of responsibility being placed on our shoulders. But all I see is either bright, eager expressions or somber, businesslike neutrality.

"One by one, you will be called forward to kneel for your king and make your oath to Helston. Captain Jory will then fix the silver crest to your tunic, and you will be, hereafter, a squire of Helston."

She looks so pleased with herself. Like this is a surefire way to save Willow from the mutterings of the court.

It is going to be a *really* long day.

There are *so* many of us, and me and Edwyn are stuck right in the middle. Even on a good day, I can't stand still that long, and I'm already fidgety beyond control. I wonder how long it will take for Edwyn to snap at me.

I wish Willow was down here with us. I wish Elowen hadn't stayed back to keep Neal company. I wish we were on the outside of the line so at least I could amuse myself with watching the grown-ups, but I'm too short to see anything except the back of the boy's head in front of me. He doesn't even have interesting hair.

"This is ridiculous," I whisper to Edwyn. "I don't see why we couldn't've done it in batches instead of making us all stand around like this."

"So leave."

I whip all the way around to come face to face with Peter, who's standing right behind me. Because of course he is. I bet Adan told him to pick that spot specifically, just to plague us.

He looks right down his nose at me. "No one's making you be here, *Calliden*. If you don't like it, leave."

I open my mouth to tell him to shove it, but Edwyn's hand locks around my arm and steers me back into place with a hiss. "Do not let him ruin this for you, Callie."

I take four long, calming breaths. He's right. I'm not going to waste my dream on the likes of *Peter*. He is *not* worth it.

But Peter's the kind of kid who, once he's started, just doesn't stop.

"You know," he continues under his breath, "It would probably save you a good deal of humiliation if you gave up now. I heard a rumor that they're not even going to give you your pin when you get up there."

"Squeeze my arm and don't give him the satisfaction," Edwyn tells me right when my heart starts hammering dangerously. "He's lying to get a reaction."

I focus on breathing *slowly*. In, two, three . . . Out, two, three . . .

It is going to be a *long* day.

One by one by one each page is called by name, and I zone out long before they even reach the end of the first row.

At the very least, we're gonna bulk up Helston's numbers.

I wonder how many of us will still be here this time next year. Next month. Next week.

I'm not afraid.

This is what I've always wanted. I can't be afraid of my own dreams.

"You know . . ." Peter's voice is as insidious and annoying as a mosquito in my ear. The urge to slap him—*splat!*—just like a bug with a belly full of blood is nearly too strong to resist. "Even if you do make it long enough to get out into the field, everyone's got bets on how long you'll last. You too,

Edwyn. There's a wager going round the barracks. And I'm going to win. Want to know how?"

Neither Edwyn nor I give Peter the satisfaction of a response, but unfortunately that doesn't seem to matter.

He leans so close I can feel his spit in my ear and whispers, "Because I'm going to take you out myself."

I burst out laughing before I can control myself. I don't even care when heads turn to glare at me.

"You can't even best me on the training field," I sneer. "I would love to see you try to 'take me out.' Look, I'm sorry you feel so threatened by my existence. There's enough of you who feel that way to start a support group, so maybe go and work through it and stop bothering me."

Peter's face goes red with anger. "You should be *thanking* me. I'm doing you a favor and warning you. You have no idea what Captain Adan has planned for you. For *both* of you."

Edwyn's fingers spasm on my arm, pinching so hard I nearly yell.

"Captain Adan can suck it," I grit out through the pain. "And so can you. You're both pathetic and cowardly, and quite frankly it's embarrassing. If you don't leave us alone, I'll deal with you and Adan just like I dealt with Peran, and I'll win. How does that sound?"

"Everyone knows you cheated," Peter hisses back. "You've got the witch on your side and she cursed him. That's the only way you won."

I roll my eyes so hard I see the back of my skull. "Whatever makes you feel better."

"You're only getting away with it because you cursed Her Majesty too," Peter prattles on. "But she can't protect you forever. Your spells will be broken and you'll be exposed for what you really are."

"Yeah, sure, okay."

"And then you'll be locked in the dark with your dragon friend for the rest of your cursed lives. You and your girlfriend and the witch's spy. And you." He fixes his wild, triumphant eyes on Edwyn. "Captain Adan told me what you are," he says. "Your father kept you a secret, but he's not here to protect you anymore."

Only I notice the lump in Edwyn's throat as he swallows around his words: "I don't know what you're talking about."

"Liar." Peter grins. "You lie because you know it's wrong. It's *disgusting*. And you're ashamed. You should be."

I'm sharply aware of how much attention we're getting from the pages around us as Peter cares less and less about keeping his voice down. All eyes within a ten-kid radius are fixed curiously on us—our argument a million times more interesting than the ceremony.

I'm also aware that Edwyn is starting to tremble.

"Save it," I snap at Peter. "You want to fight this out, fine. But save it for later when I can actually punch you in the face."

But Peter ignores me, every ounce of his gleeful satisfaction focused on Edwyn as he raises his voice: "I would be ashamed too if *I* was magical."

"What?"

"Magical?"

"Who's magical?"

"Edwyn."

"Edwyn's magical?"

"Edwyn's magical."

It's like a spark caught by dry leaves, bursting into an instant, unstoppable flame that spreads and grows and engulfs *everything*.

Magical magical magical . . .

And now I understand why Edwyn didn't want to admit it yet.

Tolerance is not the same as acceptance.

It doesn't matter that the rules say it's okay. He's allowed to be who he is.

It doesn't matter how many speeches the queen makes or how hard she forces Helston to accept Willow.

Progress is slow and nothing has changed.

And a magical boy is still an abomination in the eyes of Helston.

Beneath their scorn, Edwyn cowers.

I need to get him out of here. The ceremony doesn't matter. We'll beg another chance later. But right now—

"No, you're not running away from this."

The tight ranks of pages have already begun to break in the rising commotion, the proceedings at the front forgotten.

Jory shouts for order, Papa starts moving toward us, and Peter grabs Edwyn.

Lightning cracks across the ceiling and everyone around us ducks.

"Don't touch him!" Elowen screams.

Pages scatter as she strides toward us, magic crackling on her fingers, her whole body radiating rage. She goes straight up to Peter, nose to nose, less than an inch between them. "Touch my brother again, and I will kill you."

She means it. Every syllable.

Peter falters, but I don't have time to enjoy the look on his face before Adan roars, "Arrest the girl!" and soldiers charge to grab Elowen. Four, five, six grown men against one girl.

"Stop!" I yell, trying to shove my way between them and El. "Wait! Papa!" Where is he? I can't see him! He's got to do something!

One of the soldiers elbows me back. "Stand down, kid."

I do not.

"Let go of her!" I shout right up into the soldier's face. "She didn't do anything wrong! If you're gonna arrest anyone, arrest *him!*" I jab a finger at Peter, who's not looking as thrilled as I expected him to be.

But Elowen doesn't need me.

The fire flashes blue and bright. Elowen stands her

ground, daring them to take another step, one hand out to keep Edwyn back.

"Leave us alone," she commands, the blue light flickering on her face. "Don't take another step."

Even I'm afraid of her. She could bring the whole ceiling down if she wanted to.

And by the looks of things, everyone else knows it.

"Dumoor has infected her."

"A witch's weapon."

"A spy."

"*Dragon.*"

"Move!" I hear Papa snarl. "Get out of my way."

He wrestles through and grabs me. "Go home," he orders. "*Now.*"

"But—"

"Not asking, Callie, telling." He pushes me to emphasize the point. None too gently either. "Let them through," he barks at the crowd, which parts just enough for me to squeeze past, my heart pounding so hard I might puke.

"Ewella," Papa calls to the queen. "Tell these men to stand down!"

But his voice is only one against a hundred, all whispering the wild theories like they're true. And the louder they get, the more certain they become.

"They'll poison our children just like the witch poisoned them!"

"That kind of magic, it's catching."

"Dangerous."

"Like Princess Alis."

"Just like Alis."

"Just like Peran warned."

"Should've listened."

"Her Majesty should've listened and taken action."

"She's protecting them when she should be protecting us!"

"She's one of them."

"The boy too."

"The prince."

"Dumoor has infiltrated Helston."

I want to scream at them not to be so ridiculous.

Queen Ewella raises her voice so loud there's no way she's not using magic. "Captain Adan, take them down to the chambers and secure them."

Papa's voice rises in horror. *"Ewella—"*

"The welfare of Helston is my first priority. Anyone who threatens our peace must be detained."

"No," Edwyn pleads as hands close around him. "Please, I—I'm sorry . . . we didn't mean—"

"Leave him alone!" Elowen screams. "Sir Nick, help! Don't let them—"

"Move, witch!"

"El, do as they say," Papa tells her, his strong voice wavering. "It's going to be okay, love. I'm going to fix this. I promise. Just . . . don't do anything rash."

Edwyn's pleas turn to a hoarse whimper. I don't hear Elowen again.

"Callie—"

I startle when Willow grabs my hand and drags me into a dark corner. He's divested of his robes and crown, everything that makes him stand out. He looks a little more like himself.

"I know where they're taking them," he whispers. "Come on."

"They'll miss you."

Willow shakes his head. "I told Mother I wanted to leave. She thinks I'm returning to our quarters. Besides"—he casts a bitter glance at the court—"they're too distracted to notice us."

He's right. All the grown-ups are shoving into the center of the room, grabbing for their kids, yelling at Papa, at the queen, everyone fighting to be heard and no one listening to anyone.

We will not be missed.

CHAPTER
SEVEN

No one pays us any heed. We don't even need to use the secret passages.

Willow grips my hand tight. His fingers are cold, his hand clammy, and I can feel the wild flutter of his pulse in his wrist.

He leads me quickly through the palace grounds like he's walking a well-trodden path. When we step out of the grounds, I finally ask, "Where are we going?"

"To the caverns," Willow replies, never slowing. "We have to go the back route. It's longer but if we follow them directly, we'll be caught in a heartbeat. This is the safe way. I don't think anyone knows it but me."

"And this is the way you used to come when—"

"Yes."

We turn a sharp right, cutting out of the street and heading straight for the sheer drop of cliff falling into the sea.

My stomach turns. "We don't have to swim, do we?"

Willow glances back with amusement playing on his face. "Of course not. Well," he amends, "probably not. Unless the tide is unusually high."

Thankfully it isn't.

Not that I wouldn't swim great depths for El and Edwyn, but still.

"Careful." Willow puts his arms out and gingerly starts down the incline. "I've yet to fall, but I've come close a few times. At least it's daytime."

"So you, uh, did this a lot, then?" It's hard to talk *and* focus on my balance. The sea's not even that tumultuous, but it feels like Helston's trying to tip us right into it. I *hate* heights.

"Every day," Willow says quietly. "Once I found my way out. And that took a while, of course. I wasn't really expecting to find an escape, I was just wandering the caverns." He jumps down a shallow drop and lands on a small outcrop, then turns to offer his hand.

Anyone else and I'd have rejected the help in contempt.

I accept Willow's hand and hop down next to him. It's colder, windier, and from what I can see, we're just facing blank rock.

"Is there, uh, supposed to be a door?"

"These caverns were originally built to retain the magical." Willow turns back to the cliff and sets about tracing the rock gently with his fingertips, searching every jutting stone for something invisible to my eye. "I suppose it makes sense someone found a way out. But it's been a while—*Ah!*"

Something clicks, and Willow steps back with a delighted grin.

I cover my ears, which I'm pretty sure are bleeding, as the stone begins to screech. I'm also pretty sure all my bones are grinding in solidarity. Sure feels like it, with the ground juddering beneath us.

"Seriously? You did this *every day*?"

Willow shrugs. "It was a small price for a scrap of freedom. Besides, if I hadn't, I would never have met you."

A small price indeed.

Little by little—because I guess ancient stone is allowed to take its time—the cliff parts, each rock nudged aside to reveal the smallest hole. It's so dark, if I didn't know it was there, I would never have noticed it.

Willow drops to his knees and crawls inside without hesitation or problem. It's like the hole shifts to fit him perfectly.

"Come on," I hear him say, voice muffled and echoing. "Don't be scared. I know the way."

"I'm not scared."

But that's not quite true.

The grass is scrubby and sharp on my palms and knees, and when I tentatively touch the stone, it's unyielding. I don't think I can fit. More to the point, I don't know if I'll be able to find my way out again. It's like an open mouth, waiting for me to jump right in and get swallowed whole.

But Edwyn and El are trapped inside, and I'm willing to bet my fear is nothing compared to theirs.

I take a deep breath like it's gonna be my last for a long time, and I follow Willow into the darkness.

—————

Even illuminated by the small light in Willow's palm, every step is the same; every turn leads into an identical passage to the one we just left. And only being down here for a moment, my chest feels already like it's being compressed. I have to check consciously that there's still air in my lungs every few steps. I'm fine. I am. But it doesn't feel like it.

Forget magic; this place would suck the soul out of me if I was trapped down here, even just for five minutes.

"How did you survive?" My whisper is painfully loud in the thick silence.

"I don't know. For a long time, I didn't think I had. My body still worked but the rest of me was gone. But that wasn't because of this place. That started when Jowan died. When Father left. I was already dead by the time Lord Peran brought me down here."

I suck my lip *hard*. The words don't sound like an exaggeration in Willow's voice. I remember the first day we met, the dead-eyed boy perpetually apologizing just for existing. It took a lot of work to bring Willow back to life.

We walk for what seems like miles. These caverns have got to take up the whole of Helston's underground, winding around and looping back, because Helston isn't all that big.

It's like they're designed to be a trap and we're the mouse who's walked right into it.

I just hope we can find our way out again.

It doesn't help that the farther we go, the paler Willow's light dwindles, until it's barely a glow in his hand.

"What's happening?" I ask. "Are you okay?"

"Magic needs light and air. There isn't enough of either down here to sustain it. We're nearly there, though."

"How do you know that?" It comes out more irked than I really mean it to but I don't much like the thought of being gulped down into pitch darkness.

"Look." Willow closes his fist, extinguishing the last flickering remnants of his light, and points.

Around the next bend are dancing amber shadows.

But even with the torches hung in brackets, the cells are a void—sucking the light into the darkness and snuffing it out. Except in one—

My breath catches in my throat as something in this cell glints. Eyes. Bright yellow eyes.

The Dumoor kid.

I stop at the bars, my fingers going around the chilled iron. "Hey."

There's a shuffling, a clink of chain, and the kid creeps closer, peering at me as curiously as I'm peering at them.

Their hair was once some shade of blond and some kind of curly, but now it's a filthy mat on top of their head. They still bear the marks they arrived with but if they were in a sorry state before, now it's dismal. Beneath the dirt and bruises, their skin is parched and their lips are cracked. They're so thin their eyes are like globes in their face.

I wouldn't be surprised if they haven't been fed since they arrived.

"What's your name?" I ask, my whisper loud in the silence.

The kid has to give it a couple of goes before they manage a hoarse, "Teo."

Willow joins me. "We'll come back," he promises. "We'll help you. We'll—"

Then, in the near distance, there's a crack and a yelp, and Teo cowers back.

Elowen and Edwyn.

"Callie, no!" Willow grabs me before I can pelt toward the sound.

"We have to help them!"

"I know. We will. That's why we're here. But if you charge in, all that will happen is you'll be arrested and I'll be sent away."

"So what?" I hiss. "We're just gonna wait and let Adan—" I swallow. "Do whatever he likes?"

"If you confront Adan down here, he will kill you," says Willow flatly.

I stare at Willow. I don't understand how he can say this so easily, like it's just some kind of fact I have to accept.

A thud, a whimper, and a tear-soaked snarl that I recognize as Elowen.

"Stop it! Leave him alone!"

And Adan. "Learn to shut your mouth, girl, and I will consider sparing your worthless brother."

My chest heaves, adrenaline coursing through my blood. If I had Satin, I would be in there, my blade at Adan's throat. Every molecule inside me is ready and wanting to *fight*.

But Willow is right.

Adan would snap my neck, and a dead Callie isn't useful to anyone.

I have to wait. I have to stand here and listen and do . . . nothing.

I close my eyes.

"It's been a while since we were here last, hasn't it, Edwyn?" Adan muses. "Isn't it nice to fall back into familiar routines."

The *thud* of the blow rattles through me like my own body took it.

"Get off him," Elowen begs. "I—I meant what I said! I'll—"

"You'll what?" I can hear the grin on Adan's face. "Go ahead, snap your fingers and see what happens. Down here, your tricks can't help you, girl. Down here, all we have is the truth."

"L-leave her alone," Edwyn mumbles, hoarse and thick like his mouth is full of soup. "Please. Do whatever you want to me, just . . . d-don't touch her."

"Now, that is a bargain I might consider."

Elowen's fury drowns out most of the other sounds, but I hear enough, and my head fills with hot red rage. Only Willow's pinching fingers keep me in place.

"You are lucky," says Adan after what feels like a thousand years. "If it was up to me, I'd do everyone a favor and rid Helston of the both of you. Be. *Grateful*."

There's the thump of something heavy hitting the floor, boots retreating, the squeal of old hinges, then Adan's voice one final time: "Anyone asks, the boy fought. Understood?"

"Yes, Captain," a second voice replies, blank, unaffected by the cruelty he's witnessed.

I hold my breath, listening to the disappearing footsteps and counting the seconds before I let myself break free and run.

Willow is less than a pace behind me.

On the other side of the salt-worn bars, their cell is small, dark, and damp. Edwyn is slumped against a glistening wall, his face a mess of blood and blossoming bruises. He ignores Elowen as she reaches for him. He ignores us as we approach. No, "ignores" is the wrong word. It's like he doesn't even know we're here.

But El's eyes go wide and her fingers curl around the bars. She, at least, is free of damage; the only outward sign of her ordeal is the mess of her hair and the dirt from the cell.

"Callie!" Her voice is a rasp from screaming. She coughs, harsh and wheezy. "Willow . . . you shouldn't be down here."

"We weren't going to leave you on your own." I wrap my hands around hers. Her fingers are frozen and rubbery, like she's been out in the winter rain for too long. I swallow hard, trying to keep my head. My sadness isn't going to help her. It's not my turn to freak out.

Willow crouches beside me and whispers into the cell, "Edwyn?"

Nothing. Not even a blink.

We need to get him out of here. Both of them.

I let go of El and search for the lock. It's a cruel, rusted thing that might as well laugh at me when I pull at it.

I swear through my teeth. "Willow, help me."

The prince joins me but there isn't a flicker of magic left in his fingers.

We are powerless.

"I hate him," Elowen snarls, stalking the cell like a caged wolf. "I will make him pay for what he's done. I will make him feel every ounce of what he did to Edwyn and then double it."

"And I'll help you," I vow. "Soon as we're out of here, we'll go straight to Her Majesty and show her—"

But Elowen's contemptuous bark of laughter shuts me up. "She'll what? Help us? Punish Adan? This was on *her* orders."

Willow's head jerks up. "No! That's not . . . El, she didn't mean for this—"

"I don't care if she meant it or not! She sent us down here

87

with him. She lets him do what he likes. She didn't help us! And nor did Sir Nick. They both just—"

"Papa tried to help."

"He didn't try hard enough!" Tears roll furiously down Elowen's face. "No one ever tries hard enough for us. No one has *ever* put us even close to first. We're just collateral in their little political games and I'm so . . . *sick* of it." Her forehead hits the bars with a *thunk*. "If we ever get out of here, we're leaving. I don't care how. I don't know where. But Helston is *not* our home."

I can't tell her she's wrong. Nor can Willow, though it's clear he desperately wants to.

"They promised things would be better," she continues. "They *promised* we would be safe. They promised and we were desperate enough to believe them."

"They meant it, El," I say slowly. "Papa and the queen . . . They mean it, it's just things turned out more messy than—"

Elowen rounds on me with a snarl. "That's not our fault! So why are we the ones being punished?"

I want to tell her she was right to believe, that the promise still holds true and this was all a big mistake. Just one bad day, soon to be over.

Except it feels like a lie.

I want to tell Edwyn sorry for what they did to him, for the queen, who let it happen, for Papa, who couldn't stop it, for not realizing what was happening before it had already happened. For the kingdom he was about to pledge his life to, which failed him.

I want to, but that means admitting those things are real, and I don't know how to do that and keep being me. *Sir Callie, Champion of Helston.*

So I say nothing.

I do nothing.

And the nothing floods my body like poison.

Willow slumps against the bars, eyes squeezed shut.

"What're you thinking?" I ask softly.

"I'm thinking I hate this," he says. "I'm thinking I can't believe Mother would . . . I can't believe she'd allow this." His shoulders begin to shake, and when he speaks again, it's through gritted teeth. "I—I never told her about what Lord Peran did to me. She never asked and I didn't know how to bring it up. She thinks it's all over and done with, but it isn't. Not nearly." He opens his eyes and looks across the cell at Edwyn, a silent broken bundle in the corner. "Nothing has changed because no one believes it needs to. And they want me to rule this place."

Willow stands up straight and stares around at the dungeons, at his friends on the other side of the bars, at me. There are tears in his eyes. "This . . . isn't my Helston, Callie."

The statement is small—a guilty confession that would be treason in the wrong ears—and raises bumps all the way along my arms.

"Nor mine," I whisper, and I wonder what that means for us, the prince and the champion.

But before I can ask, raised voices charge through the stillness.

"This cannot be the Helston you are willing to fight for, Ewella!" Papa's voice is a boom, louder and angrier than I ever knew he could be. "How can a kingdom where children are treated like criminals be one you are proud of?"

"Those children threatened my court," Queen Ewella snaps back, just as sharp. "They gave me no choice! I had to make a show of it. To *protect* them! I don't know how to make that clearer—"

"Protect whom? Not the children. Certainly not your son!"

"Everything I do, every choice I make, is to create a safe world for Willow and those like him."

"By criminalizing the very thing that makes them special?"

"By drawing attention *away* from the elements that put them in the most danger. Please," she begs. "I need you to understand. I need you on my side."

"I cannot support you if it puts my children at risk, Ewella!"

"I am trying to help them!"

"You are *failing*. You are failing them. You are failing Willow. You are failing yourself if you think that submitting to the court's fragile sensibilities, a court who *still* believes in Peran, is the way forward. You are the *queen*. You need to stand up—"

"Yes, I *am* the queen, and you do not have the authority to give me orders, Nick! If it was Richard, you would never dare."

"Richard would never allow this to happen!"

"Richard left us!" Queen Ewolla roars. "He left me on my own, and I am doing my best to make a safe world for my last surviving son, and everyone—from every side—is telling me I'm wrong, that I'm not good enough. Well, I am your queen, and for once in your life, Nick, you will do as I command!"

The grown-ups round the corner and nearly plow straight through me and Willow.

Papa curses loudly at the sight of me.

The queen, on the other hand, is silent in her fury.

And that makes it ten times scarier.

I'm suddenly way too aware that this is kind of a big deal— not just a matter of being caught sneaking in where we're not supposed to go, not just something that can be wiped away with an apologetic grin, but actually illegal.

And we're in *big* trouble.

The queen turns on Papa, jabbing a finger toward me. "I told you," she hisses. "This is exactly what I'm talking about, Nick. Your children run wild! They make it impossible to de-fend you against the court. *This* is why Elowen and Edwyn are in here. *This* is why I cannot allow Willow to—"

"Wait, what?" My heartbeat spikes and I don't care that I'm being rude. It's not like I can get in more trouble than I'm already in. Right? "Can't allow Willow to what?"

Queen Ewella purses her lips with a quick glance at Papa. "Willow is the future king of Helston," she says carefully, like we don't already know that. "I don't need to tell you that this kingdom . . . struggles with different, Callie. Even on his own, he stands out—"

"Why's that a bad thing?"

"It isn't a bad thing. Not by itself. His father and I have *always* supported and loved him for exactly who he is, against all the advice of the council. I wish this was a world where Willow—where all of you—could be safe exactly as you are, but it is both foolish and dangerous to pretend it is. The simple fact of the matter, child, is that association with you is a risk I am no longer able to excuse."

It takes way too long to understand her. My head's buzzing too loud, and those words are too big to make sense of fast enough.

But I get it all the way through when Papa growls, "Ewella, you go too far."

"I am sorry," she tells him, me, and Willow, not sounding very sorry at all. "It is my final word on the matter. It has to be. Look at where we are and what has happened. If we don't curb it now, this will be Willow, and I can't allow—"

"But you'll allow them," I say, my throat thick. "You'll let Elowen get blamed for defending herself and her brother. You'll let Edwyn get beaten up because Peter outed him in front of the whole court. You'll allow everyone to think they're the wrong ones just 'cause you don't want people to be mad at you." My fingers curl into fists. It's getting harder and harder to breathe. Harder still not to cry. "You said you would make things better. You said you would be on our side. You *promised!*"

For a fraction of a moment, I think I catch a glimmer of regret in the queen's deep brown eyes. But then she goes cold again. "It was a deal, Callie. A transaction. And you have not maintained your end of the bargain."

"What *deal?* It was my prize for winning the duel!"

"No, your prize was sending Lord Peran away. The deal was tacit."

"I don't know what that means."

"It means unspoken. Implied."

"That's not fair! You can't just make up rules and get mad when they're broken!"

Queen Ewella glares at me. "You wanted to be a knight. I assumed you understand that meant abiding by the rules."

"Not when the rules are wrong!" I explode. "Rules aren't right just because they're rules! How do you not get that? When the rules hurt people who aren't allowed to stand up for themselves, the rules are *wrong!* And if being a knight means pretending that's okay, then maybe I don't want to be a knight!"

Willow sucks in a breath.

I don't look at him. I can't look at him. I can't move; my own words are ringing so loud in my head, they're all that exists.

I meant them, though. Every syllable.

That's the scariest part.

"Nick," the queen says quietly, never breaking eye contact with me. "Take Callie home."

"Not without my other kids."

"They are not your children! This was probationary to see if it would work, and quite clearly it does not." She takes a long moment, closing her eyes and breathing slowly. When she speaks, it is low and firm. "They will stay here tonight. I cannot have such a threat to my court go unpunished. And tomorrow they will return to their mother."

"No!" Elowen yanks on the bars. "You can't do that! You promised! Sir Nick—" She looks desperately to Papa. "Please. Don't let them. We can't go back—"

He goes immediately to her, dropping to his knees on the damp ground and gripping her hands through the bars. "Elowen, listen to me, it's going to be okay. We're going to fix this. I'll get you home. I'll get you safe. I swear to you." He looks past her and reaches a hand toward Edwyn. "Hey, kid, come here."

The order is so soft, not really an order at all, but Edwyn reacts like it was a barked command. He uncurls from his corner and approaches, stiff and reluctant like he has to convince every muscle in his body to obey individually.

When the light finally catches his face, Papa balks.

Even the queen flinches.

"Edwyn," Papa breathes. "What happened?"

"What do you mean, what happened?" Elowen glares

through the bars. "Adan happened. He'll tell you we fought. We didn't. We couldn't. He just wanted to hurt us."

"He hurt you, El?"

She shakes her head. "He didn't hit me. But I wish he had. He's just like Father. He hit Edwyn to punish me." She turns her tearstained fury up at the queen. "And you'll let him get away with it the same way you excused Father."

The queen's gown trails on the ground as she moves to stand behind Papa. "No, Captain Adan will be held accountable for the misunderstanding—"

"It wasn't a misunderstanding!" Elowen shouts, yanking at the bars. "*You* let this happen! *You* ordered him to bring us down here!"

"For your own protection, Elowen—"

"Look at my brother and say that again!"

"You are the only person who believes that, Ewella," says Papa. "You know what this will do, don't you? You have validated every anti-magic sentiment in the palace. You say you did it to protect the children, but you have only put them in greater danger. Your son especially. You need to make a statement. You *need* to make this right." He stands up to face her, one hand still holding tight to the bars of the cell. "You want me as your chancellor, as your chief advisor, so listen to me now. This Helston you are growing is not one I am proud to serve. It is not one in which I am happy raising my kids. This is not the kingdom I pledged myself to when I took my oaths."

I suck in a breath and hold it, and the queen whispers the words that are running through my head: "That is treason, Nick."

"It is the truth," Papa tells her. "And if the truth is treasonous, so be it. If you want me on your side, Ewella, you need to prove you are on the right side. Until then—" He glances to me, to the twins, to the queen, and smiles. "I am taking my children home and I am looking after them. And yes, they are mine. In all the ways that matter." Papa turns back to face Elowen. "I need you to be brave," he tells her. "I need you to be patient, and I need you to trust me. I will not stop fighting for you. You hear me?"

"I hear you," she whispers.

"Thank you." He dips and kisses her chilled fingers. "Sit tight and look after your brother. You'll be home before you know it."

"Promise?"

Papa holds up his little finger. "On my honor."

Pinkie promises are binding.

I watch the queen watching the exchange, and I try to read her face.

I can't.

I can read Willow, though, clear as a book.

His chest heaves and his eyes dart, and he's thinking so hard his thoughts dance like pictures in the air.

The queen holds out her hand to him. "Come. Let's go home."

But Willow tucks his hands in his armpits. "No."

"Willow—"

"Let them out. Let them go home with Callie or I'm not going back with you."

She stares at him, eyes wide with hurt and shock. Then, carefully, "We will discuss this at home."

"No."

"It is complicated—"

"It isn't! And Sir Nick's right—this isn't a Helston I am proud to serve. This isn't *my* Helston."

Queen Ewella flinches, and I can't tell if she's about to give in to her tears or her anger first.

She keeps both under wraps.

"I am not willing to have this conversation with you here, Willow. We will discuss it at home." She turns her pitiless gaze on me and Papa. "You have five minutes to say your goodbyes before I send guards down. I suggest you make no more promises you will not be able to keep."

See you later, Willow mouths at me as his mother sweeps away with her hand firmly on his shoulder.

I really hope so, but the heaviness in my gut says that's a wishful lie too.

CHAPTER EIGHT

"**P**ack your things," Papa orders as soon as he shuts and locks the apartment door behind us. "You and Neal are going back to Eyrewood. Only take what you need. I don't want you laden down." He strides past me before I have time to process, searching for Neal.

I run after him, my insides trembly. "And you too, right? And El and Edwyn. We're gonna spring them, right? We're gonna break them out and get out of here and—" I stop short, frowning. "You said you'd fight. You told El you would. You promised."

"And I meant it, Callie. Every word. But sometimes the best way to fight isn't with swords."

I stop and stare at him, not understanding. "Talking doesn't work," I say slowly. "That's what you mean, right? You're gonna stay and you're gonna talk until they agree. But they're not gonna. That's never gonna happen."

"Callie, we don't know that. We have to believe the best—"

I sidestep his reaching arms, shaking my head. "No. No we don't. Not when they've proven over and over and *over* again that this is what they want and we've just gotta do what we're told. You're gonna stay and argue and you're gonna lose 'cause the council's not gonna listen and the queen's not gonna upset them, and El and Edwyn are just gonna be stuck down there and then afterward they're gonna get stuck up here with their mum and that's not right! You said you would *fight*!" I'm crying now and I don't even care. "You're supposed to be the greatest knight in all the realm, and you won't even *fight*! You're a coward!"

I wait for him to yell at me, my face hot and my fists bunched.

I wish he'd yell at me.

Instead, Papa is quiet, his mouth curved all the way down, and when he breathes, it's unsteady. Finally, he says, "I know. You're right. I just . . . I don't know what to do. A quick solution is a short-term solution, and all I see is . . ." Something snags in his throat and he scrubs his eyes with the back of one hand. "I cannot risk you, Callie. Not for anything in the world. Even El and Edwyn. I have to put you first, before all else."

"I don't want to be first."

"I know, kiddo, but that's not your call."

My whole chest feels like it's about to crack—my heart and my lungs smashed inside me. How many hours have I spent, promising the twins that they've got equal shares in this family, that Papa and Neal love them just as much as me because blood doesn't matter; assuring Elowen over and over that it's not conditional or temporary, and Edwyn that there isn't anything in the whole wide world that could ever change it.

The queen's not the only person breaking promises.

"What happened?" Neal's voice comes softly from behind me.

I don't want to tell him. Papa doesn't either.

"Nick," says Neal more firmly. "Where are the twins?"

Papa draws in a deep breath and moves to Neal, squeezing my shoulder on his way with a murmured, "Pack your things, Callie." And, to Neal, "We need to talk, love."

I stay where I am until they disappear into the privacy of their bedroom, every muscle in my body rigid with anger. They shut the door and shut me out. I'm not part of this conversation.

I'm just a movable piece in someone else's game.

⊷━━━

I stare at all my things laid out on my bed, divided into two piles—Helston stuff and non-Helston stuff. I hadn't realized how much I'd accumulated since we settled down here. I haven't been careful. I thought we were staying. It's the start of a whole life here.

A life I'm leaving behind.

I wait for my anger to simmer down into something more manageable, wait for the slow, steady thrum of reason to come. Usually I hate that feeling, and the hot guilt that comes with realizing I was wrong. But today I want to be wrong. I want to understand and trust Papa's plan.

But I don't.

And the understanding never comes.

This is wrong.

The thought starts small as a murmur, but with every repetition, it gets louder, stronger, until it's a drum pounding in my head.

This is wrong.

It is wrong to leave. Wrong to run. I don't care how dangerous it is, we stay together. That's the deal. That's what family does. We stay together. *All* of us.

My fingers trail over the soft new fabric of my Helston tunic, tracing the gold brocade sparkling in the lamplight. I worked so hard for this tunic, for the pin, for the chance to fight and die for this place that hates me and everyone I love.

Sir Callie, the Champion of Helston.

I fold it carefully, smoothing out the creases until it's crisp and perfect, and then I put it away. I cannot serve a place that hates me and hurts my friends. If that's what being a knight means, then I don't want to be a knight.

I am no longer a Helston page.

I'm just me.

Just Callie.

This is the first time that thought hasn't given me strength. I have always known myself, and been proud of that. I have always known that I'm different, that I'd have to carve out my own paths where others follow well-trodden ones. I was always okay with that. Except it was a relief when my dirt path met the ancient cobblestones of Helston. It was nice to have company, to slip in beside everyone else and not have to beat down bracken at every other step.

I got comfortable. Complacent.

This is all my fault.

"Callie?"

I look around at Neal's soft voice and meet his dark, anxious eyes. My throat closes up.

"Hey."

"Can I come in?"

I nod.

He slips in, quietly closing the door behind him, and we meet each other in a hug, his hand on the back of my head. "I'm so sorry."

"'S not your fault."

"It's not that kind of sorry, kiddo."

I cling harder. "I don't want to go. I don't want to run away."

"I know, but retreat isn't the same as fleeing. And your dad's right. We need to keep you safe."

"What about Edwyn and El? And Willow?"

"Nick will protect them."

"Like he protected Teo?"

"Teo?"

"The Dumoor kid. We found them when we were looking for El and Edwyn. They've been down there this whole time. Papa didn't protect them. Maybe he tried, but if he did, he failed, and he's gonna fail the twins too and he's gonna stay here forever and nothing's gonna get fixed and this is all *wrong!*" I pull back with a glare, my vision wobbling. "I can *fight!* I've already proven myself a thousand times over! Why won't he let me fight?"

"No one doubts your ability," Neal says. "But, Callie, you have already had to fight far more than you should've had to. This isn't the life we want for you. Even as a page—even as a *squire*—you're a kid first. You should be learning and playing, not fighting for the right to exist. This battle is not yours, it's ours. Let us fight for you. Let us protect you."

I back up, shaking my head. "You sound like Papa."

"Good. He's right."

"I thought you were on my side."

"We are all on one side, Callie—"

"That's not true!"

"I know it doesn't feel that way, but—"

"Stop telling me that what I'm feeling is wrong!"

Neal freezes, and for a quarter second I feel bad.

It's a small quarter.

I turn away from him with a mumbled, "I gotta pack if we're leaving so early. You should go to bed."

"Do you need help?"

"No." I grab a pair of breeches and fold them messily. It's not even a pair I want to take. I don't want to take any of it. "Good night."

A pause, then, "Good night, Callie. I love you."

"Love you too." I can't not say it back, no matter how angry I am.

And when he shuts the door behind him, I know it's the last time I'll see him for a long while.

I wait until Papa's snores rumble through the wall, then I lace up my boots, buckle Satin to my side, and leave the apartment.

The palace is dark and silent. Deserted. But that could change at any second and I am not willing to let my guard down. The longer I can manage without drawing Satin, the better. I don't much fancy meeting Adan on my own on a dark night.

But I'm barely away from our apartment's corridor when I collide with something soft.

Some*one*.

I draw Satin.

"Hey! Stop, it's me!"

"Willow?"

"Shh." He pulls me by the elbow, his other hand glowing with soft amber light.

"What're you doing?" I hiss once we're around a corner into a less-exposed hallway. "Your mum's gonna kill you."

Willow casts a quick glance back to make sure we weren't followed. "I was coming to look for you. What're *you* doing?"

I sheathe Satin and wait a beat for my heart to calm down, leaning hard against the wall. I don't know if my nerves can take this adventure.

"Callie?"

"Papa was gonna send me away," I tell him. Even just saying it out loud rekindles my anger. "Me and Neal. He says it's not safe here."

The prince's face is somber in the light of his own flame. "He isn't wrong."

I scowl. "I know that. But I can't go on my own. I can't leave them down there."

"So, what?" he asks. "You were going to spring them by yourself?"

"Not like anyone's gonna help me."

Willow arches an indignant eyebrow. "Excuse me?"

"I didn't mean it like that. You're the crown prince."

"So?"

"So . . . It's not like you can leave."

"Can't I?" Willow's voice is hard. "I meant what I said down there: This isn't my Helston. I'm coming with you.

Besides"—he gives a crooked smirk—"how do you expect to break that lock with *your* magic?"

I pull a face. "I figured I could, I dunno, bash it about a bit."

"And summon the guards and get caught? Fabulous plan, Sir Callie."

"Shut up." I punch him lightly on the arm. "You're really sure you want to do this, though? This isn't something we can go back on once it's done. Even if we succeed. And that feels like a really big if."

Willow gives a single firm nod. "I have never been more sure about anything. And I don't want to just rescue Edwyn and El."

"Teo too?"

"Yes. We get out together."

For the first time in way too long, my chest fills up with something other than dread or anger. Excitement. Hope. The thrill of adventure.

I grin and hold up my little finger. "We can do this."

Willow locks his with mine. "You and me."

The prince and the champion.

CHAPTER NINE

"No, this way," says Willow when I start off in the direction we went in before. "If we take that route, we'll be out of magic before we find them. We're going to need every scrap of magic between us if we're to have a hope of succeeding."

My stomach drops. "Hey, if we're depending on *my* magic, we're in trouble."

"No we're not." Willow fixes me with a stern Neal-like look. "You're not as bad as you think you are."

"I really am, though—"

He stops so abruptly I nearly bash into him. "Callie, you need to believe in yourself right now. We all need you to believe in you, otherwise you're right—we're in trouble. It isn't over until it's over. Got it?"

The nerves jellifying in my body say no, but I make my mouth say, "Yes. Got it."

We go around the back of the barracks where most of the pages live, and every window is dark. The door Willow leads me to is almost as secret as the hidden door in the side of the cliff. If I wasn't looking for it, I'd miss it completely.

It's little more than a shadow; blackened wood lined with ancient iron, same as the lock—a huge, brutal thing that looks more impenetrable than the palace itself.

I plant myself a few steps away to keep guard, and Willow pushes his sleeve up all the way, ready to get to work. He blows into his hands and rubs them together hard and fast until sparks fly between his palms. It's impossible not to gawk, and even more impossible not to be tremendously proud of him. It wasn't so long ago that he was afraid of his magic, apologizing for every tiny accidental instance. Now Willow and his magic are strong and confident, and any doubt I had in him fizzles out the moment he shoves the sparks deep into the gaping maw of the lock. The mechanism squeals in protest, and I cast an anxious eye behind me to the sleeping palace, expecting the whole of Helston to be exploding out of the doors, summoned by the noise.

But Willow stays calm, all his focus on the spell, his face and breathing impossibly steady, like the stakes aren't doubling every moment. Like we're not committing the biggest crime in *both* our lives combined.

Satin's leather hilt squeaks in my sweaty grip. Every

second Willow takes, I'm certain I can hear the distant stirring of guards, the pounding of fifty pairs of boots all heading in our direction, that the next moment will be our last. I can hold my own against any single person in this kingdom, but my odds of winning when it's one against fifty are not good.

"Come *on* . . . Got it! Callie, let's go!"

Willow's halfway in and beckoning me with his whole arm. I hesitate.

The damp, stale stench is already strong, and the dancing shadows from the flickering torchlight do nothing to make me feel better about heading back down into that cursed pit.

But this wouldn't be a rescue mission if it was fun.

I steel myself, gathering every scrap of my courage around me, and follow Willow through and down, pausing only when the heavy door slams shut on its own, cutting off the last natural light.

"Don't worry," Willow calls back to me. "We're not leaving that way."

Leaving.

Could be we never come back here, never see the palace again, never call Helston home.

I spent so long aching to be in Helston, to be accepted, wanted.

It's scary how something that takes so much work can all be lost in a moment.

"Callie?"

"Yeah . . . I'm coming."

The narrow, spiraling staircase is so long that by the time we hit solid ground I'm dizzy and ready to puke, but I don't have time to get my bearings before Willow's grabbed my hand and we're sprinting; rushing as our magic drains with every pounding footfall.

All I can do is trust that Willow knows which way we're going.

Of course, he does.

It's different coming this way—less desolate though just as depressing.

Elowen scrabbles to her feet the moment she sees us. "You came back—"

Willow gets right to work on the lock, face set in fierce concentration as he applies all the magic he can before it fizzles out.

I focus on Elowen. We reach for each other through the bars. Her exposed skin is cold and clammy. "Of course we came back. We're getting out of here, El. All of us together."

"Us?" Elowen echoes, and she searches behind me. "Sir Nick and Neal, are they here too?"

The hope on her face brings a lump to my throat that

won't go down. "We're, uh, we're gonna meet up with them later."

Elowen freezes, then her eyes narrow and I know she knows. "Tell me the truth," she whispers.

I'm a really *bad* liar. Especially when it comes to El.

I grimace. "Look, there wasn't time to wait for permission but I figure we'll write once we're safe, and—"

She turns stiffly away, moving to Edwyn. He's in the same corner as yesterday, curled up in the same tight bundle. He doesn't move when Elowen approaches.

"Stand up. We're getting out of here."

There isn't a glimpse of life until she reaches down and shakes him roughly by the shoulder. "Get *up*, Edwyn." He cringes away. Or tries to. He's already crammed into the corner; there's nowhere else for him to go.

I catch Willow's eye and he quickly busies himself with the lock.

"Hey, Edwyn." I crouch and call to him. "It's okay. We've got a plan. We're leaving Helston and getting somewhere safe. It's going to be okay. But you gotta come quickly."

Edwyn stares like he doesn't understand me. "L-leaving? How? Where?"

"It doesn't matter. Anywhere." I stretch a hand out toward him. "Come on. Willow, how's it going?"

The prince's brows are knitted tight. "It's going . . . I think I've nearly . . ." The *click* of the mechanism, and Willow slumps with relief.

I would too if time wasn't so tight.

I take over, wrenching open the cagelike door.

The hinges scream but I don't care. I dart and pull Elowen out like the door might slam shut again at any moment, then I go back for Edwyn.

The way he stares at the open door, it might as well be an open mouth filled with teeth.

I crouch a few feet away so as not to spook him. "I know it's scary, but going isn't as scary as staying, right?"

Edwyn's chest heaves. "He'll come after me."

"Adan?"

The name sends him cringing back into his corner, face screwed up.

"Let him try," I tell Edwyn fiercely. "I'm serious. I'm not scared of him. We took down your dad, and Adan's not half as scary as him. Right? We won before. We'll win again."

"Callie," Willow calls. "We have to go *now*."

"I know. Edwyn, come on. You have to get up. It's not far but if we don't go now—"

"I can't." His voice is small and high. "I'm not allowed."

"Forget 'allowed.'" I try my best to keep my own voice free of fear, caught between needing to be patient and needing to be urgent. "The only person who gets a say is *you*. And you deserve better than this."

"No I don't. This is where I belong. What I deserve. I was stupid to think otherwise. To . . . To let myself believe—"

"Don't say that word," I growl. "Don't use that word, not

for anyone but *especially* not yourself. You're not stupid, Edwyn, and anyone who tells you that you are is wrong." And I don't need three guesses to know who put that word in his mouth. I take a deep breath, curbing the worst of my anger. "I know it's hard, especially when you've had so many voices telling you you're not allowed good things, that you're not worthy, that you're *stupid*. I know those voices start to sound like your own. But they're lying, Edwyn. And five lies are still lies. Listen to me if you can't listen to yourself. You deserve to live, just like the rest of us."

When he raises his face, the bleakness in his eyes chills my blood.

He really, genuinely believes he deserves what they've done to him.

Well, tough luck.

"Come on." I lock my hands firmly around his arm and pull. "I'm not letting you go. If you wanna stay here, then we're staying together, but I'm not letting you go. You want El to be here when Adan comes back? And Willow? We're going together or not at all. Up to you."

I grin at Edwyn's furious glare. "On three."

I drag him up and Edwyn staggers to his feet with a groan, legs wobbling precariously beneath him. I chew my lip. He should be in a healer's bed, sleeping for a week, not running for his life, but I comfort myself with the promise that as soon as we're across the bridge we can pause and breathe and do what we need to do.

Just not yet.

Willow and El go on ahead, and I stay back to help Edwyn hobble out of the cell, fingers pinching painfully through my sleeve. We take it agonizingly slow, one step at a time.

"You don't have enough magic," I hear Teo say around the corner. "You don't have to do this—"

And Willow, hoarse and stubborn: "Yes, I do! I can do it! I—I have to. I just need—" He twists around and reaches for me with one hand. "Callie, help me."

I transfer Edwyn's killer grip from my arm to El's and run to Willow's side.

His magic is barely a fraction of what it was a few minutes ago, the glow dim and dwindling. When he shoves it into the lock, nothing happens.

"I'm not leaving him," the prince mutters, relighting the embers over and over again like his hands are wet kindling. "Help me."

The thought of *my* magic being all that stands between freedom and doom is not a pleasant one.

"*Callie.*"

"Okay, okay."

I close my eyes and breathe deeply, reaching all the way inside myself to gather the tiny scraps of magic lingering nearly beyond my touch. Then I rub my hands together, drawing the heat up and out. Faster and faster, and harder and harder, until my skin starts to burn.

When I open my eyes, I gasp with surprise and delight.

There are stars dancing on my fingertips.

I grin and open my mouth to say, *I did it!*

And then I hear something and my magic shrinks back, like a snail retreating into its shell.

Footsteps.

Boots.

Someone's coming.

I look back at the others, hoping it's just my anxious imagination playing a cruel trick on me.

It isn't.

They hear it too.

Edwyn whimpers.

Teo touches my magicless hand through the bars. "Go. You should go."

And it's everything I need to keep going. I won't give up. I won't let us lose.

"We're not leaving you," I growl. "Willow, keep trying. We can do this."

I don't know if that's true but I have to believe it is. There is no other choice.

Willow and I take long, deep breaths and rub our hands together.

I don't listen to the approaching footsteps. I don't listen for the moment they pause not so far away, or to Adan's roar when he finds the cell empty.

I don't listen and I'm not afraid.

Magic flares in my hand and I don't wait to doubt it before I shove it deep into the lock.

It mixes and melds with the last scrap of Willow's magic and—*somehow*—it's just enough.

The lock breaks and the magic snuffs out.

I lunge into the darkness and grab Teo. "Run!" I yell, drawing Satin and planting my feet. "Get out! I'll hold him off as long as I can."

"Put the sword down, Calliden."

I fight to keep my head and my nerves in check as I face Adan. The torch in his hand sends sharp shadows chasing each other across the stone wall, only emphasizing how narrow these passages are. How little room there is to escape.

But we won, I remind myself, adjusting my grip and readying myself for the fight. Edwyn and Elowen are free. Teo too. Willow can get them out. And I can take on Adan.

"My name is *Callie*."

A smile stretches slowly across Adan's mouth. "By the time justice is served, no one will remember your name, whatever you wish to call yourself." His gaze slides to Edwyn and Elowen behind me, and his smile sharpens to a brutal point. "Where do you think you can go?" he asks them softly. "You'll be run down the moment you touch the bridge. And even if you survived long enough to cross it, there is nowhere in this world for the likes of you. If you're lucky, if you're *good* and *sorry*, maybe your worthless lives will be spared."

"I'm not good and I'm not sorry," Elowen whispers, fierce and trembling all at once. She holds tight to her brother. "And I'm done pretending that I am. I am done letting people like you rule us. I am done existing on permission! I am *done!*"

Adan's smile drops and he takes one slow step forward. "You have forgotten your place since your father's been gone. What do you think he would do if he heard you talking like that?"

Elowen holds her ground. "Father isn't here and I am not afraid. Not of him, not of you, not of any of the cowards running this kingdom. I know my place, and it isn't here. It never has been. We aren't wanted and we don't want to be here, so why not let us go?"

"That's not the way it works, girl."

When Adan advances again, I raise Satin in warning. "Take another step and I'll run you through."

"Big words for a little kid."

"Do you want to test that?"

Adan laughs, and the sing of his sword sends ripples through my nerves. It's enormous. As heavy as it is sharp, and as likely to cave in my skull as it is to slice me up.

"I'm not above delivering you to Nick in pieces. Maybe it'll serve as a warning of what we do to traitors. Of what will happen to that witch's *pet—*"

Satin clashes with Adan's blade before I can get my head together. "Leave Neal alone!"

"He should never have dared set foot in Helston." Adan

shoves me away so hard I trip backward and crash to the ground. Pain rings through my body. Falling on stone is a *whole* lot different than taking a tumble on the training grounds.

I grope for Satin, but Elowen grabs her first.

She levels the point right at Adan's nose, gripping the sword too tight in both hands.

"Run," she tells us, her eyes never leaving Adan's face, voice as sharp and brittle as broken glass, and twice as dangerous.

There's no way on earth I'm leaving her on her own.

I pick myself carefully up. "Get Edwyn and Teo out," I tell Willow. "We'll find you."

Willow casts one anxious eye at Adan, but the captain makes no move to stop him. All his rage and attention is fixed on me and Elowen. He would let the others go, I realize, if it meant getting the chance to put us back in our place.

It's a sacrifice worth taking.

Adan's eyes follow the three of them away, casual as anything. And then he turns his attention back to us. "Do you want to know what's going to happen next? Even if they make their way out, there isn't a single inch of Helston where they can hide. If they're lucky, the hunt will be long and fun. Give the dogs a chance to practice. But your brother knows full well that there is nowhere to hide in Helston. And if they're not lucky, well"—he shrugs—"accidents happen when children wander around where they shouldn't after dark. A slip off a cliff, a tumble into the sea ... Such a tragedy. Still, it's for the best. Magical boys really should be drowned at birth—"

Each word is like a blow. I clench my teeth and weather the storm, refusing to let Adan's poison seep into my skin.

But Elowen absorbs it all, and she *explodes*.

It's awful.

Her snarl fills the caverns as she strikes with her whole body and strength, and Adan is more than ready for her. This is what he wanted. When the returning blow knocks Satin right out of El's hands, Adan darts in and grabs Elowen's wrist, forcing her down to her knees.

She cries out as he twists her arms behind her back, harder and harder until she gives up and goes limp.

"Don't move," Adan warns me softly as I try to reach Satin. "If you don't want me to break your friend's neck here and now, you will do as I say."

I step back and put my hands up. My heart batters against my rib cage. I have no doubt at all that Adan means it. People like him don't make empty threats.

At least the boys are being given time to run. Maybe they'll make it across the bridge. Maybe they'll survive this. Even if we don't.

All I need to focus on is Elowen.

Her head is bent down, face hidden behind the curtain of her hair. Her body shakes.

"Let her go," I tell Adan slowly. "And we'll do what you want."

"You'll do what I want because you have no choice," he snaps back. "You have nothing to bargain with."

He's right, I realize. We're caught. Trapped, at his mercy. If he even has any. We've lost.

But then I catch Elowen's eye. Barely a glimpse of blue through her hair, but it speaks far more than if she said it out loud: *I have a plan.*

And I know immediately what I have to do.

I make my body give in, forcing out all the fight, all the defense, until there's nothing left on the outside but defeat. I lower my gaze and tell Adan, "Yes, sir."

The triumph on his face turns my stomach, but it's what we need. The complacency of the win, of absolute dominion over his captives. He relaxes.

Fool.

Elowen slams her elbow straight into his crotch.

It's a simple move, but effective.

Adan drops like a sack of potatoes with a guttural groan.

Elowen barely manages to scrabble free before he crashes right on top of her. "Get the keys!"

I obey automatically, avoiding Adan's groping hands to snatch the heavy chain right off his belt, then together me and El batter him right into Teo's cell, never allowing him a moment to get his footing or catch his senses. It takes both of us, and his flailing fists knock me more than once, but we make it.

We make it.

I slam the cell door shut and I shove the key right into the place my magic was just a few minutes ago.

Relief catches me in the throat and I nearly sag to the ground. The lock is secure and we have the keys. We won. We're safe.

I still flinch when Adan swipes at us through the bars, his face red and twisted with rage.

"I'll find you," he vows, spit flying to splat on my cheek. "I will track every step you take from Helston to the end of the world. I will hunt down that pretty little prince and I'll do what should've been done the moment he was born. As for your brother—"

He startles back when Elowen lunges, grabbing the bars right in front of his face—fearless and furious. "Lay one more finger on Edwyn and I will kill you."

"El, come on, let's get out of here."

But she ignores me one moment longer.

"I hope no one comes looking for you," she tells Adan, her voice low and shaking. "I hope you *rot*."

Then—*finally*—she turns her back on him and, together, we run.

Adan's roar follows us through the darkness.

CHAPTER
TEN

The cavern spits us out, and we stumble into the moonlight.

I gulp huge lungfuls of fresh air like it's the last I'll ever have.

"What happened?" I hear Willow ask, and I've never been more thankful to hear his voice. He got out. He's safe. "Are you okay?"

"We have to go," Elowen replies. "We have to get out of Helston *now*. Edwyn, can you walk?"

It's Willow who replies for him: "I'm nearly done with the healing. Just give us a few more minutes—"

"We don't have a few more minutes!"

I take one more deep breath and push off from the wall, forcing my eyes to focus in the pale light.

Elowen looks worse out here, her hands bunched into

sharp-knuckled fists. Bruises on her bare arms. Blood on her dress. The blood is not her own.

Everyone looks worse out here, and I'm aware of how much my body hurts.

Teo lies a little way away, chest heaving. I can't even imagine how it feels to be outside after days in the darkness.

"How're you doing?"

Edwyn looks up blearily from his place on the ground. He looks like he just got dragged out of a heavy sleep and still hasn't properly woken up. The left side of his face is a swollen disaster. I guess Willow's been focusing his efforts on the important bits. It's easier to run with a messed-up face than a busted leg. Doesn't account for the inside bits, though, and I think the inside of Edwyn's head is in far worse shape than anything on the outside.

All I want to do is take him home and shut the door on the world. Papa can make bad soup and Neal can gently put all the fallen pieces back together.

But that's not an option.

Forward only.

El's right—we don't have a few minutes.

I push for a smile and my lips wobble. "Come on, let's take this party over the bridge."

Edwyn flinches from the hand I hold out to him and shakes his head. Hard. "I—I can't."

My heart and my hand drop. "What d'you mean *can't*?"

"This is all he's said since we got out," Willow murmurs. "He didn't want to let me touch his leg."

Edwyn's glare is dark and deep. I know that look. I remember that look.

I crouch down, painfully aware that we should be running right about now. "We're leaving," I tell him firmly. "We're leaving Helston and everyone in it and we're never coming back." Spoken out loud, the words shudder through me. "Everyone" includes Papa and Neal. But I can't think about them right now. They can take care of themselves. I can only think about my friends. "They're not gonna catch us and they're not gonna hurt us again. You got that?"

"That's what you said before. And it wasn't true."

I grimace. I mean, he's not wrong. "This is different," I tell him firmly. "This time we're not asking permission. We're not making a compromise. This time we put us first. End of story."

Edwyn's throat bobs, eyes darting toward the palace. "They'll catch us. They always catch us. And I . . . I—I can't."

"This is the only chance we'll ever have." I twist to see El standing over us, arms set firm across her chest. "I'm going. I'm leaving and I'm not coming back. It's up to you if you stay or go but I won't wait for you."

I gape at her. Even as a hollow threat, that's beyond cruel.

But it makes Edwyn move. "Elowen—"

"I mean it," she tells her twin. "We've spent our whole life trying not to be noticed to evade trouble. Being *good* and *still* and *quiet*. And what good has that ever done us? What difference did any of it make? Maybe if we go back now and kneel and beg, they won't kill us where we stand. If we're lucky—luckier than either of us has ever been—things will return to normal and we'll be back with Mother, and you'll be working under Adan and it'll just be a matter of waiting for the next thing until we're right back here. I'd rather fight and lose than give up. You choose for yourself, Edwyn, but I am not going to give my life to fear anymore."

"Come on," says Willow, approaching carefully with soft magic bright in his hands. "We need to go and I need you with me. We stick together from now on."

Edwyn clenches his teeth and turns his face away, but he doesn't resist as Willow applies the magic once more to his leg.

"What about you?" I ask Teo. "Are you able to run?"

Teo's eyes crack open, and they sit up.

This is the first time I've gotten a good look at Teo and I *know* I'm staring.

I've never seen anyone like them, not here nor in Eyrewood, but I can't put my finger on what it is that sets them apart. They're taller and lankier than I am, though that's not hard, and their filthy clothes remind me of the ones Rowena used to spend hours lovingly stitching by the fire—all deep browns and greens with sparkling flecks like stars or fire embers. There's something that looks suspiciously like a wolf's fang dangling from one ear, and their dirty-blond hair is a mess of wild curls. Their skin is lighter than Neal's but more tan than mine, and there're hints of something on their face that I'd thought were freckles but definitely aren't.

They're more like . . . scales?

"I can run." Their voice is hoarse like they swallowed smoke.

I nod slowly, trying to figure out the question that's been rising steadily.

Helston folks have been calling this kid "he," but I know with a deep certainty that it's not as straightforward as that.

They're like me, my gut whispers. But I don't know how to ask without being rude, and what if I'm wrong?

Better to ask and know. That's what I'd want.

"Hey, uh, what're your words?" I wince at the awkwardness of the question, but Teo's whole self lights up, despite the blood and the chaos and the danger, and I know immediately I was right.

"'Xe/xem.'"

I grin. "I've never heard those before! Like, 'xe,' 'xem,' 'xir,' and such?"

Teo matches my smile, and I recognize the relief on xir face. "What about yours?"

"'They/them.' And my name's Callie. And that's Willow, and they're Elowen and Edwyn. Willow and Edwyn use 'he/him,' and El's 'she/her.'"

Teo's yellow eyes go wide. "I know you," xe breathes, staring at each of us. "Your names are familiar in Dumoor."

All the good feelings drop away, heavy as stones. I had almost let myself forget this kid is a Dumoor kid. Part of the witch's army. On the side of Kensa the dragon.

The enemy.

"If we don't go now, we'll be caught," Elowen is growling at Willow, whose hands are still pressed to Edwyn's calf, brow knotted in fierce focus.

"Okay, I know. We're ready." He helps Edwyn stand and test his legs. They're still wobbly, but it's the best we're gonna get.

Time to run.

The journey up the cliff is a nightmare, and it's nothing short of a miracle when we all make it to the top in one piece. Well, "one piece" is debatable given that none of us are in one piece ourselves. We make it by sheer force of determination alone. There is no choice *but* to make it.

Willow, in the best shape of all of us, reaches the top first and lies on his stomach to help pull us the rest of the way. And there we huddle in the scrubby brush, hiding like hunted rabbits.

The bridge is close, and so are the watchtowers looming

over it. It's common knowledge that watch duty is the worst job in Helston, the most boring, the easiest to mess up simply because it's so easy to stop paying attention. Of course, that was before things started happening. I don't even know who's on duty today. It's weird to think that soldiers I've been friendly with, who I've sparred with, are tasked with taking us down.

"What if we don't run?"

I stare at Willow. "What're you talking about?"

His eyes are fixed on the bridge. "If we take it like we have every right, like we're not doing anything wrong, we'll draw less attention to ourselves. No one will hear us if we walk. And maybe . . . maybe they don't know yet. Maybe Adan hasn't been able to alert anyone." His gaze flicks anxiously to me. "You left him secure, didn't you?"

"Of course we did. No way we'd have escaped otherwise."

"That's what I thought." Willow swallows hard, fingers tapping a fretful beat. Then, softly, just for me, "We're really doing this, aren't we? We're really leaving Helston."

"Yeah. We are."

"Are you scared?"

I nod. "You?"

"Yes. But it's the right thing to do."

"It is."

The bridge has never looked longer, the other side a million miles away. And below . . . I bite my lip. Hard. The water churns, leaping up the rocks like a snapping dog trying to bite our ankles and pull us down. Hungry. Suddenly Helston guards don't feel like the scariest threat. I can fight with the best of them, but if I fall, I'm done.

Even the wind is vicious, like nature itself is working against us.

And what are we walking into? Unforgiving, unending moorland. Wolves. *Dragons*. I can't shake the little question in my head about Teo and what if xey're leading us right into a new danger.

I guess it comes down to which enemy is scarier.

The enemy at our backs or the enemy before us?

With one sword between us, how do we survive either?

It's Willow who takes the first step out of the brush.

Moonlight glints silver in his hair—a crown of stars—as he turns his face upward and looks out across the bridge toward the moorland waiting for us. "Time to go."

At least we're shielded by darkness.

One step, two steps, three steps, four . . .

Enough to tease at hope and half make me believe we stand a chance.

The salt-worn wood complains with every footfall, and I have to remind myself over and over that if this bridge can hold whole companies of horses and armored knights, it can hold five kids.

And then the warning bells ring.

High-pitched and angry, they are nothing like the low pulse of the funeral bells. They are a call to action: *Rise, Helston, and fight!*

Fight us.

"Run!" Willow screams the moment before the first arrow thunks into the wood at my heel.

I grab Edwyn and *drag* him, apologizing internally every time he trips. We stop, we die. The end.

"Turn back!" a man's voice booms, amplified from one of the towers. "Turn back and you will be shown mercy! Halt!"

"Don't listen! Keep going!" Elowen yells as Willow falters. "They're lying!"

I don't know if the watch would knowingly shoot down the crown prince, but the not knowing cinches it. I grab him with my free hand.

And then the thunder starts.

The pounding of boots, the thuddering of horses' hooves. Adan's promise that he would hunt us down ringing in my head, louder than any bell. Did they really find him already, or are these someone else's orders?

The bridge feels endless, like every step we take, two more get added onto the other side.

Even if we make it across the bridge, they're not gonna stop. Even if we could run for a hundred miles, they can run for a thousand.

The thought is so heavy it nearly crushes me.

We were so close.

Solid ground feels like a blessing, but there's no time to relish it.

"Go!" I shout, dropping the boys' hands and drawing Satin. "I'll hold them off as long as I can. Split up if you must, just keep going!"

Edwyn stares at me in horror. "You can't fight them all on your own!"

"I know that," I snap back. "But I can fight some. It might not be much but it might give you enough time to—" I stop.

Willow and Elowen stand with me, fierce magic flaring on their fingers; their faces set hard in identical determination.

Even Edwyn, barely able to stay upright, stands by my side.

"We stay together," he says when I open my mouth. "And we go together."

We don't have as much as a hope, but we have each other and we stand together as Helston's army bears down upon us.

We're ready to fight and ready to fall, but then Teo pushes through our ranks and plants xemself between us and the bridge.

I move to drag xem back. "Hey—"

But I stop as xir body starts to shift and change.

It's small, barely noticeable, but xir ears lengthen—poking out from the crop of xir hair—and what I thought might be freckles become undeniable scales, glinting metallic in the glow of the magic exuding from xir whole body.

The word hits me—*Dragon!*—half a moment before fire bursts from Teo's body and devours the bridge.

I shield my face with my arms. I can't look. Even if I wanted to, it's too hot to open my eyes. My blood feels like it's boiling; my skin and hair singeing. The roar of flames mingles with the men's yells and horses' screams.

Someone grips my arm, fingers pinching, and when I force my eyes open, Willow is staring at the burning bridge in horror, tears streaming from unblinking eyes. Elowen and Edwyn stand together in identical shock, unable to believe the picture in front of us.

Fire races across the boards and beams, eagerly consuming every inch until there's nothing left but ash that disappears into the wind.

The impenetrable bridge. Helston's greatest defense.

On the other side of the ravine, through the smoke and the flames, we are reflected by the soldiers in horror and hopelessness. There's nothing they can do. They can't reach us. They can't touch us. They can't hurt us anymore.

We are safe.

I drop to my knees on the scorched ground.

We are safe.

CHAPTER ELEVEN

The air is thick with smoke that stays burning in our lungs long after we make it to the other side of the hill. We don't stop until we cannot see Helston any longer. And then we collapse.

A stream bubbles not very far away, but none of us have the energy to do anything more than lie in the stubby grass and breathe.

My lungs hurt. My chest hurts. My eyes hurt.

My heart hurts.

Papa and Neal will be awake now, summoned in a panic by the bells. They'll look for me and I won't be there, and I wonder what they'll think. I wonder what they'll be told.

I wonder if they're disappointed in me, and my stomach cramps.

Elowen and Edwyn lie curled up together, so still they

might be sleeping. Willow is a shaking ball, bundled beneath his cloak. I don't know how to comfort him. I don't try. I don't have enough to give anyone else.

Only Teo stays upright, looking out in the direction of the sea.

Dragon.

The word is a warning in my head. One that means—has always meant—*enemy*, and rage starts to roil in my gut.

It's Teo's fault, a little voice whispers in my ear. If xe hadn't attacked and got caught, Helston would've left us alone. If we hadn't wasted time rescuing xem, we wouldn't've been there when Adan found the twins missing.

And if it wasn't for Teo, we would all be dead right now.

Xe has xir back toward me, allowing me to stare without guilt. Xir horns are small but blatant, the same color as xir dirty-blond hair. The patches of scales have a strange blue hue. Xir clothes are what I'd assume to be human clothes, the same loose-fitting tunic and breeches that I like to wear. Teo looks like any other kid. Not a dragon at all.

Dragons lie, Papa told me. *Everyone knows that. Never trust a dragon. They change and trick you soon as look at you. That's how they lure you in.*

Is that what Teo's doing? Taking the shape that would make us trust xem the most?

But that doesn't feel right. That doesn't make sense in the puzzle of my head.

If Teo was tricking us to help xem escape, that was a big gamble. Xe never asked us to help. That was my and Willow's idea, all by ourselves. Xe told us not to risk it but we did anyway. Teo could've gotten away on xir own once we were out of the dungeons.

But xe didn't.

Teo stayed with us and ran with us.

And saved us.

If there is a lie there, I can't find it.

I let all the burned air out of my lungs and close my eyes.

In my dreams, I hear the dragon's song, but this time it's not calling for me.

Private, desperate. Keening. And I feel like I'm eavesdropping on a conversation not meant for my ears.

There are no words, just a whistle that sounds like none I've ever heard before. Not a person or a bird. Not even the wind. It's high and low all at once; a trilling bird and a moaning tree. It seeps through my skin and into my bones and resonates there until I'm trembling.

I am in the middle of the moors on an open plain, surrounded by sky and long grass that bends and bows to the tuneless song; the clouds rushing away like they're being chased. There is no wind.

I crane my neck, searching for their hunter.

I see nothing but the shadows of dragons.

They swarm and swim, slashing the clouds with blade-like wings and snapping them with glinting teeth. Their eyes burn bright in the darkness of their looping silhouettes.

And then one of them pauses in the air and turns to stare at me, great wings flapping slowly.

This dragon isn't a shadow.

Its scales glint red. Blood and fire and burning bridges.

A smile stretches across Kensa's face.

So, little knight, you did it. I knew you would.

You don't know anything, I want to yell. I try to. I open my mouth, but my tongue has forgotten how to make letters. All that comes out is a smoke-scorched rasp from the bottom of my throat.

Don't worry, says Kensa. *You will find your voice again. Be patient. Give it time.* Then the dragon twists in the air, fluid as a snake. *Be seeing you, little knight. Very, very soon.*

─●──

When I wake up, I splash into the stream and I drink and drink and drink until my belly is full. Then I lie in the water, clothes and all, and let the sweet, fresh water soak into my skin.

It's the best bath I've ever had.

I push my fingers through my hair, carefully combing

out as many of the knots as I can, then I rip out a handful of spongy moss and *scrub* until I remember what clean feels like.

It's cold in the early dawn, but I don't care. It feels good to shiver after a night on fire.

I sit on a rock and rebraid my hair, looking back at our makeshift camp. No one stirs. I'm glad. I hope they sleep long and hard.

Mostly because I don't want to even think about what we're supposed to do next.

I let my feet wander and they carry me to the edge of the cliff.

The water is peaceful, shallow waves lapping lazily over the sand like all is well with the world. Like there isn't still smoke in the air. I wonder if I'll ever get the smell out of my nose.

"Hey." Edwyn eases himself down beside me, long legs dangling over the edge. His hair is slicked back and dripping, the blood and soot scrubbed from his skin. If anything, he looks worse now that the bruises and shadows are uncovered. There's a cut in his lip that's still oozing. "You should be sleeping. We've a long day ahead."

"Says you."

He laughs softly. "I've never been much of a sleeper. It takes a long time to fall asleep, and I always wake up early. And it still never feels like there are enough hours in the day."

"There are for people who don't try to fit a week's worth of stuff into one day."

I mean it as a joke, but Edwyn doesn't laugh. "I suppose that's accurate."

"How're you doing?"

Edwyn hunches down. "I'm okay. This may or may not shock you, but I've had worse days. And few that have ended so triumphantly." He catches my eye and hesitates. "I . . . wanted to thank you. I know how much you have left behind on our behalf. I underestimated you."

I can't unknot my frown. "Huh?"

"There's an order to things," says Edwyn jaggedly. "All things. And I . . . I—I've never been at the top of anyone's list." He flushes heavily. "You put me and Elowen first. Above those you love more. Above your fathers and the dream you fought for. You gave all of that up. For us."

I scrunch my face with literally no idea how on earth I'm supposed to respond to this. Even thank-yous are excruciating. "No big deal."

"Yes big deal," Edwyn insists. "Very big deal. I know what you left behind."

My shrug goes up to my ears. I don't want to think about what I left behind. "Anyone else would've done the same," I mumble.

"I know you know that's not true, Callie."

I suck my lip between my teeth and bite. *Hard.* Yeah, I do know. And that's the worst part of all of it. It was so simple to me and Willow. Straightforward. Black-and-white. There was no need for the grown-ups to treat it like it was some complicated, fragile thing.

"It wasn't a choice," I tell him bluntly. "And you don't need to thank me. It's not like we . . . stopped him from—"

"Regardless. Thank you. And thank you for not giving up on me when I was . . . not at my best. I know it would've been easier to leave me behind."

"El didn't mean it. She would never really go without you."

"Elowen is, rightly, sick of making sacrifices on my behalf. She stayed in our parents' apartment when she could've left to live in the Queen's Quarters. She would've been happier. She would've been safer. She stayed for me."

"A choice isn't the same as a sacrifice," I say, nudging his shoulder with mine. "And you need to stop being so shocked that folks are willing to fight for you. You deserve it, no less than everyone else."

He still doesn't believe it, I realize when he turns his face away. To him, they're just words; the kind of hollow placation people tell you when they want you to shut up.

We sit together on the edge of the cliff, looking out to the endless horizon, as the sun rises to warm us. It's a long while before Edwyn speaks again.

"What happens next? Where do we go?"

"I dunno," I admit. "Didn't really think that far, to be honest. The odds were low that we'd even get out. Anywhere you want to go?"

Edwyn shakes his head. "I never gave much thought to the world on the other side of the bridge. I knew I'd cross it once I became a knight, but I'd go where they told me and I would always go back. Father said everything on the other side of the bridge was dangerous. Cursed. Lawless."

"Has your father ever been right about anything?"

Edwyn gives a soft laugh. "Just because you don't like him, doesn't mean he wasn't right about a lot of things."

My eyes narrow. "Like what?"

Edwyn tenses, all wide-eyed like he's been caught doing something he shouldn't, and his fingers start fidgeting. "It doesn't matter."

"Of course it matters!" I take a deep breath, doing my best to keep my irritation out of my voice. "Look, two wrongs don't make a right. Just because your dad *and* Adan—"

"And the whole court."

I grimace. "Okay, a hundred wrongs don't make a right. It wouldn't matter if the whole entire world agreed with Peran, he was *wrong*. Period."

The fiddling gets faster. "Okay."

I want to yell in frustration and shake Edwyn until he gets it. But somehow I don't think that'll help much. I wish there was a place we could go that would prove to Edwyn that the whole world isn't as cruel or bitter as Peran painted it . . .

I perk up so suddenly, Edwyn startles.

"What?"

"Eyrewood!"

He blinks. "I . . . don't know what that is."

"It's home! Or, at least, it was before Papa and me went to Helston. It's the best!" The more I think about it, the more perfect the plan is! It was Eyrewood that pieced me back together and helped me work myself out and let me be messy and make mistakes and loved me the whole time. That's what Edwyn needs. That's what we *all* need. "It's not so far," I tell him enthusiastically. "Well, actually it's pretty far, especially if we're walking, but it's absolutely worth it! And they'll love you!"

Edwyn winces slightly. "They?"

I launch into an enthusiastic description of the family we left behind—Faolan and Rowena, Josh and his *awful* cooking, and Pasco the pirate, and the home they cobbled together in Eyrewood Forest out of nothing, where everyone is welcome. Unconditionally.

"Nothing is unconditional," says Edwyn bitterly, and I deflate.

"I know it seems like that, but—"

"*Everything* comes with conditions, Callie. That isn't a criticism, just a fact. And I'm not going to be foolish enough to let you convince me otherwise again. I—I don't mean that badly," he adds quickly, catching the look on my face. "I understand why you wanted me to believe it the way you believe it. And I understand how you're able to. But we're not the same, and it was my own fault for forgetting that."

I don't tell Edwyn he's wrong. I don't argue that the

twisted world Peran and Adan created for him is the false one. I don't promise better on the other side of this adventure.

I just hope, with everything I am, that I can prove him wrong.

"I'm glad you're here with us."

"Me too. Thank you for not leaving me behind."

"Nothing to say thank you for. We're family. Family sticks together." I elbow him lightly until I pull a smile from his lips. *"Unconditionally."*

CHAPTER
TWELVE

Willow and Elowen are up and stoking a small fire by the time Edwyn and I head back.

"Teo's gone to catch breakfast," says Willow before I can ask. And, "Callie, there's something you need to know—"

"Xe's a dragon. Yeah, I worked it out last night."

Edwyn says, *"Dragon?"*

Just as Willow says, "Xe's?"

"Yes, dragon. And Teo told me yesterday xir words are 'xe/xem.'"

I swear, every time Willow goes starry-eyed, they get brighter. "That's *pretty!*"

But Edwyn has gone a sickly gray color. "Dragon ... Xey're a ... a dragon."

"Xey're not bad," says Willow. "Xe's on our side—"

"But a *dragon!* Dragons are—"

143

"What we are *not* doing," says Elowen with a sharp glance at her brother, "is making rash assumptions."

"*Elowen.*"

"Edwyn."

The twins glare at each other, and I've never agreed with two differing opinions so heartily.

Dragons are the known enemy of humankind—the villain of all the best ballads, and the worst insult folks sling around. The greatest accomplishment a knight can achieve is slaying a dragon. Everyone knows this. And it's not like our previous experience did anything to change that opinion. Fangs and fire and flame . . . But El's right too. Teo is different. Or *seems* to be different.

Dragons lie, Papa's voice echoes in my head. *Trust your gut.*

But I don't know what my gut thinks.

My gut is *hungry.*

"Dragons are the enemy," Edwyn insists. "Don't you remember the last time we encountered one? How do we know Teo isn't trying to lure us into its nest?"

"Do dragons even live in nests?" Willow muses.

"Not the point," says Edwyn. "We have a plan and it doesn't include partnering with a *dragon.*"

"It's not really a *plan,*" I amend when Elowen and Willow raise questioning eyebrows. "More of a direction. I figured we could head north, toward Eyrewood. I know we'll be more than welcome there, and it's far enough away from Helston that it'll at least *feel* safe."

Elowen hugs her middle. "There isn't anywhere far away enough from Helston to feel safe."

Willow pokes at the fire. "I wonder what they're doing right now. It's late enough they'll be awake—"

"I'm pretty sure burning down the bridge was enough to wake anyone up last night," I say. "I wonder if they've found Adan. I wonder what they told Papa and the queen."

Willow winces. "I'm sure they're worried."

"I'm sure they're *furious*," says El. "Wherever we decide, we should start moving as soon as we can. I don't believe for one moment that a broken bridge will be enough to stall Helston for long."

I sit forward. "Seriously? I thought the bridge was the only way in or out of Helston."

"It's the only *easy* way," Willow says, almost apologetically. "It could never be the only way, precisely for reasons such as these. There weren't always protective wards up. It isn't impenetrable. Not truly. There always needed to be an escape."

My head aches. "So they could be after us. They could be tracking right now. We need to go!"

"No one has used the boats in years," says Willow. "*Decades*. If they're even serviceable, it's going to take a while. We have time to breathe."

That's not what the panic in my chest says.

"And if they catch us, we are not helpless." Elowen's voice is quiet but sharp, edged with anger. "We fought and we won unarmed. I am not afraid to face them again. In fact, let them try." She raises her face with a flash of something fierce and a curling smile that makes me uneasy. "Let them come close enough that I may take revenge."

"Revenge?" Willow echoes. "Against Helston?"

"Don't you want it too? After everything they've done to us?"

Willow catches my eye.

"I think we got a pretty healthy dose of revenge last night, El."

But she shakes her head hard. "Not enough. Not nearly enough."

Luckily we have to put all revenge talk aside in favor of breakfast when Teo returns, triumphant, with a whole armful of limp rabbits, which xe promptly starts to skin with one deadly-sharp claw.

"And I was certain we were going to starve," I muse, unsheathing Satin in an attempt to help out.

"The moors provide," says Teo, finishing xir second in less time than it takes me to get halfway through one. "So long as you know where to look." Xe grins, showing off glinting fangs. "Lucky you've got me to help, huh?"

Can't exactly argue with that, dragon or not.

Willow takes charge of the cooking like he's a seasoned camper and not the future king who, until a few hours ago, lived his whole life in a royal palace. He skewers the rabbits on sticks Edwyn sharpens with Satin while I take the time to study Teo properly.

It's so obvious what xe is now, I can't imagine *not* seeing dragon in xem.

"Did they know?" I ask. "Adan and his lot. That you're a dragon."

Teo shakes xir head. "No way. I would *definitely* be dead if they did. The first thing any dragon learns is how to hide what they are." Teo reaches to touch one of the pale horns sprouting from xir head like xe's confirming they're still there. "It feels good to be me again." Then Teo pauses, pointed ears twitching down, and xir eyes dart anxiously between us. "It's not a . . . You're not gonna . . . We're allies, aren't we? Friends?"

Xe's scared, I realize in shock. Not just scared—*terrified.*

A *dragon* is scared of *us.*

"Of course we are," says Willow quickly when my silence stretches a little too thin. "We're indebted to you."

Teo screws up xir face. "You're the ones who saved me."

"We saved each other," says Elowen. "I don't think it can get much more equal than that."

"At least let me repay you in some way," Teo insists. "I don't know what your strategy is, but there's a haven for you as long as you want it. *If* you want it."

I frown. "A haven?"

The dragon nods eagerly. "A sanctuary. A safe place for all those who wander the moors in search of a home. Everyone is welcome."

Edwyn's eyes narrow. "And the conditions are?"

Xir head cocks. "Conditions?"

"Nothing is free," says Edwyn with a bite of impatience. "And we don't have anything to give."

"No conditions," says Teo, shaking xir head emphatically. "I swear."

Dragons lie.

"How do we know to trust you?" I ask. "How do we know you're not just leading us into some kind of trap?"

Hurt floods Theo's face, and I fight against the guilt. But it's a fair question, isn't it? We might've been through a nightmare and back, but that doesn't mean we know each other. And when it comes all the way down to it, knights and dragons are natural enemies. There's no point pretending otherwise.

"I know it's risky," says Willow softly. "And it seems illogical to willingly go into the heart of enemy territory, but El's right—whose enemy? We don't know anything about anything. Friends are enemies and enemies are friends, and I say we give xem a chance. Besides"—he twists the hem of his tunic—"maybe it would be useful to make contact with Dumoor. *Positive* contact. Maybe if we help Teo get home, it might go some way to repairing the relationship between Helston and Dumoor."

Something inside me sparks and explodes. *"You wanna go on a diplomatic mission? Are you kidding me?"*

Willow flushes. "We're not on anyone's side anymore, but maybe we can use that to stop this war before it begins. If we can show Dumoor that Helston isn't that bad, maybe they'll make amends with Helston. And Helston will see that magic isn't the problem and their fears are unfounded and—"

"You can go home," I finish for him.

Willow winces. "Is it awful to want that, after everything?"

El says, "Yes!" just as I say, "Of course it isn't."

"Helston was your whole life," I continue to Willow with a hard look at El. "It's not always easy letting it go, no matter how bad they treat you."

"It isn't just that," says Willow bleakly. "I've been thinking a lot, even before yesterday, for a long time now . . . Helston is *my* responsibility. Even if I'm not crown prince anymore, even if they hate me. If there's a way to help, I have to do it."

"You don't *have* to do anything."

"But I want to," he insists. "I'm not saying I want to go home or I think we shouldn't have left. I'm not saying I want things to go back to the way they were. But if there's an opportunity to do some good—to be better—I *want* to take it." He sighs. "Regardless, we need a direction, and this is the only one we have."

"What about Eyrewood?" I ask. "It's farther, but at least we know it's actually safe!"

"Eyrewood's a *long* way," says Teo. "If you're going to make the journey, you're going to need supplies. Please, come back to The Roost with me. Let me repay you in food and shelter and supplies."

"What's the roost? Is that like a collective of dragons? Thought that'd be a 'swarm' or something."

"I think the actual term is 'horde,'" Teo muses, either ignoring my jab or not understanding it. "But there's never been enough of us for that. Dragons are pretty rare. Or, at least, mostly unknown. It's not a very . . . fun thing to be."

Which sounds like the biggest lie of them all, because who *wouldn't* want to be a dragon? To fly and breathe fire and shape-shift . . . to be the most powerful creature in the world. Unstoppable. If I was a dragon, no one would ever give us trouble again.

"Anyway," Teo continues, "The Roost is home, the heart of Dumoor's community. It's the safest place in Wyndebrel, founded as a haven for the lost and wandering. *Everyone* is welcome."

Teo's assurances do nothing to make any of feel less uneasy. Things that feel too good to be true usually are. Like Edwyn said, there isn't anything in this world that is truly unconditional, especially toward strangers.

It's El who asks, "At what cost?"

Teo's yellow eyes blink. "There is no price," xe says with half a question in xir voice. "We help anyone who seeks it. There is no condition or obligation. No price."

"But that's not true," I say. They all stare at me. "What? Remember, we know someone who got out of Dumoor. Who escaped and told me *everything*."

Teo's ears twitch. "Who?"

I suck my mouth shut. I don't want to tell xem about Neal. It feels too risky, like a secret that isn't mine to spill. "Doesn't matter who," I say. "But he told me all about Dumoor. He said that nothing is ever free and the price is never worth it."

Hurt flashes across Teo's expression. "Someone said that about us? Are you sure?"

"Yes?" But I can't keep the question out of my voice. Maybe I'm not sure. Maybe there's more to Neal's story than he let me believe.

I give a rough shrug and scowl. "I dunno. Maybe you're from a different bit of Dumoor. Maybe the Witch Queen is separate—"

"The Witch Queen?" Teo asks, perking up. "You mean Alis?"

"Yeah?"

The dragon grins, fangs flashing. "She runs The Roost! She's in charge of all of Dumoor."

My heart sinks like a thrown stone. That is exactly what I feared.

"I don't think we would be welcome there," says Willow carefully. "There's a history . . . We're not exactly on good terms."

Teo's ears droop. "But you're different. You're not Helston. And everyone is welcome, no matter what. Besides, she's so busy she probably wouldn't even know you're there if you're not planning on staying. Please, let me do this for you. Wherever you're going, you're going to need more than you have, and The Roost will always provide. The beds are the most comfortable, the fires are the warmest, and the food—" Teo groans in longing. "My mum, she was the best cook in our whole village, but hers is nothing compared to what I've eaten since I joined The Roost. I promise, it'll give you all the strength you could possibly need for your journey and then some!"

I don't even need details—my mouth is like a waterfall already, and once I start thinking about food, there's no hope of stopping.

But still—

"How're you gonna convince us this isn't a trap or a trick?" I demand, crossing my arms tight. "For all we know, this could all be a grand conspiracy. Why should we believe you?"

Teo hesitates, gaze flicking between us. Then xe bows xir head and holds out xir hands, one cupped within the other. "By the feathers that fly and the rain that falls, by the end of days and the rise of the moors, I swear it."

The spell is a softly spoken incantation but the magic is sharp, a true and tangible thing as it wraps around my wrist and *pulls*.

I try to jerk my hand back but the dragon holds on.

"From my heart to yours and all the truth in my soul, I swear it. Break my word, break my heart."

The magic that presses into my skin, into my veins, into my blood, is warm and reassuring. It feels like Neal's arms wrapped around me. It feels like Papa's kiss on the top of my head. A truth I can trust.

"I will not lead you to danger," Teo intones. "I will not ask anything from you that you are not willing to give. You have my oath, my life, myself. By the moors which bind us, it is done."

And suddenly the magic isn't just Teo's. It is the moor's.

Ancient power stirs and shifts in the ripple of grass and the brush of wind, turning the air bright and hazy around us, like sun through fog. Around me, the others rise almost as though an invisible hand is coaxing them up. Elowen sits forward, fascinated, and Willow's eyes go huge with wonder. Even Edwyn stares, more intrigued than afraid.

And me . . . This promise feels like the first true thing to me in far too long.

"What was that?" I breathe when the spell is complete and I feel the magic release me.

"An oath," the dragon replies. "And the moors will hold me to my word. We do not make promises lightly in Dumoor."

I rub my arm where the remnants of the spell still tingle on my skin. I'm surprised it didn't leave a mark. "You didn't have to do that. You don't owe us anything."

"It's not about owing or having to," says Teo earnestly. "I want to help because I believe in you. And I made the oath because I understand how hard it is to trust a stranger."

My breath loosens a little, then a little bit more. Xe's not telling me what I want to hear just for the sake of it. Xe's not lying. Xe's giving us the best truth xe can. And I believe xem.

I believe a dragon.

CHAPTER THIRTEEN

I will never not be thankful that it isn't winter, nor the cool spring we get down here, full of surprise snow and bitter chill. I'm also pretty relieved it's not the middle of summer, when the air is thick and sweltering and every step brings a new bucket of sweat.

I count the things I'm thankful for as we start our trek in earnest, trudging up and down hills and across barren moorland, eyed by the soaring falcons, which wonder if we're prey.

I keep my hand on Satin every step, endlessly thankful that I had the forethought to bring her with me. We don't have much, but together we can do anything.

Ish.

We do our best, and every one of us is determined and stubborn, but I know my friends. Their little tells of weariness and pain, hunger and fear, as we walk farther and farther away from the only home they've ever known. Even if it was a home that hurt them.

Only the dragon has a spring in xir step.

Teo grows a little stronger with every mile we get away from Helston; ears pricked and eyes bright, there's a smile always twitching across xir lips.

I still can't decide how I feel about trusting a dragon.

My heart is all in, but my head won't shut up—going over and over everything anyone's ever told me about dragons, and I can't find anything good. Not a single detail.

But even if all dragons are bad, there's got to be exceptions, right? And why shouldn't we find ourselves friends with the single exception?

Even if it does seem impossibly unlikely.

"You okay?"

I startle out of my grimace at Teo's voice. "Yeah. Sure. Why?"

"You look like you have a stomachache."

"Wow. Thanks. You know, walking a hundred thousand million miles without breakfast will do that."

"You had breakfast."

"Barely."

"I can catch more—"

"We don't have time to waste."

"Eating isn't waste."

"It is if we get caught and killed."

"You think that's what'll happen?"

I shrug up to my ears. "Dunno. Not worth finding out."

We continue in silence. I glare at the scrubby grass beneath my feet, at the bracken marking a crude path beside the trickling river, and I feel Teo's eyes upon me. I grit my teeth. Neal told me about Dumooi. He warned me about dragons and their unkeepable promises, and the deals the witch demands of anyone fool enough to get sucked in.

But everything Neal told me—everything *Papa* told me—feels like it's crumbling to sand in my fingers, and the harder I try to grasp it, the faster it trickles away.

"So . . . how'd you get yourself captured? If you're a super-powerful dragon, I mean. If I was you, I'd have obliterated them the moment they touched me."

Teo's shoulders sag on a long sigh. "I'm not a proper dragon yet," xe admits. "What happened at the bridge . . . I've never done anything like that before in my life. I didn't even know I *could* do that yet—I just knew I had to try." Teo offers a guilty smile as I gawk at xem. "Yeah, I know. It was a risk."

"No kidding . . ." I don't want to think about what would've happened if Teo's magic had given out. If the soldiers had managed to make their way across the bridge and run us down. Our fate hung on a thread so fragile, one breath in a different direction could've snapped it.

"I'm still learning how to be"—xe makes a vague gesture to xemself—"*me*. With all my dragonish potential. And it's all still new to me."

"Yeah?" I look at xem with interest. "Tell me about it?

157

How'd you become a dragon?" Because, not gonna lie, I wouldn't mind taking those lessons myself.

"Oh, that's easy," Teo chirps. "Dragons are born, not made."

"Like out of an *egg*?"

"That's a common misconception."

I grimace. "Sorry. I thought I knew about dragons. All the stories make out like they're lizards."

Teo laughs. "It's okay. I didn't know about dragons either until not so long ago."

"But you *are* one . . ."

"But I didn't know *what* I was," says Teo. "Only that I was different. I didn't know I was a dragon until these came in." Xe touches a finger to the sharp tip of one horn. From a distance, they look pale blue, but up close they shimmer with a whole spectrum of colors, pearlescent in the sunlight. "My parents didn't know what I was either. They took me to see a healer in the city of Fairkeep who specializes in curses. They thought I must've upset a powerful witch and got myself in trouble."

"Wait. Your parents aren't dragons?"

Teo shakes xir head. "Nope. Just me. No one knows how it happens, just that some people are dragons." Xe glances away. "The healer . . . she told my parents it would be safest to kill me. Safest for them and a kindness to me. No one looks kindly on dragons and, fully grown, we're the most dangerous beings in existence." Teo gives a crooked smile, fangs poking out. "Wouldn't think that to look at me, I bet."

I shake my head numbly. On the outside, Teo looks just about as dangerous as Willow. Though I guess that's an illusion too.

Teo continues, "But my parents weren't going to be scared off. They told her they didn't care. They loved me and would help me, no matter what I was." Xe sighs. "They should've lied and promised to do as she said."

"What happened?" I make myself ask, because of all my guesses surely the truth can't be worse.

"She told our village leader that my parents were sheltering a monster," says Teo. "And one day they came for me. My parents protected me. I escaped. I shouldn't have. I should've stayed. *I* should've been the one protecting *them*. But I didn't know what to do. I ran. I hid. And when I came back—"

I dig my fingernails hard into the soft part of my palm. "They died?"

Teo nods, tears dribbling down xir face. "They were killed. Because of me."

"No," I say fiercely. "Not because of you. It wasn't your fault."

But that's not 100 percent true, is it? In all the epic ballads and sweeping stories of knights chasing down the evil dragon who terrorized the villages and stole the princesses, slaying the beasts and bringing bits of their bodies back as trophies . . . I always imagined them the way they're stitched onto tapestries—fearsome, bloodthirsty beasts who hatch out of their eggs already murderous. Who should be destroyed

159

on sight before they even get the chance to live up to their reputation.

Papa's slain dragons.

I wonder if any of them looked like Teo.

And if a human had stood between the sword and the dragon, what would've happened?

I know what would've happened.

The same thing that happened to Teo's parents.

"You couldn't fight back?" I ask in a breath. "You could've destroyed them, just like you did the bridge—"

"I didn't have my magic then," Teo replies. "At least, I didn't know how to access it. Metamorphosis is a slow process. My eyes changed first, then my horns came in and my scales developed. I didn't learn any magic until The Roost found me."

I stare at xem, unable to even pretend not to. Some moments xe looks totally human, others I can't believe I could ever mistake Teo for anything other than what xe is.

"If I had learned about myself sooner, I would've been able to hide," Teo continues. "The first thing I was taught was how to change my body, to pass for human. No one ever needed to know. But there's no school for dragons. No books to learn how to be one. Only ballads that call us monsters, where the hero vanquishes us. Maybe there's more of us, everyone's just hiding and no one dares admit it."

I gnaw my lip until the tang of blood slicks across my tongue. I know those ballads. I grew up on those tales. Papa told them as though they were true. And—right up until this moment—I believed them.

I should know by now that there are two sides to every story.

"If you can change your shape and hide your dragon-ness, why don't you?" I ask. "You could live a normal life as a normal kid and no one would ever know—" I stop short at a particular look from Teo.

"Is that what you would want, Callie?"

I flush heavily. No. It isn't. A life pretending to be something you're not is no life at all. Why should that be any different for a dragon?

Teo gives a small smile. "I learned how to hide, but I also learned how to be myself. I learned how to fit into the person I was made to be. Not a human hiding, not a monster to be defeated, just me. And I've found a home that accepts me as I am, where I can be useful as myself."

"But aren't you mad?" I ask. "About what happened to your parents? If you're getting stronger and stronger . . . Do you ever think about revenge?"

Teo's ears flick. "Revenge?"

"Yeah . . ." I try to gather my scrambled thoughts together in some semblance of order. "I mean . . . If anyone hurt my dads, I'd be mad. I'd want to pay 'em back. Hurt them like they hurt me."

The dragon balks, shaking xir head hard. "No, not once. It wouldn't help. It wouldn't bring them back. It wouldn't make things right. I . . . I figured the best thing I can do is live." Xe blushes, turning xir scales a blue-green-pink gradient. "I know that sounds selfish, but that's what they wanted for me. And that's why they . . . did what they did. Yes, I'm mad, but the most effective form of revenge I can take is to be myself, 100 percent. There's nothing humans hate more than the thought of a dragon living their best life." Teo gives a crooked smile. "That's what Kensa says, anyway."

I stop short. So fast, Willow nearly barrels right into my back. I don't care. Every nerve on my body is on fire. "Kensa. You know Kensa?"

"Of course I know Kensa! Xe's my mentor!"

It makes sense. Obviously it makes sense. But that doesn't stop my head from spinning or my stomach from roiling so hard I'm pretty sure I'm about to puke on my boots.

"I know it was bad, when you met before." Teo's voice is distant through the buzzing in my ears, like there's a hundred feet of water between us. "But Kensa's not like that. Not normally. Xe told me about you. About all of you."

"You didn't tell us," says Elowen. "You should've told us."

"I know. I'm sorry. I didn't know how. And I thought, if I did, then—"

Edwyn's voice is brittle with anger. "Then we wouldn't come with you?"

Teo gives a tiny nod. "I'm sorry."

"If Kensa told you about us, you know xe tried to kill us!"

"No! That isn't what happened! I mean . . . On the outside it was, but xe would never try to kill you! I know Kensa," Teo insists. "And I know the mission."

Willow steps forward. "What mission?"

Teo's gaze darts nervously between us. "To . . . save you."

CHAPTER FOURTEEN

"**S**ave us?" My laugh is an uncomfortable twisted thing on my tongue. "Are you *kidding*? Kensa tried to *obliterate* us!"

"No!" Teo insists. "We don't instigate. We don't kill. We defend! We protect!"

My nerves finally give out and my temper *snaps*. I draw Satin and level her right at Teo's chest. "Liar. Everyone knows dragons lie and you nearly tricked us into thinking you were different. There's no such thing as a dragon's oath, is there? You're just continuing Kensa's *mission,* trying to lure us in to . . . to what? Recruit us? Curse us? *Kill* us?"

Teo raises xir hands, shrinking back as I advance. "Of course not! I meant every word, I swear it!"

"Why should we believe you?" I demand. "You're on the enemy's side!"

"We don't know that."

I whip around at Elowen's soft voice, and she meets my stare squarely.

"Xe should've told us right at the start," she pushes on. "But xe's done nothing but help us. And I think it's worth finding out for ourselves who is the enemy and who isn't. You really want to go by Helston's assumptions? Teo's right—if Kensa's goal was to kill us, xe could've done so. Easily."

"*Who cares!*" I explode, startling a small flock of gulls into the air. "Even if the actual out-loud purpose wasn't *murder*, you can't in any way say that xe didn't attack us! I'm not about to get tied up in semantics debating a dragon, El!"

But Elowen stands her ground, strong as if she was taking root in the earth itself. "Semantics are important," she says. "The details *matter*. Otherwise we're no better than the council, who craft their own reality. I believe you," Elowen tells Teo. "And I want to go with you."

My jaw drops. "El—"

"You can decide for yourself what you do," she says. "That's what freedom is. But I'm going with Teo to this Roost place. I want to find out the truth for myself."

I gape at her like a fish, then shut my mouth. All my instincts tell me to *run run run!* But when I think about where those instincts came from and why . . . Well, Elowen's right, isn't she? There's no point pretending we know anything about anything anymore. The only way to know is to find out for ourselves.

"I agree," says Willow. "And I trust Teo not to lead us into danger. If we go and it's bad . . . well, we escaped Helston, didn't we?"

I nod slowly, keeping one eye on Edwyn, who looks like his body's seizing up the way it does around Adan. "And we won't stay for long," I add for his benefit. "We'll go, we'll rest, and then we'll leave. We're there on our terms and our terms only. Right?"

Elowen and Willow nod. "Right."

Edwyn presses his lips together in a hard line and says nothing.

The sun sets and we keep walking. Darkness falls and we keep walking, the magicians leading the way with lights in their palms while I trudge behind them with Edwyn behind me.

Everything is so twisted around and confusing. It has been for ages, long before it all fell apart yesterday (how is it only yesterday?). Ever since Papa and I arrived in Helston that very first day, everything I thought I was sure of has been proven wrong. And it won't stop. It's not gonna stop until there's nothing left apart from me. Just me. And I'm terrified I'm gonna lose myself too. Maybe I already have. I've wanted to be a knight for as long as I can remember. A *Helston* knight. Without that compass pointing my way, I don't know where I'm going.

It's impossible not to think about the fact that we're literally walking into the arms of the enemy, toward the dragon we ran from and the infamous banished princess. Everything and everyone we were warned against. And not just by folks I know not to trust, but by those I do.

By those I did.

I clench my jaw until the ache distracts me.

⊰—⊱

The moon is high in the sky when we finally stop beneath the canopy of a tree so ancient and sprawling, its branches reach out in a wide embrace that seems to go on forever.

When we sit down, it feels safe. Like nothing can touch us here. It feels like when Papa and I camped inside the ancient stone circle, guarded by the moor's wards.

I can breathe.

Willow curls up and falls asleep easily between thick, gnarled roots; cocooned in his cloak, with Teo on one side and Edwyn on the other.

Elowen doesn't even pretend to sleep, sitting up with her arms wrapped around her knees, occasionally tending to the small fire. I take my place beside her, and we sit with our heads touching in silence until, one by one, the others start snoring.

Then, softer than a murmur, "Callie, I need to ask a favor of you."

"Anything," I tell her immediately, honestly. "Anything at all."

Her fingers find mine and our hands twine tight together. "This is my dream. My want. I've had it ever since we escaped Kensa before. I know that I'm meant to be in Dumoor. But it isn't Edwyn's dream, and he has a right to his own. Callie, I need you to promise me that you'll help him find it."

"What're you saying, El?"

"I'm saying . . . I'm saying that when the time comes, you'll go ahead without me."

"No."

"You said you would do me a favor. *Anything.*"

"Anything but that!"

"Hush," Elowen begs. "Please. I need you to understand—"

"I understand that the point of getting out of Helston the way we did was to stick together."

"No. The point of escaping Helston was to be *free*. Free to make our own choices and follow our own paths."

"Edwyn will never leave you."

"I won't have him stay where he doesn't want to be for my sake. I know my brother. I know what he is willing to give up for me. I am not going to let him keep doing that, and I need you to help me."

"Why do you think you'll want to stay? What's in Dumoor that's worth giving up everything else for?"

Elowen's silence is thick and guilty, and she turns her face away before she speaks. "Revenge."

Every inch of my skin prickles.

Revenge.

"On who? Adan?"

"Adan. Mother. The queen. All of them."

"El—"

She swipes her hand across her eyes. "I hate them," she whispers fiercely. "Every single person in Helston. Each is as culpable as another."

I chew my lip until blood threatens to spill. All I can think of is: She's including Papa and Neal in that list.

"You think revenge will make things right?"

"Yes. I do."

Her blue eyes are fierce, gaze challenging me to argue and tell her she's wrong.

I can just about manage, "How?"

"How?"

"How will it make things right? What do you think it'll achieve?"

She stares at me like she can't understand how I don't know. Maybe I'm missing something. Then, slowly, "I want them to know how it feels to be us."

I wouldn't wish that on anyone. Even Adan.

"But that's why you have to promise me that, when the time comes, you'll go. It'll be messy. And it's not your fight. It isn't anyone's but mine." She raises her little finger and looks me right in the eye. "Promise me you'll protect my brother."

"I promise I'll protect Edwyn," I say carefully, gripping her finger in mine. "If that means leaving, so be it. But it won't come to that."

Elowen's body relaxes on a breath and she dips her head until our foreheads touch. "I hope not."

⊢——→

I dream of running.

I pelt through darkness, across terrain I cannot see, from enemies I daren't look back at. But I can hear them, snapping at my heels and cursing my existence. I can feel them, their breath hot and heavy, their feet slamming into the ground like a blacksmith's mallet.

I know it's useless. I know I'll be caught. The certainty is sharp in my chest, but desperate fear spurs me onward until the very last moment. If I go down, it won't be for lack of fighting.

Black melts into blue. Sky or sea, I don't know. Both, perhaps. I don't care.

I push my burning body faster, the last little distance.

The pounding of my heart is as loud as the footfalls on my heel and they, in turn, are louder than a war drum beating time to my hand.

The cliff catches me and I skid, almost falling.

In front is an abyss of the unknown.

Behind me, the enemy is familiar.

There is no choice.

I jump.

CHAPTER
FIFTEEN

When I wake up, I still feel like I'm being chased, adrenaline sharp and urgent and real, and the ground is shaking—

Panic kicks me up and I grab at Willow, Elowen, Edwyn. Even Teo.

"Wake up," I hiss, jostling each of them awake. "Someone's coming."

Someone. Like there could be any chance it isn't Helston snapping at our heels.

Elowen is already on her feet, alert and ready with magic in her hand, while Willow helps Edwyn rise. Teo's eyes are bright in the dark; xir ears twitching, listening.

"How many?" I whisper.

"Six. Seven . . . Maybe more. Coming from the west."

The west.

Helston.

"And . . . dogs too."

Edwyn cringes. "They're hunting us."

"Of course they are," Elowen growls. "We're just beasts to them. Less than."

"Maybe . . . maybe we can talk to them," Willow whispers, gathering up our small smattering of things. "Maybe they aren't even looking for us. Maybe it's just a hunting party, a real one, and if we explain what happened they'll help us. Or maybe Mother sent them to—"

"To what?" Elowen snaps, and Willow shuts his mouth. "We're traitors. Fugitives. Enemies of Helston. If we're lucky, we'll be captured and taken back alive. And I don't think we can count on luck."

She's right.

I take a deep breath, steeling myself back into the warrior I am. I might not be bound to Helston, I might not wear the unform or bear the insignia, but that's never stopped me before. I know who I am. I am Sir Callie, the prince's champion, and I know what I need to do.

Run, fight, protect.

In the distance, a dog howls.

Elowen grabs my arm. "You remember your promise?"

I swallow and nod. "I do."

She gives one final smile, then shoves me away. "Go! Run! Teo and I will fend them off."

She's already turned away when Edwyn starts toward her. "Elowen, what—"

I grab his hand to hold him back. "Come on, we have to go. We'll catch up with them later. Please," I beg as the storm of men and horses and dogs comes closer. "We have to at least try. She'll be fine. She's the best of us. Come *on*!"

"No! She's my sister! I—I have to—"

"You have to *live*!" Willow shouts. "That's *it*. That's all! Callie's right, we need to go!"

Neither Willow nor I give Edwyn any more chance to choose.

We take one hand each and run.

Dumoor Forest is like a gaping mouth, open in welcome and eager to swallow us down. And it's the safest place for us. We don't stop. We don't look back. We don't slow. When the gnarled roots rise to snag Edwyn's bad leg, Willow and I keep him upright. We keep each other moving. I don't know where I'm taking us, only that we need to get as far away as possible, as fast as possible.

Elowen can handle it, I tell myself over and over. She's the fiercest of us all. The most capable. She has Teo with her. They'll be okay, and they'll give us time to get away. To escape. To find somewhere safe.

And where is that? A hundred miles off in a different direction?

I push the thought away. It doesn't matter. Safety is ahead. That's it. Just keep going and don't look back.

The trees are bunched and the branches are low, twisted together into an impossible maze that forces us to duck and dip and change trajectory just to keep moving. The sounds of horses and hounds surround us. In front, behind, everywhere and closing in, and I don't know where to go and I don't know how to save us and I need Satin but that means letting go of someone's hand and I've already lost El and Papa and Neal and—

A wolf lands solidly on all four paws in front of us, teeth bared and dripping. Just like the ones that attacked us on our way to Helston. The witch's wolves. I bet it's got her mark on it somewhere.

My first instinct is to shove Willow and Edwyn behind me. But behind isn't safer.

Wolves at our front; dogs at our back.

Willow's free hand lights up but his magic is shaky—exhausted, terrified. We have fought so much, we've barely got anything left.

The wolf stalks toward us, shoulders up, breath hot, but when it finally lunges, it goes right around us. Straight for a dog, whose growls turn to a yelp.

I don't pause to look or ask questions. As long as we're in one piece, we gotta keep going.

Men shout to each other. *At* each other. Not so far away,

someone cries out in anger and pain. It doesn't sound like Teo or El. I wonder if they've been found yet. I hope not. I hope they ran in the opposite direction. I hope—

"Halt! You're surrounded!"

We freeze in unison and I brace for teeth or arrows or both in the middle of a clearing carpeted with trampled leaves and gnarly roots.

But when I see who it is, I burst out laughing.

Peter glares down at me on a horse that's way too big for him with a sword he can barely lift. And no backup.

"Seriously? Don't you have anything better to do?"

"Shut up," he snaps, jumping down and hitting the ground hard. "Didn't you hear me? We've got you surrounded. You've nowhere to go."

"It's three against one," I remind him softly. "And you've never beaten *any* of us in single combat. Just because you've been given a big-boy sword, doesn't mean you know how to use it."

Peter levels the sword right at my face. Okay, maybe he *does* know how to use it.

That's fine.

I unsheathe Satin.

My stance is firm; my heartbeat, steady. I know what to do and I know I can win.

"Let's go," I murmur. "Best of one. Winner takes all."

"And give you the chance to cheat again? I don't think so, Calliden."

The name is a knife in my throat, and I strike with a snarl and a double-handed swing.

"That's. Not. My. *Name!*"

Peter meets me strength for strength, force for force, and he smirks behind his sword. "I guess it's true what they say. Girls really are too *emotional* for battle."

"I *wish* there was a girl here to grind you into the ground," I spit. "If El was here, there wouldn't be anything left of you to take back to Helston. Lucky for you."

The next blow rings right through me. "Elowen thinks she's something she's not. Just like you. Just like *them.*" And I know he's talking about Willow and Edwyn. "You think you're better than us. You think you're *above* us." The blows get harder, faster, more difficult to deflect. "Well, you're not. You're *dirt.* Less than dirt—"

My heel snags on a raised root and I crash to the ground, my head thunking back against a tree. A sword point grazes my cheek before the stars clear from my eyes.

"And if we didn't have strict orders to take you home alive, I'd—"

"Stand *down,* Squire Peter."

The cool point drops, leaving a spark of pain and a dribble of something warm. I don't try to stand.

Peter bows quickly. "Captain Jory, I was just—"

"I saw exactly what you were doing," Jory says sharply, shutting Peter up. "You and I will talk later." The captain dismounts and rushes to me, gripping my forearm and hauling me up on wobbling legs.

"You gonna arrest me?" I ask thickly through a swallow of blood. I guess I bit my tongue on my way down. My head hurts. My cheek stings, and when I swipe at it, my hand comes away red. I shoot Peter a glare but his gaze is planted on the ground. Cowed.

A small triumph.

"Callie." Jory's urgency forces my attention up. "Where is His Highness?"

"Willow? He's—" I look around for Willow and Edwyn, but neither is here. Good. I hope they ran. I hope they got away. I level my glare at Jory. "Not telling."

Jory pinches the bridge of his nose so tight I half expect it to come right off. "Callie, child . . . Do you have any idea the trouble you've caused?"

"I've got a fair idea. But I'm not sorry. I'd do it again. Over and over. And we're not going back to Helston."

"You're not in trouble. We're not here to arrest you, we're here to help—"

"Don't lie." The grip on my shoulder is friendly and loose. Easy to escape from. I back up, Satin ready in my hand if I need her.

"Not lying." Jory puts up his hands, like that proves anything. "Your dads are beside themselves with worry. Her Majesty too." His eyes flick to something behind me, and Willow creeps out of the trees, Edwyn following reluctantly. Warm relief breaks across Jory's face. "They charged me with bringing you home safely. All of you. That's it. They just want to make sure you are all where you're supposed to be. Please," he says when none of us move. "I know you're scared and I know you think they failed, but—"

"We don't think," I snap. "We know."

"Of course. I'm sorry. I know too. It wasn't right, what happened. Any of it."

I bristle. "Then why didn't you say anything? Or do anything? Why did you just stand there and *let* them?"

"There was nothing I could do—"

"Then what's changed?"

Confusion flicks across his lined face. "Changed?"

"Yeah. What's different now? When we go back with you, what's changed to make Helston better and safer? Did the queen stand up to the council? Did Adan get banished for what he did to Edwyn? Is Willow allowed to be himself? Has El been pardoned?"

Jory's guilty swallow is answer enough.

"I didn't think so." I gather myself together and sheathe Satin. "Look, tell Papa and Neal I'm okay. We're all okay. We're doing what we need to do for us and we'll write when we can. You can tell Her Majesty that too. If you mean what you say, you won't make us go back and they will understand. Helston doesn't want us. If they really want us back, they're gonna have to make changes first. You take that message home."

"Tell Mother I love her," says Willow. "And I'm sorry for hurting her but I'm not sorry for leaving. Callie's right—if they want us back, it will have to be safe there before we return."

To my surprise, Jory bows deeply. "You are right. My orders were to see you safe, and I understand now that I would fail those orders by forcing you home. I will take your messages with me and I know they will bring comfort to your families."

"You're . . . letting us go?" Edwyn asks.

"I am doing what I should've done a long time ago," Jory replies. "I'm sorry it took all this. Go now," he says sharply. "There are others who will not understand. Be safe. We will see each other again."

"Thank you," Willow tells him, gripping the captain's hand in both his own. "We are indebted to you. I will see you honored when we return."

"I hope that is sooner than later, Highness. Look after each other, hear?"

"That was always the plan, sir."

And then there's a sound. Tiny. Barely more than a shifting insect that sounds like a *thwip*.

Jory gasps, and it's like all the breath has been suddenly stolen from his body.

I don't understand.

For the longest time I don't understand.

Until Jory falls with an arrow in his neck, blood pooling on the ground. Already gone. Already dead.

CHAPTER SIXTEEN

Willow screams.

So do I, though my voice doesn't sound like my own.

"You killed him," Peter whispers, his voice a breathless squeak. "Why did you kill him?"

"Move aside," says a voice in the trees.

"What're you going to do?"

"That is not for you to question."

"The orders were to bring them home—"

"*Move!*"

"Callie, watch out!" Edwyn yanks me down just as another arrow whistles past my ear and thunks straight into the solid trunk of the tree behind us.

I stare at the quivering arrow. The same kind that felled Jory.

In one thoughtless motion, I yank the arrow free and stuff it down my tunic.

Adan steps out of the darkness, a third arrow leveled right at Willow.

"So sad," he says softly. "So tragic. How will Her Majesty survive another loss? Her last son. The only living member of her family. I wouldn't be surprised if this killed her. How cruel Dumoor is. How valiantly Helston tried to save the children. Such a tragedy Jory fell defending the young prince. He never stood a chance against the witch's army. We were lucky any of us survived at all." He glances back at Peter, stone-still and staring in confusion and horror. "Aren't you?"

"Aren't I—?"

"Lucky," Adan prompts. "To survive."

The implication settles heavy like cold, wet wool.

"It isn't your fault it went south. The girl was foolish. If she hadn't resisted, we would've got away in time. It's no one's fault but hers that the mission failed. She put us all in critical danger."

It takes a long, dizzying moment to realize he's talking about me. And he doesn't plan for any of us to survive.

Willow scrabbles backward, glaring up at the Helston knight. "You won't get away with this," he says, voice wobbly but strong. "They'll know. As soon as you ride back, they'll know."

He flinches as Adan stands right over him.

"Perhaps," says Adan. "And perhaps they'll be glad. Perhaps it'll be a relief. Perhaps no one will ever say it out loud, but perhaps this will be the best thing that ever happened to Helston."

"I will live," Willow returns fiercely. "If only to see you brought to justice."

"Would you like to make a wager, Your Highness?"

Adan draws back the string.

I grope for Satin.

I can't find her.

The arrow is inches away from Willow's head.

A snap. A yell. My heart stops.

But it's not Willow's yell.

Magic crackles in the air.

Green magic.

Edwyn's magic.

And Adan is clutching his face with a snarl of agony, blood spraying between his fingers.

"Move! Go! Come on!"

The ground lurches beneath my feet like the forest is on a boat in the middle of a storm, rolling and pitching and trying to knock me to my death.

Only Edwyn's grip on my arm tethers me to safety.

We run.

"*After them!* Don't let them get away!"

We're not running *toward* anymore. We're running away.
Running for our lives.

The forest is alive with magic and the sound of fighting, and I have no idea who's fighting who, only that we need to get away from both sides and the man hunting us down.

Horses and humans scream and snarl; blades flashing and blood spilling. Willow stumbles. I grab at him. I miss. I can't tell the difference between dogs and wolves. They both lunge for us with snapping jaws.

And I don't have Satin.

I left her lying on the ground. Just like I left Jory.

Jory.

There's no time to grieve.

Only the living get to grieve, and that means we have to survive.

We have to—

Something scorches into my back and for a moment I think I've been hit by a wayward spell. I reach behind and touch feathers. My hand comes away slick and red.

My stomach lurches. My eyes don't understand the vision in front of them.

A crash of branches and Adan lunges after us, face contorted in triumph.

Peter looks small in his shadow.

I thought he was bigger than that.

"Callie!"

I dunno if it's Willow or Edwyn or Jory or Papa, and it kinda sounds like all of them. It sounds like dragons and wolves and hounds and my own blood rushing out of me.

I fall.

CHAPTER
SEVENTEEN

I don't dream.

I don't feel.

Is this what dying is?

Many folks believe many different things as far as death goes, but I always figured it would be a short, sharp stop.

Not whatever this is.

What is this?

In the distance, I can feel my own pain, am dimly aware of life moving around me, but I'm not a part of it. Like there's a wall between us that I'm not allowed through. And I don't want to go. I'm tired. So bone-tired it's all that I am and all that I will ever be.

And I hope this doesn't last forever. If I'm going to be dead, I'd rather stop existing at all.

Except I don't.

Instead, I dream of dragons and Papa. Of falling, of being

caught; of running, running, running from the shadows sweeping across the sky. Papa's hand in mine, pulling me onward because stopping isn't a choice, giving up isn't an option.

Fight, kiddo, fight.

I fight.

I fight until I'm beyond exhausted and sweating. Until I give everything I am and then a whole lot more. I fight the shadows and the arrows, and the men at my back.

I fight until I win.

And then I wake up.

CHAPTER EIGHTEEN

The world is bright, made only of light, and I cannot open my eyes against it. It hurts. My whole self hurts. Like I'm being held together by frayed string and if I move, it'll snap and I'll fall apart.

There is nothing to do but hold my breath and wait until, little by little, piece by piece, my body wakes up.

First, my throat and my tongue, so dry I don't remember the taste of water.

Then, when I cough, my chest. My ribs pull against my skin, emphasizing my bruises and the soft, sore parts, which spread over my sides and down my legs and into my back.

My back.

Memory is the last to come, and it flies fast and sharp as the arrow that felled me.

I got hit.

But I'm alive.

I am alive, aren't I?

I test the theory and try to move, pushing life into my limbs, my hands, my fingers—

"No, stay still."

Gentle hands and a familiar voice keep me steady, and I squint through the sharp light. "Willow?" Except it comes out as a sandy rasp from my mouth that tastes completely disgusting.

"Wait." My bed creaks once when he leaves, then again half a moment later, when he presses something cool into my hands. "Drink."

I grip the glass in two wobbly hands as Willow helps me sit up, rearranging my pillows so I couldn't fall even if I tried.

"I'm pathetic," I mumble around the rim of the glass. The cool, crisp liquid nearly makes me cry in relief when it soothes my parched throat. I'd down it all if I had the energy.

"You're not pathetic, you're hurt," Willow returns sternly, but he smiles when I glare at him. "I'm glad you're feeling better."

"Who said anything about better?"

"Well, you're not dead, are you?"

"That's a matter of opinion." I bet death would hurt a whole lot less. I feel chewed up and spat out. I'd rather be digested and have done with it. "What happened?"

Careful not to so much as jostle me, Willow settles at my side to share my pillow. "What do you last remember?"

"I remember . . ." It's hard to think through the throbbing ache in my head, harder still to pick apart the dreams from the memories when they're all tangled together like my hair at its worst. But I brush it out.

I remember blurred movements and indistinct shapes, and masses of sound I can't pick apart. I remember yelling. I remember fear.

I push back further and further, until one image sticks out clearly.

Jory.

Jory on the ground.

Jory staring right at me.

Jory dead.

My whole body revolts, and I dive over the side of the bed before I puke all over Willow.

Well, "puking" is a generous word. There's nothing inside me to come out, but I guess my body doesn't seem to care. I keep retching up spit that tastes so bad my stomach heaves, and the process repeats again and again until I'm scared my insides are gonna end up on the floor.

Willow, to his credit, doesn't balk. He just sits beside me and rubs my back in slow, soothing circles until I stop feeling like I'm going to die.

Finally, when I'm able to gulp a lungful of air, I croak out, "Tell me they caught him."

"Adan?"

Just the sound of his name makes my stomach heave again.

Willow's heavy sigh speaks volumes. "After you fell, Elowen and Teo found us. They brought backup. *Dumoor* backup. They chased Adan and the others off."

I pull myself up, wiping sweat-slicked hair out of my face. "Like . . . let them go?"

"It wasn't about fighting Helston. It was about saving us. Dumoor saved us." Willow falls back against my pillows, shaking his head. "Saved from our own people by the enemy . . . Dreams make more sense, Callie."

Truer words were never spoken.

"And that's where we are? Dumoor?"

"Yes. The Roost Teo told us about."

Dazed, I lie beside Willow and try to take in my surroundings. It doesn't feel like enemy territory.

A soft patchwork quilt is bunched up around me like I kicked my way out of a cocoon; thin curtains flutter in an open window; the walls are pale stone and the furniture is mismatched and well worn. The door to whatever lies beyond the room is unlatched. And Willow, he looks different. He looks . . . *good*. Like the best version of himself, in soft clothes that fit somewhere between a dress and a tunic in a muted color, closer to pink than red. His black hair is glossy and clean and *long*.

I jerk up. "How long was I out?"

"Little under a week."

"No way! But your hair, it's ... *How* ..."

Willow blinks, confused at my confusion, then bursts out laughing. "It's magic! Isn't it amazing? I had no idea you could use it in such a way. I mean, I suppose it makes sense. You can use magic for anything, but it never occurred to me that you could just . . . *change yourself.* Anytime you like. Any *way* you like." He sits up, all jittery and excited. "Callie, you should see the way people use magic here. It's *spectacular*! And so *normal* and—I can't wait for you to see it! And El, you should see her too! I'll go get her. And Edwyn. And Teo. Everyone's been so worried about you. For days we thought—we feared ... but you're okay. We're *all* okay!" He bounces up, pushing his fingers through his hair. "Stay here, all right? I'll fetch the others."

"Like I'm going anywhere."

Just the thought of moving more than absolutely required makes me feel seasick.

Teo bounds in and smothers me in a hug so fierce it's like we've been friends a whole lifetime and not just a few days, most of which I was out cold.

"Glad you're alive."

I hug xem back just as hard, xir body radiating a warmth I didn't know I needed. "Glad *you're* alive."

I guess that's the new "hello."

When Teo finally lets me go and draws back, I take xem in fully. Xe doesn't look like xe just escaped a prison anymore—xir clothes are fresh and clean, the colors sharp like they're new. Scales pop bright and pearly against clean skin, and I swear xir horns are longer than before.

"You're . . . dragony-er."

Teo laughs, a tired, happy sound. "I feel like myself again. What about you? How're you feeling?"

"Like I got shot in the back and died."

"Well, you look pretty good for a corpse."

"Thanks! I think."

We share the rueful smile of two people who went into the underworld and made it out alive.

"I've seen worse come through The Roost," says Teo, xir voice dipping low and serious. "The healers here . . . they know what they're doing. I'll go fetch Nina and tell them you're awake. She can fix you up without even a scar."

"I wouldn't mind a scar," I call after Teo. "Girls like scars."

"Knowing you, there will be ample opportunity for scars, Callie."

My whole body jolts with joy. "El!" And then my mouth drops open when I see her. "Whoa! Your *hair*!" Where it had once been a cascade down her back, Elowen's hair now barely tickles her neck, the cut framing her face without hiding it.

"Oh, this?" She fingers the ends where it curls just beneath her ear. "What do you think?"

"It's *amazing*!" I wish there was a better word to express exactly how much more perfect it is, even though it was entirely perfect before. Like Teo, Elowen just looks so much more *herself*. "I *love* it," I tell her with so much sincerity I'm scared it sounds false. "Did you do it yourself?"

Elowen nods. "Watching Willow experiment, I realized I wanted to too." She smirks. "Mother would *hate* it."

"Good! Wish I'd been there!"

"I thought about waiting for you, but as soon as the idea came to me, it wouldn't let me go until I did it. It was like I could suddenly feel every strand of hair on my head and I just wanted to be rid of it. I thought about shearing it all off entirely, but I didn't want to scare you too much when you woke up."

I imagine El bald. She still looks amazing. She would look amazing no matter what she did with her hair. "It's *so* good to see you, El."

Her smile gives the faintest wobble, and there's a hairline crack in her voice. "You say that like I was the one who nearly died."

"You say that like you were worried or something."

"Callie—" And then her arms are around me, a hand at the back of my head. She buries her face in my shoulder. Her whole body is quaking. "You nearly died."

"I didn't, though."

"It felt like you did."

"Sorry about that."

Elowen glares up at me, her face so close I can count the shades of blue and gray in her eyes. "You should be. Very sorry."

"Couldn't be sorrier. Promise."

"Pinkie promise?"

"Pinkie promise." She grabs my little finger so tight in hers, I wince. "Ow, El."

She doesn't let go. "Don't do it again."

I laugh. "Do what? Get shot?"

Elowen's expression is dead serious. "Yes."

"Definitely not planning on it. Even for the sake of a cool scar."

She thumps my shoulder. "Not funny."

"Ow, El!"

"Oh, stop it. You've survived worse." But she rubs my arm and plants a kiss on my cheek in penance. "I'm glad you're alive."

A tingling warmth blooms from the place her lips touched. "Yeah. Me too."

Really glad.

"Come on," I hear Willow whisper. "They're not a ghost. You don't need to be scared."

"I'm not—" Edwyn freezes in the doorway when he catches my eye, one foot on either side of the threshold. The way he looks at me, you'd think I was some terrible specter.

I push for my biggest smile, trying to look as alive as possible, and wave him over.

I'm pretty sure he's half a second from bolting when Willow grabs his hand and drags him to my bedside. He won't look at me, even when I say, "Hey."

All I get is a curt nod of acknowledgment.

Guilt curls in my stomach, except I don't even know what I need to apologize for.

"Hey."

I get another face-averted nod in return.

"Thanks for, you know, saving my life."

"Of course." He's so terse, I wince. It feels like we're all the way back to that first fight at Helston's training grounds, when my mere existence was cause for the highest offense. I don't know what I did wrong.

"How're you doing?" I try. "You seem—"

"I'm fine. I'm glad you are too."

"Yeah, sure sounds like you are."

Edwyn stiffens at my tone, then makes a short bow with a muttered "Excuse me."

Willow reluctantly lets him pass, and we watch together as he disappears into the hall, closing the door without looking back.

"What's *his* problem?"

Willow twists his hair around one finger, which I guess is his new favorite fidget. "That's the most he's said since we arrived."

"To anyone?"

"To anyone," says El with a distinctly irritated sigh. "It took all three of us to get him out of our room to visit you today."

"And it isn't as though he hasn't been worried," Willow adds. "When you were unconscious, he made sure there was always someone with you."

Elowen rolls her eyes. "He didn't need to make small talk, so it was easier. He'll be fine."

"You sound annoyed at him."

"I'm not annoyed, I'm . . ." She pauses, holding herself still as she picks out her words. "I don't understand why he's sulking. Everything is fine. *More* than fine. I understand that change is hard. I don't like it either, but being like that isn't going to make things easier."

"He'll come around," says Willow, touching El's folded arms gently. "Once he's used to things. He always needs a little extra time."

"A luxury we have *never* had." She turns away with a tight, frustrated sound. "You'd think he'd know that by now."

I catch Willow's eye, and the look on his face confirms my thoughts: Whatever's going on with Edwyn, he is not okay.

I'm half dozing as my friends chatter around me, when there's a soft tap at the door, and it opens to reveal Teo and a stranger who has warm brown skin and is wearing a butter-yellow dress; long inky-black braids woven with bright multi-colored threads hang heavy over their shoulders.

They beam when they see me awake. "Good morning, Sir Callie. I had a feeling you might be awake today. How're you feeling?"

I'm running out of ways to say *awful but alive*.

"This is Nina, and her pronouns are 'she' and 'they,'" Willow explains, hurrying to help Nina with a tray loaded with a whole collection of clean, folded bandages, a tiny vial of something sapphire blue and glittering, and most importantly—*food!* I clamp my mouth shut just so I don't start salivating like a rabid wolf. "Callie, did you know that some people have more than one set of words? I had no idea!"

My eyes go huge. "Really? I didn't know that either!"

Nina laughs. "Many folks don't feel like one particular thing, and that makes it hard to pick the right words to fit you." They look at me, amber eyes sparkling, and I feel like they've had this same conversation with others before. "Your friends tell me your pronouns are 'they/them,' right?"

I nod slowly, stunned. There's a weird feeling in my chest, like discomfort at *not* feeling discomfort? Because the way she asked me my words, it was as easy as asking my name. No question. No confusion. No weird look or demand for explanation. I'm not questioned, just . . . accepted.

It's been such a long time since anyone hasn't looked at me and assumed "girl."

My eyesight goes wobbly.

If this is what normal is here, maybe The Roost *is* a good place for us.

With Nina's help and Willow's encouragement, I sit up and lean forward and let Nina carefully pull up my tunic so they can check my bandages. "Looks like you're well over the hill into recovery. You had us worried for a couple of days."

"Teo said you've seen worse," I mumble, focusing on anything but the pain as the bandages fall away, exposing my wound to fresh air. "Can't've been that bad."

"*Not the worst* doesn't necessarily mean *good*. You survived; not all do. But it was hard work getting there."

"You had it easy," Elowen adds. "You didn't have to watch you nearly die."

I guess that's fair. In a very roundabout way.

"So," says Nina, "how're we feeling on the inside?"

"I feel . . . really tired. And hungry. Starving, actually. Like the concept of food is fictional."

"All right, all right." Willow hurries over with a shallow bowl and a spoon that looks it was made for mouths much larger than mine. "Say 'aah.'"

I try, but it comes out more of an "oomph" when he shovels a heaping spoonful of I-don't-know-what-and-I-don't-care right down my throat.

It's the best something I've ever eaten, rich and savory and spicy, with enormous chunks of soft vegetables.

Willow grins as I groan in bliss. "Good?"

I open my mouth again. "Aah!"

Willow feeds me like a fledgling while Nina continues their healing, changing the bandages and testing the flexibility of my muscles. Every touch *burns*, my body filled to

198

bursting with tension. Like all the fear and anger seeped into my muscles and stayed there.

"You are doing well," Nina says finally, letting me lie down again. "Sleeping for a week probably helped you far more than anything else. By all accounts, you're not one who sits still easily. A few more days, and you'll be allowed to be up and about. However"—Nina fixes me with the sternest eye— "your body took a beating and the only way to get back to normal is to be kind to it. That means no pushing yourself, no fighting, only *rest*."

I snort. "That's a big ask."

"Not asking, telling," says Nina firmly, and she sounds so much like Neal, a smile tugs at my mouth. "Your friends have given me their most solemn vows to help you sit still."

I glare at Elowen and Willow and mouth, *Traitors.*

They just smirk at me, entirely unrepentant.

"Drink this once you're done eating," Nina continues, holding up the vial of blue stuff and swirling it so it shimmers. "This is going to help you get your strength back quickly. Make sure they drink all of it," they tell Willow, handing it to him. Then, to me: "I will visit you every day to make sure you're moving in the right direction and following your healer's orders." But despite the severity of their tone, Nina smiles warmly down at me. "We're glad you're here, Callie. *All* of you. I hope you can find a home with us."

Nina leaves, closing the door behind them, and Elowen

perches on my bed with a smirk. "So," she says in a distinctly *I-told-you-so* tone, "what do you think?"

"What do I think of what?"

"Nina. The Roost. All of it."

I squirm. "Hold your horses, El. I've been awake for, what? Two hours?" Truth is, I don't know what I feel about anything. It all feels good, but in the way dreams do. Like I'm waiting to wake up to a colder, harsher reality. And the more I fall for this fiction, the harder it'll be.

"What about the stew?" Willow asks.

Okay, he's got me there. "The stew is *really* good."

"Wait till you try the biscuits!"

"There're *biscuits*?"

"The best biscuits," Elowen promises with a glint in her eyes. She knows *exactly* what she's doing. "Better than any I've ever tasted."

"And you didn't bring me any?"

She gives a light shrug. "I suppose you'll just have to do what Nina says and heal enough to make it downstairs. No biscuits in bedrooms. That's the rule."

I glare. "*Whose* rule?"

"Mine."

"I knew it! Traitor!"

"Just because you keep saying it," says Elowen primly, "doesn't make it true."

I glower, sinking back into my pillows. I guess doing what I'm told might be worth it for biscuits.

CHAPTER NINETEEN

Recovery is just about as long and twice as tedious than I feared, and I have absolutely no choice at all but to stay still and behave. And my friends are *not* on my side. No amount of begging, whining, or being generally obnoxious makes them relent even a little. They dangle the promise/threat of biscuits over my head like I'm some kind of belligerent donkey. Worst of all, it works. I rest and I heal, and I do the exercises Nina teaches me and I don't push myself even when it feels like progress is so slow I want to scream.

"Everything in its own time," she reminds me when I get close to snapping, and whenever she does, I think of Neal. It's hard to imagine him here, but this was home for him longer than I've even known him. I want to ask Nina if they remember him, but every time I think I'm going to, his name gets stuck in my throat.

I miss him so much my chest aches. Him and Papa. They should both be here. They should've come with us.

I wonder where they think we are.

My dreams are filled with Helston as I wish it had been, and I always wake up full of longing and homesickness. The dreams are so sweet and real, there's always a moment where I think I'm back in my bed in our apartment, with Papa's snores filtering through the wall and the smell of Neal's cooking drifting in from the kitchen.

But the snores are Willow's, who has taken to sleeping curled up beside me, and the mouthwatering smell of breakfast wanders up from the world withheld from me downstairs.

Every time I wake up, my back twinges, the wound between my shoulders never letting me forget for a moment what happened and why I can never return. And every time I wake up, I grieve my long-treasured dreams all over again.

It's hard to let go of something you wished for for so long, even if that something became twisted beyond recognition, even if it was never going to be the thing you wanted, even if your wish could never come true.

Helston was still the dream that fueled me, through life with Mama, through the impossible puzzle of working myself out in Eyrewood. Even after we arrived in Helston itself and nothing was as I'd expected, I still hoped, I still believed, I still clung to the single thing I had always known about myself: *I want to be a knight.*

I don't know that anymore.

I don't know anything.

You can't be a knight without a kingdom to serve.

Willow and Elowen don't talk about Helston or Adan or anything approaching serious, and I don't know how to bring it up. They're so happy here, safe in this magical bubble that feels like it'll pop if I dare speak my fears out loud. I don't want to ruin it for them. But not talking about problems doesn't mean they don't exist. Even if we pretend everything's fine, Queen Ewella is still preparing to ride against Dumoor, and Adan is still out there. He made it perfectly clear that he wants us dead, and he is not the kind of person to admit defeat after one loss.

If he decides to come looking for us again, I don't know what we'll do. I'm not in any state to fight, and I have no idea what The Roost can or will do to protect us. I don't care how adamant Teo is, or how kind Nina appears; when it comes down to it, we're just Helston runaways, bringing trouble to their doorstop.

I wouldn't blame them if they turned us in just to keep the peace.

The more I rest, the better I feel. The better I feel, the more my head clears. And that's not fun for anyone, because once the worries start rolling, they don't stop, and lying in bed doing *nothing* as trouble brews like encroaching fog is . . . not my natural state of being.

By the time Nina gives me the all clear, I feel like I'm going to pop.

My legs are still wobblier than a newborn foal's, and it takes Elowen on one side and Willow on the other, with my arms slung around both their shoulders, to help me up and out and down the stairs into The Dragon's Roost itself.

———

I don't know what I was expecting from an establishment called The Dragon's Roost—probably some kind of communal nest thing? But it turns out that The Roost is a pub. A *really* big pub. Like, Great Hall–sized, but half the height. Chandeliers made out of carriage wheels and dripping candles swing from fragile-looking chains; strings of tiny sparkling lights are woven across the ceiling like spiders' webs, and there is so much magic, the air glitters. Enough tables for everyone are spread out with plenty of room to walk between without having to shove or apologize with every step.

A few people glance our way, and a few of them wave in greeting, but most pay us no mind, more focused on their own conversations. We are inconsequential. We are *normal*.

I stand between El and Willow and just *stare*. I don't realize how hard I'm smiling until my face aches. This place is *beautiful*.

"Over here!" Far across the other side of the room, Teo stands on a chair and waves to us with both arms.

My entourage guides me carefully all the way to a blazing hearth surrounded by huge armchairs and sofas half filled with curious grown-ups. Just the short journey is more than enough to wipe me out, and I collapse into the chair nearest the fire with a grateful sigh and close my eyes. Music and magic and the smell of cooking herbs fill the air, and all I want to do is breathe it in until it's all that I am.

With the crackle of the fire, I feel like I'm back around the campfire at Eyrewood as Neal's sweet singing voice conjures pictures in the embers and Josh dishes up supper. The armchair is deep and holds me like a familiar hug.

The music shifts, picking up the tempo and turning into an upbeat ballad about a traveler who gets led into a bog by an attractive yet vengeful spirit. A deep baritone voice takes the lead and, one by one, more voices join in until the whole of The Roost is filled with raucous singing and clattering of dancing feet on wooden boards.

I open my eyes to see Willow and Elowen trotting into the fray and joining the dance—bouncing and twirling completely uninhibited, keeping pace with a tempo that gets faster and faster and faster until it stops abruptly and they collapse with laughter and applause.

I watch hungrily. I don't dance, not in regular life, where there are steps to memorize and an expectation of delicacy that I do not possess. But this isn't like any dancing I've seen before. This looks . . . *fun.*

I can't wait to be well enough to join in!

"So, what d'you think?" Teo asks, perching on the arm of my chair like some kind of bird. I wonder if dragons have hollow bones too.

"It's amazing," I tell xem. "Is it *really* as good as it seems?"

"It is," xe replies with total sincerity. "I know it's hard to believe. Most folks who find their way here struggle for a long while, because how can it be? How can anything be this good?" Xe looks fondly around The Roost. "It was hard for me too. But it's real, Callie. What you see is what you get."

I follow Teo's gaze, absorbing it all. I want it. I want to be part of this. I want to live and grow here with my friends. But there's still a hard knot of doubt in the middle of my chest that refuses to loosen.

"I don't understand. . . ."

Head tilted, Teo sits forward with an easy smile. "Wanna talk it through? Maybe I can help."

I suck my lip. I don't think I can find words that won't spoil everything the moment they leave my tongue. This place, these people . . . they're supposed to be the enemy. Not just Helston's, but the way Papa and Neal talked about Dumoor made it sound like a secret cave filled with bloodthirsty wolves in the middle of a cursed forest. Not a warm inn, an unconditional sanctuary to any and all who wander this way. A haven for the lost.

The two pictures in my head are so drastically opposed, they ping right off each other.

Finally, I manage, "Are you . . . sure this is Dumoor?"

Teo's ears twitch. "What d'you mean?"

"I mean . . . I thought I knew Dumoor. I've been here before. Twice. And it was awful both times. I've heard so many stories—even from someone who used to live here—and this isn't at all what they made me imagine. I know I don't have the greatest imagination, but it's not *that* bad! There's got to be something else. Something you're not telling me." I meet Teo's eyes, begging the dragon to tell me the truth. "I just want to protect my friends," I tell xem. "That's it. Please help me do that."

Teo's smile never falters. If anything, it only gets warmer. "I know it'll take a long time to really believe, but you have nothing to fear here. That's the point of The Roost. Even the fighting and everything going on with Helston, it's all kept separate up at Pioden."

"Pioden? What's Pioden?"

"Alis's castle. It's where all the big things are decided and the conflict strategy—all the scary things—take place. Alis is determined to keep it separate from the rest of The Roost, to protect those who don't want to be a part of the fighting."

"So it's a choice? A *real* choice?"

"Of course," says Teo, fangs poking out of xir crooked smile. "No one's forced to fight."

"What about you? You *chose* to fight that day?"

"I did." Though xe looks away when I narrow my eyes. "I

did choose. I *did* agree. It wasn't my idea, but when it was presented . . . I was glad for the chance to pay my way. Dumoor has given me so much. And if she thought I was ready—"

"Who? The Witch Queen?"

Teo nods. "It's a huge honor to be noticed personally by Alis. Apparently she used to be more present in The Roost, but since the fight with Helston got worse, she rarely leaves Pioden. She doesn't have time to meet every single person herself. If she knew about me, it means I'd stood out." A proud flush ripples across the scales on Teo's cheeks. "I know some who have offered their services for years but never received an invitation to Pioden. I got lucky."

"Doesn't sound very lucky," I reply bluntly. "You got captured, and no one came looking for you. How's that lucky?"

Xir smile drops. "It wasn't supposed to be like that. It wasn't supposed to be a battle. We got taken by surprise and I panicked. That was my fault. I could've said no. I *should've* said no. Kensa tried to warn me, but I was too excited. I figured if Alis thought I was ready, it meant it was true. She trusted me. I didn't want to betray that trust, and Kensa always worried extra about me. I figured they'd never think I was ready. I wanted to prove them wrong. It was my fault. I should've known myself better."

My heart thrums furiously in my chest. It feels too familiar. Grown-ups taking advantage of kids. Making them feel special and grateful so they can't say no.

"She shouldn't have put you in that position," I growl. "Grown-ups in power . . . they're just the same everywhere."

"That's not true, Callie," Teo insists. "Alis isn't like that. She would never make anyone do anything against their will. I didn't get tricked. You wait till you meet her and then you'll understand! You're gonna love her. Everyone does! And I know she's going to love you."

It still doesn't sit right, the thought of the Witch Queen knowing we're here in her domain. In my mind, she's a fearsome shadow with big teeth, looming over the moors like a storm cloud full of thunder.

"We'll be gone before then," I say with as much conviction as I have energy for. "We're not sticking around."

Teo's ears flatten with disappointment. "You're really set on that?"

"Yes. That's the plan. That was always the plan."

"Oh. Okay. I guess I was sort of hoping you'd stay once you learned what it was really like here."

I grimace. I want to. It feels so perfect, and El and Willow are so *happy*.

But . . .

"It's not safe," I tell Teo. "Not for us and not for you. Helston's coming, if not tomorrow, then soon. Look, the day you got captured, it was like the whole place exploded. They're all totally convinced that it's a matter of kill or be killed, and we may have slowed them down, but not for long. Helston's coming, and we can't be here when they do. They mean to get revenge."

Teo flinches. "Revenge for what?" xe whispers. "We haven't done anything."

"How can you say that? You've killed just as many of our people, if not more!" I freeze the moment the accusation falls from my tongue, and my face burns. *Our people.* As if I can possibly claim any part of Helston as my own anymore. As if me and Teo are on opposite sides of the bridge. "I'm sorry," I mumble, sinking deeper into my seat. "I didn't mean that. It's not your fault. It's not your fight. I just mean . . . Dumoor's not innocent either. It takes two sides to start a war."

"Is it yours?"

I squint up at Teo. "My what?"

If the dragon's offended by my explosion, xe doesn't show it. "You said it's not my fight. Is it yours?"

I shrug. "Dunno. Maybe." Everything is too loud and too bright, and there are too many people and I can't *think.* "It was, at least."

"What changed?"

Everything. Everything changed.

Or maybe it didn't and I just woke up from a long, convincing dream.

I wish I could go back to sleep.

"I think I'm gonna head to bed," I mutter, wriggling out of the armchair that seems determined to consume me. "I'm wiped out. Will you tell El and Willow where I've gone so they don't think I've wandered off on my own?"

"Of course." Teo hops off xir perch, eyeing me anxiously. "Do you want me to help you upstairs?"

Xe's already reaching, about to take my arm, when I step away. "Nah. Thanks, though."

Teo's hand drops. "If you're sure."

I am.

The stairs are a monumental undertaking, and I just about make it to the top with enough energy left to get to my room. But the second I touch the handle, I pause. Every door down the long corridor is open and empty except one. And I know who's hiding inside.

Edwyn is the only person between Helston and Dumoor who might understand a little of what I'm feeling right now.

I'm so exhausted by the time I reach his room, I'm just about ready to slide down the wall and fall asleep right here on the floor. Luckily, slumping against the door achieves the same goal as knocking.

A soft click and the door cracks open less than half an inch.

I grin blearily at a single dark blue eye. "Hey."

The eye narrows, and when the door opens fully, I tumble

into the room, landing solidly on the rug. I'm not even cross about it. It feels so good to be horizontal.

Edwyn peers down at me, and I can't tell if he's confused or annoyed. Probably both. He's usually both. "I thought you were Willow."

"How'd you figure?"

"Elowen doesn't knock, and I didn't think you'd— I thought you were Willow."

"Sorry to disappoint."

"No, it's . . . That isn't what I mean."

"I know. Relax. Teasing."

He closes his eyes like he's praying for enough fortitude to deal with my nonsense. "Of course you are. What can I do for you? Why are you here?"

I lever myself up onto my elbows and fix him with a look. "Everyone else is downstairs having the time of their lives, and you're up here—what? Being a goblin?" It sure feels like a goblin cave—dark and stuffy, with the curtains drawn and the window closed. Nothing like the light, airy bedroom I was gifted. "Truth is, I'm feeling pretty gobliny too, and I figured you might relate. Except now I am worried about you. You look *terrible*."

It's true. He looks all pale and waxy, like he hasn't seen sunlight in a hundred years.

"*Thanks*," says Edwyn tightly. "But there's no need for concern. I'm fine."

"Sure you are."

The smile he gives me is the worst I've ever seen. "I'm

fine," he repeats in a voice that sounds like a poor imitation of Willow's. "See? I'm happy. Nothing to worry about."

"Well, now I'm double worried. What's going on?"

"Nothing." His voice gets sharper and higher, and his chest is starting to heave as he struggles to breathe. "Callie, please, I am fine. Go back with the others before they come looking for you. I can't be around them. I'm just . . . tired."

"No, but same, though," I insist. "It's way too much down there. Like, it's great. But it's a lot. Exhausting. I'd rather just hang out up here and be a goblin with you. Is that okay? We don't even need to talk."

Edwyn stares at me, utterly baffled that I would choose his company over anyone else's. "If you . . . really want to."

"I do. Your floor's comfier than mine."

He shakes his head hopelessly and returns to his nest of a bed, which looks like he hasn't left it in days, where he lies on top of the blue-and-brown patchwork quilt and gazes at the ceiling.

I keep my promise of not talking for an impressive eighteen seconds before I blurt out, "Is this what you've been doing since we got here?"

"Yes."

"Why?"

"Because I want to," says Edwyn in his dry monotone. "Isn't that the point of being here? So we can do what we want?"

"The point of being here is to heal and rest. At least, that's what people keep telling me."

"You don't believe it?"

I lie back down and copy his position, counting grooves in the ceiling. If I relax my eyes, patterns start to form. I guess this is pretty entertaining. "No, I do. It's good here. It's . . . weird. And the others don't seem to get how weird it is."

"This is what Elowen has always wanted," says Edwyn softly. "Willow too."

"Not you?"

"I don't think about things like that. Never have. Wanting hurts when you don't get it, and when you do . . ." His voice cracks, and when I sit up to look at him, his hands are fists in his quilt and his face is screwed up in pain. "I—I can't do this. I shouldn't be here. I don't belong here. I'm going to ruin it. Just like I ruined everything at Helston. You should've left me behind."

I sit up properly. "You really believe that?"

Eyes squeezed shut tight, Edwyn nods. "I was thinking of going back. To Helston. But I'm . . . not even brave enough to give up."

"Adan would kill you, Edwyn."

"Yes. I—I know."

I relinquish my comfy place on the floor and stand over him, hands on hips. "You are not going back, and you do belong here. Just like everyone else."

Edwyn snorts, turning his face away. "As though you would ever tell me anything else."

"Hey!" I'm glad he's got his eyes shut so he doesn't see me wince. "You think I'd lie to you? You think I'd go through all that if you weren't worth saving? Give me more credit than that. Willow might lie to save your feelings, but I wouldn't."

Edwyn cracks one eye open to fix me with a scowl. "Why aren't you angry?"

"Angry? With you? About what?"

I can hear his teeth grind before he answers. A tear makes a track all the way down to his ear. "I ruined *everything*. I ruined your dream. You worked so hard. You had everything you wanted. So did El. And I ruined it."

"You didn't—"

"I *did!*" Edwyn shouts, sitting up to face me properly. "Stop lying to me, Callie! It *doesn't* help! It *doesn't* make me feel better when I already know the truth!"

"Which is what?"

"That I'm . . ." He shivers. "Poison."

I hold myself very still and very calm and breathe through the worst of my anger before I tell Edwyn softly, "Those aren't your words. Those are your father's."

More tears follow the first. "Maybe they are. Maybe he's right. Maybe we need to stop pretending that he was wrong about everything."

"He was wrong about *you*."

"That's not true. I let you convince me it was. I made myself believe it. I thought once he was gone, everything would be better. I thought *I* would be better. But he was gone and I *still* ruined everything. That means it was me."

"Edwyn, what happened, it wasn't your fault. It was Peter and Adan and—"

"I can't keep blaming everyone else!" Edwyn snaps. "Besides, I'm not talking about that. At least, not entirely. I'm talking about the apartment. Everything Sir Nicholas and Captain Neal did for me. I couldn't be happy with what I had. I made everyone feel awkward. I spoiled it for Elowen. I ruined it for you. And it will all go the same way here. I can't do that. I *won't* do that. You deserve to be safe and happy."

"So do *you*!"

Edwyn covers his face with his hands with a frustrated growl. "No, I don't! Don't you get it yet? How do you not get it? *I'm* the corrupt one. *I'm* the abomination. Stop trying to turn me into something I can never be! It won't work! That's why everything is broken! Just let me fix this in the only way I can, and leave me alone!"

His raw fury freezes me. He's so determined, I almost believe him. All the good—all the little stitches we made since Peran left Helston—they've all came undone, leaving Edwyn's wounds gaping and exposed. The scabs grown from a lifetime beneath his father's fist, a small protection against the rawest wounds, are gone. We did that. We knocked them off before he was ready. We half healed him and left him more vulnerable than before.

"I'm really sorry, Edwyn."

His hands stay plastered to his face. "Don't. Don't apologize."

"I hurt you. I'm gonna apologize."

"It was my fault," he mumbles. "I should've been smarter. I should've been more careful. I should've listened. I should've stayed away from you and Elowen and Willow. Everything that happened was because of me. My fault."

I don't even know if he's talking to me or if he's caught up in the perpetual whirlpool of blame and guilt. I know that feeling. I recognize those thoughts.

I stick my hand right into the middle of the pool and hold tight.

"My mama used to make me feel like that."

Edwyn peeks between his fingers to glare at me.

I settle on the very edge of his bed, folding my legs up beneath me. "For years and years, I was sure I was the problem. *I* was the reason we couldn't get along, and everyone looked at me weird. The reason that my parents argued and Papa always looked like he was on the battleground even at home. Everything bad was because *I* was bad. That's how she made me feel, even when she didn't say it. And she *did* say it sometimes. That kind of stuff sticks to you like hot grease and stays burning a long time afterward. I reckon I've still got burns even though I haven't seen her in nearly three years. Sometimes I think I'm all fixed, totally scabbed over, but then something happens and one scab gets picked off and I'm all the way back there. But that doesn't mean she was right. It just means that big hurts take a long, *long* time to heal, and sometimes they never go away completely."

Edwyn's hands drop like they're too heavy to hold up anymore, and he looks so utterly defeated my heart twists. "I don't know how to fix it," he whispers. "I don't know how to be what everyone wants me to be."

"Which is what?"

"Happy."

Oof.

"Well," I say slowly, "I know for a fact that you can't force happy, and trying just goes the opposite way. *But* I would bet a fair amount that holing up in the dark with only yourself for company probably isn't helping all that much. Look, you're not gonna poison the air and ruin everyone's lives. Even if that *was* a thing, it would totally get canceled out by all the joy leaking from everyone else." I grin. "It is frankly disgusting, and I definitely need a grumpy ally to fend off the worst of it. Wanna do battle with me?"

"You . . . really want me on your side?"

"Edwyn, you are on my side whether you like it or not. Might as well accept your fate."

I hold my breath and *hope*. Those deep, wretched feelings in me took so long to disappear, and I had time and space and Neal. I don't know if I can do the same for Edwyn by myself.

But—miracle of miracles—the slightest crack of a smile breaks across his lips. "I accept."

I punch the air with a triumphant "*Yes!*" Then I hold out my hand to him. "I promise, cross my heart, you can goblin out whenever you like."

He takes my offered hand and lets me haul him up. "That is all I ask."

CHAPTER TWENTY

We are enveloped in the world of The Roost as seamlessly as if we were always a part of it, exactly the way Papa and I were welcomed when we first arrived in Eyrewood, lost and displaced.

On the third day of our joining society, Teo introduces us proudly to his brood, which is the Dumoor word for "family": little pockets of people who make a home together in this collective. Turns out that they've basically adopted us too!

Sulio is the oldest, with dark brown skin and a soft, curly gray beard covering his chin. He immediately pulls Edwyn into a passionate conversation about birds—the species that can be found in these parts and the pigeons that are infamous in Helston and did you know that they're actually more similar to crows than regular pigeons? To everyone's surprise, Edwyn meets Sulio point to point, and I don't think I've seen him so invested in a conversation. Ever.

Dolan is younger, though not by much, with forest-green hair that falls long over their shoulders—long and thick enough to wear as a cloak if they want to. Colorful tattoos speckle their tanned arms like rainbow constellations, and he and Elowen dive deep into a lengthy conversation about elemental magic that results in lightning sparking from their fingers and nearly setting the sofa alight.

Feena and Inis are a pair so in tune with each other, I can't imagine them ever being apart. Their harmony is so fluid, even in their differences, just like Papa and Neal. They remind me of El, and I wish I could work out how to ask her thoughts on them. Feena is tall and pale, with freckles spattering every inch of her skin. Her fawn-colored hair is short and spiky, and if I didn't like my long hair so much, I would *definitely* copy her. Inis, on the other hand, is short and stout, wearing loose brown breeches and a waistcoat made up of all the colors of the sea. I like her immediately. There's a certain understanding only short people can have with each other.

Turns out Inis is responsible for the increasing length of Willow's hair and the elaborate braiding styles he's been practicing. On first glance, her shoulder-length hair is black. But in the right light, with the right movement, it flashes a dark rainbow, like the underside of a bird's wing. She grins when she catches me gawking and winks. "Now, *that's* what I'm going for!"

They are all so completely at ease with themselves, with each other. With us.

Dolan conjures a speckled feather in the air, blown up three times its normal size to show Edwyn the particular pattern on the underside, and no one in The Roost even turns a head at his display of magic. The affection between Feena and Inis is uninhibited and on full display, and I am the only one who can't stop staring. They love each other *so* much; it's clear in every breath they take and every word they speak. And they don't care who sees, because it doesn't *matter* who sees. There's no one around shooting them dirty looks or muttering behind their hands. Trust me, I know the signs. They're allowed to just . . . be.

Not just tolerated but *accepted*.

Feena catches me staring, and I must look a right fool, because she laughs heartily at me. "I don't suppose you see many lesbians in Helston, do you, kid?"

"Les—?" The word feels vaguely familiar, but I can't quite place it.

"That's our word," Inis explains with a gentle smile. "There are countless words people choose from to describe themselves if they want to. Folks around here tend to get specific with their words in a way that most beyond Dumoor don't."

"Or can't," Feena adds, and Inis inclines her head in agreement.

"Why can't they?" Willow asks, shuffling over to join our conversation.

"Danger," says Inis. "If you proclaim yourself different in a way folks don't like or don't understand, that puts you at risk.

222

But even if you choose not to identify yourself out loud, that doesn't change who you are on the inside. There're no rules." She grins. "That's kind of the point. But words have power too, and there's community in them. And comfort, knowing there are others just like you when maybe you've been made to feel strange or alone before. It's up to you."

Willow's eyes bug right out of his head. "What words?" he asks breathlessly. "Tell me the words. All of them! I want to pick mine!"

This conversation goes *long* into the night, so late that we're the last ones up.

I'm tired, but I don't care. Obviously, I knew there were different kinds of people beyond girls and boys, males and females, and it's not just ladies and men falling in love with each other, but I had no idea there was a whole dictionary of words to describe them!

I'm nonbinary, and that means I'm not a girl or a boy. *Nonbinary.* It fits me like a glove made just for me. A word, finally, for who I am, when I thought I was by myself for such a long time.

"What does that mean for me?" asks Elowen, folding her arms. "If Callie was a girl, I would be a lesbian. If Callie was a boy, I would be straight. I don't think 'bi' fits me. I don't like boys. I just like Callie."

My mouth drops and I can't shut it again. She just . . . *said* it. Out loud. In front of *everyone.* Like it's no big deal. When actually it's a *really big deal!* The *biggest* deal! And what am

I supposed to say? That I like her back? Because I do, obviously, but my head's full of bees and I can't make my voice work and if I don't say it back right now, what if she changes her mind? And Willow's grinning at me something awful and Edwyn's staring at El like she's suddenly started talking a whole new language.

And Elowen's just *sitting* there like everything's normal and fine.

Then she catches my eye and smirks, and my face burns so hot I'm surprised I don't set the whole Roost on fire. I'm a useless nonparticipant as the others hash it out.

"If you're not comfortable with the more specific labels, there are broader ones you can use, like 'queer.' But if you feel 'lesbian' fits you, Elowen, it's yours."

"But Callie's not a girl," Elowen insists. "So that can't be right."

"I know some trans men who still identify as lesbians, and plenty of nonbinary folks who do too. It's about what fits *you*."

Willow sits up. "What are trans men?"

"Men who were born into a female body," Inis explains. "And trans women are women who were born into male bodies."

I bob my head, trying to keep up. "And nonbinary is neither, right?"

When Sulio nods to me, Willow asks, "But what if . . . what

if you might be both?" His fingers fidget in his lap. "Some-times one, sometimes the other, and sometimes . . . both. Is that allowed?"

Sulio squeezes Willow's shoulder with a smile as warm as soup on a cold day. "Whatever and whoever you are, it is al-lowed. Everything you just said, Willow, that's exactly what Dolan said when they were working themselves out."

Willow's eyes go wide and round with wonder. "Really? You're like . . . me?"

Dolan winks, grinning. "Pretty neat, isn't it, not to be special?"

"*Yes*," Willow breathes. "Though I don't think 'they' fits me. Not yet. Maybe not ever. I like being 'he.' Even on days when I don't feel much like a boy. Is that okay? Or is it cheat-ing? It sort of feels like cheating."

"I promise you it isn't," says Dolan, laughing. "I promise you also that that feeling is *very* common among those com-ing in new to all this. You don't have to *earn* the right to be yourselves. There isn't an exam, and there are no rules, and just because you feel a certain way one day, that doesn't bind you to that identity for the rest of your life. People grow and change, and their words change with them."

"Like shoes," I whisper, and Dolan dips his head.

"Just like shoes."

Willow's hands flutter excitedly, his legs bouncing. "And perhaps I have two pairs of shoes. And some days I like to wear one, and some days the other. And perhaps there are days when I might wear one of each." He beams when Inis claps her hands. "I wonder what Mother would think if I told her."

"She would tell you to keep your mouth shut before the council lords overhear," says Elowen bluntly. "And she would cut off all your hair and retailor your tunics so they couldn't be mistaken for dresses. What?" she says when I elbow her with a glare. "It's true. Isn't that exactly what happened?"

"Yes," I hiss. "But that's not the point."

El opens her mouth to argue, then catches sight of Willow and winces.

He has, to be very specific, withered; sinking heavily back into the deep sofa so it nearly swallows him whole.

"Willow, I'm sorry, I didn't mean—"

"No, you did," the vaguely Willow-shaped lump in the sofa mumbles. "And you're right. Mostly. I just . . ." He sinks in deeper. "If we weren't in Helston, I *know* she would be happy with whoever I was. I know she would love me. She *does* love me. She's just . . . scared."

I snort so hard it's more like a sneeze. "Funny way of showing love. Punishing *you* because other people suck."

"Callie." It's Elowen's turn to scold me, and I pull a face.

"Sorry. It's complicated. I get it."

Feena kneels beside Willow. "It's hard when the people we love the most don't seem to want us to be our best selves. And, yes, most often that stems from fear. They can believe with their whole hearts and all the love in the world that they are protecting us, when really they're the ones who are hurting us the most. We can understand that they love us, and we can love them too, but their intention doesn't lessen the pain they cause. It's okay to feel different things—even opposite things—about one person."

"I'm sorry that happened to you, Willow," says Sulio, and the other grown-ups all nod and murmur their agreement. "Maybe one day you can see her again as your whole true self and show her that she doesn't need to be afraid on your behalf."

"I'd like that," says Willow from inside the sofa, just as I'm thinking that I never want to set foot in Helston again, no matter how strong I am.

The arrow, fletched with Helston crimson and gold, the colors I was ready to pledge my life and my loyalty to, shot right between my shoulders . . .

They don't deserve any of us at our best.

"We were thinking and talking," says Feena when Willow stretches with a yawn that makes me realize how tired I am too. "And obviously it's unconditionally up to you, and you don't have to decide right away . . . but if you wanted a home here—something other than The Roost, which is mostly just a temporary place for new folks—you're more than welcome to become part of our brood. All of you. There's plenty of room."

"We can *make* room," Inis corrects her. "It's a little tight and *much* smaller than what you're used to. But it's home, and if you want it, it's yours."

The dragon nods enthusiastically. "Yes! Come and stay with us! It'll be so much fun! There're *hammocks*!"

As tempting as the promise of sleeping in hammocks is, none of us make any move to accept; we trade uneasy glances that are, for once, unanimous. Even El, basically ready to swear fealty to Dumoor, holds back. It's one thing to pledge allegiance and make friends, but it's something else altogether to commit to the hospitality of strangers. Living in someone else's home feels . . . scary.

"Maybe later," I say. "Thanks for the offer, though. We definitely appreciate it. And maybe later. If we stick around."

Teo's ears start to droop in disappointment, but Sulio squeezes xir shoulder and nods, understanding. "Everything in its right time."

The familiar words are a punch I hadn't seen coming, and my throat closes around tears I can't stop.

"Callie, what's the matter?" El asks.

"I dunno . . ." I scrub my eyes hard, but it's like a flood's been released. "That's something Neal always said. And this place—all of this—just keeps reminding me of him."

Dolan sits up so sharp it's like he's been struck by lightning. "Neal? You know a Neal who was once here?"

"Yeah." Thinking about Neal is bad enough, but talking about him . . . I *really* don't want to start bawling. "Neal's my other dad. He's the kindest, smartest person in the whole world and he's really good with magic and he taught me how to be my best self, and Papa and I met him in Eyrewood after we ran away from Mama, and now they're both in Helston and probably in trouble 'cause of me and I'm here and—"

Inis makes a sweeping motion with her hand, turning the air into a pale, blank canvas upon which she paints a portrait of a young man, maybe even a teenager, with a fierce wariness in his dark eyes and long, wavy hair the color of rosewood. He looks different—thinner, angrier, less sure of himself—but he is, undoubtedly, my Neal.

I lose the battle with grief and guilt and burst into tears. Real, ugly sobs that feel more like an earthquake than something that could fit into my body.

"How did you know Neal?" I hear Elowen ask close by my ear as she puts her arms around me.

Feena's voice matches the feeling in my chest. "He was part of our brood for many years. The gap he left behind is impossible to fill."

"Not that it wasn't understandable," Dolan adds. "Or a long time coming. As sudden as it felt to us."

"What d'you mean?" I ask through my snuffles.

Sulio opens his mouth but shuts it again on a small shake of the head from Dolan.

"It isn't our story to tell, child," he says gently. "We don't

229

possess all the information to give you a fair picture of what happened."

"Kensa does," says Inis. "Kensa and Neal, they were close as anything. If you have questions, you should ask xem."

"You're wrong," I blurt out. My face burns as they all stare at me, but I hold my ground and take a deep breath that's way more wobbly than I'd like. "Kensa and Neal weren't friends. They're *enemies*. We met Kensa months ago, and xe tried to kill us, and when Neal stopped xem, xe tried to kill Neal too. That is *not* what friends do. And Neal explained everything to me after. He told me all about Dumoor and Kensa and why he left and what Dumoor is. I don't need answers," I say when Inis opens her mouth. "I know everything. Maybe . . . maybe you're the ones who don't know. You said it yourselves: You don't have the whole picture. Maybe Kensa lied to you. That's what dragons do, anyway, isn't it? Dragons lie."

It's not until the last syllable leaves my mouth that I realize exactly what I said.

My stomach flips. "Teo, I didn't—"

Teo's ears are flat to xir head, yellow eyes huge with hurt. "Is that what you think of me, Callie?"

"No! Of course I don't! That's not what I mean. I don't think *you* lie. You're different, you're not like—" *Other dragons.* I grimace. "I'm really sorry."

"How many dragons have you met?" Feena asks. Her voice doesn't *sound* cold, but the guilt twisting my gut sure makes it feel like she's yelling. I cringe.

"Two. Just two. Kensa and Teo."

"And what does your experience tell you? Your own *lived* experience, not the tales that get more and more twisted from person to person. *Your. Own. Experience.*"

The Roost is stone-silent, with my friends, old and new, and the grown-ups all watching me and waiting for my response. I owe them a thought-out answer.

"Kensa tried to hurt us and trick us into joining Dumoor," I say slowly. "But Teo helped us. Xe kept xir word and we're alive because of xem. I consider Teo one of my best friends. I'm really sorry," I tell Teo again. "Truly. It was a rubbish thing to say. I wasn't thinking. It's just . . . that's what everyone's always told me. *Always.* Dragons lie. Dragons are bad. But that's not true. And I *know* that's not true. Not always. And . . . and humans lie too."

"And even if it isn't their intention," says Inis, "folks can think they know something when really they don't. That's how dangerous rumors start and wrong assumptions are made, and soon enough, a whole species is being condemned by those who have no experience of their own to know it's wrong."

"Dragons are not the only reviled beings," says Dolan, putting an arm around Teo's shoulders. "But they are the least understood, and the rarest. Most dragons live their whole lives never revealing themselves. The ones who do are usually hunted and killed. Very few dragons live long enough to reach their full power."

"How old's Kensa?" I ask.

"As old as the moors themselves." Sulio gives a crooked smile. "At least, that's what Kensa says if you ever ask xem."

"Apparently if you count the ridges on a dragon's horn, that's how old they are," Teo adds, touching xir own. "It's right for me, at least."

I don't think I ever want to be close enough to Kensa to count the ridges on xir horns, but I'm glad Teo's still talking to me.

Every moment away from Helston, I'm realizing that I don't just know nothing; what I *do* know is wrong. *Especially* about dragons.

Sulio catches sight of my knotted frown. "Don't worry, Callie. Learning takes time, and *re*learning takes longer. Give yourself some grace."

I grimace. It's way easier to give grace to other people than keep any for myself.

CHAPTER
TWENTY-ONE

I lie awake that night, my thoughts tumbling and tripping over each other, too big to find their own space without displacing another.

Neal and dragons and Helston and Dumoor and Teo and witches and friends and enemies and—

It's too much.

My head is too small. This room is too small. This *world* is too small.

All my thoughts are bunched together, crowded around my bed, taking up all the air.

I can't breathe.

My legs are still a little watery, but they work and that's enough.

I stumble out of bed, out of my room, out of The Roost.

Moonlight floods the glade like spilled milk; stars speckle the sky, bright and free.

I suck in lungfuls of cool night air, my face turned up toward the stars. They are the same stars that can be seen in Helston and Eyrewood. I can pick out the same constellations Neal used to point out to me.

"See that one there?" he said, one arm around my shoulders, the other reaching to the sky. "He's called Orion. If you're ever lost, look to the stars and he will lead you home."

I don't think that's true anymore. How can Orion know where home is for me when I don't even know myself? I don't know if it's Eyrewood, where I felt safest, or Clystwell, where I was born. I don't know if it's with Papa and Neal, or here with Elowen and Willow and Edwyn, among a community that embraces us exactly as we are.

Home is where the people who love you are, but what about when they're scattered? Am I supposed to choose? *How* am I supposed to choose?

You already made your choice, a little voice in the back of my head reminds me. *You made your choice the moment you left Helston.*

I guess that's true.

I chose my friends over my dads.

I chose to put my faith in a dragon's promise.

I chose to step into Dumoor, and I have chosen, so far, to stay.

I have chosen to stay.

The thought is small and fragile, but the longer it lingers, the more certain it grows.

These people are good people.

There is a war coming.

We can help them.

We *must* help.

We *must* fight.

For Dumoor. Against Helston.

I tremble in the cool air, my back hitting the rough gray stone of The Roost, and close my eyes.

I see the bridge burning and I remember being glad.

You are not the first, nor will you be the last, little knight.

My eyes fly open and I jump into a combat stance, my hand automatically searching for Satin. She isn't there.

"Good evening, Callie," says Kensa, xir eyes a glow in the darkness. "I'm so glad you have finally found your way to us."

CHAPTER
TWENTY-TWO

I remember the fire. I remember the fear. I remember my hair burning and my blood boiling as Kensa opened xir jaws wide, teeth longer than Satin. I remember being certain Neal and El were dead. I remember being helpless as Edwyn and I struck the dragon with our useless blades.

I raise my fists, knowing it isn't enough. I am unarmed and alone. If Kensa decides to finish what xe started, I don't stand a chance. "Stay back."

Kensa puts up xir own hands. Human hands, free of claws or scales. Xir skin is reddish brown, xir hair scorched black, and xir eyes . . . like Teo's in shape, with narrow pupils, but instead of the warm sunshine yellow, the irises are every shade of fire. This is xir true form.

"I mean you no harm," says the dragon, voice low and sincere through the rasp in xir throat. "I heard you were here. I heard what you did—"

"We didn't do anything," I say shakily. "And we're not staying. We're not here to make trouble—"

"And I needed to thank you."

My fists drop just fractionally. "You want to . . . *thank* me?"

"For Teo," xe says. "For bringing xem home. For saving xir life. When news came that Helston had captured xem . . . I was certain xe was lost forever. A dragon of my years is not surprised easily. I know men. I know Helston. And I know the way the world treats us. But you, little knight, you surprised me. So, thank you."

And Kensa *bows*. To me.

"I am indebted to you, little knight. You succeeded where I failed. Whatever you need, it is yours. You have my solemn promise."

"I don't need anything," I make myself say. "And I didn't do anything. Teo's the one who saved us. If anyone owes a debt, it's me."

"Do not be so quick to undersell yourself."

I shut my mouth.

"You have come far and have far to go," Kensa continues. "There are many dangers ahead of you. You must arm yourself any way you can."

"Why does that feel like a threat?"

"Because you have been hunted and you are still being hunted, and every breath signals danger now."

That hits the mark so sharp and true, I grit my teeth. "You don't know me."

Kensa smiles. It's not like the smiles that haunt my dreams, full of fire and threat, but instead is one of warmth and reassurance. A little like Teo in the fangs poking out one side of xir mouth, and a lot like Neal.

Kensa and Neal, they were close as anything.

"I know that real honesty is hard for you. You are fighting a war inside yourself, and it's a battle for your life. But I know, too, that you will win."

I flush. "How d'you know that?"

"Because you are a fighter. You have trained your whole life. You know who you are and you know what is right. Even in your darkest moments, you have never lost sight of those two elements, and they will arm you better than any blade. We may not be friends, Callie, but we are allies."

"Yeah? How'd you figure?" I growl. "Far as I know, allies don't try to kill each other."

"I regret the way our previous interaction concluded," says Kensa. "I allowed my personal feelings to overtake me, and that made for poor judgment. I apologize."

I don't say it's fine, because it's not. I fold my arms tight across my chest and study the dragon carefully. "Actions speak louder than words, and I'm not gonna trust you just 'cause you tell me I can. It doesn't work like that. You wanna apologize, you can do it by showing us you're on our side. You can *prove* it. Got it?"

Kensa inclines xir horned head. "I do."

I keep going. "And I don't speak for everyone, just for me.

You want to make amends with the others, you gotta talk to them yourself. We're four separate people."

"Of course you are."

"And . . ." I suck in my lip, not sure if even *I* have the daring required to make my next demand. "You gotta swear it. Oaths are binding in Dumoor, right? That's what Teo said. So, make an oath saying everything you just said. 'Cause else it's just words."

Kensa hesitates, and xir eyes flash. "You are a sharp one, little knight." Then xe holds out xir hand, palm up. Xir nails are somewhere between claws and fingernails. They could slit my throat easy as anything.

But faith goes both ways, fragile as it is.

Pushing back the fear prickling through me, I place my hand in the dragon's palm. Xir long fingers curl around to grip me tight.

Xir hand is warm to the touch and not rough like I was expecting, though. The scales are soft like skin. Like *my* skin.

Warm turns hot so fast I only have time to flinch as our joined hands burst into flame. Real fire, full of red and orange and yellow snapping and crackling on my skin. Except it doesn't hurt, and I didn't think my head could get any more twisted around.

Kensa's face remains placid as the flames curl and lick around our wrists like chains binding us together.

"You have my oath," Kensa tells me over the rush of air being sucked into the furnace. "My word, my life." Bright magic flows from the dragon's hands into mine, strange and cool, and ties us together. "By the moors which bind us, it is done."

Kensa releases me and I inspect my hand, my wrist, my sleeve. No burns. No scorch marks. Just the lingering tingle of magic. Of a dragon's promise.

"Anything you need, little knight," says Kensa. "It is yours."

A dragon's favor ... There're a million things I could use it for, and I can't think of a single one.

"Why?" I call after xem as xe turns away. "After everything that happened ... Don't tell me it's just about Teo."

The dragon pauses, moonlight glinting off xir horns. "No," xe says, "it is not just about Teo."

"Then what—"

But Kensa is already gone.

CHAPTER
TWENTY-THREE

The moment the sun rises, I call an emergency meeting of the Helston contingency.

We sit on the floor in Elowen's room, which is the biggest, with a slightly-but-not-really-stolen plate of biscuits between us. And, yes, they are the best I've ever had the pleasure of putting in my mouth. I eat and talk and ignore the disapproving looks Elowen sends my way.

"You talked with *Kensa*?" Willow breathes in horror. "Callie . . . you could've been killed!"

I wave off his concerns with a casual, "Nah," ignoring the fact that I had very much feared that exact thing the whole way through the conversation. "It was fine. It was weird, but it was . . . fine. Xe's not like Teo, obviously, but xe's not *not* like Teo either. Really, what I'm saying is—" I take a deep breath. Even with all the certainty in the world, it's still hard to say. "I've been wrong about a lot of things. And I've known that for a while, even before we ran away, but talking to Teo's brood last night, then Kensa . . . I can't pretend anymore. Even for the sake of my pride. Shut *up*, El."

She raises her hands innocently. "I said nothing."

"You didn't need to. Your face says it all."

"There is nothing I can do about my face."

"Moving on," says Edwyn wearily.

"Yeah, moving on. What I'm trying to say is, these are the things we know as facts." I start counting them off on my fingers. "Dumoor has been kind to us, against everything we thought we knew. Two, Teo is our friend. We are friends with a dragon."

Willow frowns at his own fingers. "Is that three?"

"No, still two. They're joined."

"All right."

"Three, Adan holds a grudge and he's gonna come after us, somehow, sometime. And it's personal. Four, Helston is bringing a war against Dumoor. That's not personal, but we're mixed well into it. Helston's army is going to attack, even if we don't know exactly when. We know, too, that everything is kept in separate boxes here, and The Roost has nothing to do with the fighting and the killing and such. But Helston's not gonna care. They see magic, they see the enemy. Each one of us is proof enough of that."

Elowen nods, her face somber, while Edwyn hugs his knees.

Willow's fingers dance a fretful beat in his lap, midnight-blue skirt pulled over his knees. "If she . . . If Mother knew what it was really like—what *they're* really like—I know she would understand. At least, I think she would. I believe she would. If she could understand that they are just like us—"

"Helston and Dumoor are not alike," says Elowen. "I'm sorry, but they're not. If they were, do you think we would be welcomed here? Do you think we would have stayed one moment? There are not two people farther apart, and comparing The Roost to *Helston*—" She gives a contemptuous hiss. "I know you are homesick and guilty, Willow, but you cannot let your personal feelings cloud your senses."

"Hey," I say when Willow flinches. "That's a bit much, El."

Her sharp gaze flashes to me. "No it isn't. It's true. And I am glad you've caught up, Callie, because I feared you were going the same way. It's easy for both of you to sit comfortably in the middle when you still have people you love back in Helston. But it's not fair or right to diminish the damage Helston has done or the role it plays in this war." Elowen looks from me, to Willow, to Edwyn, holding us each steadily in her gaze for a long moment as she speaks: "In a world of black and white, Helston is the villain, and each of us needs to decide where we stand."

I take in Willow, wilting and miserable. "You really think it's that simple, El?"

She nods, once, firmly. "I do."

Silence sits among us, unbroken except for the soft patter of Willow's anxious fingers. I get it. His mind is with mine, back in Helston, in the warmest, safest places in the palace.

243

Islands surrounded by tempestuous storms, the violent sea slowly eroding the land inch by inch.

Maybe we would've been safe for a while longer, but not forever. We would've crumbled and fallen eventually.

"So, what?" Willow asks in a wobbly voice. "We fight against Helston? Is that what you're saying, Callie?"

I say "no" just as El gives an emphatic "yes."

"I'm saying that *my* goal"—I thump my chest—"has always been to protect my friends. You're my friends. But The Roost are my friends too. I think I have a duty to protect them. Or at least to help however I can. We're in a unique position, right? We have information all the way from the inside that might do some good. I'm not saying fight your mum, Willow. And I'm not saying burn the palace to the ground. I'm saying we follow the knight's code. The *real* one. The *true* one. To help and defend those weaker than ourselves. Whatever is going on up in Pioden, it isn't The Roost's fight. Right?"

Willow and Elowen both nod slowly.

"What about you?" I ask Edwyn, who has neither spoken nor moved nor *breathed* since we gathered. "You're an equal part of this. What do you think?"

"I think . . ." Edwyn's eyes flick between Willow and his sister, then drop. "I think there is nothing we can do to stop Helston once they ride. It isn't just about magic and fear. It's about Prince Jowan, His Majesty, and you, Willow. It's revenge. It has *always* been revenge." He takes a deep breath. "Father says—*said*—all of Helston's problems stem from a single source. To solve those problems means to eradicate that source. Dumoor. That includes The Roost, Teo, and everyone here. Helston won't rest until the job is complete."

"We have to tell them," says Elowen, standing up. "Callie's right. We have a duty to these people. We have to warn them. We have to *help* them. We have to . . ." A flash of something that almost looks like guilt crosses her face. "We have to speak with Alis."

Her name sends a prickle all the way from my scalp to my bare toes. Edwyn sucks in a breath, and Willow says, "No."

When we look at him, his jaw is rigid with anger. He avoids our stares, glaring at the space between us. His chest heaves. "I know it's complicated," he starts. "I agree that this is a good place and these are good people. But she . . . she killed my brother, and I can't—" But just the mention of Jowan is enough to break him. He smothers his face in his hands. "I can be here so long as it's separate," he mumbles, wobbly with tears. "So long as I can pretend that she isn't . . . But it's too much to ask. It's more than I can manage—"

"We're not going to make friends," I murmur, shuffling to wrap the prince up in a tight hug. "We're not even going to be allies. This isn't about her. It's about Teo and Dolan and Inis and everyone who's been kind to us. Who have nothing to do with Helston and don't deserve to die because of someone else's fight. Look, you don't even need to come if you don't want to. No one'll think badly of you if you wanna sit this out. Right?"

"Of course," says Elowen, and Edwyn nods his agreement. But Willow shakes his head, sitting up with a snuffle.

"No, if you're going, I'm going. And I'm . . . I—I want to look her in the eyes and ask her *why*. She took away my brother and then she took away my father. I want her to know what's left. I want her to see me and know what she's done."

"Okay," I say, squeezing him tighter. "Then that's exactly what we'll do."

Teo is somehow even bouncier when xe greets us in The Roost. If xir wings were through yet, I'm sure xe'd be on the ceiling!

I don't beat around the bush. "We need to talk to Alis. Do you know how we can make that happen?"

Teo stops short, yellow eyes wide and puzzled. "You want to talk to Alis? Why? I thought you were determined *not* to talk to her."

"Yeah, well . . ." I rub the back of my head. "I guess some things have changed."

"Does that mean you're staying?"

"We're not sure what it means yet," says El before Teo can get too excited. "That'll depend on what the Witch Queen says. Are you able to get us an audience?"

"*I* can't," says Teo. "But I know someone who can." Xe looks at me, nose wrinkled in apology. "I . . . don't suppose you've changed your mind on Kensa, too, have you? Because xe's back. Xe came home last night."

"Well, actually—"

I fill Teo in as fast as I can on my weird conversation with the older dragon and our even weirder truce. "I might not understand it, but I'm gonna take it. So you think Kensa can get us in?"

"I'm certain," says Teo. "There's no one closer to Alis than Kensa, and I'm sure she's interested in seeing you. I'll go now. Better to catch xem quickly before xe gets sent off on another mission. It could be weeks before xe's back again." Teo's already skipping backward before xe's done talking. "I'm sure you'll get an answer fast. I think she's keen to talk to you."

If Teo's trying to make us feel better, it is not working.

We wait anxiously for Teo to return with a reply from Pioden. Bundled up in the corner we've claimed as our own, we don't talk to each other; the magnitude of what we're doing sucks up all the oxygen around us.

I try to focus and remember everything anyone's ever told me about Alis, Witch Queen of the Moors, Helston's banished princess. Papa told me the story that night I first met Kensa. An evil witch who preys on lost children to feed her growing army. Queen Ewella told me about her jealous rage, which flared and exploded and nearly brought the palace crumbling to dust. Neal said that Alis is not to be trusted, that she'll catch you and keep you, easy as anything. Even Elowen had her stories, court rumors of the king's sister, whose power grew too big to contain.

She is the excuse the council gave over and over for keeping us small and contained. She is the justification Peran gave for cruelty. She is the very reason we were chased out of Helston.

She is why we are here now.

I don't like that. I don't like feeling like a piece in other people's games.

I wish I had Satin, though I dunno how good a sword would be against a witch queen. Probably about as effective as it was against a dragon. Nope, we're gonna have to rely wholly on *tact* and *diplomacy* and—I grimace—*manners*.

I give a little prayer of thanks for Elowen. If it was left up to me on my own, we'd be dead in a heartbeat. It is Willow, however, whom we are most worried about. I've seen him sad to the point of miserable. Depressed. Despondent. But I've never seen him brooding before. He doesn't speak or look at us, just stares at a point in the middle distance, his expression one I can only describe as stormy.

I *know* he's thinking about Jowan.

"Hey." I shuffle right up next to him. "You really don't have to do this, you know. We can tell you all about it. If you're not up to it—"

"I am up to it," he replies stiffly. "I want to be. And I want . . . to make sense of it. For myself. Because she isn't just some fairy tale villain. She's my aunt. Father's sister. And I don't remember her, but . . . I want to know if she's like him. Even just a little bit. Mother and Father never mentioned her, but Lord Peran did. Whenever I couldn't control my magic, he'd tell me I would end up just like my aunt. He said she was corrupted. Cursed. That her magic was poison, and she was the reason I was . . . the way that I am."

"Father's a liar," Elowen reminds him from the chair farthest from the fire. Today she has picked a tunic of aggressive magenta, paired with soft fawn-colored breeches, while Willow chose a dress that looks like it was stitched from fresh leaves. Edwyn wears the closest brown to black he could find, and I'm back in my favorite shade of green. We are all dressed for battle.

"I know that," Willow insists. "But lies grow from seeds of truth, don't they?"

Elowen's mouth twists down and she looks away.

But she doesn't need to say it out loud. We all know it: The best lies contain the most truth.

The first sign of news is a commotion among The Roost's residents at the creak of the ancient latch. Heads swivel, drinks are forgotten, conversations pause, all in favor of the newcomer.

I crane my neck, trying to see, then get up to perch on the back of the sofa.

Kensa is a returning hero.

The sight of the dragon still sets my blood ablaze.

I watch with interest, noting how the dragon takes the time to speak with each person, xir demeanor calm and . . . friendly?

Teo slips through the mass with a grin. "Told you it'd be easy!" When I don't reply, xe follows my gaze and xir expression turns fond. "Kensa's always badly missed when xe's gone."

But it's more than that. More than a hero returning triumphant. It takes a while, but finally I place the strange familiarity of the scene.

It reminds me of Papa, finally riding home after an age away on duty.

"They love xem."

"Of course," Teo says. "Kensa has been here all the way from before the beginning. Xe takes care of every single person who finds their way here, and xe makes sure we all get a voice in Pioden. Xe's the bridge between Pioden and The Roost, especially since Alis rarely leaves Pioden anymore."

"But Kensa's not even in Dumoor much anymore, right?"

Teo sighs and shakes xir head. "And even when xe is, xe's mostly up at Pioden anyway." Xir ears droop slightly. "It's very different from when I first came here. It's still good. I still love it. But I miss the way it used to be. It's like the sun's setting on Dumoor." Xe gives an awkward laugh, scritching the back of xir neck. "That sounds dramatic, I know. I just wish things were back the way they were. Especially as these come in." Xe reaches around to touch xir back. Through the thin fabric of Teo's loose shirt, I can already catch shapes of wings straining against xir skin. "I need Kensa to be here so I can learn to fly."

"How long d'you think till they pop?" I imagine enormous feathery wings sprouting fully formed right out of Teo's back and *squirm*. I wonder if it's like getting your adult teeth in. I wonder if it hurts.

But if Teo's worried, xe doesn't show it. I guess the excitement at the promise of flight overrides everything else. "Could be any day now!" Xe spreads xir arms wide. "I know they'll be pretty useless for a while, but I don't care! As soon as they come in, I can start shifting fully."

"You mean into a whole dragon?"

Teo bounces eagerly. "Yup!"

I squint, trying to picture Teo as Kensa's kind of dragon. That's a lot of creature in such a small body!

"Are all dragon-forms the same?"

"No, of course not!" says Teo with the kind of laugh that makes me feel foolish for even asking. "They're as different as people are different."

I guess that makes sense. "What do you think you're gonna look like?"

"I dunno." Teo touches the blue scales freckling xir face. "Something pretty, I hope. I don't want to be too scary."

I grin. "I don't think you could be scary even if your teeth were seven feet long!" Truthfully, I don't think Teo could ever be anything like Kensa in any way at all.

I hope not, anyway.

Kensa finally extracts xemself from the crowd and comes straight toward us. Even though xir expression couldn't be more neutral, even though xir teeth are safely inside xir mouth, warning goose bumps prickle all the way up my arms.

I force my biggest smile, like we've been besties forever and not, you know, trying to kill each other. "Hey, how's it going?"

Kensa ignores the question. Up close, xe looks *tired*. "Alis has extended an invitation at your request. To all of you." Xe nods to my friends, who are lingering uncertainly behind me. "Are you ready to go?"

"Now?" My heartbeat spikes. "Like . . . right this second?"

Kensa fixes me with a fiery eye. "Alis's time is precious. Wars start and end in less than a second. You requested a meeting, and your request is being met—"

"Yeah, all right, I get it." I look back at the others with a shrug of apology. "Now or never, I guess."

Willow swallows hard, then steels himself with a curt nod.

Elowen's chin is already raised, her expression fierce. "I'm ready."

Edwyn looks like he's here in body only. I don't think we can ask any more of him.

"Oh," says Kensa. "Alis asked me to pass on a message to all of you. She says . . ." The dragon sighs deeply, the audible equivalent of an eye roll. "She hopes you are hungry."

CHAPTER
TWENTY-FOUR

Food, however, has never been further from my thoughts as we follow Kensa on the long trek to Pioden. The dragon doesn't speak. Xe barely even acknowledges our existence as we trot to keep pace. I guess we're lucky xe doesn't just transform and fly, leaving us to make our own way toward the Witch Queen's castle.

It's like dragons have a finite amount of chattiness between them, and Teo has all of it, leaving Kensa with, well, none.

And the trek to Pioden is awkward to the point of unbearable.

Out of The Roost and through the dense forest, dark even in daylight, then out onto the moors themselves.

Going from claustrophobic woods onto desolate moorland is like jumping from an ice bath into boiling water. Miles and miles of stubby grass, gnawed down by bored ponies, granting no protection from the snapping of the wind.

I wish I'd dressed warmer.

All that breaks the landscape is a teetering mass of granite that looks like it's gonna topple over at any moment.

And not a single castle-like anything in sight.

I'm not the only one casting a nervous look up at the sky, at the carrion birds sweeping and dipping beneath the clouds.

The others are just as confused as I am by the empty countryside. We shield our eyes against the sun to squint toward the horizon, searching for a hint of our destination. There is nothing but grass and stone and the distant shapes of the birds sweeping across the sky, watching us like they're waiting for us to drop down dead.

"They are not birds of prey."

Kensa's voice startles me more than I'd like to admit. Xe's neither broken pace nor looked behind at me as xe speaks.

I trot to catch up. "What are they, then?"

"Magpies."

"Oh." My knowledge of magpies is zero except what Neal says about how you're supposed to greet them respectfully anytime you cross paths. I don't know if this counts as crossing paths, since there's basically a mile of air between us, but I salute the dancing flock anyway. Better safe than sorry.

"So, how far is it to Pioden?"

"Not far."

"Sounds real fake, given there's literally nothing any-where." Irritation bubbles and pops. "Hey, just wait a sec! We've a right to know where we're going."

"I told you, little knight, Alis's time is precious. Keep up and stay close to me."

I plant my feet and *stop*.

Willow barrels straight into my back.

Elowen glares at me. "Callie," she growls. "Now is not the time."

But as far as I'm concerned, this is the *only* time. "You said we could trust you," I call out to Kensa, who is *still* going. "You need to tell us where we're going. You can't expect us just to put our faith in you without proof we can trust you. You could be leading us anywhere!"

The dragon finally—*finally*—stops, and when xe turns back to us, xir eyes are ablaze with a warning I'm doing everything in my power to ignore. "You asked this favor of me, little knight."

"Yeah, because Teo said you were the best person to help us."

"I am the *only* person who can help you."

"So . . . what?" My temper is spiking so hard and fast, my eyesight goes fuzzy. "We don't have any choice but to follow you wherever you choose to take us?"

I know that's the case. I am painfully, miserably aware that that is the case. And it feels like every other moment of heavy disappointment when you hope a grown-up will do right by you and then they're just as self-serving as the rest and—

The dragon dips xir head. "Forgive me. You are right to be wary. Of course you are. It was not my intention to make you afraid."

I fold my arms and glare. Mostly because I have no idea how to respond out loud to this. And I don't like being wrong, even when it's for the better.

"Look." Kensa returns to my side and points in the direction we've been heading in. "Do you see the line where the moorland meets the sky?"

"The horizon? Yeah, obviously."

"Between here and there sits Pioden."

Irritation pricks at me. "But I can't *see* it."

"Just because you cannot see it does not mean it isn't there. Pioden is the heart of Dumoor and fiercely protected. Only those with the key may see it. That is why you must stay close. Stray too far from me and you will pass right through it."

Sounds like a whole lot of nonsense to me, but what do I know?

Elowen being Elowen, she accepts Kensa's riddles with hesitation, and Willow follows with a resigned shrug. Not like we have much choice other than to let faith lead the way.

Only Edwyn hangs back. He stares off at the spot Kensa pointed to, so statue-still I'm worried he's forgotten how to breathe. For a moment, I think he's going to turn tail and run all the way back to lock himself in his room.

"You coming?"

"Yes." Except he doesn't move.

Where Willow fidgets when he gets nervous, Edwyn locks together. He's like that now—hands clasped so tight that the bones strain beneath his white skin.

I take a cautious step toward him. "What's up?"

"Nothing."

"Don't lie."

He shoots me a look. "I do wish you didn't know me quite so well."

I shrug. "Sorry not sorry. So, what's the matter?"

Edwyn's gaze follows Willow and his sister on either side of Kensa, and the frown between his eyes is deep and permanent. Finally, he settles on, "This doesn't feel good, Callie."

"I mean, we're walking into the enemy's lair. Of course it doesn't feel good."

"No, I know. And that would be okay if the others were . . . if they weren't . . . I—I know Willow is nervous. And I'm glad. Not that I'm happy he's nervous, only, knowing Willow—"

"He trusts so easily it's gonna get him in trouble one of these days?"

"Precisely." Edwyn sighs. "And Elowen . . . I'm afraid she's already made her mind up, and I'm scared that is going to cloud her senses."

"Elowen is smart," I say, even though I've been having

exactly the same worries. "We're going into this with eyes open. It's going to be okay."

Edwyn takes a deep breath. "I hope so."

Yeah. Me too.

"Callie, Edwyn, come on!" Willow yells, waving both his arms. "You have to see this!"

We sprint to catch up, but we see it long before we even reach them.

I stop beside Elowen—her face a picture of awe—and gape.

The tor is twice as tall as it is wide, deep gray granite as ancient as the sky.

The magic it must take to conceal . . .

"Is this Pioden?" I ask, but Kensa doesn't answer. Approaching the foot of the tor, xe bows xir head and closes xir eyes, then touches two fingers to the rough stone. Kensa murmurs something somewhere between a song and a spell and ends in a high whistle I feel all the way in my bones.

Like a duet, the tor starts to moan.

We all flinch and clamp our hands over our ears. The sound of rock shifting and grinding splits my head like a toothache times a million. And it goes on and on until the point I can't stand it anymore. And then it stops.

When I dare crack my eyes open, there's a door where plain granite was. Exactly like the escape beneath Helston, except this isn't just a hole bashed into the stone, but a nice piece of dark wood embellished with bronze. The kind of door you'd expect to find in a palace.

On closer inspection, the runes carved into the wood are birds, and when Kensa touches them, they shake out their feathers and spread their wings, and the door swings outward, presenting us to Pioden like a master of ceremonies.

I gawk. It's a castle. A real, whole castle inside a lichen-covered rock. It is a perfect replica of Helston's palace, crafted from a single piece of stone and rendered in every shade of gray. From the curving staircase to the tiled floor, it's the same. Familiar and different all at once.

I hate it.

"Come," Kensa urges, but the resemblance isn't sitting well with any of us.

The stars in Elowen's eyes have faded. Willow's jaw is tight. And Edwyn—

"It's not real," I tell him quickly as his breathing gets harsher. "It's not Helston. It's okay."

"It feels the same—"

Willow takes his hand and squeezes until Edwyn squeezes back, repeating my words: "It's not Helston."

"Of course it's not Helston," says Elowen impatiently, like she didn't freeze at the sight of the entrance hall too. "It's everything Helston isn't. Come *on*."

She strides after Kensa, chin held high, leaving us to trail along in her wake.

We follow Kensa up the stone staircase and through the stone halls; the only breaks in the granite are the dark wooden doors with their bronze fixtures. Every element that makes up Pioden is ancient, even its inspiration, but it feels brand-new.

Magic hums through every inch.

The only living, breathing souls are us, our footsteps echoing loud as a blacksmith's hammer, ricocheting from stone wall to stone wall with nothing to soften the sound.

It's eerie to the point of haunted.

When Teo described Pioden, the operational hub of the Witch Queen's realm, I had imagined Helston at its busiest, filled with knights and warriors, and grown-ups arguing about strategy over enormous maps. Keeping things separate from folks who don't want to fight makes sense, but surely Alis's army isn't just her and Kensa?

"Where is everyone?"

I don't know why I expected to get a response out of the tight-lipped dragon.

We go up two hundred and seventy-three stairs, and Kensa stops right on the landing.

Gauzy curtains hang in an archway, floating in the light breeze like tethered ghosts. Sunshine glows through the pale material, and on the other side is the indistinct shape of a person.

"Go through," says Kensa.

On the other side of the curtains is a balcony with a full view of the moors. We're so high up, I'm pretty sure we can see every inch of Dumoor, from The Roost nestled within the forest to the little buildings making up community, and all the tors dotting the landscape like sentinels. I wonder if there are castles hidden in them too.

And right in front of us, all the way to the west, a clear view of Helston. The town, the towers, the castle. The chasm where the bridge once stood.

"Welcome, finally."

We all back up as a woman comes toward us with her arms outstretched.

She's short and stocky, golden hair a tumble about her shoulders. She wears the kind of dress I recognize from The Roost—brightly colored and simple in design. She could've been there and I would never have picked her out of the crowd.

The Witch Queen. The banished princess.

Alis.

"It's been so long," she says to Willow, looking down at him with a fondness and warmth that only comes with familiarity. "You look so much like Ewella."

She has Willow's smile.

CHAPTER
TWENTY-FIVE

"I'm so glad you reached out," says Alis, her voice deeper than I was expecting. "I have wanted to see you from the moment you crossed the bridge, but I knew I had to let you come to me. And I knew that you would."

Alis stretches out a hand as though to touch his cheek, but Willow steps back, eyeing her warily. Her fingers are short and stubby and bedecked in rings bearing brightly colored jewels that seem to glint with a light of their own.

"You knew we were coming? How?" Willow asks.

"I have eyes everywhere, child. From here to Helston, there is nothing I cannot see. Even through your mother's wards."

Willow catches my eye, and his fear matches the twist in my stomach.

She saw and did nothing.

To be seen and unaided is worse than not being seen at

all. She watched us run. She watched us being hunted. She watched Jory die.

Alis redirects her attention from Willow to me, her expression just as warm and welcoming, even though I *know* she can see me bristling with suspicion.

"Callie. Your reputation precedes you, young knight."

"What reputation?" I growl, keeping well out of arm's reach.

If Alis is offended, she doesn't show it. "Your courage," she says. "Your determination to fight for what is right, no matter the personal cost. It is a rare, commendable thing. And valuable."

I don't like the way she says "valuable" like there's a price on my head. Like I'm something to be bought or bartered.

Her pale blue eyes, the color of snow at dawn, settle on the twins, and Elowen is the only one of us who doesn't balk at the welcoming touch.

"Elowen. Edwyn. I remember the day you were born. I knew you would both be special. I am so glad you have found your way here."

"You talk like we had a choice." My voice is sharp to the point of brittle, and my fingernails cut into the soft part of my palm. But her easy countenance, her friendly manner . . . It's like we're just visiting a relative who lives far away and whom we rarely get to see. But that's not true. That's not *real*. And it completely wipes out *everything* that is.

My heart thudders fast.

We're not doing this again.

I am *sick* of being around grown-ups who make up their own reality at our expense.

"You said you see everything," I say. "From here to Helston. So you *know* what we went through and why. You *know* we're not here by choice."

The Witch Queen tilts her head with a patient smile. "Fate is a strange thing, child. You were always meant to be here, whether you knew it or not."

Anger blurs my vision. "What does that even *mean*?"

"It means that all that has happened and all that has been done to you has led you right here. It was inevitable. And I am so glad. You are exactly where you are supposed to be."

She's still smiling. How can she still be smiling?

"Come, sit. Some things should only be discussed over tea."

Alis motions at a table behind her—sprung like a mushroom out of the stone balcony—and my treacherous mouth starts watering immediately.

Laid out is a feast of scones and jam and *cream*.

And all at once, every bad feeling, every ill will, evaporates.

I'm done. Sold out. The End.

I never stood a chance.

I manage to keep my composure just long enough to *not* rush at the table and face-plant right into the dish of cream, instead forcing my feet to move at a demure and excruciatingly civilized pace along with the others' more cautious gait.

The plates and cups are thick pottery—nothing like the delicate tea set Queen Ewella used—but they're all carefully patterned with the image of the same kind of bird that adorned the front door. A black-and-white bird.

"The magpie is Pioden's sigil," Alis explains when she catches me squinting. "Given our mission, it was the obvious choice."

"Thief," Elowen whispers.

"Collector," Alis corrects her. "We find the lost and bring them home. We discover the treasure among the discarded. I know what it feels like to be turned on by those you loved and who you believed loved you, simply because you don't quite fit their idea of who you should be. Each of you has been led to believe you are less than you are. Some more than others, yes, but all have fought more than you should ever have needed to just for the right to exist." One eyebrow twitches as she catches my eye. "Tell me I'm wrong."

I can't. Every word out of her mouth is true.

"I know you have already been welcomed to The Roost," says Alis. "But let me repeat: You are all welcome here for as long as you wish to stay, without condition or expectation. I hope your time here will be long enough that we might become reacquainted, that I might have the chance to make up for the time I lost with you, Willow, but I know also that some stories are not so easily rewritten. But for now"—a sweeping gesture of a hand fills each of our plates with scones—"eat. Everything else can wait. We have time."

I demolish my plateful and go for seconds. I'm on my third before I notice the others aren't really eating. Elowen is sipping her tea with lowered eyes; Edwyn's been spreading jam on his first scone for several minutes, and Willow's hands are in his lap, a frown knotted between his brows. It's only then that I remember I was angry a few minutes ago, but for the life of me I cannot recall why.

Maybe I was hangry. I'm my own worst enemy when my stomach is growling. Whatever it was, it can't be that important. Alis is nice. Dumoor is safe. And she's right, isn't she? Everything we went through led us right to this moment, and this moment is pretty okay. Maybe it was all worthwhile.

"Jowan wasn't fate," says Willow quietly. "Father wasn't fate. None of it was *meant* to happen, and it didn't make me stronger, and if I'm any good now, it's *despite* what happened, not because of it!" He glares at his aunt across the table, his eyes full of tears. "You don't get to call it fate when *you're* the one who took them away from me! It was your fault. Everything that happened to me—to *us*—it was because of *you*. They fear magic because of *you*. They hate us because of *you*! *You're* the reason why Father left. *You* killed Jowan! It is *all. Your. Fault!*"

Willow's voice rings clear and loud and sets the magpies that are coasting in the air closest to us fleeing.

None of us speak. None of us dare. I can't even swallow my mouthful of scone, turned to clay in my throat.

We each hold our breath, all eyes on Alis, waiting for the sweet façade to finally crack into something violent and vicious, like lightning breaking through soft clouds to strike us down and put us back in our rightful place.

But all that happens is a twitch of one blond eyebrow and the tilt of a golden head. "Is that what they told you about me?"

Willow doesn't answer. I don't think he *can* answer; stunned into silence by his own insolence. Elowen and Edwyn look like they're waiting and wishing for the ground to swallow them up whole. It even takes me a few good goes before I can get my voice working again.

"Yeah." I clear my throat. "Everyone knows the stories."

"Stories?" Alis repeats with an amused curl of the lips. "I do know how Helston loves their stories. Their epic ballads of daring deeds. There are none so talented in twisting a tale as Helston's elite." She reaches for her cup and raises it in a sort of toast. "Go ahead, child, tell me a story, and make it an exciting one."

I falter. "About . . . you?"

"Of course!"

I study the Witch Queen carefully. I can't tell if she's for real or trying to lure me into a trap. It feels like all those moments when Mama would sweet-talk me into telling the truth about why I had come home covered in mud with rips in my skirt; she'd promise amnesty, then punish me anyway. Truth is not always safe.

Alis smiles. "Trust me, Callie. There is nothing you can tell me that is worse than my imagination. Don't forget—I was a Helston princess once upon a time." She winks. "I know the kind of talk that gets spun through the court. I wasn't their first villain, and I'm certain I won't be their last."

"I'm afraid we may have taken that spot," says Elowen bleakly, and Alis laughs a full-belly laugh that washes away the worst of the tension so at least the air is breathable again.

"Then you are in good company. This little community we have forged, it is a haven for all Helston's enemies. Each of us different. All of us united."

"So, what? You saying the stories aren't true? They're just stuff Helston made up?"

"All good stories sprout from a seed of truth," Alis tells me. "I know the part I played in my own, and I accept responsibility." She sighs and sits back, her gaze on the teacup cradled in her lap; then she raises her eyes and asks us, "Will you permit me to tell you *my* story?"

"Yes!" Elowen sits forward in her seat so fast she nearly topples right off it. "Please do!"

Her enthusiasm is, apparently, enough to speak for the rest of us. Alis nods, pours more tea, and settles into her tale.

"Like all who were raised in the palace, Helston was my

whole world. Its rules were all I knew and all I ever expected. I was my parents' firstborn, the oldest and the strongest, but from the moment he was born, I knew that my little brother had already surpassed me. It didn't matter that Richard fumbled his lessons and could never take anything seriously; his destiny was set in stone. It didn't matter that I worked a thousand times harder and did everything anyone asked of me; I was always just the crown prince's sister. I existed in his shadow, and there was nothing I could do to escape it. Anytime I tried, I was returned firmly to my place behind him, while all Richard had to do was breathe and the court cheered.

"I accepted my frustration as part of myself. Helston doesn't change. Helston *cannot* change. But the older I got, the harder it became, and the bigger my resentment grew. It wasn't fair, and no one was interested in making it fair as long as everything stayed the same. As the princess, I had my pick of companions, but there was only one I considered my friend. My partner. With only a few weeks between our birthdays, we grew up together. We shared every moment of our lives, every secret dream, every forbidden wish. When we played, we played as queens together, ruling as one, with no one above us and no one who dared tell us to moderate ourselves.

"But it wasn't enough to keep our hopes in the pretend world. I needed them to be real. And we could do it, she and

I. We could do it together. We were the strongest in Helston, honing our magic in secret beyond anything Helston told us was possible, even if we were the only two who knew of our potential. But she was afraid. A child's game is one thing, but true rebellion—*treason*—is something else entirely. I pushed too hard, and I pushed her away. I watched her leave me, and I watched her become queen on her own. At someone else's side. In someone else's shadow."

"Mother," Willow whispers, and Alis nods, her expression deep with grief.

"We would've been great together, she and I. We would've been everything. But Ewella lost her courage. I watched her marry my brother and look at him the way she used to look at me. I watched her raise the next future king, another unexceptional boy who would never have to work for the crown on his head. And then I saw you, Willow, and I knew you were something else. Something special. Something like me. And you would be ignored and stifled just the same; crushed by a world I had helped create by holding my tongue and keeping the peace.

"I wanted more for you. I wanted everything for you that I had wanted for myself. And I knew you would never have it in Helston, the most beautiful crystal cage." A smile slips across Alis's lips. "So I broke it. I shattered the façade and I accepted my fate as the banished princess, the Witch Queen of Dumoor, Helston's greatest enemy." Pride flecks every word. She wears the titles like a crown. She wears them well. "I showed them all what they should really be afraid of."

Elowen is literally on the edge of her seat, elbows on the table, absorbing the tale like it's a life-giving elixir.

Willow, on the other hand, is not smiling. "Is that why you killed Jowan? Because you were jealous of Father?" His fingers are white where they grip the lip of the table, chest heaving with anger. "And what did you do to Father? Did you kill him too?"

Alis shakes her head. "I did not kill Jowan—"

"Maybe not personally, but you ordered him dead!"

"I didn't—"

"Don't lie!" It's a desperate plea, more pain than rage. "I am sick of people lying to me! I am strong enough to bear the truth, so tell me! Tell me what happened to my brother and father! Because *I* remember. Every moment. It was Jowan's first mission. It wasn't even supposed to be a battle, but I didn't want him to go anyway. I didn't want him to leave Helston. But he promised it would be okay. He promised he would come home. I believed him. But when the riders returned—" Willow turns his face away and grits his teeth, fighting desperately not to crack.

I know because I feel it too. The lump choking his words is in my throat too, the memory vivid and vicious. I wasn't in Helston back then. I was in Clystwell, waiting by the gate for

Papa to ride home. Just as Willow said, it wasn't supposed to be a battle, so when Papa came home war-torn and haunted, I didn't understand.

It was a long time before he told me why he was never going back to Helston, why he was retiring and why he was willing to give up everything for my sake. When he told me Jowan had fallen that day, it was like I'd lost my own brother. It didn't make sense. It wasn't right. Jowan was *good,* and good people weren't supposed to fall. Not so easily. Not so quickly.

"Sir Nick said it happened fast," Willow whispers. "That he couldn't have suffered. That's what I heard him tell Mother and Father. He said they'd been caught off guard and attacked unprovoked. That they didn't stand a chance."

I nod. "That's what Papa told me too."

"Mother as well," says Elowen. "I remember that day also. Father was gone, occupied with Their Majesties. Mother sat us down and told us what had happened. We weren't allowed to leave the apartment until Father came home. It was the longest he'd ever been away from us."

"Lord Peran was with me," says Willow bleakly. "He said Mother and Father were too grief-stricken to take care of me. He said I had to stay out of everyone's way, that I would just be a reminder of everything the Crown had lost. I didn't see them again until after the funeral. Even then, I knew they were busy making plans for what they were supposed to do without Jowan. I was the new crown prince." He raises his eyes to Alis. "Isn't that you wanted all along? Isn't that what you said? How can you tell us you didn't do it while admitting in the same breath that you didn't think Jowan or Father deserved to be on the throne? You finally got what you wanted, so just admit it!"

"I never wanted them dead," says Alis softly. "I loved my brother and I loved Jowan. Just because I didn't believe they deserved the powers and privileges they possessed merely by virtue of their birth doesn't mean I wanted them *dead*. When I heard that Jowan had fallen, I made *certain* that it was not at the hand of one of my own. If it had been, I would've ensured that they faced a just sentence. I remember that day, too, just as well as you do. As I told you, I have eyes everywhere, from here to Helston. I watched Helston ride out and I watched them attack my people. Unprovoked. I saw Jowan fall, but it was neither by my hand nor on my orders."

Willow stares at her a few moments longer, and then he slumps, defeated, head falling into his hands. I know that feeling—everyone with a different story, and the truth is getting harder and harder to grasp. Exhausted just by trying to hold on to the shards of a thousand different stories when all you need is a single truth.

I put a hand on his back and glare at Alis. "Why should we believe you above anyone else? Far as we know, everyone's got their own version of the story and *none* of them are true. What makes you any different?"

The Witch Queen pauses, painted lips parted. Then she sets down her teacup and rises.

"Because I can prove it," she says, holding out a bejeweled hand. "Because I can *show* you. Come."

CHAPTER
TWENTY-SIX

We follow Alis back into her granite palace. My legs feel weird, like they're not part of me, and my heart is racing so fast I'm afraid it's gonna run right out of my chest. I'm scared of what she wants to show us, and this isn't why we requested an audience with Alis. But every time I try to think of a way to get us back on track, my mind slides right off the thought. I can't get a grip on my own head, like my brain has turned to slick oil.

There's nowhere else to go. No more stairs, no more doors.

We stop beneath the pointed ceiling of the tallest tower, the crisscrossed eaves full of magpies, which stare down at us with cocked heads and curious black eyes.

Alis whistles a single high note and the birds take off in unison, streaming out of the single small window.

"It is better that we are alone," Alis explains, ushering

us into the tiny, round room with no doors, no furniture, no nothing except a single dip in the floor, perfectly round and filled with water so tranquil it's almost invisible. She settles on the far side, arranging her skirts around her, and motions for us to sit.

The air is so still, it feels almost disrespectful to breathe.

We each take a spot equidistant from each other, making up five points around the pool.

Willow is across from me, his face pale and somber. El sits between me and Alis, hands folded neatly in her lap. Edwyn is on my other side, gnawing on his lip.

Once we're all settled, Alis leans and touches the tip of one finger to the water's surface.

It ripples. It shimmers. It *glows*.

And then it breaks into a picture as clear as though we were looking through a window.

It's a bird's-eye view—a bird soaring over the moors below gray clouds. A summer's day, yes, but what does that even mean in Wyndebrel?

Far below, a company of tiny horses and riders trot across the countryside.

The picture pulls us in, down, closer, and my heart leaps as I recognize Papa on Bayna and, beside him—

Willow makes a choked sound. His fingers are curled tight around the lip of the pool like he's about to pitch right into it—back into a world where his brother is still alive.

Prince Jowan throws his head back as he laughs.

The sound—so familiar and forgotten; so *real*—hurts my chest.

I steal a glance at Willow, who is valiantly fighting tears as he watches his brother. What a difference it would've made if Jowan hadn't ridden out that day. Peran would never have dared even try to touch him.

"How are we seeing this?" Elowen asks, softer than a breath. "I've never heard of this magic before."

"Dragons have their uses," Alis murmurs.

So that's what this is. Not a bird's-eye view. A dragon's.

Kensa's.

"Note how it doesn't attack, only watches. My dragons are my eyes. I see what they see."

And now so do we.

And we hear only what they hear too—just the rush of air and the chirping of birds. I know that I'm on solid ground, I even press my palms flat to the floor to prove it to myself, but my brain doesn't quite believe me. I suck in my dizziness and make myself watch the scene unfold.

The riders sit easy in their saddles, unaware of the beast above them, and the dragon soars a little lower on silent wings. I don't understand how the knights don't notice Kensa. I guess dragons have decent invisibility magic too?

Lower and lower, and faces come into focus. Papa's, the prince's. Captain Jory is there too, and my heart pangs with fresh grief. There's a cluster of riders I don't recognize, concealed by their helmets. One of them nudges their horse to a trot and rides to stop beside Jory. He points into the trees, murmuring something to Jory, who shakes his head.

I lean forward, straining to hear the conversation, but there's nothing except birdcalls and the whisper of wind.

Papa notices and nudges Bayna beside them, leaving Prince Jowan behind. Alone.

My pulse thumps loud in my blood.

I know what's coming. We all do. And every second that passes is a second closer.

Everything inside me wants to look away, like somehow not seeing it means it won't happen. Like it's still possible to save Jowan.

It's already done.

He's already dead.

I glance at Willow. I wish he wasn't here. He shouldn't be seeing this. It's not too late. It hasn't happened yet.

I start to move, to open my mouth to call a halt to this whole thing because it doesn't matter. Jowan's dead. That's it. It doesn't need to be more complicated than that.

"Look," says Elowen, pointing.

The air has shifted, the riders gathering close together. Papa and Jory draw their swords first, facing the trees. No one's laughing anymore.

We hold our breath with the Helston company. I couldn't move even if I wanted to.

And then the scene explodes.

People spill from the trees like rabbits chased out by

hounds. Even from high in the sky, their panic is visible. Tangible. The Helston company wheels in shock, weapons at the ready.

But the charging people . . . they're not attacking. They're *fleeing*.

Fear collides with fear in an explosion of violence, of magic, of blades. Everyone is trying to defend themselves from an attack that never took place.

And amid all that—

Willow's cry is a broken thing, like the arrow struck him.

The arrow.

Wait—

I lean so far I nearly dive right into the water, but I have to see, I have to be sure.

The moment before Jowan falls, I glimpse red.

Not blood. Not a crimson tunic.

A red feather.

A *Helston* feather.

CHAPTER
TWENTY-SEVEN

N o one but us—two years late—notices. The battle continues around the fallen prince, and through the chaos a single figure darts in and snatches the arrow out of Jowan's back. They're gone before I can catch an identifying detail, but one thing's for sure—

"They lied," Elowen breathes. "They told everyone it was magic, but it wasn't." She raises her face from the shimmering scene, and there's a strange triumphant light in her eyes. "I knew it. Helston murdered—"

"No." Willow scrambles up, backing away from the pool and shaking his head so hard it's like he's trying to dislodge the image from his mind. "This is wrong. This is a lie. That isn't what happened!"

"A dragon's eye cannot lie." Alis rises, approaching Willow slowly and softly, gathering him into her arms. He lets her, accepting the comfort, letting her hold him up on legs that don't want to work. "I'm sorry, child," she murmurs into his hair. "It is a hard thing, when all you know is false. And I'm sorry, too, all of you, that you suffered so terribly beneath this lie. I promise you now, Helston will pay. I will not stop until reparations have been made."

"I want to help," says Elowen at once, her voice quavering with determination. "I want to fight. On your side. Against Helston. I was the chancellor's daughter and I know Helston better than anyone. Let me help you."

Alis inclines her head. "You are sweet to offer, Elowen. But this is not your fight. It is time that the four of you rest and let the grown-ups fight for you."

The words—strung together in an all-too-familiar sentence—buzz in my head.

How many times have we been told that?

How much good has it done us?

I pick myself up, my own legs trembling. "No. This *is* our fight, and we've every right to be a part of it. That's why we came up here, isn't it?" I look to the others for support, but Elowen's already made her mind up and Willow's face is hidden in Alis's shoulder. Edwyn hasn't moved from his place by the pool, and he's still staring down into the water, frowning.

I take a deep breath and face Alis. "Look, I get it. You don't know us and you feel bad and want to make things right, but leaving us out isn't the way to do it. You haven't been in Helston for forever. You don't know what it's like on the inside. *We* do. We can help. And maybe we can work out a way to get through this without bloodshed—"

Elowen wheels on me so fierce and fast, I nearly trip backward. "Why? After *everything* Helston has done to us, why on *earth* would you want to protect them?"

I stand my ground, mirroring her glare. "Because I don't believe in making innocent people suffer for one person's crime, Elowen!"

"One person? You think *one* person is responsible? It was a cover-up, Callie! They lied to give themselves an excuse! That's not *one* person! That's the *whole court*! The king, the queen, Captain Jory, Sir Nick—"

"You're wrong!" I have to clench my fists tight to keep myself from clamping my hands over my ears; my nails cut into my palms. "They didn't know! There's no way they could've known!"

"And there's no way they couldn't."

We stare each other down, our stubbornness frustratingly equal.

"Now is not the time to bicker," says Alis gently. "Whoever your enemy is, it is not each other. You all have a lot to process. Please, return to The Roost and allow yourselves to be taken care of. You have my word that we will talk again soon." To me and Elowen, she says, "I understand your passions and your eagerness to set things right, but you must let your feelings settle before making big decisions."

"We're not kids," I snap.

But the look Alis gives me fizzles out the hottest part of my temper.

"Yes, Callie, you are. Even if you haven't been treated as such. I know the way Helston treats its young." She carefully extracts Willow from her embrace, helping him stand on his own. The prince looks utterly spent, hair a mess, face blotchy. I don't know if he'll even be able to make it all the way down to The Roost. "From the moment they are big enough to follow orders, children are treated like soldiers. Girls too," she adds with a nod to El. "Obey, be quiet, don't argue. Everything you do must be for the good of Helston. That is not the way we do things here."

"What about Teo?"

There is a moment—a fraction of a second—when Alis's placid countenance flickers. I don't think anyone else notices. Maybe I imagined it, because the gentle earnestness is right back in place when Alis says, "I am forever indebted to you for bringing Teo home. When we heard she had been captured—"

"Xe," I say. "Teo's pronoun is 'xe.'"

"Of course. Forgive me." Alis dips her head. "It is a recent change. I still haven't got used to their new words yet."

My heart thudders, each wrong word like a kick to the gut. Doesn't matter that it's not me being misgendered. Doesn't matter that Teo's not here. Everyone deserves basic respect *always*. "Xir. You haven't got used to *xir* new words."

"Xir," Alis repeats, her smile taking on a strange brittleness.

"As I say, when we heard Teo had been captured, I was devastated. The responsibility was entirely mine. Teo was keen to join the scouting party, and I had been advised that Teo was ready. I should've known better, but I always like to give people a chance when they ask for it. Be assured, I will not take such a risk again. Every life is precious."

I feel myself nodding—yes, that makes sense—but on the inside I'm screaming that this feels wrong. Except that's all it is: a feeling. And one I don't have a name for.

"It's been a hard day for all of you," says Alis, a sweep of her hand ushering us out of her strange tower room. "A hard *week*. Return to The Roost and be kind to yourselves. I will be here when you are strong enough to talk."

I'm strong enough now, I want to argue, even as my feet follow her command. Except I can't get my head straight, and Willow's in no state to think about anything right now, and Elowen—

I glance at her as she strides past me, her face set rigid. Angry.

Before we talk to Alis again, El and I need to work things out.

CHAPTER
TWENTY-EIGHT

Except she doesn't talk to me. All the way back down the hill and through the forest and into The Roost and up the stairs and into her room, where she slams the door as though *I'm* the one who killed Jowan and covered it up.

"I . . . think I just want to be by myself," Willow mumbles, dragging himself into his own bedroom. "Good night."

Like it isn't barely past midday.

I stare at each closed door, unsure what do to next. I don't want to leave things weird with El, nor do I want to leave Willow miserable by himself. But neither of them wants to talk to me right now and I don't know how to fix this.

I don't know if I *can* fix this.

I don't even know what *I* feel.

There's no way it was a big cover-up like Elowen says. Papa loved Jowan just like he loves me. If he knew who'd killed Jowan, he would've seen them brought to justice. And why would *anyone* in Helston want Prince Jowan dead?

Jowan was born to rule, not just by virtue of his birth but in everything he was. Maybe I didn't get to spend much time with him—I certainly didn't know him the way Willow did—but the few summers he spent at Clystwell as Papa's squire still burn bright and alive in my memory. Jowan was brave and fair, funny and kind. He treated every single person he met equally and was always eager to help out anywhere he could, never using his status to pass off hard work to others. I didn't even know he was a prince until I overheard Papa and Mama talking one evening. He didn't fit any picture of a prince I had in my head, and now, when I think about the kind of king he would've been, I nearly cry. Jowan's Helston would've been the kind of Helston I could believe in. A Helston I would be happy to live and die for. Jowan would never have stood aside and compromised as Lord Peran and the council picked apart everything good in the kingdom.

I *don't* get it. . . .

"Callie?"

"Huh?" Edwyn's voice startles me. I didn't realize he was right there, lingering awkwardly like he wanted to say something but couldn't find the words. "Sorry, my head's all over the place."

"Mine too." He shifts on his bad leg, brow deeply furrowed.

I try to wait patiently for him to find the words, but

waiting for Edwyn to speak is like waiting for a pot to boil. Except longer.

"What's up?"

"I . . ." His gaze flicks nervously between El's door and Willow's; then he shakes his head with a brusque, "Do you want to spar?"

The request is so unexpected, I burst out laughing. "Yes! Please, yes!"

There isn't another method in the whole world guaranteed to clear my head as well as hitting things with sticks.

Unfortunately, sticks are all we have to work with.

There isn't a single sword in sight anywhere near The Roost, and when I finally decide to ask someone, they look at me like I just asked if I could personally murder all their loved ones, please?

We beat a hasty retreat.

"I guess Teo wasn't exaggerating when xe said there's a total separation between Pioden and The Roost," I mutter, foraging for two relatively sword-sized sticks in the undergrowth of an enormous oak tree.

It's quiet out here, nothing to disturb us but distant birdcalls and whispering wind, and I'm glad we came. I've never been so thankful for peace.

Especially after today.

I grasp for the tree as a fresh wave of grief batters through me and leaves me breathless.

I don't want to think about it. I don't want to know. I don't want to believe.

I don't want Elowen to be right.

"What do you think of her?" I ask Edwyn, letting my back hit the trunk and sliding down to sit among the roots. "Alis. Do you think she's telling the truth?"

Edwyn looks at me like he forgot I was there. Or that he was here. Pale and confused, he looks like he's lost.

I push the thought of Alis aside for a moment. We came out here to relax and blow off steam, doing what he and I do best: beating each other up. I grin, handing Edwyn the longer of the two sticks. "You can take first strike if you like?"

Edwyn flinches.

The way he reminds me of Willow way back when makes my heart hurt.

I drop both sticks and put my hands up where he can see them. "Hey, it's okay. What's up?"

His lips part briefly, then lock up tight like there's some invisible force keeping his mouth shut. Frustration flickers across his face, and there's something in his eyes that is begging for help.

I don't know what to do. I don't know what is wrong.

"You didn't really want to spar, did you?"

The tiniest shake of the head.

"D'you want to . . . talk?"

He nods—*yes*—but the whisper says, "I can't."

It's like there're two of him. One on the outside and one on the inside. And the one on the inside is scared to death.

"Hey, look, shall we go back? I feel like we should go find El. She'd be better at . . . whatever this is."

"No, don't." His voice is high and urgent, leaving no room for argument. "She mustn't . . . She can't—" He grimaces like there's a bad taste in his mouth, like words keep getting stuck in his throat.

Honestly, I'm scared he's gonna choke.

"No, we're going back," I tell him firmly, looking for a way to touch him without triggering another panic response. "It's been a messed-up day. Alis is right; we need to take it easy. We can come out and spar another day. Let's head back."

Edwyn grabs me.

It's so fast and unexpected, I nearly punch him.

His fingers pinch, nails sharp and biting into my arm.

I swallow my own instincts, breathing through the pain and telling myself over and over that this is *Edwyn*. Not Mama, not Peran, *Edwyn*. I don't need to be as scared as I feel.

"Tell me what you need," I grit out. "*Talk* to me."

"I . . . remember."

"Remember what?"

"I'm not . . . I can't . . ." A strange sound comes out of his mouth, somewhere between a growl and a whimper, as Edwyn grimaces, fighting furiously with himself and taking it out on my arm.

I bite my tongue to distract myself from the pain, and cover Edwyn's white-knuckled hand firmly with my own. I don't try to remove him. I don't even try to loosen his grip. I just need him to know where he is and who he's with.

"It's okay," I tell him. "Take it easy. Take it slowly. It's just us. We're nowhere near Helston. We're safe. *You're* safe."

I wait as long as it takes, and, wow, it takes a long time. I'm pretty sure I can *hear* the bones in Edwyn's fingers creak as he slowly manages to uncurl them just enough that my pain is replaced by tingling as blood rushes back to the spot.

"I think . . . I know," he says haltingly, not looking at me. "Watching the battle . . . seeing His Highness . . . But I can't get to it. I can't reach it. But I *know* it's there. Something I'd forgotten." He presses his fingertips hard into his temples like he's trying to reach into his mind to yank out the thoughts. "It hurts," he mumbles. "My whole head feels like it's about to explode. I don't understand what's happening to me. . . ."

Neither do I and, to be perfectly honest, he's freaking me out.

"You said you think you know. Do you know what you think you know?" *If that makes any sense at all.*

But Edwyn says "yes," the single syllable drawn out like he has to drag it from his lips. Like there's someone inside him trying to pull it back. "His Highness . . . Prince Jowan . . . I know what happened."

I freeze. "What d'you mean?"

"I—I know what happened," Edwyn repeats, rubbing

furiously at his forehead. "I can't find it, but I *know* it's there. I can feel it. I *know* that I know!"

I stare at him, my heart a drum in my chest. "You have to find it," I breathe. "We have to know the truth. The *real* truth. Edwyn, this could make all the difference . . . This could *stop the war!*"

Because this is the key, isn't it? Jowan's death, that was the catalyst, the big *kaboom* that sent everyone angry at each other. Helston wanting revenge on Dumoor. Dumoor wanting revenge on Helston . . . I know what it looked like, in the pool. And I understand why Elowen's made her mind up. I don't blame her. Not really. But even if what we saw was real, that was only one piece of a sprawling tapestry. And one piece doesn't tell a whole story.

Whatever is hidden inside Edwyn's head, we need it out. All of us.

"I think we should go back to Pioden," I say. "Right now. We can talk to Alis. See if we can use that pool to—"

"No. Not her. She's . . . nice."

A smile tugs in one corner of my mouth. "You don't like nice?"

"Mother is nice," Edwyn replies. "When she needs to be. When she wants something. Nice is a tool people use to get what they want and make you believe it's what you want too." His head drops. "Nice is a costume. It isn't real."

"But it can be. Not everyone is like that. Sometimes people are nice just to be nice, without any ulterior motive."

"Nice isn't the same as good, Callie."

I chew my lip. He's right. Nice and good are two *very* different things, even if they look the same on the outside. And I don't know if I can even tell the difference anymore. I wish people really were like they are in the ballads—good and bad, and obvious which is which, who is who. The knights in the stories never waste paragraphs having to work it out and getting it wrong. Kings and knights are good; dragons and witches are bad.

But that's not true.

That's not real.

And I feel like I missed a whole curriculum of lessons in how to tell the difference between the two.

But I can only go by what I know—what little that is—and what I know is that we need to find out what is wriggling around in Edwyn's head and get it into the light.

"Then we'll do it, just us," I tell him. "Lucky you're friends with the best sneaker in the whole of Wyndebrel. We'll be in and out, and Alis'll never even know!"

I don't mention how we're not sure we'll even be able to make the pool work on our own, or how Alis told us several times that she can see everything from here to Helston. If we're caught, we'll beg forgiveness and claim ignorance. We could even tell the truth. She did say we were welcome in Pioden anytime. It's not like she could easily do away with us.

It's fine.

It'll be . . . fine.

CHAPTER
TWENTY-NINE

We go quickly before our courage gives out. It feels discomfortingly familiar, slipping through the trees and praying we won't be caught, and I have to tell myself in no uncertain terms that this is *different*. It isn't Helston. Even if we're caught—even if we get in trouble—we'll be okay. Even if we don't know Alis, she isn't Queen Ewella. She'll listen. She won't lock us up underground to prove a point.

She isn't Peran.

And we aren't doing anything wrong.

Beside me, the battle inside Edwyn rages. He keeps it in the best he can, jaw clenched, expression set in fierce determination, but the effort is visible and I'm scared he's gonna lose the fight before we even get there.

By the time we reach Pioden, he's sweating and shaking like there's a fever rushing through his body.

"You okay?"

"Yes."

Three letters have never held so many lies.

As Kensa promised, now that we know where Pioden is, the illusion breaks on the horizon; the vast stone formation looms up out of the moors, surrounded by swooping magpies. But granite stays granite, even as we stop before what is supposed to be Alis's castle, and I kick myself with a curse. I didn't pay enough attention to the tune Kensa whistled. Not that it would do me any good. My whistling is even worse than my magical abilities.

I run my fingers over the rough stone, searching desperately for any kind of dip or bump that might indicate a mechanism. Which is just about as useful as searching for a particular grain of sand on a beach.

Then, from behind me, a clear, high note sounds—smooth as silk and twice as beautiful. I gape at Edwyn, the tune from his lips curling effortlessly like he's spent his whole life at rehearsal, and the door in the rock opens up in response.

"How'd you do *that*, Mr. 'I Don't Do Magic'?"

But Edwyn just gives a rough shrug. "Come on. If Princess Alis doesn't already know we're here, she will soon."

I follow quickly as Edwyn steps inside. "And you're okay with that?"

"At this point, there is no choice." Even our whispered voices echo through the witch's castle, every footfall as loud as a bell.

Sneaking was definitely easier in Helston.

Without Alis as our guide, the journey up and up and up feels *endless*. Not even exaggeratedly endless, but literally. I consider my endurance confidently above average. I know how to pace myself and I know how to get the best out of my muscles, but by the time my legs start burning in complaint and I glance backward to see how far we've come, my heart drops. It looks like we've barely made it halfway, and the thought of doing this whole climb again makes my bones *ache*.

Edwyn is struggling, too, leaning on the curved banister to hoist himself up each stair, but anyone could see the mess this is making of his leg.

I open my mouth to call it quits. This was a bad idea. We should do it the proper way and ask permission, except suddenly the topmost landing is in sight.

It wasn't there before.

I *swear* it wasn't.

Suspicion sparks through my blood, but I'm not about to reject this gift, no matter where it comes from.

With my final burst of strength, I bound up the rest of the flight and pull Edwyn up after me, and we collapse together, panting, just inches away from Alis's pool.

It feels like a miracle.

Edwyn crawls to the edge of the water first, breathing hard. I shuffle to stay close beside him. I don't know if this will work, or what will happen if it does, but whatever Edwyn is searching for is being fiercely guarded. No one should head into battle alone.

A finger hesitates over the mirror-still surface, then retreats.

"I . . . don't know what I'll see," says Edwyn. "I don't know how to find what I'm looking for, and I don't know what else is there."

"D'you want me to wait outside for you?"

"No. Don't leave. Just . . . don't tell, okay? Not Elowen or Willow. Or anyone. I can't do this unless you promise."

"I promise." I mean it too. Edwyn's business is his own, and even though I don't get why he'd want to keep secrets from Willow and Elowen, that's not my call to make. I offer my hand to him, palm up. "I'm here."

The calluses on Edwyn's hand are rough as he locks his fingers through mine.

He takes a deep, steadying breath and leans forward to touch one finger to the water's surface.

Just like before, ripples flicker across the pool, faster and faster until it breaks into an image.

And that's where the similarities end.

Where the scene Alis showed us was high in the sky, a dragon's point of view, watching from an impersonal distance, this time we fall all the way down into the deepest depths of Edwyn's mind.

CHAPTER THIRTY

"*D efend yourself.*"

Edwyn doesn't move. He cannot move. Cannot breathe. Cannot even think beyond the buzzing in his head as Father closes the slim gap between them. There is no room. No air. No chance. And all the magic has retreated from his fingertips, scared away the moment it was caught. Willow said it was safe to tell. Willow promised. Elowen told him no, but Edwyn didn't listen. He made himself believe it would be okay, that it didn't matter what Father said about Willow behind closed doors, that he would be different with his own son. That he would understand. That he would be . . . proud.

The red-stoned ring rips into his temple.

There isn't space to fall.

"*If your precious magic is worth anything, prove it. Defend yourself!*"

Blood slicks across his tongue.

He can't. It isn't. It never was. Willow was wrong. Father is right. Father is always right. Magic is worthless. Untrustworthy. An abomination.

So is anyone who entertains it.

Repent.

It's Elowen's fault. Willow's fault. Stay away from them and maybe he stands a chance of being normal. Stay close to Father. Do what he says. Everything he says. Do it before he gives the command. Do more. Do the most. Do everything and maybe—maybe—Father will stop looking at him like that.

That look . . . with every glance, Edwyn's whole body contracts. He hates it. Hates himself the way Father hates him. Understands why he does. Elowen doesn't speak to him. Willow stays away. That's fine. It's their fault— No, it's his fault. It's all his fault. He should've been smarter, stronger, should've resisted the temptation like he was supposed to. No one else falls. No one else is as weak as he is. Mind, body, and spirit.

But Edwyn knows he can do better. He can *be* better. He just has to prove it.

Work harder. Fight harder. Don't cry. Don't complain. This is his fault. It's for his own good. He knows that. Accepts that. It'll be worth it.

Worth it.

Mother doesn't look at him anymore. He's glad. Sometimes he wishes Father would stop looking at him too, but there are rare moments when he does something right and he *needs* Father to see those, to keep count, to know that Edwyn is doing his best even if his best isn't good enough. But Father is never looking in the good moments, only the bad ones, and he keeps meticulous score on Edwyn's skin.

It's Adan's fault.

Not Adan's fault—his fault—but Adan is Father's eyes when Father is busy in council meetings, with Their Majesties, and all the important work a chancellor should be focused on instead of his worthless son. Adan takes note and pleasure in every misstep, like he has a personal vendetta against Edwyn.

Edwyn isn't sure what he did to warrant such a grudge, because Adan doesn't know his secret. No one outside the family does. Father would rather die than let anyone become aware of what his son is. Father doesn't know that Willow knows. Edwyn has nightmares about Father finding out. He doesn't know who his father would kill first—him or Willow.

That's not true.

He does know. All too well.

Adan hits him.

A full-length steel sword against his small wooden one.

A weighted staff in the side.

A fist in the face.

He tastes blood and sawdust and dirt.

He deserves this. He should be stronger, faster, better.

He gets up earlier and goes to bed later. Meals are precious minutes that could be better spent. He works through the pain in his stomach and the dizziness in his head. He works until his body betrays him and he accepts the punishment for failing without complaint.

It reflects poorly on Father when Edwyn embarrasses himself.

He is the chancellor's son. Held to the highest standards with the best resources.

It is no one's fault but his own that they aren't enough.

"I don't know why he bothers with you," says Adan.

Edwyn doesn't know either.

Some days—most days—he's sure it would be easier if they just put him out of his misery. Some days, he thinks about doing it himself. Just walking across the bridge to let the dragons take him. Some days—every day—the thought of the Witch Queen of Dumoor is less frightening than waking up to another day in Helston.

One day, Elowen finds her way back to him.

Late at night, in the safety of darkness.

"Willow misses you, you know."

"Go away," he snarls. "Leave me alone."

She doesn't.

He tries everything he can to push her away. He is cruel to her, but still she won't leave, and he isn't strong enough to keep fighting. If she wants to be foolish, that's her choice.

She has become stronger, smarter. He doesn't stand a chance against her. She only comes after midnight, and she doesn't speak until she's painted a ward around his door. He doesn't know what use that would be if it ever came down to it, and every night he goes through the plan for what he'll do if tonight's the night they're caught.

"He misses you, you know," says Elowen, pressing soft magic into the muscle of the leg that was never quite right after the day Father discovered Edwyn's magic. "Willow. You should talk to him."

He knows she's lying. Willow doesn't miss him. Willow has probably forgotten he exists. As it should be. They were never supposed to be friends in the first place. Elowen only visits out of duty. The same familial obligation that protects him from being cast out of the Chancellor's Chambers. He supposes he should be grateful but he doesn't have the energy.

He sees Willow sometimes, though not often. Their paths do not cross now that Edwyn is busy with training—that's what Father calls it, "training," though his lessons are incomparable to those of his peers—but sometimes he catches sight of the two princes on the other side of the training grounds, Prince Jowan teaching Willow how to spar.

Except it doesn't look like teaching. They're just playing. Like it's just a game they can pick up and put down on a whim. And Edwyn hates them both for it. He tries not to watch, the knot of jealousy getting bigger and tighter around his heart until it's all he can think about and Adan knocks him into the dirt for his inattention.

Willow's fault.

It is all Willow's fault.

And Edwyn will never forgive him.

The stables. Hazy with hay dust and horsehair in the mid-summer afternoon. The memory sweet and sharp and *good*.

"Be gentle," Prince Jowan murmurs. "Like this. Let me show you how."

Edwyn's face burns, but the correction isn't angry. It isn't even impatient. It is soft and calm, and he speaks the way he runs the brush along his mare's flank.

"See? It's not so hard." The prince grins and holds out the brush. "Now you try."

Edwyn takes the brush and tries because that is what was commanded. But it feels like a trick. His Highness has no reason to speak so kindly to him. Edwyn is certain Willow has told Prince Jowan everything. They are close as anything, as different as they are. Perhaps the crown prince is toying with him, luring him into a false sense of security before making him pay for the way he has treated Willow.

It doesn't matter.

He cannot refuse a direct request. Prince Jowan could order him off the cliff and Edwyn would have to obey.

"Relax, Edwyn. Horses pick up on your emotions. I don't want her spooked before we even ride out."

"Yes, sir. Sorry, Highness."

Prince Jowan laughs, but it's a quiet chuckle instead of the sharp bark usually directed his way. "Nothing to apologize for. Go slowly."

He does his best, falling into the lull of the rhythm until it starts to feel natural. The bay mare relaxes and the tightness in his own chest loosens.

"That's right. Good job."

The unexpected approval catches Edwyn off guard and he smiles.

"Are you good to finish getting her ready? I'd like to see Willow before we ride out."

"Yes, Highness."

"Thanks." Prince Jowan pauses one second longer to add, "I don't know what happened between you and my brother, but I hope you two can fix things one day. I know he misses you terribly. If there's anything I can do to help, please let me know."

Edwyn is quick to nod, face burning. Elowen might have reason to lie to him about Willow, but Prince Jowan doesn't. Maybe it is true. Maybe Willow doesn't hate him as much as he should. Maybe it would be possible, one day, to—

Not in Father's world.

Just the entertainment of the hope feels illicit, and Edwyn's fingers stutter around the brush.

Maybe in a few decades when Prince Jowan becomes King Jowan. But not now. Now, Father rules supreme.

He forces his focus back to the rhythm of the brush. This is a task he can accomplish. This is all he needs to think about right now. Everything else can be set aside for a few more minutes. The mare stands still for him as he saddles her, pulling the straps tight but not too tight and fitting the bridle to her sleek nose. She is so well looked after. So loved. There isn't an ounce of wariness in her blood.

Lucky.

He is checking his work for the last time when a sound at the other end of the stables freezes his fingers. The horse's ears flick back, confirming his fears. He wasn't imagining it.

Edwyn scrabbles to make the calculations in his head. Everyone else is already in the courtyard, ready to ride out. No one else is supposed to be in here, but he counts two pairs of footsteps. Two pairs of footsteps he could pick out of a crowd.

And a voice that turns his blood cold.

Father's.

"You must not act before the moment is right."

It is midsummer—the hottest month of Wyndebrel—but Edwyn shivers, a thousand excuses cramming into his throat. He is allowed to be here. He was told to be here. He's working for the prince. The future king. Whose authority tops Father's. He's not doing anything wrong, he's—

As though any of that has ever mattered.

"If the opportunity does not present itself, do not act. Do I make myself clear?"

He's angry. Or approaching angry.

"Of course I understand," a second voice snaps—Adan. "I know how important this is. I know what is at stake."

The prince's horse tosses her head. He was holding her

too tight. He hurt her. He's sorry, but he needs her to be quiet. He needs her to understand. Just be good and silent and invisible and don't exist until they're gone.

Except they're coming closer.

"When you return," Father continues, "it is imperative the body is brought *immediately* inside and interred. I will ensure that Their Majesties understand that the magical attack rendered His Highness unrecognizable and his memory must be preserved in perfect form. Do you hear me? They must *not* see him."

"And what about Nick and Jory?" Adan asks gruffly. "They'll have seen the boy already. Chances are, they'll have seen him fall. And with Nick being as close to His Majesty as he is . . . You really think he's gonna keep his mouth shut?"

"You will ensure that Nicholas sees *nothing*," Father snaps. "On my word, Adan, if you are caught, I will *not* stand by you. *No* one can know."

Edwyn bites his tongue, straining to hear the exact distance between himself and the grown-ups, and *praying* that they'll finish their conversation and leave before they come any closer. He doesn't know what they're talking about. He doesn't want to know. Knowledge is dangerous and it's none of his business and he just wants to finish his work and leave and—

"You'd better make this worth my while, Peran. That blood is not going to wash off my hands quickly."

Since when has Adan cared about blood? He wipes it

306

from his hands on his trousers like it was worth less than water. Blood stopped being precious a long time ago.

"There isn't a soul in Helston who doesn't love Jowan."

Edwyn's heart stops beating.

Oh.

Jowan.

Prince Jowan's blood.

They're talking about . . .

About hurting . . .

"I told you I would make you captain, didn't I?" Father snaps. "And once Helston unravels, you will be at my side as I piece it back together. You want this as much as I do. Don't act as though you're doing *me* a favor. The way Helston is going . . . it is intolerable. Allowing that *peculiarity* to go unchecked as though he's normal—"

Peculiarity.

That's the word Father uses for Willow in the privacy of their apartment.

"Their Majesties are beyond advice. It is time to *act*. Do this one thing, Adan, and I will take care of the rest."

There's a long pause, silence thick, and all Edwyn can hear is the loud *thud* of his own heart beating to the tune of *Jowan. They're going to hurt Jowan.*

Then, "It will be done."

"Good."

Good? Does that mean they're leaving? It sounds like they're walking away. It sounds like he got away with it and

Edwyn knows he should be grateful, and most of him is, except—

They're going to hurt Jowan.

It buzzes in his head and snatches his breath and he can't breathe and there's too much hay in the air and—

Edwyn sneezes.

It comes too fast to smother with a sleeve, with barely a warning tickle, and the only way out is the stall's gate and that isn't an option when it's already filled with a familiar shadow grabbing for him.

"You!"

The prince's horse whickers in alarm. She isn't big enough or fierce enough to protect him.

A hand snags his collar and wrenches him out.

Even if he wanted to, even if he thought he stood half a hope, there is no time or space to fight. The thought doesn't even occur. If he fought, they would kill him. Right here in the stables. Better to be small and sorry and do what they say.

He is grateful for the straw when Adan throws him down in the empty stall. It is warm and damp and long in need of changing, but it's better than stone. Kneeling on stone is hell.

He kneels now, head bowed, waiting for judgment, the way Father likes.

Don't look up. Don't speak. Don't move.

Don't exist.

He can do that. He's good at that. Well practiced.

Even when Adan moves, a sudden, violent flash, Edwyn

doesn't stir. He takes the blow like he's been taught. Like a knight. Like a man. Biting his lip against the pain.

Sometimes it works.

Sometimes Adan takes it as a personal challenge.

"You were *listening!* What did you hear? *Speak!*"

It takes too long to make his tongue work. This time he cries out. He sees Adan smirk.

"Nothing." His voice is barely a breath. It feels like smoke in his throat. "I—I swear, I didn't—"

"*Liar!*"

Edwyn's courage gives out and he cowers.

"Calm yourself, Sergeant." Father's command is low and soft, but it is enough to stay Adan's hand. "The boy still has duties to attend to for His Highness. It will not do to send him back . . . imperfect."

Relief is dizzying. Confusing. A blessing. A trick.

Straw crunches.

"He *knows*," Adan snarls. "There's no way he didn't hear anything. You said it yourself, Peran—no one can know. The boy is a liability. Let me—"

"Edwyn knows what is good for him," says Father. "And he knows the value in keeping his mouth shut. Besides, who would he tell? Who would believe him? I would be more concerned with the beasts talking out of turn."

Father's shiny shoes replace Adan's scuffed boots in Edwyn's limited vision.

Fingers lock in his hair and shove his head back.

Father smiles down at him. "What did you hear?"

"Nothing, sir."

"And who would you tell?"

"N-no one."

"And if you're lying"—the hand on his scalp tightens—"who would ever believe you?"

"No one," Edwyn whispers.

"Quite right."

He is released, dropped like a dirty rag, like Father can't stand to touch him a moment longer than he has to.

"You see?" Father tells Adan. "The boy is inconsequential. Whatever else, he knows his place. Up."

Edwyn stumbles to his feet, hardly daring to believe his luck. Father's defending him. Father's *protecting* him. Adan is furious and Edwyn knows he'll catch it later, but right now that doesn't matter. Right now, he is safe.

"Return to your duties before you are missed."

"Yes, sir."

Father turns on his heel and walks away, and Edwyn almost laughs with heady relief.

A hand around his throat chokes off any thought of laughter.

Adan squeezes. "Open your mouth and I will cut out your tongue myself."

There is nothing inside Edwyn that doubts that Adan is anything less than serious.

He is lucky to have survived this far and too grateful to

waste the chance he has been given. Edwyn does what he does best. He shuts his mouth and keeps it closed, locking away his secrets so far in the darkness it's like they were never there at all; a closet crammed to bursting.

And he forgets.

He survives.

And when Prince Jowan's body returns to Helston just a few hours later, Edwyn is as shocked as anyone.

CHAPTER
THIRTY-ONE

The pool spits us out and leaves us dazed and breathless. The image is gone, soon as the moment ended, but I can't stop staring down at the water, wishing I hadn't heard what I heard. Wishing I didn't know what I know.

Wishing, more than anything else in the world, that what had happened wasn't real.

Except it was.

It is.

And Edwyn is the proof of it.

"It's my fault."

The statement is a hoarse confession.

"Edwyn, no—"

"Yes. It is. I should've told. I should've been braver. I was only thinking of myself. I wasn't thinking at all. I could've saved him."

"They would've killed you." From all I witnessed, there isn't a doubt in my heart that it's true.

"So?" He raises his face and there is nothing in his expression but bleak acceptance. "What kind of exchange is that? I am nothing."

"That isn't true!"

"Yes it is!" He slaps the stone floor so hard it's got to hurt, but he doesn't wince. I don't think he even feels it. "Everything they said, it's true. And I locked it away because I didn't want to know. I wanted to keep pretending. I wanted to keep believing that I stood a chance. But I was lying! And Prince Jowan died because of it! We're here because of it! Willow lost his home and his crown because of *me*! And you—"

"Stop."

If I asked, he would refuse. On a different day, I would respect that.

Today I don't.

I wrap my arms around Edwyn's body and squeeze as hard as I can.

"It wasn't your fault. I'm sorry they made you believe that it was. You didn't deserve what they did to you. Any of it. It wasn't right and it wasn't your fault."

Edwyn struggles and growls like a feral cat. "Stop lying to me! Let me go!"

I hang on tighter. It's more a fight than a hug, but it's a fight I'm not going to lose.

"Not lying. The only people who lied to you were the ones telling you that you were worthless just because you have magic. Who told you that you needed fixing. Who made you believe you didn't deserve any scrap of kindness. Your dad and your mum lied to you, Edwyn. Adan lied to you. Not me. Not El, and not Willow."

At Willow's name, Edwyn goes limp. "I can't face him," he whimpers. "He can't know."

"Willow loves you. We all do. And we're not going to let you carry this by yourself." Even with four, I'm scared we're not strong enough to bear this load, that it's still going to crush us to dust. But at least we'll be crushed together. "And I swear, on my honor, on Satin, on *everything*, they will pay for what they did. I don't know how and I don't know when, but I *know* that justice will be done." Even if I have to do it on my own.

"Yes," says a voice from the landing. "Justice will be done."

Edwyn jerks away from me and I move fast, planting myself between him and the intruder.

Alis watches us from the top of the staircase, the same gentle smile resting on her face.

My frantic pulse doesn't let up. "You said we could come anytime."

"I know. I meant it." She takes a slow step closer. "Do not fear, children. You are not in trouble."

Then why does it feel like we are?

"You were very brave to come here," she tells Edwyn. "I

know how hard it must be to unlock that door, especially when the lock only goes one way."

I keep myself as a wall between them. "What d'you mean?"

"When a closet is crammed as full as that, there is no closing it again once it has been opened." She tries to get around me. "I'm sorry, Edwyn; you are in for a rough journey."

I don't move. Even when she nearly knocks into me. "He'll be fine," I say. "He's got us."

"And you are confident in your ability to give your friend the kind of healing he needs, are you?"

The smile stays in place even as the tone shifts a fraction.

"He'll be fine," I repeat through gritted teeth. "Right now we need to worry about stopping the war. Dumoor didn't kill Jowan, and neither did Helston. It was all Peran and Adan. We heard them say—"

"I heard it too," says Alis. "I heard everything."

"Then you know this war is needless! We need to tell Her Majesty! You need to make contact. And peace. You are on the same side! We have the proof now! Edwyn's testimony, the arrow . . ." I look desperately at the banished princess. "Please, this can all end. And if you and Queen Ewella work together to bring Peran and Adan to justice—"

She holds up a hand and I close my mouth.

I'm not entirely sure if it was of my own volition.

"You have done well," says Alis. "Both of you. It is a hard thing, to face the shadows in the back of your mind, and your sacrifice will not go to waste. You have my word. But these things take time, and I must now beg for your patience as I decide the best way to proceed."

Patience.

I hold my breath for the count of one . . . two . . . three, then, "With all due respect, there's no time for patience. Helston's gonna ride out as soon as they can. Maybe we don't know when that's gonna be, but it's not worth risking. They're not gonna listen once they're on the other side of the bridge. You need to do it now!"

"It will be done in good time, Callie," says Alis firmly. "I have been in this role for many a year. Have faith. For now I must ask that you keep your new knowledge to yourself until plans can be made. I am not asking you to keep secrets," she adds when I balk. "I am asking you to be considerate. My primary goal is to protect my people, and I will not have them suffer unnecessary stress. You understand, don't you?"

I nod slowly.

"Good." She rests a warm hand on my shoulder. "You are a brave knight, Sir Callie. I thank you for your service. Go now, sleep. We will talk soon." She touches the charms on her bracelet, and one of them glows red. "I will have Kensa help you home."

"We don't need help," I say automatically. "We know the way back. Thanks, though," I add, just in case she thinks I'm being as rude as I feel. "I think it'd be better if we stick together. Elowen will know what to do. We'll be fine. Thanks."

It already feels like we've been in here too long. I wouldn't

316

be surprised if El and Willow were wondering where we've got to. It's gonna be hard to enough to explain everything to them without having to calm down a panic too.

"You came to me for help," says Alis. "So let me help you."

I step away from her. Or try to. The hand on my shoulder holds on.

"You can help by letting us go."

"No one is keeping you here against your will, Callie."

But that doesn't feel true.

"Are you ready to go?"

I never thought I would be glad to hear Kensa's voice.

The dragon pauses on the top stair behind Alis, yellow eyes assessing the scene. I don't know xem well enough to read xir expressions well, but I swear a flicker of concern crosses xir face.

Alis is still for a moment longer, her own gaze locked on Edwyn, but then it breaks and she releases my shoulder, all softness and smiles. "Very well," she says. "I understand. At the very least, let me give you this." She reaches deep into a pocket hidden in her skirts and retrieves a small green glass bottle, which she presses into my palm like it's something precious. "Give him three drops in a warm drink every two hours for the next day, and then come back and see me."

I give the vial a swirl, and it looks like the night sky from Eyrewood—flecked with sparkling, unreachable galaxies. "What is it?"

"It calms the mind," says Alis. "And helps it heal so the

317

afflicted can better deal with whatever has damaged it. Don't worry—there are no ill side effects."

"Thanks," I tell Alis, meaning it. "And . . . thanks for listening and not just being mad."

"You and I want the same thing, little knight," Alis replies. "Justice for the wrongs committed against our loved ones. I understand." She looks up to address Kensa: "Take the children to The Roost, then return here. We must start reassessing our plans immediately."

CHAPTER
THIRTY-TWO

I t is dark and cold when Kensa leads us out of Pioden. How long were we in there?

After a lungful of fresh air, everything that happened inside Alis's castle feels like a weird dream that slips a little further out of reach the more I try to make sense of it.

The tiny vial digs into my clenched fist.

I wonder if anyone would notice if I took a drop of it myself—

"Don't," Kensa growls, and I startle.

"Get out of my head."

"You have already proven yourself foolish. I am looking out for you."

I stop and glare. "Foolish how?"

The dragon rounds on me with bared teeth, eyes flashing in the darkness. "I told you to be careful and cautious."

"We didn't have time to ask permission. And it doesn't matter. We didn't get in trouble. It's fine. We're fine."

Kensa stares at me, xir anger shifting into something different, and then xe shepherds us on with a terse command: "Come. Quickly."

If it was me on my own, I'd argue and demand a conversation right here and now. But Edwyn is shivering fiercely, and if my head is messed up, his has got to be in pieces.

Everything else can wait.

But Kensa doesn't take us to The Roost. Instead of going right toward the inn, we go left toward the deepest part of the forest.

Panic flickers in my throat. "Where're you taking us? She told you to take us to The Roost."

But the dragon doesn't reply.

I wish we told Elowen where we were going. And Willow. Edwyn and I fended off Kensa before, but not alone. Not even nearly—

"I am not going to hurt you," Kensa says, xir voice a low rolling growl. "I told you I owe you a debt, and I take my vows seriously."

"Then tell us—"

"No. I cannot. It isn't safe."

"What d'you mean?"

But Kensa just puts one long-clawed finger to xir lips and lights a flame in xir other hand. The fire is rich and warm, effortlessly illuminating the trees.

I gasp.

Not just trees, but a whole village built into the branches. Walkways and ladders, hoists and pulleys. Each tree holds a dwelling.

Kensa whistles a single long note, high and low in the same breath, and just a few seconds later one of the doors opens and a figure leans over the wooden rail.

Teo stares down at us and grins, waving enthusiastically.

I raise my own hand in confused greeting as Teo practically runs down the steep stairs. But xir smile dips into a frown when xe sees us up close.

"Are you okay? What happened? Where're the others?"

"Go to The Roost and fetch them," says Kensa. "Don't linger. Be back here quickly."

Teo's ears twitch with a question that never reaches xir lips. Then xe gives one nod and takes off, sprinting silently toward The Roost.

Kensa tugs on a rope hanging down the tree, lowering a platform to the ground. "It's safe," xe says, urging us onto the boards.

I'm too tired to argue. I'd rather take my chances and trust xem than attempt the stairs. My legs would not make it. Luckily the journey up into the trees is short and smooth, and Kensa is waiting for us at the top.

I help Edwyn onto the balcony. He moves automatically, and I'm not sure he's even aware of what's going on. He doesn't seem afraid or happy or anything. He's just . . . existing.

Sulio is waiting for us at the door, as calm and somber as if he'd already been filled in and was expecting us. He greets us with a warm smile and coaxes us into the small treetop dwelling.

"Come, sit down."

Their home *is* small, but it's also huge, and my head spins trying to work it out. It's a single, round room that goes up and up and up, like we're inside the tree trunk itself. There are no windows, but light flutters in the air like fireflies, warming the home as easily as a blazing fire.

Curtains woven from brightly colored threads create doors to private spaces, and the rough wooden floors are covered with mats and carpets. Branches crisscross from wall to wall, hung with hammocks and draped with clothes in all shapes and sizes. The smell of something sweet and spiced drifts from a small alcove concealed beneath the walkway that spirals up to the very top of the dwelling, and the rest of the brood all look about when we step inside.

They're sitting on cushions around a low table filled with cups and books, a half-finished knitted garment that might be a scarf or a blanket, and empty bowls from that evening's meal.

Edwyn and I linger awkwardly on the threshold until a gentle nudge from Sulio pushes us all the way inside.

The grown-ups get to work immediately.

Inis takes both our hands and coaxes us into the warmth, plying us with cushions and blankets and all manner of soft things. Dolan disappears into the alcove to tend to whatever is cooking on the stove, and Feena joins Kensa and Sulio by the door.

The sound of their low, serious murmuring hurts my stomach. It's the tone grown-ups use when they don't want you to hear what they're saying. I huddle into my blanket, breathing in the comforting smells of woodsmoke and lavender.

"Callie?"

I peek out to see Feena crouched beside me, hand out, palm up.

"Do you mind if I take a look at that potion?"

I'd forgotten about the bottle locked tight in my hand. My palm aches when I let it go, the chiseled crystal leaving grooves in my skin.

"Thank you."

She spirits it away to where Dolan is working.

"I must return to Pioden," I hear Kensa tell Sulio. "I will come home as quickly as I can. Teo will be back with the other two soon. Don't let any of them leave before I get back."

Fire flashes through my blood. As tired as I am, I leap up.

"You can't keep us here against our will! You can't trap us!"

Inis rises with me. "No one is trying to trap you, Callie—"

"Don't lie! I heard what Kensa said!" I glare at the dragon. "What do you want with us? At least give us the courtesy of telling us why we're here!"

Kensa looks back at me impassively. "I cannot, little knight."

"Why not?"

In response, Kensa touches xir side. The place beneath xir ribs. The same place where Neal's mark lies.

The witch's kiss.

I freeze.

In Dumoor, oaths are binding, Kensa reminds me inside my head. *And my bonds choke me. I cannot give you what you deserve to know. I can only give you the resources to find out for yourself. That is why you are here.* And, out loud, "I must go."

And then xe's gone. Just like that.

It's too much.

Between Jowan and Edwyn and Kensa and Peran and Adan and the war and *everything* . . .

It's too much.

My knees fold and I curl into myself, yanking my hair until my scalp burns. There's too much to fix and I don't know where to start and I don't know how to make things better and I don't know who to trust and I don't know *anything*!

Dolan touches my shoulder. "Child—"

"I'm not a child!" I rip away with a snarl that hurts my throat. "I am a person! We are people! And I'm sick of

everyone treating us like we're nothing! Like we're not even worthy of information that concerns us! No one tells us anything! No one asks us what we want or what we think! We're just expected to trust you when we've barely even met you! Kensa tried to kill us the first time we met, did you know that? And now we're supposed to just believe that xe has our best interests at heart? It's *our* lives you're all playing with! Why don't any of you get that? You tell us what to do like you know us, but you *don't*! We have to yell to be heard! We have to fight to be seen! And it's not *fair*!"

I grind my palms into my eyes because I *don't* want to see the way they're looking at me. I don't want to feel bad and I don't want to apologize and I don't want to be placated. Nothing is right and nothing can be made right because it's all already happened. Jowan is dead. Edwyn is shattered. Willow lost everything. Elowen is filled with rage she shouldn't be expected to contain. And me . . .

I want my dads.

Neal would show me how to pick all this mess apart and how to put it back together in a way that would make sense. And Papa would be on my side, no questions asked, no conditions. They would let me rage and cry. They would include me.

I don't know how to do this on my own.

"Breathe, Callie," Dolan reminds me.

"Don't tell me what to do," I mumble, but I follow the instruction; breathing in slow and letting it out slower. It helps. A little.

The door bangs open, and Willow's hugging me before I can even look around.

"Callie, what's going on?"

I hug him back. Hard. "I don't know."

"Where were you? El and I went looking for you both, and when you weren't anywhere . . ."

"I'm sorry. I didn't think we'd be gone long enough to worry you."

"Five minutes would be long enough to make us worry," Elowen snaps.

I pull my head up and she's with Edwyn, who's hunched down like he's got a stomachache.

Feena beckons to the rest of the brood. "Let us give you some privacy. We'll be outside if you need us."

Elowen waits until all the grown-ups are gone, then her glare returns to me and Edwyn. "Talk," she orders us both. "Now."

But I don't know how. I don't know if I should. I don't know if it's safe. I don't know anything.

My eyes burn and I hide my face in Willow's shoulder before I start bawling. Willow hugs me tight.

"Here, get this down."

There's a *clink* and I blink up to see Dolan and Teo setting down four enormous mugs.

None of us move.

"What is it?" Elowen asks, not even bothering to hide her suspicion.

"Chocolate," Dolan says. "With cinnamon and nutmeg. Don't worry, there's nothing weird in it. Look—" They return with two more mugs and hand Teo the one that has *Teo* painted in huge red letters. "Cheers!" They clink and drink in unison.

Teo comes away with a full chocolate mustache. "Sulio's specialty," xe says with a grin. "It's the best cure for a hard day."

"Not a cure," Sulio amends. "But it goes some way toward helping. Especially if you're heading toward hard conversations."

I wonder how much they know, how much they can guess just by looking at us. I hate that everything inside my head is written so blatantly across the surface of my skin. But I don't have the energy to pretend to be anything except what I am.

Willow follows Teo's lead, sitting cross-legged at the low table and raising the mug to his lips. The rest of us watch intently as Helston's crown prince drinks steadily.

He doesn't die.

He doesn't even grimace.

Just beams and assures us, "It's good!"

I sniff warily at my own and the smell takes me all the way back home to Eyrewood. This is Neal's recipe. Precious and potent; brewed only in the most dire emergencies like periods and grumpiness. I close my eyes and drink deeply. It's creamy and spicy, bitter and sweet all in one mouthful.

The chocolate slides down my throat and warms me from the inside out, soothing my spinning head and slowing everything down until thinking doesn't hurt so bad any-more; a promise that everything's gonna be okay. Maybe not quickly, certainly not easily, but eventually.

When I open my eyes again, Elowen is watching me closely.

I take a deep breath and put down my cup. No point try-ing to make it pretty. "It was Peran and Adan. They plotted the murder, they carried it out, and they covered it up."

Elowen swallows and her voice shakes as she asks, "How do you know?"

"Because I was there," says Edwyn. His drink sits un-touched beside folded hands. He speaks to his fingers. "I heard everything."

Willow's mouth drops open. "Wh-what?"

"It was all laid out. How they were going to do it and how they were going to hide it. How they would make it look like Dumoor."

"You knew . . . ," Willow whispers. "You knew this whole time . . ."

"It wasn't like that," I say quickly, since it doesn't look like Edwyn's gonna give the right context anytime soon. "Wil-low, you know what Peran and Adan were like. *Are* like. They would've killed him if he'd said anything to anyone."

Edwyn glowers at me. "That's not an excuse."

"No," I return. "You're right. It's not an excuse; it's a *rea-son*. All that stuff you had to dig out, you *literally* had to forget it. That's how bad it was. It wasn't your choice to tell or not to tell."

Willow sits forward, expression stony. "What do you mean, he had to forget?"

"I mean just that," I say, looking between him and El, making sure they're listening and understanding. "That's why we had to go to the pool."

"If you'd forgotten," says Elowen, "how did you know to go looking?"

Every question sets Edwyn's shoulders tighter and tighter until he's bunched into himself. "They were still there, my memories. They exist because they happened, just . . . put away somewhere I couldn't get to them. I—I know it sounds ridiculous, but I swear, I'm not lying. Seeing . . . seeing His Highness fall, it was like kicking a chest I thought was empty and hearing something inside. I didn't know what I would find. I—I didn't know what I knew." He swipes roughly at one tear, erasing the track before it reaches his cheek. "I know I should've been braver. Back in the beginning. I—I'm sorry. I know it was my fault. I—I take full responsibility—"

"No," says Willow, and Edwyn shuts his mouth with a wince.

Willow doesn't speak again for a long while, and it feels like we're waiting for a formal verdict to be passed down for sentencing. Even Elowen looks anxious, gaze flicking between Willow and her brother.

Then, softly, "It wasn't your fault. What happened with Jowan. What happened at all. None of it was your fault. Even if it wasn't locked away and you did remember, it still wouldn't be your fault. How does it feel? How do *you* feel? Because I'm guessing it's not all going to go back in, is it?"

Edwyn shakes his head slowly, as wary as if Willow had raised his voice. "No, it isn't going to go back in. And I . . . I don't want it to."

My eyebrows shoot up so high they nearly leave my head. "Seriously."

"Yes." Edwyn's hands fidget. "It's hard, and it hurts, and there's so much more than you saw. And I understand why I made myself forget. If this had happened in Helston, I don't think I would be okay, but . . . it's like I was in a fog I didn't even realize and everything was blurry around the edges. But now it's cleared, and I can see, and there are details I've never noticed before. I—I don't know how to explain it, only that . . . something's different. Not better, not worse, just different. Seeing myself from the outside, the way others— *you*—see me . . . I suppose I can believe you now, in the way I couldn't before."

Willow's head tilts curiously. "Believe us how?"

Edwyn's lip disappears briefly between his teeth, and he can't look at us when he says, "That they weren't right. Father and Adan. It wasn't right, what they did to me. And I . . . I didn't . . . deserve it."

The confession is small, almost guilty, and it's like Edwyn's bracing himself for retribution, hunching up and holding his breath. Like just the thought is a punishable offense.

"No one deserves it," Willow says, shifting closer until their shoulders bump. "Not even you."

"I know that. Now. I think." Edwyn sucks in a deep breath, and when he exhales, all the weariness in his body goes rushing out. He leans on Willow, eyes closed. "Or I'm beginning to, at least."

"That's something," says Elowen.

"That's *everything*," I add, and Willow nods emphatically.

"Perhaps. But also . . . I—I feel so *stupid*. I should've known. I should've seen. I should've been braver. I should've . . . I—I should've—"

"You did exactly what you needed to do," Willow murmurs, moving slightly to put his arm around Edwyn's shoulders. "There was nothing you could've done to save Jowan, but you did what you could to save yourself. And I'm really glad you did."

Once upon a time, not so long ago, Edwyn would've pulled free of the embrace, deflecting the warmth with a sullen mumble.

Today, right now, he accepts it, turning his face into Willow's shoulders.

And I can breathe a little easier.

"So, what now?" Elowen asks, her clipped voice sharpening the peace. "What do we do with this new information?

What difference does it make? Father and Adan are *still* Helston."

"But if there's to be a battle for justice, holding two people accountable is way better than vilifying a whole kingdom, isn't it? This is gonna stop the war and save lives!"

Elowen meets my gaze squarely. *"How?"*

"What d'you mean, *how?"*

"I mean . . . It isn't just about Prince Jowan, is it? He wasn't the only person hurt. He isn't the only one who deserves justice. What about everyone else? What about *us?* I don't understand how this changes *anything."*

"And I don't understand how you don't understand!" I yell. "We can *heal* instead of *fight!* We can put things right. We can make Helston home again!"

I want it *so* bad, my head aches. The Helston that could've been. That *should've* been. The Helston of Papa's stories and my dreams. The Helston that came within a finger's reach—

"Helston was *never* home," says Elowen, low and furious. "I don't care if Prince Jowan walked right in here now, alive and well, it wouldn't change *anything!* It wasn't just Father and it wasn't just Adan, it was every single person who watched them hurt us and did nothing! Every single person who believed Father, who believed *Adan,* even Her Majesty, over us. Every. Single. Person. And I want them *all* to pay. Helston deserves to *burn."*

Silence rings as loud as Helston's bells.

The fire in Elowen's eyes burns as hot and true as Kensa's.

She would set the kingdom ablaze on her own given the chance.

And, for the first time, I am afraid of her.

By the looks of them, Willow and Edwyn are too.

Elowen flushes and turns away from us. "I don't want peace," she says. "I want to fight. And I don't need your blessing to seek it." She rises stiffly, tucking her newly cut hair back behind her ears, and hesitates. Then, "Freedom is the choice to follow your own path. I don't think we're on the same road anymore."

I stagger up as she steps toward the door. "What're you doing? Where're you *going*?"

Edwyn stands too. "Elowen, stop! You can't just—"

"I can," she tells her brother. "I can do whatever I choose. And I'm not 'just' anything. I have known what I want since long ago. I'm not waiting any longer. Come with me if you wish, but I will not be held back anymore. I am going to pledge myself to Dumoor."

"El, *no*—"

She's already gone. The door is shut behind her.

But I'm not done.

I go right after her.

CHAPTER THIRTY-THREE

"*E lowen!*"

She is already on the ground, walking briskly toward the moors, to Pioden.

I take the ladder so fast I nearly fall. I hit the ground hard and run. My back hurts and my head aches, but I don't care.

She ignores me all the way until I grab her arm, and then she wheels on me with a snarl. "Don't touch me!"

"Then stop and talk to me!"

"I am *tired* of talking and not being heard. You have already made up your mind. You and Willow. The moment it seems like your precious parents aren't as culpable as you thought, you are all ready to go back to Helston and just forget. Because that's the only reason we're here now, isn't it?" She gives a brittle laugh, eyes bright with tears. "It wasn't until you and Willow were about to *suffer* that you cared enough to leave."

I reach for her desperately. "El, that's not true—"

"*Don't call me a liar!* We are not fighting the same war, Callie. We never were. For you and Willow, it was all about Jowan. It's simple. *Easy.* Not for me. Not for Edwyn." Her voice pitches high with grief. "You saw what they did to him. The fire kept burning long after Father left. It isn't over for us. And I cannot forgive. So don't ask me to." She backs away, then turns from me. "We are not on the same side."

My body feels boneless, my heart heavier than a stone.

"How can you say that?" I hear myself ask, my own voice sounding like it's far away and underwater. "You told me— you told *everyone*—what you felt for me, and now you're saying we're not even on the same side? Both can't be true, so which is it? Which is the lie?"

Her throat flickers in a swallow. "Neither," she says. "Neither is a lie. I meant what I said, then *and* now. Callie, I . . . You are the *most* important person to me, but that isn't enough. I have given too much of myself for the people I love. I can't do that anymore. I need to do what's right for *me.*"

"I want that for you too, El! Don't you get it?" I hate that I'm nearly crying, because I'm not sad. I'm not even angry! I just need her to *listen*! "I want what you want! I want to make them pay. I want to protect you and Edwyn and Willow, and I want us to stay together! Because *that's* why we're here, isn't it? That's why we're doing all this. To stay together!"

Elowen freezes, almost midstep. If it wasn't for the sway of her long tunic, I might think a spell had been cast on her.

Then, softly, "I love you, but I have to do this and I need you to understand. I need you to be on my side."

I nearly trip forward with relief. "That's *all* I want—"

"Then let me go."

As much as it's presented as an ask, I know that it isn't. It's a statement. An ultimatum. If I let her go, I stand a chance of getting her back. If I keep pulling her back, I know I will lose her.

I wipe my nose on my sleeve. It doesn't help. The snot keeps flowing.

"I'm scared for you."

"You needn't be." Her voice is soft and close; her fingers gently coax my hands away from my face. Her own is fierce and certain, and I smile through my tears despite it all. "I am stronger than even you know, Sir Callie."

I try to say *I know*, but the words stop just short of my lips.

The tip of her nose is cold against mine.

I didn't know her eyelashes were that long.

I didn't know there were so many different colors in her eyes.

If we stayed like this for a thousand years, it wouldn't be enough time to count them all.

When we finally part, the air is cold.

CHAPTER
THIRTY-FOUR

It takes an age to drag myself back up to the tree house. I don't know how I'm gonna explain to Edwyn and Willow that Elowen's gone. She's picked her side and she left us behind. We have so much to talk about and decide, and I don't know how to do that without her. Elowen is the steady, sensible voice in the swirling sea of our chaos. We need her.

I need her.

I grip the smooth wooden door handle, take a deep breath, and step inside.

The stillness is shattered.

"Are you sure?" Willow is asking, his voice high-pitched and scared. "How can you be certain? Maybe . . . maybe it's a mistake. Maybe she gave it to him accidentally. I'm sure that's it. I'm sure—" He catches sight of me in the doorway and rushes to me. His eyes are blown huge and his hands are desperate when he grabs me and pulls me over to Sulio.

"When Alis gave you the potion for Edwyn, what did she say? Where did she get it? She probably picked the wrong one, right? She probably has so many, she just picked up . . . the wrong one. Right?"

"Why?" I ask. "Is there something wrong with the potion? She said it would calm Edwyn's mind. To help with all the bad memories that have just come back."

"It certainly will do that," says Sulio grimly.

"What is it?" Teo asks from the sofa. Xe is perched on the back like a bird behind Edwyn; both are twisted around toward Sulio.

Inis takes the tiny bottle, unstoppers it, and sniffs.

Her whole face puckers. She passes it back, shaking her head hard. "This won't just help you manage your new memories; this will strip them down so bare you won't be able to tell if they're real or not. This is *potent* stuff. More likely to strip your mind down to a clean slate than help you manage what you have."

"I—I don't understand," Edwyn whispers. "Why would she give that to me? It must be a mistake."

"It was no mistake," says Kensa from the doorway. The dragon's face is filled with smoldering rage, barely contained. Xe storms in, snatches the vial from Sulio, and crushes it like a beetle, the glittering glass and shimmering potion oozing between xir clawed fingers. When Kensa raises xir face, xir eyes are furnaces. "There is nothing in this world so dangerous as truth. The price is too high, the consequence too steep. Gold and glory are cheap in comparison. You're leaving. I'm getting you out of here. Come."

"Wait, what?"

The dragon stares at me. "What do you not understand? I swore an oath to you, little knight; this is me keeping it. I can get you as far as the Estebrel border, and from there you can head north. Do not cross back into Wyndebrel." Xe looks around, taking attendance. "Where is the sorcerer?"

My stomach drops, and I cringe when all eyes turn on me. "El . . . she . . . she's gone to Alis. She wants to fight for Dumoor, and I couldn't stop her. I tried, I swear, but she has a right to her own choices. . . . It didn't feel correct, but it didn't feel wrong either. I—I didn't know—"

"We have to go after her!" says Edwyn. "We have to stop her before she—" He pales when Kensa shakes xir head.

"If your sister has already made her choice, there is nothing we can do. She is on her own path now."

"No! That's not right, that's not *true!*" Edwyn insists. "We can stop her! We can make her listen!"

"Kensa's right," says Willow softly. "It's not our place to force El onto a different path. But we can help her, can't we? We can look out for her and support her?"

Kensa glances uneasily between us. "This is not a safe place for you."

"We are *not* leaving Elowen on her own," I say, and the others nod. "Whatever's going on, we can survive it. I don't know what Alis's deal is, but *we* know the truth and maybe that's enough. We don't need her to help us. We don't need her permission and we don't need to play her games." I take a deep breath and meet Kensa's eyes. "Truth is powerful and precious, and you owe me a favor. So this is what I'm asking for. Tell us the truth. Tell us everything."

The dragon recoils, xir hand touching xir side. "I cannot, little knight."

I stand my ground. "*Why* not?"

"Because I am afraid."

"*That is not an excuse!*" I bellow. "Why is your fear more important than ours? You said you wanted to help, so *help*! Or are you just like every other grown-up who tells us pretty things to hold us in line and never keeps their promises? Oaths are binding in Dumoor, or is that a lie too?"

"I am not afraid for myself," says Kensa softly. "I have flown these skies for longer than you can comprehend. I have watched kingdoms rise and fall. I have watched the world change more times than I can remember. I am immortal. My choices are my own, and I claim my mistakes."

"Then *what*?"

Kensa's gaze flicks to Teo. "It is not my life that would be forfeit, should I break my oath."

All heads turn to Teo. Xe squirms, ears drooping beneath the weight of the attention. "Me?"

"You," says Kensa. "Once upon a time, I believed I could make this land a home for our kind. I was foolish. I let my hope overcome my sense, and I failed to understand the extent of humans' capacity for cruelty when they are afraid." Xe looks at me. "You ask, why is my fear more important than yours? I ask you the same in return. Why does your fear excuse the destruction and violence committed against my kind? I watched my people hunted and killed in the name of valor. I watched them flee gleeful blades. I watched them disappear, hiding behind disguises that would protect them. Young dragons learn quickly to conceal themselves, if they're lucky to grow old enough to understand and to be born to those willing to love them. They learn that love and safety are conditional. Fragile. Dependent on lies. That is the choice we all must make.

"When I met Alis, I believed that Dumoor could finally be the haven I had dreamed of. A place for the vilified, where they could be themselves without condition or fear. We welcomed all, and I waited for my kind to find their way home. I knew it would be a long wait, after centuries of persecution, with the instinct to hide so deeply ingrained that it's near impossible to break through.

"And then a boy arrived in the forest. Angry, alone. I knew at once what he was, though he had no idea. He thought he was cursed, the desperation to hide his magic manifesting in something monstrous. I tried to teach him, to explain that he needn't be afraid of who he was. A dragon is a powerful, beautiful thing. But he had spent too long among men. He couldn't accept himself, and I pushed too hard. I pushed him away, and he fled. It was years before Teo came to us.

Younger, barely in the first stages of metamorphosis, but *excited*. Teo is everything I wished we could all be. Loving our form and our magic, and understanding how much the world could open up to us if only we had the courage to be ourselves."

Kensa pauses, xir face soft and fond, but sad, too, as xir gaze rests on Teo.

"And then Dumoor changed. It was my fault, my error in judgment. I knew the moment he appeared in the forest that everything would change. But by the rules I had created myself, everyone who finds their way to Dumoor gets a chance." Kensa gives a bitter hiss. "I should've made an exception. Within days, the very air had shifted. I don't think anyone else noticed. She kept him hidden at Pioden, fully aware of the panic his presence would cause if word got out. No one was allowed inside and she rarely left. Only I was permitted to come and go as I pleased, bound by my oath of confidentiality.

"I trusted her. We had been equal partners from the beginning, our values and mission identical. When she told me to put aside my misgivings and have faith, I did so. Against everything my heart told me, I did so.

"And then she started sending me away, on missions that took me from Dumoor for days at a time. When I started to argue, the requests turned to orders. She didn't look at me like an equal anymore. She looked at me like a beast. A creature to be controlled. And I knew she would do the same to Teo as soon as she could. I kept xem away from Pioden as long as I could, but Alis was impatient to have another dragon under her command, and Teo was eager to pay xir way.

"She waited until I was gone to summon Teo and present the offer of xir first mission like a grand privilege. By the time I returned, it was too late. The deal was done. And they made it perfectly clear that this was my punishment for disagreement. If I was good and obedient, Teo would survive. If I fought, xe would die."

"How?" My voice is a rasp. "It's not like they had any control over the Helston side. How could they dictate the outcome like that?"

"Because they did have control of the Helston side."

"What d'you—"

Then my blood runs cold.

A man who found his way to Dumoor a few months ago, who could twist something that had started so good into something so bad.

I don't need Kensa to tell me his name.

"Peran's here, isn't he?"

In Pioden.

With Elowen.

The dragon bows xir head. "Yes, little knight."

343

CHAPTER THIRTY-FIVE

"I don't get it," I whisper. "I don't understand."

It doesn't make sense! Except it does. In the wrongest, most twisted way, it almost feels inevitable. I push my fingers through my hair and *pull* until my scalp burns.

I can't breathe.

I can't *think*.

And Elowen—

"Lord Peran hates magic," I hear Willow whisper. "Why would he come here? And why would Alis let him? Everything she said . . . She knows who he is and what he's done. He is everything she is against. Maybe . . . maybe she didn't know. Not entirely. Maybe she didn't know about Jowan, and now that she does—"

"It doesn't make a difference." Edwyn's voice is as cool and still as Alis's pool. "She was there the whole time. She saw what we saw, heard what we heard. If she didn't know before, she does now." He swallows hard and looks to Kensa. "That's why she tried to keep me there, isn't it? And why she gave me that potion when I wouldn't stay. She wanted to . . . silence me, didn't she?"

Kensa doesn't need to nod to confirm what we all already know.

"I still don't get it," I growl. "They are on opposite ends of the line. How can they work together when each of them is what the other hates the most?"

It is Willow who answers. "Because there is one person they both hate more than each other."

"Which is who?"

"Mother."

Of course.

They were both banished, both humiliated, both betrayed by Queen Ewella. The reasons may be different, but the result is the same.

"Is that it?" I ask Kensa. "They're working together to get revenge on Her Majesty?"

"Justice takes many forms," the dragon replies. "The justice we once sought for the wronged used to be a force for good. Revolutionary kindness. Our friend brought something new to lay as an offering at Alis's feet. Something irresistible."

"Revenge."

"Revenge."

All I can think of is Elowen.

"We have to go back to Helston," says Willow. "We have to tell them. *Warn* them."

"And why would they listen?" Edwyn demands. "Who would believe us? We're criminals. They'll arrest us the moment they see us. Even if we make it far enough for an audience with Her Majesty . . ." He swallows hard and glares at the ground. "Father and Adan were right. No one would ever believe us."

"Papa would. Neal would. If we can get to them first, we stand a chance." I don't think about how slim that chance is. I don't think about what will surely happen if we fail, or how many obstacles we will have to successfully navigate just for the opportunity to be heard. None of that matters. "We have to try. If we can convince Her Majesty to keep Helston from attacking, that'll buy us time to convince Alis that Peran is poison. We can do that, right?" I ask Kensa. "You said yourself that it didn't start off like this. There's a chance that she can change?"

The dragon nods slowly. "I believe there is still hope, though the window of possibility is closing."

"All the more reason to act quickly."

Though mostly I want to go before we lose our courage.

"And how will you prove it?" Edwyn asks. "It isn't enough to just tell. They will take every chance to discount you. We need proof. *Real* proof. Does that even exist?"

I suck my lip, desperately trying to think of something—*anything*. To my mind, the proof is right here, in us. But Edwyn's right. The word of a few kids is not enough.

"Is there anything?" I ask Kensa. "Anything at all we can take with us?"

"Alis is careful," Kensa replies slowly. "Every deal is made with magic. Untraceable and intangible. Our friend is not so cautious."

"Father never discards anything," Edwyn adds. His hands twist fretfully together before him, but there's a new determination in his face. "He keeps every letter, every note, anything at all that could ever be used in evidence. Kensa, is he in contact with anyone in Helston?"

"Birds fly back and forth every day," says Kensa, which I assume means "yes" in cryptic dragon.

"Then we can find their correspondence," Edwyn assures us. "Real, tangible evidence that you can take to the palace."

Willow sits up anxiously. "What about you?"

Edwyn's gaze drops. "I . . . cannot go back to Helston. Nor can I leave Elowen. We stay together."

"Even with Peran here?" I ask.

He nods. "Yes. I'm not . . . I *am* afraid of Father. But it's different. *I* am different. I don't want to run away anymore. I don't want to be invisible or silent. It wasn't right, what they did to me, and I am not going to let my fear silence me anymore." He rises stiffly and makes a deep bow before Willow. "I stand with you. I fight for you. My life and my sword are yours, Highness."

Willow's blush is blazing as he shifts awkwardly. "Not really a Highness anymore, am I?"

"Yeah, you are." I elbow him in the side with a grin. "Even if it's for our own, new realm."

"Our own . . ." Willow brightens. "I like that! Our own world. A *better* world . . . That's something worth fighting for, isn't it?"

It's weird to feel so good, so *alive* in the wake of the worst news we could've possibly received. But we have direction now. Purpose. And the path forward may be perilous, but we couldn't be more prepared.

"Me too. I'm in too." Teo stands a little apart from us, xir own fire small but blazing in xir eyes. "I want to fight for my family too. For Dumoor. For what Dumoor is supposed to be. I'm already a part of it," xe says when Kensa starts to argue. "And I haven't taken the mark yet. I am free, and I can do what you can't, Kensa. I can help. I can fight."

I catch Willow's eye and he's thinking the same thought: It would be no bad thing to have a dragon on our side.

"Besides, you'll need to get to Helston fast. I can do that."

And just as if xe'd orchestrated this perfect moment, Teo tugs off xir tunic, wriggles xir shoulders, and . . . spreads xir wings.

Willow's voice is pure joy. "They came in!"

"Just today." Teo gives a twirl, showing them off in all their glory.

The wings are translucent, the bones giving them their shape visible beneath thin blue skin. When Teo gives the wings an experimental flap, I expect them to tear. They look just about as strong as wet paper.

I school my face into something less disappointed as Teo turns back, flushed with pride. "Can you . . . fly on them?"

Teo gives them another experimental flap. "I haven't tried yet, but probably."

"No," says Kensa. "You cannot. Nor can you try before they are fully formed. If you work them too hard too quickly, you will damage them permanently. Final transformation cannot be rushed."

It's embarrassing how relieved I am. If Teo tried to fly with me and Willow on those things, we would crash and die. Period.

Teo huffs, steam billowing from xir nose. "I can transform. I know I can."

"Even if you can, you shouldn't," Kensa growls back. "You are not ready."

"I *am!*"

"I have been a dragon *hundreds* of years longer than you have. I know you are impatient," Kensa continues more softly. "And I know you are eager to help your friends, but I beg you to wait just a few more days until you can safely—"

"Fine. I'll wait."

The elder dragon narrows xir eyes. "Really?"

"Mm-hmm."

"Why don't I believe you?"

"You do," Teo retorts. "Else you'd make me swear."

I hold my breath, waiting for Kensa to call Teo's bluff and get out the dragon magic again.

But Kensa just sighs the same way Papa does, and says, "I trust you. Do *not* make me regret it."

If Kensa sounds like Papa, Teo's smirk is mine.

"Then what's the plan?" Edwyn asks. "Now that we've established our goals, how on earth are we going to implement them?"

"We need to get into Pioden undetected," I say. "*Really* undetected this time. Is that possible?" I ask Kensa. "Is that something you can help us with?"

"If Alis is sufficiently distracted, she won't notice your presence," the dragon replies. "But that is no easy feat. She is fiercely protective of Pioden."

"I'll do it," says Edwyn quickly. "I'll go looking for El, and they'll catch me and—"

"No," Willow and I say at the same.

But Edwyn holds his ground. "Yes. I can do this. I *want* to do this. And if I'm to face Father again . . ." He swallows, face twitching a little. "I—I want it to be on *my* terms. By *my* choice. Kensa can walk us in. Willow, you can conceal yourself and Callie. You can make it to the aviary and be out again before they ever notice you're there. I will make sure their attention is diverted."

I chew the inside of my mouth.

It's a good plan. It makes sense. I can see it working.

But I hate it *so* much.

"And then what?" Willow asks. "How do we get back to Helston? What if they chase us? What if we get lost?"

"We can guide you," says Dolan, and the grown-ups around us all nod.

"You are part of The Roost now," Feena adds. "We protect our own. We will see you safely to where you need to be."

All the way to the bridge.

The thought of going back sends prickles up and down my skin, concentrating on the wound between my shoulders.

I can still feel it, that arrow.

And the memory of pain scares me.

"Then it is decided," says Kensa. "Tomorrow, we fly."

"No," says Edwyn. "Not tomorrow. *Now.* We cannot wait until tomorrow."

"I'm afraid this is something I will not compromise on," Kensa tells him firmly. "You owe yourself more than that. You will sleep, you will eat, and by the time you go on your adventures, you will be at your best. *That* is what you deserve."

"Kensa's right," I say, surprising everyone, including myself. "We can't leave *anything* to chance. We go tomorrow, when we're ready."

As ready as we'll ever be, anyway.

CHAPTER
THIRTY-SIX

I don't sleep much but I don't mind. The gentle swing of the hammock mingled with the soft sounds of sleeping lulls me into the next-best thing. Peace never lasts more than a few minutes, though, before I'm pulled out of my guilt and worry and thoughts of Elowen.

I should've gone after her.

I should've put her first.

I should've fought tooth and nail, with everything I have, to rescue her.

Except she doesn't need rescuing. I know that. I don't doubt that. If any one of us can handle themselves alone, it's El.

I wouldn't be surprised if we arrive there tomorrow and Peran's body is cut into pieces at the front door.

Wouldn't that save some time and trouble.

Though that ignores the small matter of Alis.

I roll over and nearly roll right out of the hammock.

Alis.

She seemed so sincere. Maybe she was sincere. Maybe she meant every word she spoke.

Except the potion.

The potion.

As hard as I try, as much as I want to, I can't make myself believe that she didn't know exactly what she was doing when she passed me that little vial. She was there. She witnessed what we witnessed, saw everything that spilled out of Edwyn's head, and still wants him to carry it all by himself.

She lied.

She lied.

She is not on our side.

I guess I ended up falling asleep because the next time I open my eyes, the sun is bright through the curtainless room and the smell of breakfast fills the dwelling.

I am, it appears, the last person up.

I grimace, sliding in beside Willow and gulping down a stolen mug of tea. "Sorry," I tell everyone, wiping my mouth on the back of my hand. "I hope I haven't messed up the timeline." I look around, counting heads. "Where're Kensa and Teo?"

"First light is the most powerful," says Feena, who's

drinking out of the biggest mug I have ever seen in my life. "It'll be good for Teo's form to catch as much of it as xe can."

"They're doing dragon stuff? I'm gonna go see—"

"No," says Dolan in the kind of voice that makes me stop and listen. "A dragon's business is xir own. Xe will come back. Xe always does."

I sit back down with only a slightly petulant huff.

"I just want to go and get it over with," Edwyn mutters, shredding a bread roll like it has personally wronged him. "The waiting is always the worst. Knowing what's coming, knowing you can't avoid it, and being forced to *wait*. It was Father's favorite trick." He snorts. "It feels like he planned this."

"He didn't," says Willow softly. "He doesn't know anything."

Edwyn's lips press tight. The fiery certainty that burned so hot last night has dwindled down to embers.

"You don't have to do this," I remind him. "We can rework the plan."

"No." He glares at me sharply. "I'm fine. I can do this. I know how to do this."

"And you have allies," Feena says. "We won't let you fall, Edwyn. As soon as Callie and Willow are out safely, Kensa will bring you and Elowen home."

I look doubtfully between the grown-ups. "You think xe'll be able to? As easy as that? Peran's not gonna just let them go."

"It's not up to him, child," says Dolan. "You are all wards of The Roost now. That man has no authority here."

Hidden beneath the table, my hands fidget.

I wish I could believe that.

"Come," says Kensa before the door is even fully open. "It's time."

Not even a "Good morning, how'd you sleep?" but I guess centuries-old dragons don't really do preamble.

I chug the rest of my tea and rise.

Willow's hair is long and loose down his back, his tunic a soft, light lilac. Edwyn has chosen a pale green, the same color as his magic, for his battle garb.

As for me, I wear the deep forest shades of Dumoor. Rich browns and bright greens that clash brilliantly with my hair.

We look good. We look like ourselves.

The best way to head out into battle.

But before we step outside, Kensa stops us.

"It has to be now."

"What does?"

Xe looks to Willow, who nods grimly and blows into his hands.

Soft silver sparkles fill Willow's cupped palms, shimmering like fish scales.

The invisibility spell.

"Ready, Callie?"

No. It feels so final. Like we're really riding into battle and once the spell is cast, there is no going back.

Edwyn stares at the magic, face gray.

I squeeze his shoulder. "We'll see each other again soon."

"Do you really believe that?"

"I do." I have to. "Tell El we love her. Make sure she doesn't burn the world down."

Edwyn gives a wet laugh and swipes at his eyes. "There's no one alive who could stop her." He takes a deep breath that rattles his chest, and hugs me. "Be careful."

It's the first time Edwyn has ever instigated a hug, and I squeeze him back hard. "You too."

Willow and Edwyn's parting is complicated by the spell Willow's holding on to, and I wish I could take it so they could say goodbye properly.

"Stay yourself, all right?"

Edwyn nods. "Not a chance I'll let him take that away from me again. And if you see Adan . . . kick him where it hurts for me?"

Willow bursts out laughing. "I'll do my best!"

Adan.

Adan deserves far more than a kick.

"Time to go," says Kensa.

Willow nods and gently blows the magic onto me. The air sparkles and tickles, like a thousand butterflies are settling on my skin.

Edwyn's eyes go wide. "It worked!"

"Yeah?" I don't *feel* invisible. Not that I know what invisible feels like. I look to Willow. I can see him, but he looks more like a ghost than a person, all grayscale and shimmering. "Did you accidentally kill us?"

He grins. "I promise I did not."

"How can I see you?"

"We shared a spell." Like *that's* an explanation.

"Come." Kensa ushers Edwyn out beside xem, and Willow and I follow.

Invisible and ready to do battle.

CHAPTER
THIRTY-SEVEN

Kensa and Edwyn don't acknowledge me and Willow from there on. We tail them like a shadow, hands locked together. We don't speak. The spell conceals our physical forms, but our voices are intact.

One slipup, one sound, and it'll all be over.

I've never wanted to talk more.

When we reach Pioden, Kensa whistles the key but there's another note added to the end of the phrase that I haven't heard before.

"The staircase will work for you if you need to find the bathroom," xe tells Edwyn pointedly. "Otherwise you'll be climbing forever and never get anywhere. But don't go too far. If you take a wrong turn left, you'll end up among the birds."

I touch Kensa's arm in thanks and we step inside the witch's castle.

There is nothing to suggest that anything is different or wrong. The air is still, silent, as immovable as the stone itself.

Kensa guides Edwyn left through the foyer and away from the staircase, one clawed hand resting between Edwyn's shoulders.

Neither looks back.

Willow's hand is clammy in my own. Or maybe mine is clammy in his. Maybe we're both sweating up a storm.

Most likely that one.

Get in, get out.

We take the stairs fast.

The higher we go, the narrower the stairwell grows, until it feels like we're being squeezed through a tube. Round and round and round and—

We're spat out into a circular room with an open door, rafters crisscrossing the vaulted ceiling and filled to bursting with magpies, their black eyes all staring straight through the spell, right at us.

But that's not the worst of it.

Willow's hand spasms, a whimper catching in his throat.

Seated at a desk so cluttered it could be Papa's, back toward us, is Peran.

It doesn't matter that his hair is shaggy and flecked with gray instead of the sleek, careful crop of unbroken brown, or that he's clothed in garments I recognize from The Roost, all patches of rainbows that don't look right on him. It doesn't matter that he's smaller than I remember. Thinner.

Even with my eyes closed, I would know it was him.

Peran might have had a long, hard fall from grace, but he still holds himself like a lord chancellor.

I try to catch Willow's eye, to silently ask, *What do we do?* But every ounce of Willow's attention is on Peran. He's frozen, flung all the way back to the beginning.

I need to get him out of here.

We can regroup away from Pioden. Find another strategy.

I pull on Willow's hand, urging him away. Then I tug. Then I *yank*.

And then the birds start to shriek.

Every single member of the flock takes wing and swarms us in a rush of fury and feathers, tiny beaks ripping at our clothes, our skin, the spell; picking apart Willow's carefully crafted magic like descaling a fish until we're left wrecked and exposed.

By some miracle, we're not bleeding and our clothes are intact. But the spell is gone.

"Good morning, Calliden. Your Highness. Isn't it a little early in the day to be engaging in treason?" Peran lays down his quill pen and takes his time folding the parchment he was writing on. Only after he's sealed it, presented it to one of the birds, and watched it disappear into the sky does he finally grace us with his full attention.

He smiles and I want to puke.

"Come in. Tell me what you're looking for. Maybe I can help you."

Behind us, the door slams shut and both Willow and I flinch.

There is a flicker of something bright on Peran's finger.

"You . . . don't have magic," I say shakily.

Peran rubs the light between his fingers, examines it with mild curiosity. "Everyone possesses a little magic, Calliden. You should know that better than anyone." He admires the glimmering light for a moment longer before extinguishing it in a fist. "You are not the only ones learning more about yourselves in this place."

Usually learning is good. I love that folks can change and grow. But somehow I don't think that whatever growing Peran's been doing is in the right direction.

"So, what? You don't hate magic anymore, is that it? You've had some big revelation and now you're good? No way. People like you don't change. Whatever you're doing here, however you made Alis trust you, it's gonna fall apart. You know that, right? She knows who you are and what you've done. She's gonna tear you to shreds."

Peran cocks his head, assessing me with glittering blue eyes. "Would it surprise you to learn that I have been nothing but honest with Princess Alis from the start? She knows who I am. She knows what I have done. The promise of power and vengeance overcomes all." He smiles. "I believe my daughter is coming to a similar realization. It's curious how old animosity fades when enemies discover mutual ambitions. It is . . . heartwarming that she has found her way back to me."

"Elowen would never work with you," I hiss, staggering up. "She's gonna gut you in your sleep for what you've done to Edwyn."

"Elowen is smarter than you give her credit for. She knows what she wants and she knows how to get it. And priorities change, Callie. Desire is a far greater force than love."

"If that's what you think, you don't know El."

Peran chuckles, and the sound is as cold and sharp as ice. "Elowen is my daughter, in blood *and* spirit. She is more like me than even she knows. I cannot wait to help her reach her *full* potential. As for my son, thank you for returning him. The work needed to break his new bad habits is inconvenient, but he'll be back to normal soon."

Something inside me snaps.

No. *Everything* inside me snaps.

I don't have Satin. I don't need Satin.

I hurl myself at Peran with a yell.

He hits me. I hit him back.

This time, there is no queen to stop me, no Papa to hold me back, no Helston etiquette to tell me that *I'm* in the wrong.

I go for his throat, and every blow he lands kindles my strength.

I am relentless. He doesn't deserve a single moment to catch his breath.

He killed Jowan. He beat Edwyn. And he lied and lied and *lied!*

We crash to the ground together, the alarmed shrieks of hundreds of magpies blowing out my ears. I don't care. I don't feel it. I don't feel any of it. But I'm gonna make sure Peran does. Every. Single. Bit.

I am distantly aware of Willow sidestepping us, rushing to the desk, and ripping out drawers to rifle through papers. Maybe if I can distract Peran long enough, Willow can get away, get to Helston, complete our mission alone. Maybe there is still hope.

"Callie!"

I grit my teeth. I will not be distracted. Not even by Willow.

Except that's not Willow's voice.

"Callie!"

It's Teo's.

Willow gasps, the joyous sound so disconnected from everything else, I look up.

There's a dragon at the window.

Tiny. Turquoise.

Teo.

Peran grabs my hair and yanks.

I scream.

"You are not going anywhere," Peran growls in my ear. "You are staying right here, and I will make you watch as your friends are hunted down like the beasts they are."

Then something other than me hits him in a place I can't

see, and Peran howls and drops me, and Willow is hauling me up and dragging me to the window, to Teo, and the window is tiny but we're small too, and Willow pushes me out first and I don't even have time to be scared of *how bloody high up we are*, or how much Teo drops when I land on xir back.

Willow is halfway out the window when Peran grabs him.

I reach for him. Teo's thin wings beat furiously, fighting for enough height to help.

Willow kicks back. If his kick lands, it doesn't make a difference.

And then there's a *snap* that sounds like lightning and Peran yells in pain.

He drops Willow.

And Willow falls.

Our fingers just miss each other.

"Catch him!" I scream at Teo, and the dragon dives.

The air is so sharp, I can't see. I grope for Willow, wishing and wishing and promising not to wish for anything else so long as I live. My hand finds his wrist. His hand finds mine. And we're still falling. The three of us hurtling down and about to crash but at least we're together and—

Teo's wings catch a current and it is just enough to slow us down before the ground comes up to meet us.

A giggle bubbles in my throat, and once it bursts, I can't stop. The grass is itchy beneath me, and my body hurts so bad *something's* got to be broken. But we made it.

We made it.

Except we didn't.

"Run!" Willow drags me up by both arms. "We have to go!"

"Get on my back," says Teo. "I can get you to Helston."

"You can't carry us—"

"I can. I will," says the dragon fiercely. "I won't let you down."

Teo is about the same size as Flo—minuscule compared to Kensa's monstrous form. Willow and I could just about fit on xir back, but Teo's wings . . .

"Kensa said if you push yourself too hard too soon, you won't develop right."

"I don't care," says Teo, yellow eyes blazing. "If this is the only thing I ever do, I want to do it. Get on my back."

What choice do we have?

Willow and I share a last anxious look, and we mount the dragon.

CHAPTER
THIRTY-EIGHT

I squeak the moment Teo moves. Xe might be the size of my horse, but xir anatomy is *completely* different. Willow and I are squished between Teo's neck and xir wing joints, trying not to get impaled on one of the many sharp spikes jutting along Teo's spine.

Dragons were definitely *not* designed for riding.

Each step Teo takes rocks us nearly out of our seats. Willow clings to my middle and I cling to Teo. If we make it halfway to Helston in one piece, it'll be nothing short of a miracle.

And that doesn't even account for flying.

Teo spreads xir wings wide, gait speeding up, into a gallop that rocks us violently.

I'm 99 percent sure we're going to die.

"Hold on!" Teo calls back, like we weren't already hanging on for dear life, and then xe leaps.

I scream, locking my eyes so tightly shut I don't think they're ever gonna open again.

My stomach feels weird and the air is freezing my scalp, and I know we're climbing higher and higher but I don't dare look.

And then we stop. At least, it feels like we stop.

I crack *one* eye open a fraction of a millimeter and gasp.

Okay, so that's pretty cool.

Wind ripples around us as we soar above Wyndebrel, between birds below and clouds above. There's no more jarring motion about to pitch us off, just smooth, flawless flight.

I open my other eye and risk a look down.

I can see everything.

The great, dark expanse of Dumoor Forest; the miles and miles of moorland. Glittering sea to the north, south, *and* west. And right on the farthest tip of Wyndebrel, Helston.

From up here, it doesn't look so far away. Like I could just reach across and touch it. It's weird to think there are only a few miles between Dumoor and Helston. It feels like leagues.

"I wish we could stay up here forever." I don't realize I'm speaking out loud until Willow hums in agreement.

"I wish we didn't have to land."

"I wish we could turn around and fly all the way in the opposite direction."

"We could." Teo's long neck twists back so that xe can catch my eye. "If you wanted to."

I suck my lip. It's painfully tempting, made worse by how easy it would be.

As the grown-ups keep telling us, this is not our fight. They don't want us involved. It's not our responsibility.

But, as we keep telling them, that's not true.

This is our world and our lives, and we are the only ones who are willing to do what must be done to set things right.

"No," I say. "Keep going."

Even though Helston doesn't look far away from up here, progress is slow.

"I can't go faster," says Teo when xe senses my anxiety. "I'm sorry."

"Don't be." This is still way faster than if we were on foot. "When we get to Helston, we're going straight to Papa," I tell Willow, making the most of the time we have to strategize. "If we land on the beach, maybe no one'll notice us."

"What about the wards?"

"The wards?" I curse viciously. I'd forgotten about the wards. "They alert the watch, right? Is that it?" If we have to battle a few soldiers, so be it.

"The wards were erected to keep magic out," Willow explains. "The more someone has, the bigger the consequence. I—I'm not sure exactly what that entails. Dumoor's never tried to infiltrate directly, as far as I know."

"Teo got through before, though. When they first brought xem in."

"Mother lowered the wards to let them through."

Of course she did.

I lean down across Teo's neck. "If you land on the hill beyond the bridge, we can walk the rest of the way."

"Nope," says Teo, coasting left to dip below a flock of confused gulls. "Even if I were willing to leave you—which I'm not—look at the bridge."

Willow and I peer down through the haze of clouds.

Helston's once-proud bridge stretches over the gulf, held up by an elaborate framework of scaffolding. A huge chunk is still missing from the middle.

"They haven't finished fixing it yet," Willow breathes.

I can't take my eyes off the skeletal structure. "You make it sound like that's a good thing."

"It is," he insists. "The army cannot move out until the bridge is fixed. That means we still have time to stop them."

He's right.

We still have time.

There is still hope.

Teo soars around Helston, searching for the right place to make first contact. There's no good place, not when they'll know we're there the moment Teo's wing tip touches the wards. We have to just go and deal with whatever consequence occurs.

The scariest part is always not knowing.

On the ground, Helston is readying itself for war.

The palace grounds are packed with horses and people moving as busily as ants. And they're all looking up at us.

Suddenly, landing doesn't feel like such an attractive idea.

Then Willow points and yells. "I see them, Callie! Mother and Sir Nick!"

I follow his finger, scanning the faces coming into focus the closer we get. And I see them too, distant but distinct figures far below us.

My heart leaps.

"Get ready," says Teo, angling down.

Willow holds on to me and I hold on to Teo, and the three of us brace for impact.

Far below, our shadow is *huge*, and it isn't long before Helston starts to notice and panic. Tiny figures run and scatter. Others point to the sky. I can hear the distant shout of command, ordering men to their positions, ready to defend against the enemy.

I wonder if they know it's us.

I wonder if it would make a difference if they did.

Close up, Queen Ewella's wards shimmer like the surface of the sea on a summer's day.

Before, passing through the wards was like being doused in cold water.

This time, it's like smashing through glass.

Teo cries out in pain, and our smooth flight cracks and stutters. Xe fights desperately to get more height, flapping and writhing like a wounded snake, all the while trying to keep me and Willow on xir back.

The bells start to toll before the ground comes up to meet us.

It comes hard and painful. I skid, gravel ripping into my chin and my hands. I groan. But I don't have time to lie there and catch my breath or take count of my injuries.

Orders are thrown through the air and the whole force of Helston bears down on us. I find Willow and Teo. Willow's face is bleeding, his cheek one huge gash of blood and dirt, but he's on his feet too, with magic ready and blazing in torn hands.

Teo, on the other hand, is in a bad state.

Xe lies on the ground, wings limp around xem. Red blood stands out stark against xir beautiful blue-green scales. Xir eyes are wide and wild.

I move to help, to comfort, to do *anything*, but a barked order—"*Don't move*"—freezes me.

We're surrounded on all sides, but not by knights and soldiers.

By kids.

Pages I trained with, done up in full battle gear, and younger ones I don't recognize, who must've started their training after we left. Ten years old. Eleven at most.

They hold their swords in unpracticed hands, their ferocity a fragile front.

Is this really how Helston plans to win?

Willow stands up tall and stares down the length of the

sword pointed right between his eyes. "We didn't come here to fight. I am the Crown Prince Willow, and I demand to see my mother, the queen. You will put down your weapons and you will allow us to help our friend."

The sword's owner—an older boy with straw-blond hair and a pale, spotty face—falters. "Prince Willow . . . Prince Willow is dead."

"Do I look dead?" Willow snaps. "Take me to Her Majesty at once. I have time-sensitive documents she *needs* to see."

For a single sweet moment, I believe it's enough.

A murmur rumbles through the pages, and the swords and arrows aimed at us start to drop.

"They're *lying!*" Peter snarls, barging his way through the crowd and scattering kids like pins. "Prince Willow fell in Dumoor Forest. I saw it with my own eyes!" He glares at me. "Callie too. Whoever these infiltrators are, they're wearing their skin to trick us! Don't be fooled!"

I stare at Peter.

He looks *awful,* like he hasn't slept since that night in the forest. He looks like Edwyn at his worst, and it's impossible not to feel horribly sorry for him.

"I know that's what Adan told you to say." I keep my voice soft and low, like I'm talking to a wild horse. "And I bet I know what he said to keep your mouth shut, but if you help us now, we can help you. That's why we're here. To put an end to his reign. His and Peran's. We have all the evidence right here."

Willow reaches into his tunic and pulls out a whole sheaf

of papers. Letters. This is the first time I've seen them, and there are so *many*. A whole story, told from beginning to end.

"It's all here," says Willow. "Lord Peran has been in communication with Adan in a plot to overthrow the queen and take control of Helston."

A single flicker of hesitation crosses Peter's face, and I hold my breath, hoping and hoping and—

Peter turns to the pages, their eyes huge and nervous. "You see the lengths Dumoor will go to try to trick us? This is what we're up against. Do *not* be fooled!"

Disappointment finally snaps the last thread of my patience. I storm right up to Peter and grab him, jerking him round to face me, our noses nearly touching. "You already have been fooled if you think Adan is on your side! You were *there*. You saw him murder Jory! What did he tell everyone when you got back, hmm? That it was Dumoor? Did he recycle the same lie he and Peran concocted when they murdered Prince Jowan? *You* are the liar, Peter. *You* are the fool."

"Step *aside*."

Pages scatter like mice beneath Queen Ewella's booming command. Even Peter falls back, bowing quickly. "Your Majesty."

She doesn't even acknowledge him, every bit of her focused on Willow, her eyes blown wide, mouth open in shock, in horror like he's some kind of apparition.

Willow takes one cautious step forward. "Mother—"

373

And she takes two back. "How dare you?" Ewella whispers. "How dare you come here, wearing his likeness?"

Willow flinches. "I—I don't understand—"

"You think I do not know my own son?" The queen's fury makes everyone in the vicinity cower. "Have I not lost enough? Have I not been tortured beyond *anyone's* limits?" She snaps her fingers, lighting a dark flame on the tip. "Show me your real face," Ewella commands. "You will die in your own body. Not my son's."

"Stop!" I shove between Willow and his mother, arms outstretched like that could do anything to protect him from the full extent of her magic. "It's not an illusion. Please! You've got to listen! He's real. We're both real. We're not the ones lying to you. We came to give you the truth; we just need you to listen! Just for five minutes!"

Something sharp, like a handful of claws, grabs my face and throws me to the ground.

I don't stay down.

I *won't* stay down.

Every bit of me hurts and I'm bleeding, but I can't tell where the blood is coming from.

The world tips around me, but I find my balance and keep it. "Where is Sir Nick?" I demand, spitting blood. "Where is my dad?"

Ewella isn't even looking at me. "Take them away," she orders. "Secure them sufficiently. I will deal with them myself when our kingdom is not under imminent attack. Ensure that Nick doesn't see them. He has suffered enough."

"And the dragon?"

"Chain it up belowground."

"No!" Just the word "it" sends me writhing, desperate to get to Teo, to protect xem from people who can't even see xem as a person.

It's no good.

The more I fight, the harder they hold on to me, gloved fingers squeezing my arms until I'm scared they'll snap.

"Of course, Your Majesty," Adan murmurs. His gaze roves over me and his eyes glitter with satisfaction at my uselessness. "Take the boy," he orders Peter, who moves at once to obey. "I have a feeling the *girl* might be too much for you to handle."

"I'm not a girl! Leave Teo alone! *Don't touch me!* Papa! It's me! I'm here! *Papa!*" I scream for him as Adan locks my arms behind me, a knee in my spine forcing me forward through the sea of staring pages. They shrink away, faces filled with fear and confusion. I know where we're going. I know where they're taking us. It was all for nothing. Everything we did. As close as we got. Everything we gave up.

We're all the way back to the beginning, and none of it mattered.

"Ewella, what is going on?"

My head jerks up. I know that voice.

"Don't, Nick. It will only hurt you. Just another of Alis's cruel tricks."

Nick?

Papa.

I search for him. For Papa. But there are too many people between us and I can't see anything.

"Papa!"

He answers immediately. "Callie?"

"It isn't them, Nick—"

But he ignores her, pushing through the crowd.

I squirm in Adan's grip, desperate to get free and reach my dad. "Papa!"

The moment we see each other, I burst into tears.

"Let them go," Papa snarls at Adan. *"Now."*

Adan's fingers dig into my arms. "You are not my commander."

"Let them go or you'll feel my sword through your neck."

"You really want to play this game again?" Adan asks softly. "After you lost the last round so badly? You're out of playable pieces, Nick."

One moment of distraction is all I need.

I kick back, driving my booted foot right into Adan's crotch, and I send a little wish into the air that somehow Edwyn will know I kept my promise.

Adan buckles with a curse, swiping for me.

I run for Papa and he catches me.

"I can't believe it's you. I was sure we had lost you," he

mumbles into my hair. "They told us you fell, and when they brought back Satin—Callie, if I'd known you were alive, I would've come after you. I wanted to. We tried to." His hands roam my face like he can't trust his eyes. "Where were you? What happened? How did you survive Dumoor?"

"Dumoor saved us." My throat hurts, but I raise my voice, making sure everyone close can hear me. "They took us in. They healed us. They're not what everyone thinks, Papa. Everything has been turned around wrong. That's why we're here. To tell you the truth. To tell you who's really—"

"Enough!" Adan shouts. "We will not allow this performance to continue any longer! Your Majesty, the council has been trying to convince you of Sir Nicholas's questionable loyalties ever since he brought the witch's servant into Helston. Is this not evidence that he is working for the enemy? The children fell. I witnessed it with my own eyes. This is a trick, and Nicholas is part of it."

Papa stares at Adan in true confusion. Maybe they were never friends, but Papa has always believed they were at least on the same side. "What are you talking about?"

Adan jabs a finger at us, his face lit with glee. "Admit it! You have been working with Dumoor this whole time. You and that *dragon*! You should've been locked away with it and left to rot!"

I flinch at "dragon." It's been so long since I've heard it spat out in that tone, like it's an insult, a *slur;* like it's the worst thing you could call someone.

As though dragons aren't just another kind of person.

But that's not how Adan thinks. That's not how *anyone* in Helston thinks. When they say "dragon," they don't mean Teo, who would do anything for anyone. They don't even mean Kensa, bound tight by xir own loyalty. They mean "monster." Traitor. *Enemy*.

And they're wrong.

I face Adan with my own fire blazing, Papa's hands a solid reassurance on my shoulders. "You can say what you like, you can call Neal all the names in the world, but the real traitor is *you*. And we have the proof. Right here. Your Majesty." I turn desperately to Queen Ewella, hoping and hoping she isn't completely beyond reach. "Your Majesty, please, hear us out. I know it's hard when you've been lied to for so long to believe anything else, but that's why me and Willow came as soon as we could. As soon as we found out." I wave Willow over, and he hesitantly leaves Papa's side. "We brought everything we could," I continue as Willow pulls the papers from his tunic. "Peran's at Dumoor. Working with Alis. And he's been talking to *him*." I jab a finger at Adan. "And they've been planning it all together, just like before when they . . ." But Jowan's name catches in my throat and I can't. Not without crying. And, no matter the reason, crying is *always* seen as weakness.

But Willow is able to take over for me. "Adan and Peran murdered Jowan," he tells his mother without a waver. "Then they framed Dumoor to create dissent and fuel the war. It was Adan's arrow that killed Jowan, and it was Adan's arrow that killed Jory and hurt Callie. All on Peran's orders. And that's what they're going to keep doing until Helston has fallen and there is nothing left." He brandishes the papers like I would brandish Satin—assured in his strength and ability to strike swift and true. "Letters to Peran from Adan and Lady Anita, containing everything from transcripts of your council meetings to battle plans to maps of Helston. Mother, please, you *have* to believe us. We knew the dangers of coming back. We knew we would not be welcome. But Helston is my home too, even if it doesn't want me, and I won't see it destroyed just because—"

"Let me see these." Adan snatches the papers from Willow's fingers before anyone can stop him. He scans them quickly, one after the other, barely more than a second each, then crumples them with a dismissive hiss. "These are poor forgeries, Your Majesty. An unconvincing attempt to discredit me and humiliate you. Nothing more than a ploy to distract us from the real issue." He glares at me, still addressing Queen Ewella. "I did warn you that they would attempt such tactics."

"Give those back!" I spit. "If you were so innocent, you wouldn't care if anyone saw them!"

"They're right, Adan," says Papa softly. "Let Her Majesty make her own judgment."

"We don't have time for this," Adan hisses. "Dumoor is advancing at this very moment, and every second we waste is one second closer to defeat."

"Every second you keep talking is a second closer to defeat."

Adan rounds on me, and Papa shoves me back before he can strike. It's close and it sets my heart racing with a fear I didn't feel before we left Helston. I know Adan better now. I know what he can do. I know what he has done. It would be different if I had Satin.

"You see?" Adan turns to the queen, practically quivering with triumph. "I have been telling you for *months* that Nicholas is working for the enemy. How could he not be? Ever since the children *supposedly* defeated a dragon and returned with the witch's dragon, everyone in Helston knows there is more going on than meets the eye, and here is the result. An infiltrator wearing the dead prince's face. With all due respect, Your Majesty, if you permit this, how can your people ever trust you again?"

Papa lunges with a face full of thunder and draws his sword in a single whistling motion. "You dare speak to your queen like that?"

Adan doesn't even flinch. "You lost your authority the moment you were seduced by the enemy, and you have been trying to do the same to Helston ever since. You should've been turned out. You should've been put down before anyone ever let you near Helston's children. You are the reason Helston lost Prince Willow and Peran's kids, and you won't rest until every single one of our children is lured to the other side."

"Can you hear yourself?" says Papa. "Can you hear the words coming out of your mouth? Ewella, for goodness' sake, you can't believe any of this!"

Queen Ewella looks at us warily, like she can't trust her own eyes, her own instincts. I don't blame her. Not really. She has been lied to by so many for so long.

"I have lost everything," she whispers. "I will not lose my kingdom too." She turns sharply on her heel with a final, "I will not fall prey to ghosts."

"Then we're done!" Papa calls after her, his voice shaking with anger. "I forfeit my titles and my position and my loyalty to Helston. I will do what you are too afraid to, what I should have done right from the beginning, and I am putting my family first. We won't bother you again."

"And what about your *pet*, Nick?" Adan calls after him. "You know the condition of his release. Are you really going to leave him here for us?"

Papa's hand clenches around my shoulder so hard I wince. "Let. Neal. *Go.*"

Panic thrums through my chest. "Neal? They've got Neal?"

Papa never takes his eyes off Adan's smirking face. His entire body quakes with rage. "When Adan returned to Helston and told us you'd ... fallen, Neal didn't believe it. He was certain you were still alive. He tried to leave, to go after you. And they arrested him."

"*Why?*"

"Were we to let a known enemy return to his master?" Adan scoffs. "I don't think so. We'd let one dragon escape. We weren't going to let another go. Besides, your dad needed a little . . . motivation to stay in line."

"They've been using Neal against me ever since," says Papa. "On the promise that once the battle is won, they will free him." His voice cracks. "Callie, I already thought I had lost you. I—I couldn't lose him too."

I breathe deeply. I know what I need to do.

No one's getting left behind. Not again.

This time we go together.

I catch Willow's eye and mouth, *Cover me.*

Concealing his fingers by his side, Willow counts down on them: *Three, two, one—*

And then it's like he brings the sky down on Helston.

Thunder. Lightning. Thick darkness that sets chaos in motion.

I take off, ignoring the clash of swords and the yells and the magic flashing through the air. When I trip, I pick myself right back up and keep going. There is no choice. I cannot think about anything other than Neal.

Papa and Willow are two of the strongest people I know.

They will be okay.

I have to believe that.

Neal in the dungeons, trapped in the dark as the damp sucks out his magic—he needs me.

Helston is no longer familiar, but my feet know their way

around the palace grounds. I zip past the stables and up the hill toward the barracks. The farther I get, the quieter it is.

Everyone is down the hill.

"Stop!" Peter yells not far behind me.

I curse through my teeth and push on.

He isn't worth the breath it takes to argue with him.

I wish I had Satin. My fists will have to be enough.

"Callie!"

The moment he's close enough, I wheel and punch him—a single crack to the nose.

Peter gasps and stumbles back, blood already spilling between his fingers.

And then I realize he doesn't even have his sword drawn.

It hangs untouched at his belt; the pommel a beautiful deep green, detailed with copper.

I recognize it with an outraged cry. *"Satin! That's my sword! Give her back!"*

His fingers are already scrambling at the buckle, trying to undo the scabbard before I hit him again, and she's back in my hands and the weight of her is such a relief I could *cry*.

Except I don't.

And I'm not letting Peter off so easily. The thought of *anyone* touching my sword, let alone *him*—

"How did you get her?" I demand, leveling her tip not too far from his nose.

Peter puts his hands up in surrender. "You dropped it, back in Dumoor Forest, remember? Adan brought it back as proof you'd fallen. Everyone knows how much you love that sword. After that, I . . . borrowed it. Look, I don't have one of my own. Not a good one. And I figured it was better to use it than let it get lost or rusted or—" He deflates with a sigh. "It doesn't matter. She's home now."

"Yeah. That's right. But if you think this makes up for everything you did, to Edwyn, to *Jory*—"

"I—I didn't want him to die," Peter insists. "You've got to believe me. I didn't know Adan was going to kill him. I didn't know Adan was going to kill *you*. I—I thought we were just going to scare you a bit, to put you back in your place, but I didn't . . . I would never—"

"But you did!" When I turn on him again, Peter recoils, covering his face with his hands. Good. He should be scared. "Like it or not, you're his accomplice. You let them believe we were *dead*!"

"He said you were!" Peter insists. His once-white cuff is bright crimson. "He said if we didn't get to you, Dumoor would. I didn't know you were alive. I swear!"

"Your oath is worth less than the dirt on my boot."

"You said you would help me—"

"I *said* that if you helped me, I'd help you. I don't see you doing your part."

"What about this?" He digs into a pocket and pulls out a thick iron key.

I don't take it when he holds it out. "What is it?"

"To your father's shackles."

My heart jumps into my throat. "Neal's?"

Peter nods, not meeting my eye. "I don't have the key to the dungeons, but you have magic. You got Edwyn and his sister out. I figure you can do it again. But this is my contribution."

The thought of Neal chained up and underground nearly has me snatching the key right out of Peter's fingers. But I force a pause.

I cross my arms and glare at him. "And what do you expect in return?"

"I expect nothing, but—" Peter swallows, glancing back down the hill with a whispered, "They're all going to die. Every one of them. Captain Adan thinks I don't hear them making plans, but I do. They're sending out the little ones first, as a distraction. They don't care who lives or dies so long as the battle is won."

My stomach flips so I nearly puke. "Why didn't you tell anyone?"

Peter gives a weary shrug. "Who would I tell? Anyone who is in a position to do anything is part of the strategy. Besides, who would listen to *me*?"

I chew the inside of my cheek. He sounds like Edwyn.

"But if you have friends on the enemy side," Peter says, pushing on, "you can tell them not to fight. To stand down. Or at least . . . don't hurt the kids. It's not their fault. They don't understand."

I give a wry smile that trembles on my lips. "You talk like you're not one of those kids."

A whole head taller than me, Peter scowls. "Does that mean you'll do it?"

"I would do it without the key." I snatch it from Peter's palm and pocket it before he can change his mind. "But this helps. Thank you. Sorry about your nose."

He waves the apology away with a dismissive hand. "At least, if it comes to it, I can say I put up a fight."

I smirk. "Even if it means admitting I beat you?"

"Don't push it, Callie."

I would *never.*

The palace looms up, as silent as though it's been abandoned.

I've never seen it like this before. The courtyard is always busy, with nobles and knights on their way to the next important appointment; the front doors into the grand entrance are always open; the Great Hall always loud through the stained-glass windows.

It doesn't feel like Helston, either in my dreams or in what I have come to experience. It feels like we've been gone so long that everything has changed; fallen apart and gone to seed. Or maybe we've just grown up.

Either way, I can't wait to leave.

I let the dream wind its way through my blood and fuel me from the inside.

Just a few short hours and we'll be flying away from here.

All of us. Me and Willow and Papa and Neal, letting Helston disappear behind us. Together we can get Elowen and Edwyn away, and we can finally escape this ridiculous war. Let them fight it out if they must, but keep us out of it.

You cannot help people who will not help themselves.

Just a few short hours . . .

I shove all my desperate hope right into that rusted lock and it crumbles in my hands, easy as anything.

Down, down, down into the darkness. I don't waste my magic on light. I've been here before; I can find my way again. My hand trails along the damp stone, helping me count corners as I sink into the underground labyrinth and fight to keep my courage.

Every nerve in my body sparks with the warning memory of the last time we were here.

I'm not afraid.

And if I am, it doesn't matter.

It's worth it, to find Neal.

I pass the cell that held the twins, and the room that Willow told me had once been his. Close by is Teo's cell, where we locked Adan.

I wish no one had bothered looking for him.

I wish we had buried him.

"Neal? Are you here?"

I strain for any sound of life, no matter how small, trying not to think about worst-case possibilities. Trying not to fixate on them when they lodge in my head. Trying to breathe through the terror of the certainty that I'm here too late and Neal is already—

Breathing.

I hear breathing other than my own and hope is a flame in my heart.

I chase it, my fingertips scraping along the rough stone walls, skidding in puddles of who-knows-what that have been here who-knows-how-long.

"Neal?"

The breathing is loud and steady but no one answers my call.

I fly around the last corner and stop.

Curled in the farthest, darkest, dampest corner, with a thick chain shackling him to the wall, is a dragon.

CHAPTER THIRTY-NINE

It's too dark to see anything but a shadowy shape, even as I creep closer.

But my heart knows.

Neal.

Adan wasn't just throwing insults around when he kept referring to Neal as "dragon."

He meant *literal* dragon.

Neal's a . . . dragon.

I don't understand. . . .

But I don't need to.

Not right now.

Neal is Neal, no matter what he looks like.

I crouch until my knees are wet and reach out a hand.

I'm surprised by how unafraid I am.

"It's me. It's Callie."

His scales are warm and alive and soft to the touch.

His dragon eyes fly open and roll in alarm, his body thrashing against the chain, trying to escape beneath my fingers. Trying to escape *me*. His long tail whips through the air, nearly hitting me.

"Neal. Neal." I say his name over and over, hoping it can bring him back to me. "It's okay. It's Callie. Neal, it's Callie. I'm okay, just like you knew. I've come to help. I've come to rescue you. We're gonna get out of here. You, me, and Papa. Just like it's supposed to be. Look, I have the key. Let me free you."

I keep talking, focusing on my tone instead of the words, trying to approach again, to soothe with touch; running my ripped-up palm along his smooth scales until he calms down.

One large eye focuses on me, the color of a summer sky during twilight.

"Callie." His voice is his own, and I nearly cry with relief.

I wrap my arms around Neal's long neck and cling, scales rough against my cheek just like his stubble right after he's shaved. "I'm sorry I didn't come sooner."

His neck curves around me like the safe circle of his hug. "They told us you were dead."

"Humans lie."

Way worse than dragons.

The key and lock are so heavy, I can hardly lift them together with just my two hands. But there's no way I'm giving up. Not ever.

Neal shakes out his body when I finally haul the chains off him and hurl them in a pile with a satisfying clang; he stretches his neck and wings the same way I've watched him stretch out the crick in his shoulders every morning. He is smaller than Kensa and bigger than Teo, though in these cramped cells, everything feels enormous.

Why didn't you tell me? I long to ask, but now isn't the time.

Instead, I tell him, "Papa and Willow are in trouble."

Neal dips his huge, horned head. "Then it is time to help them."

The thought of a dragon rescuing the knight is poetry better than any ballad I've ever heard.

I have no idea how Neal's huge form manages to squeeze through the narrow tunnels and back up the stairway, but there's no point in questioning magic. And the same way cats are 90 percent fluid, dragons are 90 percent magic.

When we finally break out into the sunshine, Neal's whole body shudders, huge wings stretching and quivering with relief.

I gape.

He is *so* beautiful. His scales are almost black until the light catches them and makes them shimmer with a pearly forest green. The undersides of his wings are bright, shimmering emerald, and two dark brown horns curl up out of his head, the same color as his eyes.

Eyes that I recognize as Neal's.

"Are you angry with me, Callie?" he asks, his familiar voice coming from the dragon's mouth.

I start to say *No! Obviously not!* but that's not what we do. We tell each other the truth, even when the truth is hard.

"I don't know," I tell him. "You didn't tell me you're a dragon. I'm hurt that you kept it from me, that you felt like you had to. But I'm not angry. Not at you."

His long neck curves as he twists to look at himself. Even on his dragon face, I can read his miserable expression. "This isn't me. I kept it from you because this isn't how I wanted to be."

"I'm not angry," I promise again. "I'm just glad you're okay. I missed you so much, and I've *so much* to tell you. But we gotta get out of Helston before anything else. Can you really fly?"

Neal stretches his wings again, and I grimace as the bones crack. "Climb up, kiddo."

For the second time today, I mount a dragon.

Neal is a whole lot easier to ride than Teo. For one thing, there's more room to get comfy and secure, and for another his wings are clearly fully formed in a way that Teo's aren't. They aren't translucent in the slightest, and every movement is full of power and confidence.

Neal might hate this shape, but he wields it well.

I feel like the most powerful knight in the whole world when we take flight. With Satin and Neal, no one can stop me.

War rages below us. Helston against Helston. Papa and Willow against Adan and his men. I see Willow's magic first, bright and fierce, blasting the oncoming swords.

"Go lower," I call to Neal, and his wing dips obligingly, letting us sail low over the raging battle.

I jump off before we touch down and rush into the thick of the fight, Satin drawn. I don't attack, though, just beat off anyone who comes near me; battling my way through to Papa and Willow.

They both look exhausted.

"Get to Neal!" I yell. "He's gonna fly us out of here!"

"Fly?" Willow repeats. "What do you mean 'fly'?"

"You'll know when you see him! Where's Teo?"

"I don't know!" Willow shouts back. "I haven't seen xem for a while."

I scour what little I can see, but I don't glimpse Teo anywhere. Maybe from the sky.

I shove Willow in Neal's direction and pull on Papa. "Neal's waiting, come on."

Neal is surrounded the way ants surround a fallen apple.

He snaps and bats at anyone who comes too close, never hurting anyone even if he could destroy Helston and everyone in it in a single flame-filled breath.

Half of me wishes he would.

A *big* half.

But Neal is still Neal, whether he's a dragon or a human.

Willow freezes at the sight of him. "That isn't—"

"Yup. It is." I push him onward. "You can ask questions later."

With one last confused glance at Neal, Willow blasts a way through the army with a firm force, more like a heavy wind than magic. He grabs one of the curved spines sticking out of Neal's green scales and hauls himself up, settling firmly before leaning down to help me.

I twist in turn, waving Papa on. "Come on!"

"I'm coming!"

Except he's not. He's turned back to the fight, searching for someone he doesn't have time to look for. "Ewella!"

Seriously? I'm not gonna lose now for the sake of a queen *who is literally the reason we're in this mess*!

"Papa, we have to go *now*!"

He ignores me, diving into the mass of people, and drags out the queen—dazed and disheveled—and he shoves her up onto Neal's back.

I begrudgingly give her my hand.

"Now can we go?"

Papa nods and starts the climb up Neal's side.

Wings beat down on either side of us, in the air the moment Papa's feet leave the ground. It couldn't feel more different than riding Teo.

Teo . . .

I search desperately for any glimpse of blue scales.

"Willow, where's Teo?"

He shakes his head, body trembling behind me. "I don't know I—I tried to keep xem within sight, but it was too much. They took xem when I wasn't looking. I'm sorry—"

"We'll come back," I vow. "We'll set things right."

I just hope Teo can hold on until then.

Behind Willow, the queen leans to help Papa up. "Careful, Nick," she says, soft like they weren't at each other's throats half an hour ago.

Through a huff, Papa winks at me. "Bit harder than a horse, isn't it?"

I start to smile back, to laugh and make a joke about how he's too old for this.

But the first word turns into a scream on my lips.

Because Papa gasps and jerks, eyes blown wide with shock. And I know that look. I know what he feels because I felt it too. I watched Jowan wear the same expression.

I watched the prince fall.

Just like I watch Papa fall.

An arrow in his back.

CHAPTER
FORTY

"*Turn around!*" I scream, yanking at any part of Neal I can. Nothing makes a difference. "Go back! We have to go back! We have to save him! We have to—"

Willow's arms are locked chains around my waist, the only thing keeping me from launching myself right off Neal's back. "Callie, they'll kill us if we go back."

"I don't care! *I don't care!* Neal! Go back! You have to go back."

"Callie, stop! You're going to fall!"

Good. I want to fall. If they're not going to turn around, let me fall and I'll save him myself.

"Please," I beg, sobbing. "Please, Neal, you can't leave him there. Papa—"

"Wants you to live," says Neal firmly. "We failed you before, we won't do it again. I will go back for him, Callie, I swear to you, but first I am doing what I should've done the moment I got here. I am getting you safely out of Helston."

I don't want it. I don't want my safety at the expense of Papa's. We stay together. That's the deal. We're family. *We're supposed to stay together!*

The ground gets farther and farther away. I can't tell people apart anymore. They're just a blurred mass, with Papa lost among them.

This isn't right.

"*Callie!* No!"

I'm flying.

No, I'm falling. Slipping down Neal's side. We're higher than Pioden's tower. Farther to fall. Few chances I'll survive. It's hard to care.

Willow screams my name and snags me with a net of magic, dragging me back up into the safety of his arms.

I writhe and spit, cursing him and Neal and Helston and Dumoor, and I want my dad!

Willow doesn't let me go. Just holds on until I run out of fight, then lets me sob into his shoulder, his mother safe at his back.

"I'm sorry, Callie."

CHAPTER
FORTY-ONE

We fly until Helston disappears over the horizon.

We fly until Neal can't fly any farther.

I don't speak when we land.

We could be five kilometers away or a thousand miles. We could've been flying for a moment or a lifetime. It makes no difference.

I have to go back.

We left him there.

I left him there.

And I don't know if he's . . .

I crouch in the grass, scrunching my body up like I can make it disappear, and vomit.

I don't want to live in this world.

This isn't how it was supposed to go.

We left Elowen and Edwyn with Peran.

We left Papa and Teo in Helston.

If this is safety, I don't want it.

I don't want it.

"Callie?"

"Leave me alone."

I jump up and stalk away. Willow should've helped me. We were supposed to be in this together. He isn't on my side. He's on Neal's. And Neal's a liar. Dragons lie. *Dragons lie.*

I lean hard against a tree, eyes closed. My whole body hurts, inside and out.

"Callie—"

"I told you to leave me alone."

Willow does not leave me alone. He stands his ground. "We need to talk about it."

"I don't want to."

"Tough. It's not just up to you. You're not the only one who—"

"You got what you wanted," I spit. "You've got your mother, your freedom. *Everything!*"

"I know what it is to lose someone—"

"Papa's not lost! I know where he is! And I have to go back! You should've let me!"

"You would have *died,* Callie. We all would've died! You think that's what Sir Nick would've wanted?"

I clamp my hands over my ears like a child who doesn't want to be told no. "Don't talk about him like he's gone!"

"Okay! I'm sorry! I didn't mean that. Only that he wants you to live! If you had died for *him*, he would never have forgiven himself!"

"And how am *I* supposed to forgive myself? It's *my* fault! If I had been faster, if I had fought better—"

"You did your best and your best is *always* enough."

Tears burn my eyes. "It doesn't feel like that."

"I know." Willow wraps his arms around me and squeezes, burying his face in the crook of my neck. "I'm so sorry, Callie."

"I don't even know where we are. How're we supposed to get home if we don't know where we are?"

"We'll find a way," says Willow. "That's what we do."

We stand together in this unknown place beneath a cloudy sky, clear of gulls and magpies and dragons. Far away from the sea. I look back at the grown-ups, at Ewella pressing soft magic into Neal's limp wing.

I have to face her. I have to face them both. We have to talk and come up with a plan, but just the thought of it makes my chest constrict and my throat close up.

"Don't," Willow murmurs. "Just breathe. Right now, that's all we can do."

He's right. Of course he's right.

I close my eyes, and I breathe.

ACKNOWLEDGMENTS

Having named every person I'd ever made eye contact with for the acknowledgments of Book 1, my goal for Book 2 is to keep it short and sweet. Make no mistake: There are even more humans I am indebted to this time around!

Always first, thank you forever to my wife, Christine, for her endless love and support and ability to catch typos even after ten pairs of eyes have missed them! And to Delta and Lexie for the infinite cuteness that sustains me through the darkest days.

Thank you eternally to Callie's immediate family: Megan Manzano, Liesa Abrams, Emily Harburg, and Lili Feinberg. I am truly the luckiest author in the world to be blessed by a team who loves and cares for my fictional children as much as I do (and puts them through less grief!). Thank you to every person who has given their time to make this book what it is and to make sure it has the best shot, from the sales reps to the marketing team to the copyeditors and designers. You made this messy Word doc beautiful, and the Labyrinth Road team is an incomparable force!

Thank you, Bob Diforio and Pam Pho, for being the solid foundation holding up my career!

The words on the page are only one way characters come to life, and I am so thankful to cover artist Kate Sheridan and audiobook narrator Dani Martineck, whose talents completed the magic and made my imaginings real!

My deepest appreciation for all the booksellers I have been lucky enough to meet during my debut year, who have truly championed Book 1 and worked hard to get it into children's hands. Special thanks to the Novel Neighbor for hosting my preorders and my launch party (and not being annoyed when I spilled two drinks on the books); Main Street Books, St. Charles, for guidance and wisdom; and the Chesterfield Barnes & Noble for providing a comfortable place to work and caffeinate! Shout-outs to Kassie, Stephanie, Haley, Emily, Austin, Star, Sarah, and Amy. Bookish people are the best people!

Love to my dear friends Cat, Dorian, Simone, Amanda, Britney, and Marilyn for always cheering for me! To the Class of '22 Debuts, we made it! It's been an honor to be included in such a stellar group of authors, especially Maria Tureaud, George Jreije, and Shawn Peters. To all my writing friends, Forgers, and Sub Solidarity, there's no one else I'd rather face this wild industry with! My endless gratitude to Alder, Nic, Elm, Mol, and Elle for existing and championing queer kidlit. The world is a better place for your presence.

Thank you to fellow Labyrinth Road authors Megan Reyes

(*Heroes of Havensong: Dragonboy*), Terry J. Benton-Walker (*Alex Wise vs. the End of the World*), Andrew Auseon (*Spell-binders: The Not-So-Chosen One*), and Deb Caletti (*The Epic Story of Every Living Thing* and *Plan A*) for your support and camaraderie. Our editor has excellent taste in people!

Thank you to my family, blood and chosen and work, past and present. I am so grateful to have each and every one of you in my life. And an enormous shout-out to the incredible street team who took up the challenge and made sure their local bookstores and libraries knew about Callie. Thank you for all your hard work!

Extra love to my fellow KinderCare teachers for your continuing support and patience, especially Grace, Jean, Alanna, Melissa, Kelly, Savannah, and Christy. There's no one else I'd rather spend time away from my computer with!

Thank you endlessly to all of *Sir Callie*'s early readers who loved it enough to yell about it to the universe, especially those who were kind enough to blurb and review. It will never not blow me away that folks enjoy spending time in my imagination!

On that note, thank you to *all* who have picked up *Sir Callie*, who have read it and shared it and recommended it. Seeing my book in the wild, especially in the hands of kids, continues to be like a wonderful dream I never want to wake from. To all the reviewers, big and small; to the librarians and teachers on the front lines; to the grown-ups who understand how important books are: thank you for seeing value in my stories.

And finally, thank *you* for continuing to love Callie, Willow, Elowen, and Edwyn! I can't wait to continue this adventure with you.